RED

THE LEGEND OF THE AKAKUCHIBAS

GIRLS

WRITTEN BY KAZUKI SAKURABA

TRANSLATED BY JOCELYNE ALLEN

HAIKA SORU

SAN FRANCISCO

Akakuchibake no Densetsu
(English title: Red Girls: The Legend of the Akakuchibas)
Copyright © 2006 by Kazuki Sakuraba
English translation rights arranged with TOKYO SOGENSHA CO., LTD.
through Japan UNI Agency, Inc., Tokyo.

English translation © 2015 VIZ Media

Love Vacation
Words by Tokiko Iwatani, music by Hiroshi Miyagawa
©1963 WATANABE MUSIC PUBLISHING CO., LTD.

Cover and interior design by Fawn Lau

HAIKASORU
Published by VIZ Media, LLC
P.O. Box 77010
San Francisco, CA 94107

WWW.HAIKASORU.COM

Library of Congress Cataloging-in-Publication Data

Sakuraba, Kazuki, 1971–
  [Akakuchibake no Densetsu. English]
  Red Girls : the Legend of the Akakuchibas / written by Kazuki Sakuraba ;
translated by Jocelyne Allen.
    pages cm
  ISBN 978-1-4215-7857-6 (paperback)
  I. Allen, Jocelyne, 1974– translator. II. Title.
  PL875.5.A39A7713 2015
  895.63'6—dc23
                                      2014047827

Printed in the U.S.A.
First printing, April 2015

PART ONE

THE LAST AGE OF LEGEND

1953–1975: MANYO AKAKUCHIBA

1. THE SUMMER OF FUTURE VISIONS

O ne summer, when she was ten, Manyo Akakuchiba saw a man flying up in the sky. Manyo was my grandmother, and because she was still an uncivilized country girl back then, this being before she married into the old money of the San'in region's Akakuchiba family, she didn't actually have a last name. In the village, they just called her "Manyo."

As far back as she could remember, my grandmother had seen strange things. She was a large, solidly built woman, with black hair the color of wet crow wings hanging down to her waist—although in her later years, as you might expect, her hair was snowy white—who would *naaaarrow* her wide eyes and sometimes stare up at the mountain peaks off in the distance. She had very good eyesight; she also saw things invisible to the eye. The story of how she came to be called the clairvoyant madam of the Akakuchiba house is still ahead of us—I'm trying to tell the story of my grandmother's childhood here—but it was clear from when she was small that she occasionally saw the future.

At times, this would manifest as a prediction spelled out in the spontaneous rearrangement of inky black characters carefully inscribed on the hanging scroll in a traditional-style parlor; at others, it would be a dead person coming into the room and gesticulating the future at her; and at still other times she would see the future as an image the meaning of which she didn't understand. Manyo didn't really talk to the people in the village about these things. She was just that strange "outlander" child to them, which caused my grandmother to feel a small measure of pride and an anxiety about the fact that she was not like everyone else.

This summer of Showa 28—1953 on the Western calendar— Manyo was probably ten years old. I say probably because no one in the village knew her exact age, not even Manyo herself. One day, in a remote region of Japan known as San'in, a narrow strip squeezed in between the black chain of the Chugoku Mountains and the gray sheet of the Sea of Japan, a land where the weather was always bad, she had appeared. It was as if she had tumbled down from deep in the mountains. Manyo didn't remember it herself, but the outlanders had left her in the village when she was three or maybe not quite.

"Outlanders" is the name I settled on while writing this tale. The people of the San'in region—that is to say, our ancestors—had for a very long time already been living hidden deep within the mountains, and unlike those of us living in the village, rather than being given any sort of proper name, these traveling people were referred to as "that" or "them" or "those mountain people." In recent years, folklorists have apparently given them names like "Sanka," "Nobuse," and "Sangai," but these names, at least in the village of Benimidori in western Tottori Prefecture where we live, have never been used.

For who knows how long, probably hundreds of years—no, much, much farther back—there have been people living in hiding deep in the mountains, the wind pulling their long, jet black hair out behind them, their skin dark like tanned leather, solidly built people who did not stop in a single place, who lived free in the mountains in this or that area according to the season. No annual tributes, no convening, and none of the taxes of recent years, but because there was also no state, they had to take care of themselves.

No one in Benimidori or in the villages of distant Izumo and Tottori has seen any trace of them for the last maybe fifty years, though, so I don't know if they still live on in the Chugoku Mountains. In any case, little Manyo came down to Benimidori some sixty-five years ago with the adults of the tribe, the last generation of outlanders to enter the village, and then for whatever reason, these outlanders left her, alone among the houses, when they retreated back into the mountains.

Since the majority of the people who remember this time have already joined the roster of the dead, I don't know the particulars, but during these last few hundred years, when hands were needed in the village, the outlanders would descend from the mountains like a black wind and lend theirs. Of life's major ceremonial events—wakes and weddings, festivals, rites of adulthood—they were in fact needed for the funerals.

When a young person died accidentally (suicide), the villagers burned a bundle of *tokonen* grass, which sent up a purple smoke. The outlanders then came down during the night to make the funeral preparations. They cut wood to make a box, and at dawn, they snap-snapped, and broke the thighs and shins of the stiff body of the deceased, and crammed it into the square box. This task finished, they always then took the box and threw it in a ravine deep in the mountains while singing some kind of incantation. When the outlanders came, the villagers simply waited for them to disappear into the mountains taking the youthful deceased. Not even the head priest at the temple could interfere in the process.

Which is why, on that morning some sixty-five years ago when they left Manyo, there must have been someone who had died young there. Even now, I'm not entirely sure whether breaking the legs and jamming the body in there was a calculated move to keep the body from transforming and escaping, or if the perfectly square box held some mystical meaning. We can leave that question to the folklorists. Either way, after "they" departed with the deceased stuffed in a box, a lone girl—Grandmother, dark, solidly built, long black hair, very much an outlander—was left behind, plopped down on the ground, a doll leaned up against the side of the well in front of someone's house, bucket wrapped in the vines of pink morning glories.

"I s'pose they forgot me," Grandmother said with a sigh some sixty-five years later, not long before her death.

"They couldn't have just forgotten you and left you behind."

"Then I wonder why they did leave me there."

No one knows the answer to that, even now. Just that this was how little Manyo found herself growing up alongside the children of the village of Benimidori.

The young couple three houses down from the side of that well and its pink blooming morning glories took Manyo in. The girl was a little weird, she looked a liiittle different from us, but still, the young couple took care to raise her like everyone else.

The people of the San'in region from Benimidori down to around Izumo, we all looked the same: fair-skinned, thin lines, slim waists. With narrow eyes and oval faces, our countenance was imperial to put it kindly, or like a stunted unripe gourd, to put it not so kindly. According to one theory, the individuals in this area came over from the Korean Peninsula in the Yayoi period and taught the Japanese the art of *tatara* iron production, so maybe that's why we look the way we do.

In contrast, the outlanders who had abandoned Manyo and disappeared into the mountains were dark-skinned and big-boned. Manyo looked out of place in the village and when she went into town, but the young couple took care of this strange child, occasionally severe, occasionally affectionate with her. They also sent her to school, but for some reason, Manyo could not manage to learn her letters. "I can't read," "I can't write," she would say; her studies were of no use.

She would instead make strange predictions every now and then. At that time, the Third Jurisdiction Corps of the National Police Reserve (later known as the National Safety Forces), which was created by MacArthur after the war, was stationed in Izumo in Shimane Prefecture, and each member carried a carbine thanks to a loan from the US military. The corps was basically made up of young people of that generation, born in the area and also coming in from other regions, who had missed out on deployment to the front. The carbine, a mysterious weapon from which fire erupted, naturally terrified the villagers. Even now, the provincial culture of the Edo period lives on in the village. When someone commits a crime, the people rally at the village headman's house, use spears and nets to catch the criminal, and then turn the offender over to the authorities.

When the young men in their khaki uniforms swaggered into town, clutching their carbines, little, illiterate, dark-skinned Manyo pointed at one of them, and said, "Be bright, scatter."

The young couple didn't think anything of it at the time, but when they were told that the gun of a National Safety Forces soldier had exploded late that night, killing the soldier, they cocked their heads to one side. All Manyo said when they asked her about it was, "'Be bright, scatter.' I saw it." This was a child talking, and so the young couple decided not to concern themselves with the matter any further, but the point here is that Manyo could, from time to time, in some strange way, see the future. Perhaps this was the real reason the outlanders had left her by the well that morning.

Every now and again, Manyo saw the future. This apparently happened most often when she was in a high place. She had seen the bright scattering of the dead man while the husband of the young couple walked around with her on his shoulders. And whenever they went up the mountain or to the top of the hill to a prosperous area known as Takami, the future would abruptly pass before her eyes. People died, were born, had serious accidents. Little Manyo simply watched it happen. She was a child, after all, and given the young couple's reaction when she saw the dead man brightly scatter, she figured it would be better not to talk about the visions too much. In the majority of cases, Manyo kept her mouth shut. And most times, the future she saw wasn't clear; she often didn't know what was happening.

And then the summer she was ten, Manyo saw the man flying up in the sky for the first time.

This man was not young. Or rather, although he looked young, Manyo later thought he was probably middle-aged. In any case, it wasn't as if there were all that big of a difference between the ages of twenty and forty to a ten-year-old girl. He was an adult man who seemed sad somehow. That was Manyo's sole thought. He was wearing clothing the color of dry leaves. Small in stature, he had just one almond eye in the flat, pale face characteristic of the region. That is, only the left eye was open wide; the right stayed firmly shut, looking like it had merged into the smooth skin around it.

The man hung lightly in the faintly peach-colored dusk.

His thin lips parted, and he whispered something.

"Cap. It. Al. Em!"

A *phantom*, Manyo thought. Though attending school, she was still illiterate. She had a hard time making any friends, looking as strange as she did and basically unable to do anything in class. The wind played with the black hair flowing down to her waist as she walked briskly along the village road. She was taking a shortcut, so she was halfway up the hill to Takami when the man suddenly appeared before her eyes.

He floated in the air facing downward, almost as if he had fallen from the sky, both hands spread out, and he stared intently at Manyo from directly above her. The man stayed there for a while, against the background of the peach sky, but he eventually receded and then disappeared, sucked into the darkening evening sky. About to call out for him to wait, Manyo snapped her mouth shut. She knew that this was the future. She didn't know what it meant, but the one-eyed man was flying. She understood that it would happen someday. That evening, when she saw the one-eyed man flying, little Manyo for the first time became conscious of the fact that she was Manyo, seer of the future, clairvoyant, freak. And that one day, she would meet the strange man with one eye who had appeared before her as a phantasm.

That was perhaps Manyo's bizarre first love. Fall came after, then winter, then spring, and still Manyo thought about this phantom man. She named him "One Eye." When evening fell, she would climb the hill to Takami, wondering whether she might not see some other future too, and she would focus her eyes off in the distance. But this phantom did not show itself to Manyo again. It was another ten years before One Eye, who lived peacefully in Manyo's heart, appeared in front of her in reality as a man with an actual, genuine body.

And it would be a looong time after that before the man would "fly" the way Manyo saw him fly.

Back then, there were two large houses in Benimidori, Tottori Prefecture. The people in the area called them "red above" and "black below." And it is this "red above"—which housed the old and established Akakuchiba family—where this tale is set, where my grandmother went to marry, and where I was born and raised.

Since days so far in the distant past that even members of the family themselves were unable to retrace their history, the Akakuchiba family had lived here at the foot of the Chugoku Mountains. The village of Benimidori itself came to be because the progenitor of the family had cut into the mountain to build a tatara ironworks there, and the settlement had sprung up around it. Or so I was told. The Akakuchibas' ancestors had crossed the ocean from the Korean Peninsula and washed ashore in this small island country. They then came across land on the upper stretch of the Hino River where they could extract high-quality iron sand, settled there, and thrived with their iron production technology.

In addition to the meaning of "heat further" in the ancient Korean language, *tatara* apparently also means "heat" in ancient Sanskrit. A long time ago, so long ago it's impossible even to imagine it, this iron production technology was transmitted bit by bit from India through Jiangnan in China to the southern part of the Korean Peninsula, and then to the Japanese archipelago. This old technique using a pair of bellows and a primitive furnace was employed at the tatara ironworks owned by the Akakuchiba family until very recently, but then Western iron production techniques arrived together with the Black Ships. Iron production was inseparable from war. Techniques improved as Japan became a military regime, and the country saw more and more large factories pop up with their deep black German-made blast furnaces, gray smoke streaming high into the air. Similar to Yawata Steelworks in Kyushu, the large modernized ironworks of the Meiji era, and more recently, Kawasaki Steel Corporation in Kobe, the updated public-private enterprise, Akakuchiba

Steelworks, the village's "red above," was also a large-scale facility, which benefited the entire village.

According to people who remember this period, Akakuchiba Steelworks thrived after the war. The blast furnace, a dark skyscraper symbolizing the modern age; the iron river, like flames spewed forth from a dragon; the bundles of black smoke rising thickly from countless smoke stacks, lined up like discarded iron teeth, to blanket the light gray sky always full of the sluggish clouds so characteristic of the San'in region. The stark red rapids spilling out from the blast furnace; the mechanical roar echoing, the howl of a beast; the crimson flames projected onto the faces of workers covered in oil and sweat. All a mere shadow now of what they once were. What I, living in the present day, know is simply a black, dried husk of a city, where the fires stopped as the times changed, a dead place covered in red rust, transformed into an enormous ruin.

For the young people of the San'in region after the war, the Akakuchiba Steelworks factory, the blast furnace in the sky built after the old tatara bellows were shut down, was one of the top workplaces.

Back then, the people working at the steelworks got paid a decent wage, worked hard, and reveled in their youth in their off time. Many young people came each spring when it was time to recruit new workers for the steelworks, munching on sticky mochi rice cakes to put on the pounds because there was a weight limit. "Spring is mochi-eating season," they used to say. The workers, wearing uniforms the color of new leaves, were assigned two-room suites in lodging houses complete with backyards, which was where they lived. The husband of the young couple worked at the ironworks while the wife took care of the house, and on days off, the pair would go out for a satisfying meal or to see a play. As a life for your average person in Japan after the war, this was apparently a fairly satisfying one.

It was one such young couple that took in and raised the young Manyo.

The lodging house they lived in was squeezed in neatly among others, on stepped earth like a tiered platform cut into the foot of the mountain. Right in the middle of this platform was the steep hill of the main road linking the top of the mountain to the bottom, fifteen lodging houses on the right, twenty-five on the left. These houses were lined up in order; people toward the bottom were lower on the social ladder. Although they worked at the same factory, those from the region were assigned houses higher up, while people from elsewhere were given ones lower down. Even further up stood several large houses belonging to the people who managed the ironworks, the so-called white-collar workers. And still further, at the top of the main road, was the large, bright red manor of the Akakuchiba family, where it had stood since some long-forgotten past.

This mansion was elephantine, with a slight lean to it as if it were trying to hide among the groves of trees and the land of the mountains, as if the hand of a giant were pushing it down, seeking to bury it into the soft mountain. Red tiles sparkled on the roof beyond brownish-red gates. In summer, from the hill of the main road, Manyo and her sharp eyes could see quiiite clearly the painting of the Sea of Japan and the school of bright red snapper swimming so lifelike in it that covered the open *fusuma* sliding doors of the Akakuchibas' large reception hall. Just as the first character of their name would have it, the Akakuchiba house was indeed red in every way. Dark, almost the red of maple leaves just beginning to decompose, naturally proud up on the peak of the mountain, majestic and imposing, with a slight lean to it.

The bottom of the tiered platform was the earthly world; the higher you went toward Takami at the peak, the closer you were to heaven. Black smoke and oil blanketed the world below, the air of such poor quality that the people who lived there couldn't hang their laundry to dry in the backyard, but the sky in Takami was always clear. The celestial world, the red gates of heaven. This was how the large gates of the Akakuchiba house looked to the villagers down below.

The people of the Akakuchiba branch families had built small—but naturally red houses—halfway up to Takami, where they lived, managing the ironworks, and they didn't often get the chance to see the people of the main family. Occasionally, someone from the main house would race down the main road in a large, black foreign car at an incredible speed. The inside of the car was dark, making it hard to make anything out. Even Manyo's sharp eyes were unable to discern the faces of the main Akakuchiba family members hidden in the car, and so, they remained a mystery.

This was everything Manyo knew about "red above" back then. As she gazed up at the lodging houses, a tiered platform continuing toward Takami, Manyo thought that the world must be made of stairs.

And since around this time she lived in a black-smoke-covered lodging house at the bottom of the bottom of these stairs, she was much more familiar with the "black below" that was the Kurobishi family than she was with the Akakuchiba family above.

The Kurobishis were not an old family or anything like it. They were nothing more than poor shipbuilders highly valued in the Nishiki neighborhood by the port in this oblong San'in region wedged in between the chain of the Chugoku Mountains and the Sea of Japan. Before the war, the Kurobishi children had apparently been in the same miserable state as the other villagers, running around in bare feet and wearing the same clothes every day. Shipbuilders prospered, however, with Japan's transformation into a military state, and before they knew it, after the war, the Kurobishis were the freshly minted *nouveau riche*. They built a mansion like an enormous Buddhist altar near the sea on a piece of land jutting out slightly, peninsulalike, with keynote colors of gold and black to tie in with the first character of their name, and dressed their child in splendid kimono. This child was a girl around the same age as Manyo, called Midori.

Midori was not very beautiful, round eyes popping out of her flat face, and she was a jealous girl on top of that. Dressed up in brand-new, Sunday best, black and gold kimono, she paraded around the smoke-stained Benimidori, the wind sending the long sleeves of her *furisode* kimono fluttering.

The families of the men who worked for the "black below" shipbuilder and the families of the workers at the "red above" ironworks did not get along. The reds looked down on the blacks as simple pawns of new money, and the blacks complained that the black smoke from the ironworks was dirty and smelly. Because these people, although leading such similar lives, held each other in mutual disdain and quarreled at every opportunity, they ended up living almost completely separate from each other, after more than a few unfortunate fights nearly led to bloodshed in the bars where they went to drink and the parks where they took their children. Something like an invisible line was drawn in the postwar San'in region, between red and black, seashore and mountain.

The quarreling spirit of the adults naturally infected the children just like that. The red children bullied the black children. The black children set pop-eyed Midori Kurobishi, clad in her black and gold furisode, several ornate gold hairpins jabbed into her hair where they glittered, up on a pedestal like a princess and tried to protect her from the red children. The red children called Midori "the Goldfish." Understandable, since seen through the cruel eyes of children, it wasn't a stretch to note that with her face, the dark swaying of her long sleeves, and the bubbling of baubles on her head, she looked just like a goldfish.

Unable to read although she went to school, Manyo didn't understand the majority of the things she was taught—this is definitely not to say that Grandmother was stupid; she was, in fact, rather clever, but she did have trouble with math problems. Her brain was likely simply configured in a way that was different from everyone else's—so she stood out from both groups of children. In the way that children do, the Goldfish deemed this Manyo to be a lesser being, and on the way home from school, she would often lie in wait with her underlings to throw rocks at Manyo or run up to her and pull her hair.

"You're a stray!" The Goldfish repeated the same thing over and over as she followed Manyo home from school. She was surprisingly persistent. "Stray cat! Stray cat! Your skin's black! Gross! And your hair's too black. Right?" Goldfish cocked her head, and her underlings nodded their agreement in unison, chanting her words at Manyo.

The Goldfish, delighted: "You're poor!"

When Manyo didn't respond, she stamped her feet, clearly vexed, and kept at it.

Soon, they would arrive at the invisible barrier, the line between red and black. Manyo knew they couldn't chase her beyond that point, so she told herself to put up with it until they got there and just kept walking home with her mouth shut tight, every day.

Now then, Manyo's tenth year. The start of the last age of legend for Benimidori. There are three incidents I should share.

The first was Manyo seeing One Eye, the flying man.

The second is a small thing involving the Goldfish, aka Midori Kurobishi.

The road home from elementary school continued to be a trial, and Manyo came to thoroughly despise the Goldfish, so when she had to go into town on an errand, she avoided the industrial road that served as the main street for the Nishiki port where she might run into the Goldfish strutting along, flunkies in tow. She would slip down the narrow alleys pregnant with the smell of the sea, pushing and shoving her way through hanging screens of *kombu* seaweed.

That winter. The moist wind from the Sea of Japan gusting in, Manyo, sent out for three sardines and a bit of *wakame* seaweed for the next day's miso soup, ran into the Goldfish in a small park in a corner of the wharf looking out on the gray ocean as snow fluttered down and scattered softly.

The Goldfish was wearing a winter *chanchanko* vest over her black kimono, staring vacantly out at the sea, minus her usual entourage of dirty boy lackeys. Manyo tried to hide, slipped, and fell, landing on her face in the park sandbox to end up covered in sand. Turning around at the sound of her fall, the Goldfish was at first surprised to find Manyo there, but she was quick to open her mouth in her usual sneer. Then she closed her mouth and wiped tears from her face.

The Goldfish was crying. This face, so out of character for the ill-tempered girl in her fancy kimono, startled Manyo, and she stared up at the other girl, mouth hanging open, still on her belly in the sandbox. Tears fell in large drops from the Goldfish's protruding pop eyes. *They look salty*, Manyo thought. For no reason, she felt as though the tears and sweat of an ocean girl would be extra salty.

"What's wrong?"

"Waitin' for my brother," the Goldfish replied curtly. She wiped and wiped at her tears, but new ones kept coming. Heaving with sobs, "Still hasn't come home from Siberia."

"Siberia?"

"Interned there. An' he's pretty like a girl, so I'm worried. Boys who are pretty like girls, y'know, they're weak like girls. Can't wear furisode kimono, though, so they're no good for nothin'. My brother's weak, he didn't even used to get on the tuna boats. He'd get all sick and start throwin' up all over the place. He only ever managed to get on the little squid boats, but he'd be saying stupid stuff like 'the poor squid', an' he almost never caught nothing. I guess a girly boy like him's not gonna make it in Siberia, huh?" the Goldfish said all at once and wiped at her tears again.

By 1953, eight years had already passed since the end of the war, and the people coming home came, those who didn't didn't, and those who had survived were starting their new lives. Soldiers and civilians combined, more than six million people had, over a period of several years, returned home from the continent of China, from the southern islands, and from Siberia. The black shipbuilders and the red steelworks also had their fair share of repatriates and demobilized soldiers.

Manyo quietly approached the sobbing Goldfish. "You remember your brother? I mean, you were pretty small when he went off to war, weren't you?"

"I saw him in a picture. An' my mom and dad, that's what they say. And if my brother don't come back, then I'm the heir."

"Ain't that all right?"

"It's not." The Goldfish wiped at her tears. "I saw my brother in a picture. I want that pretty brother to come back home. That's it."

Another humid wind blew in from the Sea of Japan. The snow that fell and fell was almost sucked into the gray surface of the water and disappeared. The waves roiled and rolled.

Wait a minute, Manyo thought. *Do demobilized soldiers come home from the ocean? Don't they come by land? From way, way over there on the other side of the Chugoku Mountains, they go over all them steel bridges over all them valleys, on the train that comes to Daibenimidori Station every day*. Sometimes, just when everyone was on the verge of forgetting him entirely, a demobilized soldier would abruptly show up at the station.

But the Goldfish continued to stare at the sea, so Manyo stood next to her silently and gazed out at the restless waves. She was so afraid of the Goldfish that she did her best never to come anywhere near the coast, but she definitely didn't hate the view in this area. And more importantly, down here near the wharf, far from the high elevations, Manyo never saw visions. She could relax here. She completely forgot about the Goldfish crying next to her as she looked out at the ocean, and the Goldfish glared at her, eyes dry of tears now.

"You not worried?" She yanked on Manyo's wavy, waist-length hair.

"Ow! I'm not worried. Bully!"

"Stray!"

"I said ow!"

"You don't even have a brother. You're prob'ly jealous of me?"

"I'm not jealous or nothing. I got enough."

In the moment, she herself had no idea what she had enough of, but Manyo never did have much in the way of what you'd call desire. The young couple made sure she had everything she needed, and she had seen far too many visions to want for luxuries or have any worldly desires. She had been abandoned by her real family, the outlanders, and though she might have been poor with her family now, in her estimation, she had basically enough.

"You don't got enough of nothing. And your hair's too black. Why don't you put it up, make yourself look pretty? You ain't no natural beauty, after all."

"I don't want to look pretty and stuff."

"You're all talk. Girls wanna be pretty. They wanna wear furisode."

"But . . . I like being like this," Manyo replied quietly, and the Goldfish gasped in surprise. She threw her head back, and the gilded brilliance of the many ornate hairpins jammed into the hair on that head swung from side to side. She bit her lip. And then the Goldfish stretched out a hand and yanked hard on Manyo's black, shiny hair.

With a loud rip, the Goldfish yanked fifty or so hairs from Manyo's head. Startled, she turned around to find the Goldfish grinning happily. One of her front teeth was missing, so Manyo could see the pitch black cave beyond them. She pressed both hands against her aching scalp and ran out of the park, nearly tripping over herself.

"You're poor!" the Goldfish, jet-black sleeves swinging wildly, shouted to split her throat. "Stray cat! Savage! Drop dead already!"

The terrifying abuse chased endlessly after Manyo, coiling itself around her, snakelike.

And that was the second incident Manyo remembered from the winter she was ten.

The third was the Ebisu incident. It was that same winter, the season when the snow is starting to melt.

School was out for spring break, and the children were busy with chores at home or going to play together in town. The young couple raising Manyo was busy as always. The husband came home completely black from the ironworks at night. The wife did laundry during the day, went to fetch water from the communal well, and grew vegetable seedlings in the backyard. Manyo loved the couple, so for the days of the break, she plopped herself down on the porch, legs swinging, to watch her mother standing and working, or helped look after the little brothers and sisters who were the couple's own children.

Her mother was so busy, she didn't pay much mind to the children, but from time to time, when she passed by Manyo, she would slip a hand into the pocket of her apron and pop a roasted bean into Manyo's mouth. "Is it good?" she would smile, as the girl crunched away, and Manyo would nod. Her mother would then rush off somewhere and disappear again.

It was a day like this, just like all the others.

As she left the entryway of the house, she saw a black car going down the main road. Manyo knew that this was the car that carried the important people from Takami. She had started to wander out toward the road when she heard a fierce, almost popping sound.

Peeking out from the shadow of the house, she saw that the car had stopped, the hood was up, and smoke was drifting up from it. The uniformed driver quickly jumped out of the car to begin inspecting it.

Manyo cocked her head to one side and stared. Despite the fact that the road was usually filled with the families of the workers in the early afternoon, at that moment, as if some kind of magic spell had been cast, there was no one on the main road. As she stared, the back door of the car exploded open. And then a phantom she had never seen before disembarked.

A small, roundly plump woman. Her skin was snow white, her face circular to the point of surprise, and her eyes and nose were snugly tucked into soft flesh. Eyes as thin as threads were further flattened by the meat of her cheeks. *She looks just like the god Ebisu*, Manyo thought. She wore a simple but fine kimono, and on her small feet were toy-like *zori* sandals in red and black plaid. Her black hair was coiled up and held in place with a single lacquered comb. She was perhaps forty years old.

It's a vision of the god of fortune, Manyo thought. *A female Ebisu*. She didn't even entertain the idea that such a funny-looking woman could be a real human being. The lady Ebisu clambered—almost tumbled—out of the foreign car and came rolling squarely at Manyo in the shadows without a moment's hesitation.

Instinctively, Manyo fled.

There was no way a middle-aged woman, much less one who was fat like a ball, was going to catch up with a nimble ten-year-old girl. Panting at every step, Lady Ebisu chased after the fleet-footed Manyo but soon tired and came to a stop. Then she called out in a voice that was soft like cotton candy.

"Yoo-hoo! Little mountain girl who was just here! Come on, come out now!"

At that moment, Manyo was crouched like a wildcat under the shrubbery of the fifth house up. Lady Ebisu ran on, the sleeves of her kimono flapping wildly as she continued to call out, "Little girl! Little girl!"

Manyo held her breath.

Finally, practically rolling, the female Ebisu passed right in front of the shrubbery where she was hiding. The wonderful red-and-black-checked *zori* flashed in front of her.

"Little girl! Little girl!"

Just when her voice was growing distant, it came close again. The small footsteps. How could she be that fat and yet her footfalls be light like the wind? The wonderful zori returned, and then a large face tucked into flesh popped up to fill the dazzling sun-soaked scene Manyo could see from under the dim shrubbery.

She gasped.

"My my my!" Lady Ebisu laughed happily. "So *this* is where you were hiding yourself."

"Vision! Go away!"

"Vision? Is that your name?" Lady Ebisu pulled a handkerchief from the sleeve of her kimono and wiped away the sweat like beads of white sesame seed oil springing up on her broad widow's-peaked forehead.

"I'm Tatsu."

"Tatsu?"

So then this isn't a vision, but maybe a person? Manyo thought suddenly. It was hard to believe that someone could be this fat in these times, times of shortage, but she didn't feel that hallmark of her visions, the quiet chill like a dead person, like an ice wind blowing, from this rotund Lady Ebisu. The pale fat woman calling herself Tatsu wiped her forehead again. She wiped and wiped and still the white sesame seed sweat formed its beads. Manyo finally crawled out from under the shrubbery.

Tatsu brushed off the dust and the corpses of tiny winged insects covering Manyo when she emerged. Then she bent over to look right at Manyo's face. "Little girl. I'm Tatsu Akakuchiba," she said softly.

"Ah-kah-koo-chee-bah?" Manyo questioned in return. In that

moment, she didn't have a clue what they were talking about. And then her mouth dropped open and she looked up at the sky.

She looked at all the worker lodgings lined up on the tiered platform, and then at the above of the above of that. The mansion towered up beyond the deep black oily smoke rising up again that day, a deep red like fall leaves on the verge of decomposition. Red gates, the gates of heaven.

People from another world.

It made sense. If she was from the heavens, it wouldn't be at all strange for there to be more than enough food, to the point where a woman could fatten up into a ball even in these times.

"'Red above.'"

"What's that?"

At the returned question, Manyo was at a loss for words. And then, being a child, she earnestly explained how the situation—that for the villagers, Akakuchiba Steelworks and Kurobishi Shipbuilders were above and below, and the children whose parents worked at re and the black children did not get along—looked through a child's eyes.

"Goodness, then the little Kurobishi girl bullies you, does she?"

"Uh-huh. She's a demon."

"Oh my. That girl certainly is naughty."

Even the words this person from above, this Tatsu Akakuchiba, used were different from the words they used down there. An elegant, mysterious way of talking. Manyo started to get nervous. The car was still vomiting smoke on the main road, so Tatsu began tottering down the hill, Manyo in tow, and at the coffee shop a little way down, she treated Manyo to a frothy *bukupuku* tea and a chestnut *yokan* jelly.

"Do you like bukupuku tea?"

"Uh-huh."

This bukupuku tea was a treat introduced to the San'in region. You put sweet roasted sugar-covered *goshikimame* beans in a teacup, poured in the tea, and mixed it well to create a frothy foam. You drank the tea and picked out the beans with a toothpick.

Manyo alternated between the tea and the jelly. Tatsu Akakuchiba watched her, smiling.

"Back there, when the smoke started coming out from the hood of the car, well, I thought it was a sign of some kind. After all, the car has never stopped before on that hill."

"A sign?"

"That's right. And then there you were outside the car. I heard that the mountain people left a child in Benimidori, and I suppose that would be you. You do, after all, have the same black face as the mountain people. I knew it was you right away."

"..."

"I'm the daughter of an Akakuchiba branch family, and I married the eldest son of the main family, Yasuyuki. I live in that mansion you pointed at earlier."

"..."

The woman of the Akakuchibas, the people of the heavens who couldn't be seen even with Manyo's sharp eyes, tilted her rounded, plump face to one side and stared at the young Manyo. "Do you know Yamata no Orochi?"

Manyo nodded silently.

Yamata no Orochi was a legendary creature in the San'in region from Japanese mythology. A giant snake so enormous that it straddled eight hills, it had eight heads and eight tails, its eyes were red like winter cherries, pine trees grew from its back, and it was slain by the god Susano'o. But why would the Akakuchiba lady start talking about something like that?

The lady looked down at Manyo drinking her tea and said nothing further on the topic. Then she asked, in an even smaller voice, "What do they call you?"

"Manyo."

"And your last name?"

Manyo herself didn't have a last name, but the last name of the young couple who had taken her in was Tada, so she gave that one. The lady nodded. And then, Manyo having finished her frothy tea, Ebisu led them back up the hill. The necessary repairs to the black car seemed to have been made without any further problems.

As she was about to get in the car, the lady, for some reason, spoke. "Manyo Tada, when you grow up, you come marry my son. Does that sound good to you?"

"Uh-huh…"

Manyo stared back, stunned, and the door slammed closed. She couldn't see anything on the other side of the black-tinted windows. As the car pulled out, the main road, previously devoid of people, returned to its normal bustle as if a spell had been released.

Soon after that, the age of legend began to recede even in this mountain village, a relic in the modern era, and the air of mystery that had always enveloped it naturally began to disappear. Just as the enormous Western blast furnaces and large factories had come to the tatara steelworks that sat along the river in ancient times, the holy trinity of household machines—television, washing machine, refrigerator—gradually began to creep into the households in the area. Because of the modern culture television created, the sprawling Japanese islands rapidly shrank, making it so that a national culture could be absorbed by everyone. In the end, this little village in the western part of Tottori Prefecture was no different.

This region was still a tiny island separate from this spreading culture, a place where traces of the age of legend lingered until about ten or so years after the end of the war. Pushing ahead another ten years, the outlanders would disappear deep into the mountains.

Thanks to her mysterious gift, Manyo remembered quite clearly the day she met Tatsu. And at the very top of Benimidori, Tottori Prefecture, a village in the process of modernizing, the Akakuchiba house, symbolic of a legendary world, stood as it always had, deep red with a slight lean to it, and continued its reign thereafter as well.

2. YOUR HEAD FLIES OFF AND YOU DIE.

Now then, our story jumps ahead seven years from that year of 1953, partly because Manyo didn't remember this period very well. She did manage to go on to junior high school, but still unable to read or do the simplest calculations, and with the Goldfish gang's bullying only getting worse, she thoroughly disliked this earthly life. The things Manyo said she remembered quite well from this time were that she saw again—just once—a vision of One Eye, so she chased after it, practically tumbling down the hill road, and narrowly missed being hit by a three-wheeler; and that the *yamaoroshi* that blew in the spring of 1955 was the strongest it had ever been.

The yamaoroshi is a fierce, humid wind that blows down the mountain. This wind crosses the Sea of Japan from distant China, unhindered until the large wall known as the Chugoku Mountains thwarts its flow; once it hits the mountains, it releases the moisture it holds onto the region. Thus, this side of the mountains, a region where the air feels clammy and the sky is perpetually a pale gray, is called San'in, or "mountain shadow," and the other side of the mountains, a land that is bright and clear, Sanyo or "mountain sun." The yamaoroshi, blowing down from the Chugoku Mountains, lapping up this land to escape to the sea, becomes especially strong in spring, but this is a land where the wind is strong all year long. The majority of the farmhouses, erected in the middle of the rice fields, had fences of thick, high beech to protect the house and the storehouse from the wind. All these fences around all these houses grew into a strange bent shape, from the mountain to the sea, like legions of signposts. The wind was that strong.

The spring of that year, this wind blew stronger than ever, and Manyo very nearly had her feet swept out from under her and flew off into the sky as she walked along the hill of the main road. The puppy that the child in the house five doors down had gotten came flying along whining, and Manyo, without even the time to check if it was a vision, thrust both hands out and hugged it to a stop. The image of the dog was accompanied by an actual body, and this barked in Manyo's arms and then licked her arms sloppily with its hot tongue. As she held this warm, wet, weighty creature and stood her ground against the gale, her sharp eyes caught sight of a surprising scene.

At the very limit of what she could see, the bright red Akakuchiba mansion stood with a lean to it, way up the mountain. In the wide open reception hall, the strong wind raged and pulled up two of the tatami mats on the floor, lifting them lightly into the air. They stood and slammed against each other for a while as if wrestling, but when the wind died down, the energy drained out of them and they fell back down to the floor. Manyo was stunned; she marveled at how fierce that year's yamaoroshi was. The petals of the many flowers blooming in the gardens of the houses of Takami scattered on the wind and fluttered down to Manyo and the puppy at the bottom of the hill, creating a multicolored design around them.

"So pretty," she murmured, when the owner of the puppy dashed out yelling "That's my dog!" and snatched the puppy from Manyo's hands.

That's it, that's all I remember, Grandmother said. And if that's the case, then so be it. After she finished junior high school, my grandmother took care of the younger brothers and sisters born one after another to the young couple who had raised her—who were naturally very much not young anymore, but because they were the sort of people with enough heart to take in an abandoned child, their spirits were always young. Taking a break from babysitting, she would sometimes go help out a neighboring farmer and come home having earned a bit of pocket money. Manyo loved the couple, so with a young girl's earnestness, she hoped to live with them in the small lodging house forever, if possible.

The modernization that came with the era continued apace, pushed along by a strong tailwind. This was quite clear looking at just the Akakuchiba Steelworks. The elderly men who had once been proud workers at the tatara ironworks before the war spent their days idle and unoccupied at the bottom of the bottom of the hill in little shacks, their bodies smaller now. Something called the Village Traditional Craft Preservation Society was launched, and an exhibition room was built to house the old wood-burning furnaces, the bellows used in the Edo period, and panels showing how the iron sand was collected. The Society called the old workers in, and they taught the village children who came on Social Studies field trips about the old way of making iron while humming the tatara song. The little boys were delighted. However, the art from days long past that they would exalt—of apprenticing with a master and training to learn the trade over dozens of years—was already something far off in the distant past.

The workers who toiled at the state-of-the-art ironworks, with its enormous German blast furnaces soaring like iron towers, were the ones who swaggered about town now. Their pay was good, and they were welcomed warmly in the evening town. The "mama" owners of the bars competed to count the greatest number of workers among their regulars, and these men were also in great demand as marriage partners for the young women. Unlike the craftsmen of the past, they toiled in a workshop outfitted with a great deal of machinery, with the workers themselves becoming atomic gears, one with the enormous engines. They were young laborers, skilled and proud in line with a new post-war sense of values. After the war, they were industry itself, the poster children for modern rationalism. The progress of their own individual lives could even be seen as the road to a bright—or as bright as it could be—future for this defeated nation.

It was the spring when she was seventeen. Manyo went to town to buy rice and miso and kimono for her brothers and sisters. When evening fell, the workers in their uniforms the color of new leaves and the men in their Self-Defense Force uniforms—the Japan Defense

Agency had been launched a few years earlier, and with that launch, the National Safety Forces had changed its name to the strange-sounding Self-Defense Force—filled the town, drinking, gambling, shelling out for the imported Western clothing and shoes in the department store downtown, buying women in the bar district of Yoimachi Alley. As sunset approached, the men became ruder, but although they stared at Manyo, thinking her strange, they didn't make any easy passes at her, so she had no fear of being out in the evening town. She was hurrying along clutching her rice and miso when the sunset sky abruptly went dark. By the time she realized that the sun hadn't set, but rather that clouds, jet black rain clouds, had blanketed the sky, it had already started to rain. Worried that the miso, which was wrapped only in oil paper, might melt and stream away, Manyo dashed into a nearby storefront.

It was the bukupuku tea shop. In the storefront, Manyo and a parent-child pair of *tanuki* that had wandered down from the mountain stood all three looking up at the dark sky. Then the shop owner came and kicked at the raccoon dogs, chasing them out into the rain. He then turned to Manyo, her hair dripping, her face devoid of makeup, and told her that if she wasn't a paying customer, she had to get out. Having come shopping with no extra money for herself, she didn't have the price of a tea, and so, having no other choice, she readied herself to dash back out into the rain, as if to chase after the tanuki.

At that moment, she heard the voice of a young man from inside the shop.

"You there, come in. Hey, you!"

Manyo turned around.

An extremely tall man with long hair was sitting in the corner. His flat face was very much characteristic of the region, but his almond eyes were sharp and his lips were strangely red. He wasn't bad, but he was not quite what one would call handsome. His hair was too long, he was too tall, his arms were too stretched out. Maybe it was the slightly weird, ghostlike air these features gave him.

On the table before him were a cup of bukupuku tea and a thick book. He had started in on both the tea and the book, both on hold as he stared at her as if dazzled.

"Oh, um…"

"Sit down. Uncle, a cup of bukupuku tea for this woman too."

"She says she doesn't want to go outside because her miso will melt."

"Well, that's only natural. Sit down. Hey, you, you really do look strange."

The young man looked up at Manyo approaching timidly and laughed out loud. With the innocence of a child, he tugged at Manyo's long, wiry hair. Then he brought his pale face closer and stared intently at her strange, finely chiseled face, so obviously different from that of the people of this region.

"Well, you're a mountain person."

"Uh-huh."

"If you'd like anything to eat, just say so. I like unusual things. Like this book, or a face like yours. Here, the menu."

He gave her the shop menu, almost flinging it at her, so she hurried to accept it. Enumerated there were the characters she could not read no matter how desperately she wanted to. Reddening, Manyo said to the strange young man, "I can't actually read."

The man also blushed. "You didn't go to school?"

"No, I did, but I can't read and I can't do numbers neither. Just won't go in my head for some reason."

"Huh…"

The man was quiet for a while, but when the old man brought over Manyo's bukupuku tea, he said gently, "Don't be shy, drink it." And then he began reading the menu aloud as if talking to himself. "Bukupuku tea. Kombu tea. Roasted green tea. Coffee. Black tea. Chestnut yokan jelly. Sweet potato yokan jelly. Black bean yokan jelly. *Goshikimame daifuku* rice cake…"

Manyo laughed, so the man, seemingly relieved, read the menu from the beginning once more. He brushed his long hair away from his face and said, thin, scarlet lips trembling, "Stay here until the rain stops, Manyo Tada."

"A-all right, thank you." Manyo bowed her head.

The man whose name she still did not know then picked up the book he had started to read and dropped his eyes to its pages once again. It was written in characters she had never seen before, ones that went from left to right, so she thought maybe it was a novel or something written in English. She spent some moments fishing out the beans swimming in her frothy tea, but then suddenly, strangely asked, "How do you know my name?"

"Mama told me."

The man lifted his face briefly and looked at Manyo. His long, thin eyes grew even narrower as he took a sip of tea. "Mama told me down below, there's a mountain girl called Manyo Tada. She said she doesn't care how many girls I run with, but I have to marry the mountain girl."

"What's 'mama' mean?"

"Oh, it means 'mother,'" the man answered, tapping his index finger on the hard cover of the Western book. Manyo nodded her assent, thinking this was no doubt some fancy word from the other side of the ocean.

Outside, the heavy drops of pouring rain turned into sheets. The water thundered into the ground in a pounding rhythm that made it hard for Manyo to hear the man. The master closed the front door and lit the lamps. Two orange paper lanterns began to glow inside and in front of the shop.

"I'm Yoji Akakuchiba," the man said languidly, flipping through the pages of the tome he held. "You've probably heard the name before."

"I haven't, actually." Manyo was quick to shake her head, and the man—Yoji, the heir to the Akakuchiba household and profligate son— looked at Manyo, disappointed.

"Well. And here I thought I was popular with the girls of the village."

"You might be, but I don't really talk to anyone."

"Well. You don't?"

"So then, does that mean you're Tatsu's son?"

"Uh-huh. We probably look alike, hm?"

Manyo was silent. She looked over Yoji's tall, slender form, the long slits of his eyes, his lips bright red as if he were wearing lipstick. Then she tried to imagine if Tatsu would look like this if she lost weight.

When she still said nothing, head cocked to one side, he continued. "I basically do what she tells me to."

"Uh-huh."

"Which is why, Manyo Tada, I am going to marry you."

"But someone from the Akakuchiba family can't marry some orphan. Even if Tatsu did tell you that, unless the people in your house allow it—"

"There's not a man in the main family or any branch family who'd go up against Mama. She's scary, you know?"

"What?" Manyo recalled the fat, middle-aged woman who got out of the broken-down black car that time on the hill. Little, tiny Tatsu Akakuchiba, wiping away sesame seed oil sweat, the spitting image of the god Ebisu. She had a hard time believing that this woman was so scary that no one in Takami could stand up to her.

On the other side of the window, the sudden evening shower had stopped. In its place, the wind picked up, blowing in through the gaps in the closed doors and snuffing out the fire in the paper lantern. The bukupuku tea shop promptly went dark. The light of the moon coming in through the window hit the white neck of the tall, gourd-faced young man seated across from Manyo, causing it to shine wetly like an albino rat snake.

"I'm going to marry you. We're going to be together until we die, so it'd be good if we got along. But I don't know how things will actually go."

Slim throat pale in the moonlight, he swallowed, and his Adam's apple leapt up and then fell back down. While she was taken aback by his declaration, the shop owner relit the paper lantern, and with the blooming of the fire flower, the inside of the shop was bright once again.

This isn't the sort of love story young girls swoon over, but Manyo had never had anyone say anything about marriage to her before, so her cheeks were colored with surprise and shyness, and she said nothing. Dropping her eyes to the table, she took the menu she couldn't read in hand and fiddled with it.

As she did, as occasionally happened when she was flustered, the characters written on the menu began transforming into other characters with a strange dragging sound. They wriggled and squirmed as if alive, becoming eight large characters. Manyo stared hard enough to burn a hole through these new characters, but she couldn't read what she couldn't read. Borrowing a pencil from Yoji, and then lick, licking the lead, she printed them carefully on the back of the bill.

Yoji peered over at the eight awkward, copied characters with great interest. Taking the bill, he read in a loud voice. "Your head flies off and you die."

Manyo was shocked, and the face Yoji raised was pale. In that instant, she saw the future. What she thought was snow was a storm of light peach-colored sakura blossoms whirling into the shop and enveloping the two of them. Manyo saw his head ripped off to be sent flying somewhere like a toy. The hair now hanging down his back had gray mixed into it and was tied up on this future self. The head of this slightly aged Yoji came off and winged its way through the air, smile on its lips, and for a moment, he looked like a rocket gushing flames, the spray of Akakuchiba-red blood vivid from the cut. For some reason, the swirling sakura petals flapped like a kaleidoscope of butterflies, forming a squirming tornado that engulfed the headless man. And then, as if this tornado had reversed time, the head was back, the flower storm disappeared somewhere, and the man before her was once again restored to the original young Yoji Akakuchiba.

Manyo pressed a hand to her chest and said nothing. Yoji stared at the eight characters curiously.

"So…what's this? Pretty weird that you can write when you can't read."

"Uh-huh."

"You sure don't talk much, huh? Although I guess that's better than being too chatty. Anyway, this is your answer to me proposing? Ha ha! You really are funny."

Manyo shook her head and replied in a small voice that that was nothing at all. When she thought that someday the young master of the Akakuchiba house would have his head torn off and die, her heart started pounding. And then she had the thought that she would be all right with being this young master's bride and having a good life with him just like Tatsu Akakuchiba wanted until his head was ripped off for whatever unknown reason.

The rain having finally stopped, Manyo went outside and started walking, clutching to her chest the rice and miso and new clothes for her brothers and sisters. As she climbed the main road up the tiered platform, paper lanterns shone hazily outside the entryway to each lodging house, offering her a magnificent view.

Because the workers, toiling on a three-shift system without regard for day or night, often came home late at night, the wives would make sure that there hung in their entryway a large paper lantern with their last name and family crest written on it, to ensure that their husbands did not get lost in the maze of identical lodging houses. When these lanterns were in the entryway and the insides of each house lit brilliantly with electricity, people in the town below would look up at the tiered platform each night and know that business was good at the ironworks.

A black car passed Manyo on this brightly lit platform, heading toward the red gates even further up. She wondered if it carried the young master from before. And then she suddenly thought what a curious man he was, not out drinking and buying women, but sitting alone in a teahouse in the evening, drinking tea like a schoolgirl and reading such a thick book. And she thought about how his long black hair flowed smoothly down his back like black silk, unlike the stiff stuff faded from washing that hung from her own head.

"We ain't nothin' alike..."

Cocking her head, Manyo hurried along the hill road wet from the rain and returned home.

This period when Manyo was living through her adolescence was the turbulent time following the war, a time of many changes. To begin with, repatriates were coming back from all over the world and assimilating into the groups of people who had remained in the land. The magician MacArthur from America, one of the war's victors, rebuilt this nation into a new shape and departed, leaving behind the words, "Old soldiers never die; they just fade away." The US-Japan security treaty was concluded, and the economy started to develop. The children of the provincial towns left the nest for the capital when they graduated from junior high school, the so-called "mass employment" movement. These "golden eggs," these children, were in actuality merely forced into long hours of hard work for low pay. Reality was often bitter.

In the San'in region, business was good at both the red ironworks and the black shipbuilders, and the young people of the village managed to find gainful employment without leaving for the capital. The girls got married when they reached seventeen or eighteen years of age, either because the couple loved each other or because their families had decided on a match for them, and quickly became the mistresses of their own homes.

Outside of her meeting with the curious young master, no one was talking about wanting to make her a wife, so Manyo's days were carefree. And she had her hands full with her brothers and sisters. She fixed them dinner, did their laundry, and on holidays, took them by the hands and brought them to the department store. They would watch an enka singer's show on the roof, she would feed them the kid's lunch in the cafeteria, take them by the hands again—occasionally, piggybacking a brother who got tired and fell asleep—and head home to the tiered lodging houses.

She had grown distant from her classmates since graduating from junior high. But she would from time to time descend from the mountain and walk along the wharf, window shopping at the stores of the showy arcade recently built in town, which was when she saw the Goldfish, aka Midori Kurobishi, albeit only twice.

Manyo didn't call out or anything, just stared with her farseeing eyes; the Goldfish hadn't changed from when they were children. She swaggered along the arcade, luxurious, long, black furisode sleeves swinging, hair full of ornate gold pins, *geta* sandals clacking. The boys who had formerly served as her hangers-on had apparently long ago left to work and were no longer with her, since the Goldfish was alone both times. The way she stood tall like a man, sleeves dancing back and forth as she walked, had a definite appeal to it, and her carriage was surprisingly beautiful. Manyo was surprised and astonished; the girl who had been such an ugly bulldog had turned out really beautiful. The times Manyo saw the Goldfish, it had been evening and night, the woman walking slowly against a backdrop of the dusk ocean dyed a dark rose, an incredible photograph.

However, although everyone believed that this was her, with the long black sleeves and the gold pins, the truth was that this Goldfish was not the real Midori Kurobishi and hadn't been for who knew how long. To this day, Midori herself and my grandmother are the only ones who know the truth. Well, the Kurobishi family probably knew, but none of them said a word about it; it was a secret they took to the next world.

This Goldfish's true identity was, in fact, Midori's older brother.

One night, Manyo, on her way home from an errand, took a shortcut and cut across the abandoned factory yard in a corner of the wharf. The night sky was very clear, a uniform ultramarine, in the middle of which the pale moon shone down on the remains of the factory. Just as Manyo caught sight of what appeared to be the Goldfish running out from the sloping barracks, black sleeves swinging, the girl in question abruptly yanked up the hem of her kimono, humming a quiet song.

She wasn't wearing an undershirt or anything under the kimono, and Manyo could see two legs covered in thick hair, at the base of which grew something she had never seen before. Still humming softly, still standing up, the Goldfish began to piss noisily. With each hum, the golden hair ornaments swung to the right and then to the left. Manyo stood rooted to the spot, dumfounded, as the Goldfish finished pissing, dropped her hem, and still singing, disappeared.

Manyo watched gaping as she vanished when someone suddenly squeezed her shoulder. It was a small hand, like that of a child. She let out a short cry and whirled around.

A small girl stood there. Round eyes popping out, pale skin. Thin, scrawny shoulders. Manyo realized that this was the real Midori Kurobishi. Almost a different person from her old self, the Goldfish was wearing a black kimono with a subdued splash pattern, her hair pulled back in two tails. She hadn't gotten the least bit beautiful.

"You tell anyone what you just saw, and you'll be real sorry," she threatened in a small voice as she glared at Manyo resentfully.

"Who was that?"

"My big brother. He came back from Siberia," the Goldfish said, sing-songy. The moon lit her face brightly, and that face was curiously expressionless. Like her brother in the furisode kimono walking off to nowhere in particular, she cut through the abandoned factory at a trot. Unthinkingly, Manyo followed.

"He came back different. I mean, a boy who can't get on a tuna boat, he sure can't go off to war or nothing like that. The whole thing made him pretty weird. He finally came back last year."

"Weird…huh?" Manyo nodded, thinking back on the bizarre sight she had just seen.

The Goldfish bit her lip. "It's actually amazing he came back alive," she said, following her brother fluttering along.

"Uh-huh."

"He had a girl promised to him. We'd even done all the engagement gift exchange stuff, but he's in such a state, we can't go and tell them he's still alive. Better if we just say he's dead, and she can go be someone else's wife. We keep him in the storehouse, but he pretends he's me, sneaks out wearin' some furisode. Father hits him, we lock him in, but he still manages to get out somehow. So now it's like I can't go walkin' around no more. You get that? People'd smell something fishy, two Midori Kurobishis."

"It's true, I did think it was you struttin' around."

"Lately, all I do is walk around after my brother like this. Can't leave him on his own. So I can't wear furisode no more," the Goldfish said angrily. "Once my brother settles down, I'll take a husband."

When her repatriate brother finally fluttered through the jet-black gates of the Kurobishi house, the Goldfish also went home, seemingly concerned about any eyes that might be watching.

That night, Manyo—among the workers and farmers and men in suits climbing the large steps, shoes clacking loudly, among the steps of modernity and the faces lit up by hope—dreamed of the man in the black furisode kimono tumbling down alone, soundlessly.

After the war was the era of men. The era of manual labor, of the strength of men. Beautiful feminine men, slipping on the steps. Midori's older brother. When she woke from the nightmare, someone was standing in the small room in the lodging house where she slept in a huddle with her family.

Someone wearing a large kimono. A kimono she had thought was black, but which in fact had a red pattern on it.

She started to ask who it was, but then realized it was a vision and closed her mouth. Approaching softly, she saw that the kimono was empty. Something like scattered entrails stuck to the garment in places, creating a pattern like red oil stains glistening wetly in the dark.

"What's the matter, Midori's brother?"

The kimono writhed.

"Did something happen in Siberia?"

The kimono cried. Bits of entrails trickled down like teardrops. Wet blood dripped.

"You were beautiful. You cut such a lovely figure. The furisode suits you so much better than us girls."

The kimono shuddered and the room swayed. She heard the throaty voice of a man. The kimono kept on sobbing.

Entrails flew off and scattered. The thick smell of blood enveloped Manyo. She remembered the two legs thick with hair and the man's thing that had hung its head dejectedly after his piss that she had seen when he flipped the hem of his kimono up.

The kimono was still crying. It was howling. In the vision, it scattered entrails all over the room. "Burn some tokonen grass."

Manyo nodded firmly at the voice that she could just barely hear. In the midst of this bizarre smell of blood, like none she had ever smelled before, the vision disappeared with the dawn, and she endured the vision she saw this night for three months without telling anyone, not even Midori Kurobishi.

And then one silent, frozen night after three months had passed and winter had come, the ears of the sleeping Manyo picked up the sound of a pebble hitting the glass of the window of the lodging. She stood, careful not to wake her family, and opened the window to see Midori Kurobishi standing there, the salty tears of a woman of the ocean streaming from both of her bulging eyes.

Manyo pulled a padded kimono on over her nightdress and dashed outside. "What's wrong?" she asked, running over.

The Goldfish grabbed Manyo's shoulders and shook her with a force that was almost scary. "Do you have a shovel?"

"A shovel? Uh-huh. You came in the middle of the night to borrow a shovel?"

"Do you have a bucket too?"

"Uh-huh...What's this about, Midori?"

"My brother's dead. Dead and scattered all over the place, so we need a bucket and a shovel to get it all together. Can you burn some tokonen grass and call the mountain people?"

"Tokonen grass..." Manyo stood stock still.

Tokonen grass was burned to call the outlanders when a young person died accidentally in the village. Since no one had seen an outlander in the last fifteen years or so, she didn't know if anyone would come even if she did burn the grass to send up the purple smoke. But Midori seemed to think that if Manyo, who was their child, were to burn it, they would definitely come.

Either way, however, burning tokonen grass meant that Midori's brother had committed suicide. Manyo had guessed it when she saw the future dead in her vision, but confronted with it in reality, it was all the more heartbreaking.

Manyo went down the big road with the Goldfish, bucket and shovel in hand. The night was still and frozen, and their white breath reflected the light of the moon.

The Goldfish told her in a low voice that they had to keep the fact that her brother had died wearing a furisode a secret. "I don't want anyone to know that my brother was walkin' around pretending to be me. I just don't want that."

"How'd he die?"

"Just a bit ago, he jumped in front of a freight train. Died. All in pieces." The Goldfish continued in a strange, inflectionless voice. "If we tell Father, he'll end up tossed out without any funeral or nothing, like a cow after it's been chopped up. No one in our house thinks of my brother as my brother. They don't think of him as a son. He's an embarrassment. He prob'ly w-w-w-won't get a fu—neral…"

Without realizing, Manyo had fallen into a trot as if pulled along by the dark thoughts of the Goldfish stammering "wuh-wih-wuh."

The Goldfish stopped on the deserted railroad tracks that connected Daibenimidori Station with the depths of the Chugoku Mountains.

Over a span of a few dozen meters were scattered entrails and blood and all sorts of things; you couldn't tell if they were human or animal. A wooden box the Goldfish had apparently brought was set off on its own, damp with night dew. Trembling all the while, Manyo hunted down some tokonen grass and then set fire to it with a match.

The flame made a slim purple line, snaking leisurely up into the night sky, and flickered as it continued up to surprising heights. It was a strangely sturdy smoke, a purple rope you could grab onto and climb up who knew how high.

Midori came back with her brother's head, smoothly peeled of skin, staggering as if it were heavy. She put it in the box. In the long, glossy hair remained still a number of golden hair ornaments. Then she came back dragging a hairy leg and heaving with sobs. Shocked and overwhelmed, Manyo came back to herself, and together they pulled the leg back, which had been cut off at the base. They put it in the box and ran along the tracks again.

"Lots of tanuki coming down from the mountains get hit by trains here. It's night an' all. The driver don't even realize yet it was a person he hit. But once morning comes, he's gonna know from the blood and guts stuck to the freight train that what he hit was a person. And then the grown-ups are gonna come around here. We gotta clean it up before then. I don't want people knowin' my brother's shame."

"But even putting it all in the box, what—"

"The mountain people'll take him away for me. My brother's young. Accidental death. I know they'll take him an' hide him up in the mountains. They will, right? Manyo, I'm definitely not gonna let my brother be a laughingstock. After all, he was the heir to the Kurobishi house. He was a good man."

"Midori…"

Having made her curt declaration, Midori's eyes, perhaps because of the strength of her resolve, reflected the faint light of the stars and shone brightly. She picked up a black sleeve, stained with a red pattern of blood and entrails that resembled oil stains. An arm was still in it. She put it in the box and, covered in blood, looked up at the moon and laughed loudly.

Manyo wondered in mute amazement if Midori had gone insane. Then she walked over and patted her shoulder.

Midori made strange sounds as she laughed and then started to wail and sob again.

When the two had gathered up all they could and put it in the box, they sat down, leaning against each other, exhausted. The night was still far from over. Stained with the thick stink of blood and guts, Manyo fell asleep as if passing out.

When she opened her eyes at dawn, the blood had dried and the smell was gone. The tokonen grass fire was also gone. She poked Midori awake and turned back in the direction of the box.

The box with Midori's brother in it was gone.

She looked up at the mountains, which were a faint peach in the day-break sky. Snow had already settled on the peaks. There was no sign of any person. No voices sounded. Were those people still in the mountains or not? Manyo couldn't tell. When she went to stand up, she noticed that a single wild rose—out of season—had been placed on her knees.

They came, she thought. *They exist. They'll have a funeral for Midori's brother.*

In Benimidori after the war—mechanized as it was and attacking the modern age with force—in this age of power, feet planted firmly on the ground, a feminine man was an embarrassment. But they would have a funeral for the big brother. Manyo yanked on the hand of the dumbfounded Midori and hurried to leave the spot behind them before the sky became fully light. She hid the traces of the tokonen grass being burned, hid their blood-soaked kimono, as if fleeing a crime scene.

At the road that was the barrier between red above and black below, they waved and separated. When Manyo said, "Don't tell anyone," Midori spat, "Of course not." And then the two split into up and down and ran off.

Manyo returned to the lodging house, washed the bucket and shovel, and then scrubbed her own limbs hard until the smell of blood disappeared. And then, she put the wild rose in a cup of water and set it out near the window.

That year, the prime minister of the country was Hayato Ikeda, a lively man past middle age, who made a good showing with a bold speech about a "national income-doubling plan" to increase the income of citizens two-fold over the next ten years. The vision of the burnt fields from when they had lost the war at once grew distant, and the people shouted about more mass production, the modernization of agriculture, and greater personnel capability. This was the era that saw the economy start to rise like a wave, centered on steel, the automobile industry, and the construction business. People parroted that bit about success in life being the dream of the people, like some pet saying, and well, anyway, they worked haaard. It was an era when people, starting with the youth, woke up from the postwar shock and started to believe that economic development was the road to the future.

People just kept scrambling to be first to climb up the tiered world.

3. LOVE VACATION

Ooh, your kisses make me sigh

My girlish heart's dreaming an innocent dream of sweet love

On hot sand, sparkling gold

Let's love each other naked like mermaids

Oh, the joy of love, the rose-colored days

When I saw you for the first time.

Love vacation

1963, Manyo at twenty years old. The San'in region was gray with the black smoke puffing up from the blast furnaces, the water flowing in the Hino River was the same dull shade, and the people worked hard, of course, dreaming of prosperity. The radio played the hit song "Love Vacation" by The Peanuts, young twin singers, over and over.

Manyo had belatedly met girls in town she could call friends, so she would meet them at the bukupuku teahouse and chat in front of the black and white television set up there, staring at the screen as she picked the beans from her tea with a toothpick.

Heroes of men befitting the era of men began to appear. More and more people had televisions, which meant the entire country was receiving the same culture from the center of the nation on electromagnetic waves at exactly the same time. Famous moments in professional baseball played out on the screen; everyone watched and watched and watched the flamingo leg kick of Sadaharu Oh—the Home Run King. And in pro wrestling, a huge, strong man who went by the name of Rikidozan triumphed in battle, day in and day out, his clear voice ringing out in victory. With each conquest, the people in the teahouse would be as one and cry out in triumph. The king hit balls impossibly high into the sky, and Rikidozan defeated his opponents, lifting to absurd heights the spirits of the people who watched them. Men were strong and woman fell in love with these strong men; inside and outside the television, people believed this absolutely without pretense. It was a simple time.

One evening when Manyo was watching the television with her friends, she ran into the Goldfish for the first time in a long while. The pair, eyes meeting for the first time since they had walked away from each other without so much as a wave of the hand on the boundary of the hill road separating up and down, nodded silently at each other.

"Uncle, coffee," the Goldfish said to the shop master, perhaps sick and tired of bukupuku tea. As always, she cut the glittering figure of the nouveau riche, black dress sparkling with gold beads, gleaming earrings patterned after the magic hammer of lore. She had a permanent wave in her hair and eye shadow painted along her spherical, popped-out eyes.

"Hey, stray cat!" the Goldfish called over to Manyo, dropping countless cubes of sugar in her coffee. Around her, Manyo's friends gasped and looked back and forth between the two women.

Manyo nodded coolly. "What, bulldog?"

"I'm getting married."

"What's the guy like?"

"Strong, hard worker. Crude." The Goldfish's eyes were vacant, looking up at the distant black and white television. Rikidozan did karate chop after karate chop after karate chop, and each time, the customers in the tea shop immediately cheered.

It was too loud in the small space, so Manyo moved herself next to the Goldfish, chair and all, and brought her face close. She leaned an ear toward the other girl as if to say "I'm listening" and the Goldfish's eyes popped out even further as she peered into Manyo's small, dark ear. She swallowed hard once as if fearing she might find the flames of hell in the small hole.

"Look, Manyo."

"What?"

"I chose a strong, hardworking, crude guy."

"That's what you said before."

"I'm the heiress to the Kurobishi Shipbuilders. I can marry whomever I want. So I went with the one who seemed strongest. I didn't go by looks."

"Uh-huh."

"I'm gonna take good care of my husband."

Stirring her coffee violently, the Goldfish fell silent. Someone changed the channel, and a popular song started playing. Lovely girls in white dresses sang into a mic stand. Refined, toylike women, the kind you didn't see in the provincial towns. "Love Vacation" started playing, and the girls in the teahouse began singing along, imitating the dance, and being generally delighted.

The Goldfish sipped her coffee, scowling as if suddenly troubled. She jabbed her spoon into Manyo's bukupuku tea uninvited, scooped up a bean, brought it to her mouth, and chewed it up, still with the pained look on her face. Then, as if squeezing the words out, she groaned, "I... loved...my brother naked. I like pretty boys. I'd rather look at a pretty boy than in the mirror."

"Midori..."

"To make the country richer, all right, if we work real hard, do what we can, then maybe when our daughters, our grandkids, when they grow up, maybe girls and boys won't hafta die young. You think maybe?"

"Dunno, Midori. I don't know what's coming next either."

"If you don't know, Manyo, then I don't neither." The Goldfish popped her eyes out and laughed, making a weird *ee-shee-shee* sound.

That was the entirety of their conversation when they met this day for the first time since that morning. And then, it was again a very long time before Manyo and the Goldfish crossed paths once more.

In summer of that year, the Goldfish took a husband over two meters tall, a man who resembled Rikidozan; no traffic was allowed onto the big industry road where the wharf was while Midori paraded

a whole kilometer along the road in a gold-brocaded satin damask wedding costume.

"An' she wore a headdress with a gold *uchigake* tie, one of the ones
like a folding screen. Hair all tied up *nihongami* style, just stuffed with
gold combs and pins. Undershirt, *tabi* socks, all gold. Black zori sandals.
Such a beautiful bride, like something straight outta a magazine," the
people of "black below" declared as one.

The head of the nouveau riche Kurobishi house bragged long and
hard about how beautiful the bride was marching down the industrial
road with the comings and goings of cars stopped, how she glittered in
black and gold, even going so far as to tease that she was more dressed
up than a family altar. The large groom swept the glittering Goldfish up
in his arms and crossed the threshold of the house with her. The Goldfish was apparently quite delighted at this, kicking golden-stockinged
feet out with glee.

"I heard her new hubbie's a real big one."

In the "red above" lodging house halfway up the tiered platform
where Manyo lived, the young couple—although they were obviously
no longer young—enjoyed the gossip. The little brothers and sisters had
apparently gone down to the industrial road to watch, and a little sister
played the Goldfish with her brother in geta sandals as the groom; their
graceful sauntering was interrupted by squeals and giggles. The children
had also picked up some of the gold leaf mochi rice cakes being handed
out in celebration, so that evening, they had mochi for the first time in a
while. They got plenty of gold leaf stuck to their front teeth, and the little
ones laughed as they bared golden teeth at each other. It was a joyous day.

That night, the radio on the tea cupboard the young couple had bought on installment played the news and *rakugo* stories and hit songs. The love songs she had already heard countless times that year leapt again into the small ears of twenty-year-old Manyo, chin in hands on the low dining table, head cocked to one side.

On hot sand, sparkling gold
Let's love each other naked like mermaids
Oh, the joy of love, the rose-colored days

I loved my brother naked, the Goldfish's voice came back to her. *So by love, I guess she means that*, Manyo wondered idly. *But I dunno, the Goldfish, she's so fashionable an' all, I guess she reeeally adored that pretty brother of hers.*

Maybe the way we live and the choices we make do create the future. Manyo had never thought about this before. *The men, their job, their responsibility is to work, and us women, we gotta be the shadow in the shadows.* With this in mind, she lived her lazy days. The Goldfish's words—the idea that if they worked real hard and the country became richer, then things would be better in the time of their children and grandchildren—had shocked Manyo and given her a mysterious sensation like heaven and earth reeling. But Midori had probably been talking like that in an effort to find her footing again after her brother's death.

"So Midori's hubbie's a big one, huh?" she murmured to herself and looked up at the radio. The sweet voice dragged out the "vacation" part and then the song ended.

That summer when everyone was excited about the gilded splendor of the "black below" wedding, not a single person in Benimidori expected that another, even more dazzling and elegant wedding would take place in the village that same year. Even the very bride herself, Manyo, was drifting through lazy days, looking after the little brothers and sisters; the thought that she could ever be the beautiful bride never even crossed her mind.

One night, the husband of the young couple got turned around in the lodging house alleyway despite the fact that they had lit the paper lantern and were all waiting for him. "Looks like a fox went and bewitched me," he said when he finally made it home, wiping and wiping the sweat dripping from his brow.

Oh, Dad's home! His wife and the adopted Manyo and the little brothers and sisters bustled into the entryway to receive him with a "Dad, welcome home."

As he took off his work uniform, once the color of new leaves, now stained with sweat and black smoke and oil, the husband said, "Now, you. Tomorrow, you're going on up to Takami."

"Me? Why would I?" the wife asked in reply, but the husband just shook his head, jumped in the bath before the rest of them, and went to bed. Then, the next morning, he made his wife put on her best kimono, putting on a rare suit himself, and they climbed the hill together.

The couple had a whole herd of children, and there was always a baby who needed looking after, so Manyo worked tirelessly, changing diapers and washing them, pulling weeds out of the garden. It was past noon when the wife returned to the lodging house, face drained of color.

"It does look like a fox went and bewitched us," the couple said, and went up to Manyo hanging diapers to dry in the garden.

"Manyo, hun. Come sit here a minute."

"What's wrong, the both of you?"

"Nothing to worry about, just sit, sit right here."

After she had finished hanging the diapers, Manyo went back inside. The black smoke from the plant grew worse in direct proportion to how good business was, so that some days, depending on which way the wind was blowing, there was no way you could dry your laundry outside. *We're above the wind today, so I'll let the sun shine on those diapers and sterilize 'em real good*, she thought.

"What? Now when we finally got a good laundry day?"

"You don't need to do the laundry or nothing. Seems like you're gonna be the missus up at Takami."

"Huh?"

"The missus at Takami. And the one right at the top. I don't really understand it myself, but they said they want you up with the Akakuchiba boy, the young master. Can't understand it at all. Manyo, hun, you friendly with the boy?"

"No, not at all." Manyo shook her head. She told them about meeting Tatsu Akakuchiba way back when, over ten years earlier, in the middle of the hill, and about meeting the young master, Yoji Akakuchiba, in the teahouse where she was taking shelter from the rain three years earlier, and both the husband and wife cocked their heads.

"Don't really understand it." The husband scratched his head. "But they called us up to Takami and said they'd be glad to have you. We told 'em we can't give you no kind of dowry, we're just workers on the steps, but they said, you just bring your daughter and that's good enough. But if you don't like the idea, you just say so."

"Uh-huh." Manyo nodded. "Well, I don't hate the idea."

Manyo had, up to that point in her life, never had a love like in the popular songs, like fireworks in the night sky, and she felt that such a fashionable sort of feeling would not be any part of her future either. She remembered what the young master had murmured that evening three years earlier when she was sheltering from the rain—*I'm going to marry you. We're going to be together until we die, so it'd be good if we actually got along*—and she said, just like that, "It'd . . . be good if we actually got along."

"Well, that's why you get married."

The young couple spontaneously met one another's eyes and smiled. The little brothers and sisters became quiet, watching to see where this would go. Manyo didn't hate the idea, and any way she looked at it, she'd be marrying up in a serious way, the kind of marriage you never heard about on the steps, so when night fell, the husband set off to tell Takami that they formally accepted.

"You're going to be the wife of someone pretty big," the wife sighed. "And here we had you washing the diapers." She gently took the now dry diaper Manyo had started to fold from her hand. "Someone else's business when the Kurobishi girl was all golden down there not too long ago, hm? Peanuts compared with an Akakuchiba wedding, and to the young master of the main house no less. Them down there's nouveau riche shipbuilders, but here, here's the real deal, a proper old family. I don't know what we'll do. Never even dreamed we'd be showing our faces at something so grand."

The little brothers and sisters fell asleep, leaving only the adults awake in the house. The wife looked out at the garden suddenly. The old communal well sat under the overhang of the house three doors down. Water pipes had gradually been laid out not that long before, and the well was basically used to chill tomatoes and watermelon and sodas and cool off in the summer, so it looked a little forlorn now. The side of the well that little Manyo had been leaned up against like a doll had already disappeared under the abundant bloom of the morning glories, and the ivy, about to wither, writhed like an inauspicious omen, rustling dryly in the wind.

"You...were right over there," the wife whispered, like she was telling secrets. Her face was properly, appropriately aged, burnt in the sun, wrinkled. But it was a face that brimmed with vitality, shining so brightly it was almost strange.

Manyo stared hard at the old gray well where the wife was pointing. As she stared, she felt as if the child of the dark outlanders was still there now, abandoned, propped up against that well, anxious.

She seemed like a bad omen, not cute at all, a curious something someone dropped. Manyo felt strange then—or rather, she had always been strange, but now, she asked the wife something she had refrained from asking before.

"Mom, why'd you take me in? You were young back then, you prob'ly didn't have any money to spare. And it wasn't like they left me in front of your house or nothing. I mean, it was the well three doors down."

"I s'pose so." The wife thought about it and then replied, "The war started when I was a kid. There was no food, and we were poorer than we are now. Life here's heaven. Back then, the men all got snapped up, went off to be soldiers, and the women just had to give birth, make more. At any rate, they used to say children are treasures. Compared to back then, we've been rich since we come here, and well, children really are treasures, I s'pose."

The night wind blew, and the mosquito net above them and all the sleeping little brothers and sisters fluttered gently. The vegetable shoots and cosmos flowers in the garden swayed from side to side.

"We just figured someone had to raise you," the wife said without hesitation, inside the child-filled mosquito net. "And we were the youngest an' all. Best thing for a man is to work hard and for a woman, to have babies and raise 'em right, I s'pose. I've lived my life believing that. Doesn't matter if you birthed the child yourself!"

The wind blew hard, noisily, and the mosquito net shook even more. Manyo felt this wind was a bad sign. An ominous premonition shot through her dark body abruptly, that a time would come when this way of life the wife was telling her about would no longer be a self-evident truth. Occasionally, the wind would blow on the clairvoyant Manyo and a premonition would leap into her heart. Although she never had any idea if it would come true or not.

Not noticing the sinister darkness of the damp wind, the wife wrinkled up the corners of her eyes into a smile. "Manyo, you make sure you have lots of babies too, and take good care of that boy who picked you to marry. A debt like the one you owe the Akakuchiba people now, about all a woman can do is have babies and raise 'em right."

"Mom…" Even as she murmured this, Manyo understood for the first time at that moment that this kind woman was not related to her by blood, that she was a total stranger. Once again, there was an enormous distance between these two souls, the mother who raised her and the orphaned girl taken in. *Mom's a village woman. And I'm a mountain woman. This kind village woman took me in and raised me, but there's no way I can be a woman like her, coming from the mountains like I do.*

So then why did the small, Ebisulike madam of the Akakuchiba house dare to choose Manyo, the child of the outlanders, to be her son's wife? The night wore on and Manyo was unable to solve this particular mystery. From the evening until the morning three months later when she married her new husband, she lived in the worker lodging house, feeling a curious isolation she had never felt before.

Now, the young couple's house was in a state of feverish activity until the wedding day three months later. Everything they needed to prepare for the big day had been given to them by the people up on Takami, but the people from the neighborhood came to ambush them with questions, and they tried to clean the inside of their small lodging house as best they could, and then do something with Manyo, this girl from up in the mountains. They put her in the bath every night, and the wife scrubbed her black hair and patted powders and things on her body, so that every night she collapsed into sleep, completely exhausted. The husband was restless and sat on the veranda, staring up at Takami and sighing.

Two months before the wedding, the go-between the Akakuchibas had appointed stopped by. Someone from the central government with deep ties to the Akakuchiba Steelworks, who came with his wife, handed Manyo the marriage contract. On behalf of illiterate Manyo, the little brothers and sisters, peeking in from either side, read the contract out loud in high-pitched voices, voices so loud they could be heard three doors down, and the people of the neighborhood gathered in front of the garden.

MARRIAGE CONTRACT

Whereas, it is the will of the Lord above that man and woman join together as one and begin a new life; people shall obey this will and receive this happiness.

Whereas in this unity, the woman recognizes the man as husband, and the man recognizes the woman as wife.

Whereas the husband shall appreciate and love the wife wholeheartedly, and has a responsibility to continue to do so, while the wife shall respect and love the husband wholeheartedly and has a responsibility to support him.

Given these, as of August 1963, Yoji Akakuchiba and Manyo Tada agree to wed each other, and print their names here as evidence of this intention.

Yoji Akakuchiba

Manyo

In the midst of the neighbors chattering and wondering what this was all about, Manyo took her cues from the people around her and managed somehow to write her own name where she was told before handing the contract back to the go-between. The young couple watched the proceedings from one corner of the room, as if frightened.

And then another two months later, the morning of the wedding, servants who came with the dawn from Takami barged into the lodging, roused Manyo, and began the bridal preparations.

They boiled water and washed her, and the hairdresser combed out her long, wild hair before cutting it straight across at her waist. The woman then took plenty of camellia oil, spun the hair up with her hands, and in no time flat, had tied Manyo's hair in the traditional *takashimada* style. Manyo was then made up with a thick layer of white powder and just the slightest bit of crimson on her lips. The snow-white bridal headdress hid almost her entire face. Popped into a white kimono, gold zori sandals pushed onto her feet, Manyo was turned into a glamorous and sophisticated bride in the twinkling of an eye and set into the palanquin that eventually came along, to begin her slow, graceful ascent toward Takami up the hill in front of the lodging house.

The palanquin's progress was at a turtle's pace, so slow that although they departed in the morning, it was past noon when they reached the red gates of the main house at the very top. The palanquin rocked Manyo back and forth, and the chilly fall wind blew over her as she waited intently. Those surrounding the palanquin were in olden dress, and the all-men Japanese-style band—the flute player, the cymbal crasher, the old man blowing a conch—ceaselessly made merry around the bridal litter.

The vehicle advanced ever so slowly, finally arriving among the houses of Takami just when it was getting to be noon. From the palanquin window, she could clearly see the outside. On the steps below, the eyes of the people who came out in front of the workers' lodging houses, as if to watch a festival, had been curious, but the gazes bathing Manyo now on Takami were slightly different, strangely quiet, as if they were afraid of her. Men wearing expensive suits with the smell of the city on them. Genteel wives looking like they had graduated from mission school. Children in arms, dressed in silk clothing. All of them stared equally fearfully at the palanquin.

For the first time, Manyo had the thought that perhaps they hated her and her mountain origins. However, as proof that this was not quite the case, several among them turned to the palanquin, clasped their hands together in prayer, and whispered something. It was a curious sight, the people of Takami in their stylish clothing and clad in an aura of urbanity. The men had short hair parted on the side, the women had theirs set beautifully in permanent waves. And these people clasped their hands and prayed to the beautiful bride, like the deeply religious old people of the village.

"I beg of you, new bride…"

One of the murmurings leapt into Manyo's little ear by the palanquin window, and an oppressive feeling of suffocation settled over her. *What were they begging of me just now?* She looked back, thinking it strange, and saw the figure of a young man in a stylish, white button-up shirt quietly turning his back on the palanquin, hands still clasped together. Manyo stared absently at the beautiful silver cuff links, something she had never seen before, glittering on the wrists of those hands.

Before she knew it, it had become surprisingly dim around the palanquin, so much so she wondered if dusk had somehow come early; the dark sky was an unpleasant shade, filled with arabesque-like clouds, the black smoke from the steelworks, and an unpleasant invisible something. People disappeared from the edge of the road in the middle of the houses of Takami, and in their place, many, so many, so many it was dizzying, small Jizo statues in red bibs stood on both sides, staring hard at the litter with stone eyes.

Stark red *torii* gates, apparently enshrining something. A single grave, standing alone. Large stones, entwined with sacred rope and splashed with water, appeared around the road. Fence exposing the reddish-black fall leaves starting to dry out on the red-tiled roof. The whole of the stark red fence was hardened into a bent shape, an arrow pointing from the top of the mountain down, because of its place in the mountains where the harsh yamaoroshi wind blew. A fierce wind howled, and the bridal palanquin inclined slightly. Dark red leaves danced in the gusts and fell like splatters of blood. Almost as if to say "Don't come this way, leave," as if it had a will of its own, the wind pushed insistently on the litter, causing resistance like a giant's finger poking at the vehicle.

The festive band dwindled. The old man had his conch ripped away, and it tumbled down the hill. One of the cymbals flew away, and the crashing sound disappeared. The flute broke as well, producing nothing but air, and finally, the bridal palanquin was advancing silently. The men dispatched to shoulder the palanquin roared and continued upward almost hugging the round basket carrying Manyo. The men of the band tossed away what remained of their instruments and helped shoulder the load.

The wind grew stronger. Men who appeared to be the servants of the branch families came running to push on the palanquin. Others came bustling from the red houses here and there, and then sturdy women, kimono sleeves tied back, housekeepers, flew out, and everyone pushed on the litter, helped shoulder it, until finally, in place of the band, the sound of voices bellowing "Heave! Ho!" rang out, shaking the mountain and ripping through the wind.

Bridal procession! Heave!
Yamata no Orochi! Ho!

So going to wife is this difficult a journey? Rolling her eyes, Manyo had, at some point, joined in and also started chanting "Heave! Ho!" with the people around the palanquin. She didn't really understand why the mythical eight-headed snake Yamata no Orochi was part of the chant, but the yamaoroshi wind was so severe, she didn't have the luxury of thinking too hard about it. As she shouted "Heave! Ho!" after the roof of the palanquin was peeled off, the round basket was crushed from the front and even the floor dropped out soon enough, so Manyo walked the rest of the way in full bridal costume, gold zori sandals clacking, and shouted "Bridal procession! Heave!" as she continued to climb the hill.

Finally, the yamaoroshi stopped dead.

I beg you, I beg you… The small wavelets of whispers from the people of Takami, who had protected and pushed and lifted Manyo, retreated. She thought she heard someone whisper "Vengeful spirit, begone," but having no chance to turn around, she adjusted her crooked headdress, fixed her white kimono, which was starting to come off, and finally slipped through the red gates of the house of the main Akakuchiba family, gold zori crunching against the ground.

She had stared up at this red mansion, dazzled, from the steps below for as long as she could remember. And now, the expansive garden spread out before her, the enormous main building sitting on the other side of this, red tiles glinting. The open reception hall welcomed Manyo with the wonderful landscape painting on the fusuma sliding doors depicting the large school of red snapper swimming in the wild waves of the Sea of Japan that she had seen from below with her keen eyes— although perhaps that had been a vision—bathed in the afternoon light, glimmering. She was a little confused that there was no one at all to receive her other than this fusuma. She took a breath deep enough to push her shoulders up and stood there for a while. As she did, a man and a woman appeared in the blink of an eye, as if they had been blown in and landed in the garden before the daughter of the mountain and her bridal procession arrived all alone with even the palanquin broken.

"Well, hello!" a voice called to her. "You made it, I see."

Hurriedly turning around, she saw standing there the man who would be her husband now, the man she had met just once three years earlier in the tea shop. As before, long-haired. Almond eyes, thin red lips. Tall and thin, long legs and arms. Yoji Akakuchiba was dressed in Western clothing, black morning coat over a silk shirt, and he casually held in one hand a thick, half-finished book. Beside him stood the small, fat woman, the female Ebisu, Tatsu, dressed properly in a kimono.

"Congratulations on making it up here. You really are a mountain girl," Tatsu said in an easy tone. Then she clapped both hands together sharply, and guests and servants came bustling out of nowhere to begin preparing for the banquet.

Having come to be married all on her own, Manyo sat next to Yoji, exchanged the three-times-three nuptial cups and swore before God, and then she sat very earnestly and quietly throughout the dinner. She simply rolled her eyes at the scene, not knowing who was who with the people from the branch families.

It was when the sun started to set that she noticed something odd. She noticed that there were too many people.

At first, Manyo thought some workers were also at the banquet, mixed in with the Akakuchiba relatives. However, that was not the case; she was, unknowingly, seeing a vision. The people she saw were workers from the steps after they had lost their lives. A worker of her acquaintance, looking a little older than he did now, wandered around without one of his hands. Spotting Manyo, he went to raise the missing hand in greeting and then stared down at his own body as if confused. Some workers were still young. As soon as Manyo noticed them, they all started to reveal bodies that were half-burned or missing legs or other parts. There were many accidents at the steelworks, and Manyo knew only too well that there were more than a few cases where a man working happily yesterday was no longer able to work today. The people here were the future injured and the dead.

"What's wrong?" Yoji asked, noticing the look in Manyo's eyes, as he drank sake quietly beside her.

"Nothing." Manyo shook her head. The banquet continued, and

when night fell and the men among the relatives lowered their heads to Tatsu before heading home one after another, the future spirits also lowered their heads to Manyo one after another and disappeared somewhere.

When the banquet was over, the young couple, Yoji and Manyo, still formally dressed, were left alone with Tatsu Akakuchiba and her husband, Yasuyuki, just the four of them in the reception hall where the large school of snappers leapt on the fusuma. Tatsu was as before—no, she was rather even shorter than she had been when they met ten years before in the middle of the steps and had put on quite a bit of weight. Yasuyuki was of a scholarly bent, thin, with glasses, a man who seemed to have little moisture in his body; he stared at this strange bride whom he was meeting for the first time, clearing his throat with a little cough from time to time.

The red mansion fell back into silence. Even the air here seemed different from the steps below. Clear, cool, freezing in places. Everyone spoke quietly and elegantly, little ripples. There were no children thundering around like little elephants, noses running.

This is the world above. I managed to get through the gates of the red heaven, Manyo thought. *I've married into a strange place.* And then, precisely because she was at the top of the mountain, she saw incessant visions. When she looked up, she saw several beams high up in the ceiling, about as thick as the central pillar, and in the middle of that gloom floated the flying one-eyed man like a fond memory. Ruined right eye and kindish left eye. Seen through the eyes of the adult Manyo, he looked to be over forty, just as she had thought.

She smiled in tired relief at the familiar vision; it had been who knew how many years since she last saw it. But a heartbeat later, she remembered that she had just married another man. This event that had actually just taken place, however, still felt hazy in her heart, like a fleeting vision.

"It's so good you've come to us." Tatsu started up a conversation abruptly, as Manyo stared up at the apparition near the ceiling with relief on her face. "I was honestly worried you wouldn't be able to make it up the hill."

Manyo hurriedly looked away from the vision and dropped her head. "Uh-huh." She placed both hands on the tatami-matted floor. "The yamaoroshi was so fierce, the palanquin even broke. But I managed to walk up somehow. The wind today was incredibly strong, wasn't it?"

"Might've been a vengeful spirit getting in your way. Right, honey?"

"I don't believe in vengeful spirits or in mountain girls," her husband Yasuyuki replied in a low voice, fiddling with his glasses. "As if there could be such things in this era of science and technology."

"But you will do as I say," Tatsu said quietly.

"I'd like to see the man who could go up against you. In any case, I leave this young lady here to you. I have to give the factory my undivided attention."

Manyo lifted her head and compared the three members of her new family. Yasuyuki had an old face and averted his eyes, but Tatsu smiled unfazed by Manyo's staring. And Yoji, who was now her husband, flipped through the Western book he had dug out of his pocket, seeming entirely uninterested.

"What do you mean, 'vengeful spirit'?" Manyo asked. She remembered hearing all the strange things about "vengeful spirit, begone" and about Yamata no Orochi as she climbed the road to be here.

"No matter how you look at it, there are too many accidents at the ironworks," Yoji said gently, popping his face up from his Western book at his perplexed bride. "The blast furnace is a gift of modern technology, but well, it's like a living creature. In fact, the longer you work there, the more you end up believing in a mysterious power. So then you get frightened people saying that where there's an accident, there's a vengeful spirit."

"Uh-huh."

"As technology progresses, the old things are smashed, the area picks itself back up, and new things are put in their place. That's how it goes. The people are probably nervous about how the old tatara plant was taken down and the blast furnaces put in. We didn't have enough land when we built the factory, so we tore down a lot of the ancient places of the gods and put new facilities on top of them, you see."

Manyo nodded, remembering the Jizo statues and the deified rocks along the way up the hill, and Tatsu began to talk about a variety of things for the edification of the new daughter of the Akakuchiba family.

In the end, no one ever did tell her the reason why the people of the main family so desired her as their son's wife, but she told me in her last years that she gradually came to understand it as she lived with them.

Yamata no Orochi is a legend told since ancient times in the mountains of the San'in region, a story written in the *Nihon Shoki*, the chronicles of ancient Japan. The enormous fire-breathing snake with eight heads and tails in this story was probably a mythological metaphor for the steel flowing from the tatara ironworks.

The lore in the village of Benimidori was that the ancestors of the Akakuchiba family had originally crossed over from the Korean Peninsula, settled in the mountains of Benimidori, transmitted the steel-making technology this country lacked, and reigned as head of the tatara plant. But this history changes a little when you take into consideration the legend of Yamata no Orochi, which also appears in the *Nihon Shoki*. In this case, Susano'o-no-Mikoto, the slayer of the great snake, becomes a metaphor for the newly arrived people, and indigenous people in this land already possessed the eight crimson rivers, i.e., iron-making technology, before the Akakuchibas crossed the ocean from the Korean Peninsula to come here. In this case, the tatara technology was originally the occupation of the indigenous people.

If this was the real story, then the Akakuchiba people were perhaps invaders who defeated the ancient people, kicked out the indigenous gods, and installed the new gods they brought with them. They destroyed the indigenous people, chased them deep into the Chugoku Mountains, and to rub salt in the wound, built a new tatara plant and reigned over the land. Then after a long period of time, the modern age arrived, and the invaders again smashed the tatara plant and the gods of the place to establish the Akakuchiba Steelworks with its German blast furnaces, which they called a gift of modern rationalism. This is somehow also a microcosm of the history of this country and modern industry.

The fear of divine punishment the people of the Akakuchiba Steelworks felt each time an accident occurred was probably because

the ancient heart of Japan beat there, and they felt a debt to the fact
that, whether anyone liked it or not, things were developing and changing to be more Western. Either way, the outlanders, living deep in the
mountains with no ties to the nation, who came down every so often,
were, for the Akakuchiba people, something like the descendants of an
indigenous people chased off a long, long time ago. Perhaps having the
abandoned Manyo—a descendant of these people who had disappeared
into the mountains with modernization and were no longer coming
back—marry into their family was meant to appease the ancient vengeful spirits and calm the fear in their own hearts of such spirits.

This is nothing more than the theory that Manyo in her later years
and I, her granddaughter, came up with while talking with one another
about the past; I don't know the actual truth of the matter. In any case,
over the course of this night when she overcame the wind and went
from being an orphan on the steps below to being the bride in the house
in the heavens at the top in the fall of 1963, Manyo became the clairvoyant madam of the Akakuchibas in the red mansion that ruled over
Benimidori.

That night, Manyo left her seat reciting in her heart all the tidbits
Tatsu had imparted to her. That night, Manyo did not know what was
where in the large mansion. She left the reception hall and walked down
a long hallway, Yoji leading her by the hand. A small woman, thirtyish, a
housekeeper by the looks of her, staring at them from the shadow of the
fat central pillar caught her attention.

When she gave a slight acknowledging bow, the servant abruptly dropped her eyes to her own toes. The name of this mature woman was Masago, and she was, in fact, a servant Yoji had made his mistress, but Manyo had no way of knowing this at that time. And because she was a late bloomer, it took her a fair while to realize it.

Anyway, Manyo, not knowing anything at that time, simply followed Yoji's lead and shuffled down the smooth, polished hallway, looking absently out at the expansive backyard spreading out to the right through the flower-shaped transom in the stretch of shoji paper doors to her left. This backyard was tended each day by several people under the supervision of older men who had once been gardeners in the city; it was an extremely artistic space.

Tuk! The bamboo *shishi-odoshi* tube in the fountain clacked against the rock. White pebbles were arranged in a pattern she had never seen before, a conflagration like a crimson lotus. Yoji told her in a dry voice that it was patterned after the flow of molten steel.

He tucked his Western book into a pocket and gradually increased his pace, pulling Manyo along with one hand and loosening the collar of his morning jacket with the other. Manyo, still in her bridal wear—complete with headdress—trotted along after him, feet getting tangled as she did. The older housekeeper's gaze slithered and coiled around them, and they pushed ahead at this quick pace as if to shake free of it, when in the middle of the long, long, endless hallway, the woman's gaze was at last abruptly cut off. They had arrived at a corner, a bend of ninety degrees along the backyard, which was probably a barrier to Masago's eyes.

Yoji turned corner after corner after corner until Manyo was nearly dizzy, running familiarly through the enormous labyrinth of a mansion, going deeper and deeper inside. Just when she thought she couldn't go on, the hallway began to slope gently. The backyard too became an easy slope, following the mountains. Crystal water flowed, a small river and a delicate toylike waterfall, and Manyo cried out softly. She liked this work of the gardener, and from the following day, Manyo would often frequent the garden, but this first night was not the time for that.

The two raced along the smooth hallway as if climbing the mountain, and out of breath, they finally reached a small Japanese-style room somewhere even deeper inside the mansion, the new couple's bedroom. Two cold futons were spread out next to each other, and by the head of the futons was a red cut-glass water pitcher.

Unconsciously, Manyo looked back at the garden. The *tuk* of the bamboo tube pushed at her heart, as if cheering her on. Yoji pulled the shoji door shut roughly and tossed his Western book onto the tatami floor. The pale moonlight poured through the flower-shaped transom onto the futons like a cold fire.

Her husband's hands lifted the headdress off, and the high knot of the takashimada hairstyle set with camellia oil was also immediately undone.

She thought she might be floating, before she realized she had been tossed toward the futon by her husband. Her long, unbound hair lingered in the air, and Manyo unconsciously stretched out both hands toward the ceiling. Her many precious memories from childhood on flickered through her mind, as if flying out of her heart and fluttering to the ground in the darkened room. She suddenly understood that the woman she was no longer belonged only to herself. She had become a man's wife; she had become a family's possession. The word *goodbye* popped up in her heart. Was it a parting from what had been hers alone, an isolated inner space? Or was this a farewell to the man in her vision who had lived so long in her heart? She saw in the back of her mind the one-eyed man she never got to meet in the ten years before she married, and she felt a fierce yearning for him in her heart. Finally, she had the flicker of an idea that perhaps this woman she was had wanted to belong to that man, but the thought was fleeting.

When she came to herself, she had fallen gently onto the soft, luxurious futon, long hair spread out on its surface like an enormous black fan. The lamplight was a wet orange. The futon was a sumptuous, crimson thing that felt to her like being on a puffy cloud, a softness she had never touched at the house of her adopted parents on the steps. Burning the color of blood, the futon caved in as if swallowing her body, enveloping her as if to say, "You belong to this house now."

From Yoji's body, now divested of the morning coat, grew a strange something, black and ferocious. Manyo remembered the one belonging to Midori's brother she had glimpsed under the kimono hem several years earlier in the abandoned factory along the sea. The ferociousness of this one was very different from the dejection and head-hanging of the feminine man. It was like the blast furnace rising up, ready to erupt even now with the crimson conflagration.

Manyo resigned herself. Her eyes closed; it was all half dream, half reality.

That night.

She felt Yoji, now her husband, so roughly, so violently, and for so long that it seemed like it would go on forever. And Manyo, at first in such pain, suffering since she had no idea what was going on, was then drained of all energy right in the middle of it and instinctively looked up into her husband's eyes, astonished. "Oh . . . what's all this fuss about?"

Yoji stopped his violent movements and stared at Manyo with a look of utter amazement on his face. He peered at the tired, fearful face of his new wife for a while, until finally, he screwed up his face and laughed lightly.

"It's no fuss. It's just everyday business. This is what we do from now on."

"Well, then."

Well then, can't be helped, Manyo thought. She felt as though it was the power of the house itself that would embrace her, rather than the man before her. She still felt the pain and uncertainty, not understanding what was so great about this fuss, but when she thought about the fact that the big red house surrounded her now, that she was deep in the mountains, she gradually, strangely calmed down.

When the thing was finally over at daybreak, Manyo poured water from the pitcher down her throat. She drank and drank, and yet she was oddly still thirsty and continued to drink water like a child in limbo on the banks of the Sanzu River to Hell, suddenly aflame. Yoji was already asleep, an elbow still listlessly planted in the futon.

And then I don't know if it was that night, or the next night, or the night still after that, but Manyo became pregnant with her first child, the oldest son and heir to the Akakuchiba main family, Namida.

The morning after the first night was very fine, and the early light pouring in through the transom was so harsh that it woke Manyo up. Pulling herself up from the futon, she made herself presentable and woke Yoji.

If she had married into some other family on the steps, she would have put the water on to boil straightaway after waking up before rousing the family and tackling a busy morning. But morning at the mansion was quiet, and she came across no one as she shuffled back down that first hallway holding Yoji's hand. When her tabi socks slipped on the smooth floor of the gently sloping corridor and she fell, Yoji said, "I'll carry you until you get used to it. The housekeepers had trouble at first too," and helped her back to her feet. The backyard glistened in the morning sun, turning the river, the fence, and the hanging lanterns into a magnificent spectacle. They arrived at a small Japanese-style room, and there she took breakfast with Yoji, the two of them facing each other over individual lacquered *hakozen* tables.

There was nothing in particular for the young madam of the house to do. Tatsu single-handedly took care of everything from managing the housekeepers to seeing to the neighbors. No one disobeyed the grande dame; Manyo realized that they were afraid of her. Once she got used to this life, Tatsu would instruct her in giving tea parties, how to take the reins with the servants, and more, but for the time being, the most pressing thing for Manyo was to memorize the layout of the mansion and get to a point where she didn't get lost in it.

Almost as if the yamaoroshi of the previous day had never happened, the weather that morning was calm and clear. Walking through the backyard, she finally reached a gate on the other side. She opened it to step outside, and the grounds of the ironworks spread out before her. Here, you could take in the entirety of the enormous factory, cutting into the surface of the mountain. A lone, jet-black blast furnace soared there like the Tower of Babel reaching up to the heavens.

For some reason, this large, bizarre figure struck fear in Manyo. As she stared dumbfounded, a young worker in a uniform the color of new leaves approached in the burning morning sun. This man stepping out from the light wore a hat the same new leaf color pulled tightly down onto his head. Following Manyo's gaze as she stared at the blast furnace, his eyes soon stopped on Manyo herself. As they did, a small laugh escaped him, startling Manyo, and she looked over at him.

"What? Why are you laughing?"

"Oh no! Ha ha ha! Just that, a girl of the mountain looking just like them that control the mountain. You look like you're the young madam of the place, standing there in such a fine kimono. It's funny. Really don't suit you none at all."

Manyo looked puzzled, as the worker clutched his stomach in laughter. He seemed to be about the same age as she was, and his youthful voice was bursting with energy.

"You know the mountain people?"

"Saw 'em once, way back when. Just one time, but no way I could forget it." The worker's voice suddenly grew serious. "My ma, she got something bad done to her by one of them Americans that came and occupied, and it hurt her and hurt her so much that in the end she killed herself. When I was a kid. And then they put her in a box and took her off into the mountains. I saw 'em then. When I think about it now, it was a strange funeral. My pa, he said that them mountain people looked like the people he saw in the Philippines when he was drafted."

"Philippines?"

"On the other side of the ocean. Place far away." The worker pointed to the sea.

They stood at a point even higher up than Takami and looked out across the large plant spewing black smoke, the hill road of the steps stretching out with the flow of that smoke, the village and plains spreading out beneath that, the glittering Nishiki port, and then the Sea of Japan an ominous gray off in the distance. The worker pointed still further beyond the sea and narrowed his eyes. Manyo could see his profile from under the hat he wore low over his eyes, and she stared hard at his spirited young face.

She felt she had definitely seen this face before. Maybe she knew him from the factory, or maybe he lived in the neighborhood on the steps, or maybe he was a friend of the young couple, although in any case, it wasn't as if she actually knew him. So why would she feel like this, something like a nostalgic fondness, for someone she was meeting for the first time? Manyo pressed a hand to her chest and stared at the worker's profile.

"Ma'am, you were just standing and staring up at the blast furnace there. What were you thinking about?"

"Oh, I—it was nothing serious," she responded simply, since she probably wouldn't have been able to properly explain the fearful sensation she had felt when she stared up at the blast furnace.

"Huh," the worker said. Then he looked square at Manyo's face. "What's yer name again?"

"It's Manyo."

"Huh. Mine's Toyohisa. Toyohisa Hozumi."

Manyo gulped and took a long, hard look at his face. It was both familiar and not at the same time. Which was as it should be. The face of the young worker Toyohisa was that of none other than the flying one-eyed man from her vision, a face she couldn't forget even if she tried. The man with both hands stretched out, floating lightly in the sky. She had indeed locked eyes with him many a time in her visions. Fondly, sadly. Meeting each other, losing each other. Manyo was silent, heart full of conflicting emotions, feelings she had never known before.

So the one-eyed man's name is Toyohisa. Toyohisa Hozumi.

Manyo etched the name deep into her heart over and over, digging it into her flesh with a sword. She felt a stinging pain. But Toyohisa in his uniform the color of new leaves was crisp, much younger than in her vision, and brimming with hope. And more than anything else... Manyo stared hard at Toyohisa's face, that spirited young face, from the front.

He had two eyes.

Just like the open left eye, the right eye was wide open, shining safely there. He had the flat face characteristic of this region, but the darks of his eyes were remarkably large, making her think of the blackness and hardness of iron. All this brought to mind the middle-aged Toyohisa, slightly older than now, she had seen with her foresight, shocking her. When she thought about the day one eye would be ruined, her heart trembled all the more in fear.

Toyohisa was again staring at Manyo intently enough to burn a hole right through her. She quietly shifted her gaze first.

"How old are you, Toyohisa?" she asked.

"Twenty."

"Oh my. The same as me."

"I know. Just that everyone was talking about you yesterday at the procession. I heard a girl the same age as me went to wife, but the palanquin got all smashed up, and so she had to walk up the hill in that heavy bridal outfit in the middle of that yamaoroshi. I thought it musta been pretty rough."

"It was. All heave ho."

"I heard that. Still, that was some yamaoroshi." The worker, who would in the distant future be one-eyed and up in the sky for some reason, snickered like a child. "Almost send a person flying, wind that strong."

"True. But I made it somehow, and now here I am, a wife."

"And thank goodness for that, ma'am."

Then, in the house, from across the broad backyard on the other side of the gate, she heard the voice of an older man. "Hey! Toyohisaaa!" Wondering where she had heard that voice before, she realized it belonged to her father-in-law, Yasuyuki Akakuchiba.

"Uh-oh." Toyohisa ducked his head. "Boss is calling me. I was just hanging around 'cause I got here early, so then I got to meet you."

"My father-in-law? Oh, goodness."

"When he's got something or other he wants from the workers at the blast furnace, he calls me. The workers won't lift a finger 'less I give my say-so."

Toyohisa looked at Manyo a little proudly, young face shining. "Best be on my way, ma'am." He waved a hand before opening the gate and dashing into the backyard.

Manyo stood and stared after that slim figure for a long time.

The period around this year, 1963, was an age when the world grew steadily wealthier and everyone believed that they could be happy, thanks to the booming postwar economy. Waves of prosperity came in the form of the Iwato and the Izanagi booms, the economic growth rate climbed, and worker salaries rose. An awareness of the concept of "middle class" spread, and most everyone thought of themselves as being firmly a part this class, rather than at the bottom rungs of society. In both work and leisure, they delighted in consumption.

On the other hand, it was also an age that saw a surprisingly sharp decline in the kind of traditional artisanal work requiring a long apprenticeship.

Living in the heaven of the Akakuchiba house, waited upon by servants, there was no longer any benefit to life on the steps below now that Manyo had gained the acquaintance of Toyohisa. One evening, when she met him by chance in the middle of the hill road, he pointed to the steps below and called out to her brightly.

"Hey, Capital M! Did you know construction's already started?"

Toyohisa knew Manyo was the "young madam" of the main family, but he still called her "Capital M," all carefree as if shouting to a friend. In those days, the factory worker was the clear star of the labor world, and it was no different at the Akakuchiba Steelworks—to keep the blast furnace running smoothly, management needed deft handling of worker relations. Toyohisa, swaggering about, made easy conversation with Manyo as well. And Manyo, as she grew accustomed to life as the young madam, gradually became good friends with those around her. Although she was timid with Toyohisa, she did start calling him "Toyo."

"What construction?"

"Knew it. You don't know nothing, hm? 'Cause you're up here. They're rebuilding the lodgings, concrete buildings. It was your husband's suggestion too, y'know."

"Concrete?" Manyo blinked a few times and then looked hard at the lodging houses running along the hill below. The wooden buildings, old-fashioned longhouses, stretched out endlessly. From above, she could see some had been destroyed, and some kind of construction had begun.

The spread of electrical appliances and apartment buildings. The Akakuchiba house was heaven above, but thanks to their economic clout, the modernization of the steps of Benimidori was quietly proceeding.

"Young master says concrete's the future. Says he's gonna make amazing apartments with rebar made from our own iron. And, well, I s'pose we can't live in little wooden shacks forever." Toyohisa then pointed somewhere on the steps. "My place's right around there." Manyo couldn't really tell exactly where "there" was, but she nodded all the same. "Capital M, the kids born in these parts, all the boys want to be workers. Although I guess the ones that get especially good grades, good enough to get into university, they'll probably go to the city and get some job where they wear a suit. Workers're popular, though. And if they get to live in an amazing concrete apartment building type deal, it'll just be more and more popular. Hey!"

As he spoke, Toyohisa started to climb the hill. Manyo trailed after him.

"The dad who raised me, he was a worker too, you know."

"Old man Tada, yeah? I know him myself. He works hard, good worker."

This made Manyo happy, and she nodded any number of times. "At home too, he's a good dad."

"Most important thing for a man." His voice was a little quieter. Wondering what was wrong, she looked over and watched Toyohisa's spirited young face cloud over. "My father, well, after my mum passed on from nerves, he really went to pieces. He used to be a tatara worker. Around ten, his master took him on as an apprentice, y'see, and just when he'd finally gotten the hang of the furnace and the iron sand and all that, the war broke out. And then when he managed to eventually make it back home, Mum had gone and hanged herself. He went back to his tatara work, but he'd only ever been taught the old way of doing things, so he didn't know a thing about the dangerous blast furnace them Germans made, and he grumbled about how he sure as heck didn't want to touch a thing like that, so he got fired from the ironworks pretty quick. And then, well, he was just all worn out. I go home, and it's just me and my dad, and I really hate it. That's why I like the time I spend working here."

"So your father used to be a worker too?"

"Yup. But workers're just garbage," Toyohisa said, surprisingly fierce, and kicked roughly at a stone at his feet. His face even lost color, perhaps in annoyance with the weak-minded father who couldn't adapt to the changing times. "Heard he was actually good at the job. But he's proud, he's a proud man. No self-awareness that he was a hired man. Us workers down on the front lines, we're different. Our job's to make a whole lot of standardized goods at the factory. We never apprenticed to any master. We're company men, employed by the factory. But the fact is us workers understand that blast furnace best, better than any fellow in Takami pulling in a big salary sitting in front of a desk, better than them college boy engineers. We're one in there with that German machine, we're skilled with the technology. We're so much a part of that machine—we'll probably even go up to heaven together with it."

He started to turn toward the factory, and Manyo managed to keep up behind him. "I can hold my head high," he told her, impassioned, "and say, I'm an Akakuchiba worker, you can trust me with anything to do with the latest blast furnace. In this day and age, how many fellows out there can say that about their own work? Me and that German blast furnace'll die together."

Manyo looked up at the sky.

Again today, the black smoke puffed up, and clouds darkened by the ironworks blanketed the sky. They went into the enormous, oblong factory, and Toyohisa began explaining this and that about the steel-making process to Manyo. When the men in their new-leaf uniforms saw him, they raised a hand or came over to say hello.

Nodding good-naturedly, Toyohisa said, "This here's old man Tada's girl, the one who married the young master. She's one of us too, so you be nice."

"Oh! The young madam!"

The workers hurried to correct their posture, making Manyo feel that, more than awe toward someone on the management side, they saw her as a mountain girl with unseen powers there to banish vengeful spirits.

"Hey now." Angered, Toyohisa gave them a kick and made them stop. "You can just settle down and relax. There're no vengeful spirits in the factory or in Takami. This is an age of science! Stuff like that shouldn't even be crossing your minds! And this one here, she's origi-nally a girl from the steps. She's one of us. Right, Capital M?"

"Uh-huh." Manyo nodded and dipped her head. Even so, the work-ers kept their distance and watched her with fearful eyes.

Toyohisa explained that work at the ironworks was divided into three parts: melting down the iron ore in the blast furnace, smelting this melted stuff to make steel, and rolling that steel, applying pressure to form it. He informed her proudly that working on the blast furnace team like he did was the most dangerous of the three and many quit, but for all that, the work of this division was also fairly rewarding.

Seeing him so youthful, Manyo blurted, "Please take care with your eyes. Your right eye."

"Huh, my eyes? Got it. Though I don't know what you're talking about." Toyohisa nodded, cocking his head curiously to one side.

They left the factory and stared up at the enormous blast fur-nace once more. Manyo again felt a tremor of fear at its black ferocity. Looking hard, she saw the little scaffolding continued upward, so that a person could climb it, like the chimneys of a bathhouse. "Can you go up there, Toyo?" she asked, and he hurriedly shook his head.

"It's dangerous, too dangerous. That's just there 'case we need to inspect. You don't go near the blast furnace when it's working. Look, everyone says it's a bad sign when birds land atop the furnace. And if you want to know why, well, that's 'cause when it's on, the blast furnace gets real hot, and you can't get anywhere near it. Birds stopping on it means business is bad, and the plant's stopped. But Akakuchiba Steelworks doing so good as it is, we keep it runnin' all the time. Us guys on the furnace team, we're on twenty-four hours, three-shift system. But you get close to that thing and you'll get burnt so bad, you'll be covered in scars. You make sure you stay away."

Another worker came running over as Toyohisa was stressing this to her. "Toyo! Boss is looking for you, all where's Toyohisa, what's he wasting time on."

Toyohisa hurriedly looked up toward the Akakuchiba mansion. "That's no good. I forgot. Met Capital M along the way and forgot."

"Is it my fault? But, Toyo, is Father calling for you again? The boss suuure does call you a lot."

"We get along is all. He's a pretty great guy. Not like my dad. He works to keep up with the times—he's the first to modernize the plant. This prosperity we're seeing, it's thanks to him."

"Goodness. Thanks to Father?"

"You bet. And I'm supposed to talk to him today about the blast furnace's summer weight loss. Here I am, the one who brought it up, and then I go and forget all about it."

The soles of his canvas shoes stained black by scrap iron crunched against the earth as he started up the hill road. The yamaoroshi was blowing again, and Manyo unconsciously narrowed her eyes. The wind swept his feet out from under Toyohisa running ahead of her, and she saw him start to dance up into the sky for a moment. This happened at the end of autumn, and instead of Toyohisa, a snowstorm of deep red leaves fluttered down from the mansion's impressive garden. *Like red snow*, Manyo thought with a sigh.

Pushed back by the wind, Manyo's return to the mansion was slow.

In the parlor Yasuyuki Akakuchiba used, she heard people talking. Apparently, Toyohisa and Yasuyuki had just started conferring about whatever the issue was.

This parlor was the sole Western-style room in the entire house. Leather sofa, table covered in white lace. A glass ashtray so big it could have been mistaken for a hat. Vase always filled with roses.

Manyo slipped into the backyard, and as she drank the water flowing from the little waterfall, voices in conversation sounded out and leapt into her little ears. She could hear the voices of Yasuyuki and the worker Toyohisa. They seemed to be arguing fiercely.

"There's gotta be a scientific reason for the blast furnace's summer weight loss. Boss, you know this as well as I do."

"Of course. Tatsu trots out her vengeful spirits or ghosts of the land for every little thing, but the majority of it can be explained with science. I know that."

"The reason there are more accidents in the summertime, it's the San'in weather. *That's* the problem. This is Benimidori. It's not like Germany. After all, accidents that don't happen in Germany happen here. Listen, Boss. San'in in the summer's real humid. So then the air we send up into the blast furnace has more moisture. I may not have gone to school or anything, but I'm with that blast furnace all the time—I feel it in my skin. The humidity, it makes the furnace shriek and contract. Who knows how much extra humidity's in there? That's what's causin' the summer weight loss, not some ancient vengeful spirit. And it's not something that's gonna be fixed by Capital M marrying the young master."

"But...he can't exactly divorce her."

"If he does, I'll take her as my wife."

"Toyohisa."

"Aha ha ha! No, no, I'm just fooling."

They stopped talking briefly.

Gulping down water, Manyo tilted her head slightly and strained her ears to hear them better. A small bird chirped its bird song. She noticed she had ruined the crimson lotus conflagration of gravel at her feet.

Still, Manyo thought, *these workers certainly do tell the boss exactly what they're thinking.* If the workers were gone, the plant was done; the force of management alone wouldn't keep it running. Manyo recalled the way the young workers swaggered along in Yoimachi Alley below.

She heard Toyohisa's low voice again.

"Boss, we're the poster children of the postwar world. It's been almost twenty years since we lost the war. I'm part of a new generation in Japan; as far back as I can remember the war's been over. And this isn't nothing against the missus, but my generation, we're not superstitious, we have to believe in modern science. And," Toyohisa lowered his voice further, "I don't understand too well couples who marry for the sake of family when the world's all in an uproar about love and romance. The young master, he's a bit of a strange one too."

"Mm. Yoji believes in his mother. He'll shut his mouth and marry whatever girl Tatsu picks out for him if it means making her happy."

"That's a bit strange. But, anyway, I think we can fix the blast furnace if we tweak the ventilator so it takes the humidity out. We'll get

it done before next summer. You just leave it to me and the engineers."
She felt as though Toyohisa stood up then.

Manyo finished drinking and stepped up into the hallway. As she
started to walk, the wind rustled the autumn garden, and a single red
leaf fell into the water of the small river, where it floated away like a
small boat. As she saw it off, Yasuyuki and Toyohisa left the parlor, and
she could no longer hear anyone talking.

A few days later.

On an afternoon when the wind was strong, she bumped into
Toyohisa just as she started to climb the hill road. They walked along
together, chatting about this and that, when a black foreign automobile
shot up the hill in front of them. They heard the sound of the brakes
screeching, the rear door opened, and a single loooong arm slowly
reached out like a ghost.

Manyo approached and the arm wrapped itself around her waist
before yanking her into the car. Toyohisa barely had time to cry out in
surprise before the vehicle took off, resuming its forceful ascent. The
long arm belonged to her husband, Yoji. He stared at her, head cocked,
black hair spread over the seat. Manyo finally realized she was in the
back seat and looked over at her husband.

"Did you go out?"

"I did. On my way home now. The wind's pretty strong, so I figured
I'd give you a lift."

On the seat was a pile of books. He had likely gone into town to
buy them. By this point, Yoji had started reading books on business

administration and the like rather than the foreign novels he had previously favored, but this was something Manyo heard in her later years from her husband himself. Given the sad fact that she couldn't read, Manyo then had no idea what kind of books kept him so occupied. She simply stared at the mountain of them in something like admiration.

Toyohisa was reflected in the rearview mirror as he continued to climb the steps by himself, gradually growing smaller until he turned into a speck in the glass. The couple didn't have anything in particular to talk about, and the air in the car was still. Finally, the vehicle slipped through the Akakuchiba gates and stopped before the main entrance to the house.

Yoji got out of the car, clutching the bundle of books he had bought in town, stepped into the house, took his shoes off, and started off down the hallway, dropping one book and then another, like a child carrying too much candy. He kept on, not seeming to pay these any notice, so Manyo walked along after him, crouching down to scoop up the book each time Yoji dropped another. Drop one. Pick it up.

Yoji stopped and looked back. He grinned suddenly at the sight of Manyo staggering along, weighed down by books.

"Say, Manyo?"

"What?"

"I never thought I'd end up marrying a woman who doesn't read. And forget *not* reading, never thought I'd marry one who *can't* even read or write."

"Me too." Manyo got a strange look on her face. "The thought never crossed my mind that I'd end up married to someone who just read and read and read all these books. I never even saw books so thick as this."

They carried the books into Yoji's study. The small room was filled with a mountain of books, and Yoji sat on a chair almost buried by them, picked up a volume, and started reading right away. Manyo quietly left the study and headed down the hall.

Abruptly, she remembered the men talking in the parlor a few days earlier. No one seemed to be in there today, so she went in and sat on the sofa by herself, charmed by the roses that decorated the room.

The room also held a stuffed lynx, an expensive porcelain vase, and a round ball-like thing covered in a strange pattern on a lace-covered table. It had something like a table leg attached to it, and was constructed such that only the ball rotated when you touched it. She was spinning it around like a cat on catnip when Yasuyuki came in, carrying a pile of papers. Barging into the room, he headed for his chair before noticing Manyo, who had snuck in at some point. "Ah!" he yelped.

Manyo leapt up and then hurriedly bowed her head. "I'm sorry, Father. No one was here, so I came in myself."

"No, no. It's fine." Yasuyuki turned and went to leave, but then as if he now felt like trying to talk a little with this odd daughter-in-law of his, he whirled back around. Cocking his head and groping for words, he said, in a quiet voice, "So you like the globe then?"

"Is that what this is?" Manyo asked in response, and Yasuyuki opened his eyes wide in surprise.

"You didn't know that?"

"No. What exactly is it?"

"What do you mean? It's miniature copy of the earth."

"The earth?"

"You, you don't know what the earth is?" Yasuyuki cried, astonished.

Manyo quickly took a step back. She realized she had made a serious mess of something, but she had absolutely no idea why Yasuyuki was so agitated.

Fiddling with his glasses frames, he stared at Manyo almost in fear. He opened his mouth as if to explain and groaned a little but failed to speak. Then he shouted, "You're worse than my wife! Why on earth wouldn't you know that? All right, hey, Yoji! Yoji!"

He called his son loudly, and eventually, Yoji appeared from the other side of the hallway, thick book in hand.

"What is it, shouting like that?"

"Your wife says she doesn't know what the earth is. I can't explain it well myself. You, take responsibility, and teach her properly."

"I'm sorry, I never learned about this," Manyo said timidly. "I went all the way through junior high, but . . . I didn't really . . ."

When she was a child, she saw so many more visions than she did as an adult, and she spent her school days in something like a trance, not paying too much attention to her lessons. She was far from worldly things like science and physics. And this would be the case again forever after as well, but on this day at least, Manyo learned about the earth. Because upon hearing this, Yoji got excited, sat down on the sofa, pulled Manyo onto his lap, and began talking, long, snake arms wrapped around her.

"Never imagined I'd marry a woman who doesn't know which planet she's on."

"Hurry up and explain it, Yoji. Then this roadblock will be broken and this girl will become a woman who knows about the earth. Hurry up, Yoji," Yasuyuki said, annoyed. The fiddling with the frame of his glasses was an unconscious habit.

Playing with Manyo's hair with one hand, Yoji stretched his other arm out lengthily and spun the small globe around, finally stopping it in one place. "This is Japan." He pointed at a long, thin shape.

"Uh-huh. I don't understand, honey."

"Japan is an island country—it's surrounded by the ocean. And it's shaped like this."

"Why would you draw a map on a ball? I don't understand how to look at it."

"This world is round like a ball, Manyo."

"That's not true!"

"It is."

Worked up now, Yoji told Manyo about the birth of the universe, the shape of the galaxy, the structure of the earth. Nose puffing excited breath, he began to introduce her to a vast wealth of knowledge. The light in the parlor mixed with that of the fiery evening sun coming in from the backyard, turning a dark peach, and the air filling the room was strangely moist.

"Anyway, take care of it," Yasuyuki said and, perhaps finding it difficult to stay in the room with them, left on unsteady legs.

Once his father was out of sight, Yoji didn't hesitate to playfully undo Manyo's kimono sash as he continued to impart his knowledge to her. She felt a chill, and her dark skin rose up into goose bumps.

As he filled her with this knowledge, Yoji, the incarnation of the house and the family, again penetrated Manyo's body. The sky was cloudy, and the soft hiss of evening rain came from the backyard. The air became even more humid, and drips and drops of water ultimately began to fall from the globe, the world shrunk into a ball. Manyo was finally able to feel something like a sad, suggestive wave brought about by the work she did in those days, rather than simply her woman's duty. Over the course of this long, long period, Yoji's lips continued to speak the knowledge that made that world go round, and that knowledge flooded into Manyo's snow white, empty cave of a brain.

That day, she learned for the first time both the true meaning of her work and the round, *kemari* handball shape of the world. Yoji, in unusually high spirits, was taking his time in finding his release, so that the sun had fully set when her work and the lecture on the earth were over and they exited the parlor. The night sky was a deep blue. Yoji returned to his study on light feet, as if nothing had happened. The middle-aged housekeeper Masago hid once again behind a blackened main pillar, although half of her body could be seen sticking out. Manyo staggered out into the backyard alone and drank from the small waterfall. Then she stood up.

She wandered around in a daze, as if sleepwalking, and walked endlessly even as she got lost; when she looked up at the dark sky, all the stars of the heavens glittered there. She felt now for the first time that she was the belonging of this man her husband, and she shivered with the conflicting emotions of sadness and a sensation like she had finally found a place to settle into as a woman. And then the night sky above frightened her all over again. It was terrifying that the sky, although it seemed like it was right there in front of her like some high, high ceiling, was actually an extraordinary cavern.

She finally made it through the backyard and slipped out through the gate. Here and there on the night street were construction sites caught midway through their transformation into square concrete buildings, and the steps glittered brightly from top to bottom with paper lanterns and the electric lights inside the houses, spotlights on a tiered platform.

Manyo smiled faintly as she looked down on the platform. She remembered when she was a child and didn't know anything. Back then she thought the world was made up of steps.

Steps, above and below. Everyone down below aimed higher and higher still. Like the country itself after the war, these steps. Work harder, get a better life. A better future. For your children as well. Now, up the steps, higher, higher.

But, Manyo thought, filled with horror, *the world isn't actually a staircase that just keeps going up forever.* It was a thought she would never have had back when she was the Manyo who only knew the sea, the port, the village in the mountains, and the place deep in the mountains. *The world's round like a ball. There's no above or below. Because it's round. Then that means, that means...*

"Then," Manyo unconsciously murmured aloud. "Then even if we run to try and get higher and higher, we're still on top of a big, round handball, so doesn't that mean it spins right around, and we end up back where we started? Is the world really such a hopeless shape? Ah, I wish I could talk to Mom! She's raised lots of kids on the steps. I wonder what she'd say!"

Both she and her family had avoided seeing each other since she left to get married, but Manyo fondly remembered the parents who had raised her and the little brothers and sisters. From up there at the very top of the steps where the Akakuchiba mansion was, she could look down on the whole of distant Benimidori. The big factory in the mountains, the lodging houses. The village farming area, the broad river where the tatara factory used to sit. The port town stretching out, the Sea of Japan beyond it.

Looking down on it all, she could see, *Oh, yes, the horizon's curved. The sea's proving it. That the earth's definitely round, all right. No matter how fast they all run and run, no matter how much them factory workers on the steps and the office workers in their suits and the men after the war believe in a bright future and give their all to the climb, the road is maybe just going to spin right around in the end and leave them back where they started. That square box holding Midori Kurobishi's feminine older brother, after he slipped and fell and died way back when. Don't we all come back to the same place as that sad box? Do we Japanese ever actually get anywhere?*

Clairvoyant Madam Manyo was rooted to the spot, trembling at this round, empty world she saw. Tears so salty it would put the women of the sea to shame poured from her eyes.

That was in the fall of the still bright era of the power of men after the war in 1963.

Noticing the crying Manyo, Tatsu, her mother-in-law, the spitting image of the god of fortune Ebisu, came out from the garden. "What's wrong, Manyo?"

Sobbing, Manyo told her about seeing the globe in the parlor and about not knowing the earth was round. "The earth?" Tatsu asked, surprised. "What's that? What? The world is round? You were just having a weird dream."

Her face then grew serious, and she drew herself up to her full height, pressed the palm of a fat hand to Manyo's forehead, and started to check for a fever.

5. CRYSTAL LENS

But a curious shadow fell over the entirety of Benimidori that autumn, when Manyo became pregnant with Namida, the heir to the Akakuchiba house, not lifting until the following year.

Around that time, things that had been hidden in the shadow of prosperity began to surface little by little in Benimidori. In Kumamoto Prefecture, one of the original centers of heavy industry, the pollution illness Minamata disease, deemed to be caused by the waste liquid flowing out from the Chisso plant, became a serious issue. Also taken up as issues of the day were Yokkaichi asthma in Mie Prefecture, caused by the smoke emitted by the oil refineries, and Itai-Itai disease in Toyama Prefecture, caused by unprocessed waste water discharged by the mines.

In tiny Benimidori wedged in between the mountains and the sea in the San'in region, this pollution issue also began belatedly to surface. The black smoke from the steelworks made people's dining tables gritty with filth and tinted white laundry gray. And yet the workers bragged that their work was supporting the country, that it was the road to the future, and they frequently clapped their hands together to offer up a little prayer of thanks to the smoke. But—according to what Toyohisa told Manyo a little later about an incident at a neighboring house—when the canary a child had kept on the family's balcony inhaled the black smoke, stopped singing, and died soon after, the child's father changed his tune, and he no longer clapped his hands together at the smoke.

"We got food on our plates thanks to the ironworks—we got a debt of gratitude there. But are our kids all right? Growing up breathing in that black smoke here in Benimidori, are they all right?"

In truth, there were many examples of excellent workers whose lungs pained them once they got past forty, leading them to retire from the line. And as the color of the sky grew blacker, the Hino River became muddier, and the sea at Nishiki port too turned a dark color.

All of these things had been progressing incrementally for some time, but for Manyo looking down at the small plain of Benimidori from up on Takami, it seemed like this virus modernity had rapidly spread in the space of a mere month or two.

The black smoke that rode on the wind caused increasing animosity toward "red above" from the people living in the wharf area and the "black below." Midori's Rikidozan-lookalike husband set out to resolve the pollution problem, while also expanding into the construction industry at the same time, realizing that the business wouldn't survive with just shipbuilding in a peaceful era. The Goldfish, even more golden since taking her husband, telephoned Manyo, now a wife up above, just once.

"Hello? Midori?" Manyo whispered into the receiver nervously. It was the first time she had spoken on the phone and the first time she had gotten a call from anyone.

"Rikidozan died the other day," was the first thing out of the Goldfish's mouth. "You know that?"

Rikidozan, the man people were so crazy about in front of the TV that year, had been stabbed by a drunk and died young, only in his thirties. His death in the evening town hadn't been a quick one either.

"Mm." Manyo nodded. "I heard it on the news. Did you call just to tell me that, bulldog?"

"I did, stray cat. Well, of course, as a Kurobishi, I actually wanted to negotiate with you people up there about the black smoke, but I guess saying something like that to you won't do no good, Manyo. You know anything?"

"No, nothing. Truth is, I just learned the earth's round not too long ago."

"You really are a dummy, huh? Anyway, I leave everything to my hubbie now. So, Rikidozan. Hey, Manyo? Hey, stray cat? You. I was shocked, y'know. Big, tough guy like that, and he can just up and die."

"Guess so." Manyo nodded. "No knives in pro wrestling, after all."

"Honestly, Manyo. You know, on the other side of the ocean, President Kennedy died too. And *that* was a pistol. Dangerous times. Honestly, you know?" After chattering on in this weirdly threatening manner, the Goldfish hung up.

Manyo stood for a while in front of the phone. With the strong economic growth, people in that era still dreamed of prosperity, but she felt like a faint shadow was beginning to fall on Benimidori. With her foresight, Manyo alone felt uneasy, wondering if the future really would be richer than the present, if it really would be brilliant with happiness.

And then this young madam saw her first New Year's with the Akakuchiba main family. The housekeepers bustled about their work, and a festive air filled the house as people from the branch families came by to offer their first greetings of the year. These visits made it obvious that Yasuyuki's bride, Tatsu, was in fact the empress of the main family.

The sons of the branch families, having gone off to the capital and returned with doubtful get-rich-quick schemes, practically fell to their knees and lost the ability to speak the instant they came before Tatsu and were then almost dragged from the reception hall by their fathers. And the children of the branch families, who ran about laughing and screaming, stopped their shrieking and fell silent at a single word from Tatsu. The grande dame laughed, her small rotund body shaking, at the spineless branch family men and the children with their mouths clamped shut like clams. The Akakuchiba people were each and every-one of them tense and scared of Tatsu. However, Manyo adored her mother-in-law, Tatsu, and was unable to really understand this fear.

And speaking of Manyo, it was clear from the state of her body that the time had come for congratulations. Yasuyuki and Tatsu both ensured that their daughter-in-law did no work and had her sit quietly in the young couple's place. "Heir to the main family?" The men of the branch families chatted happily with each other as they came one after another to pay their respects. "Wonder if it's a boy or a girl."

Things inside the heaven of the main house were as they had always been, but take one step outside and the air of the village was heavier than it had been before with pollution or something. That year, Manyo spent her time simply sitting quietly in the mansion at the top of Takami, stroking her increasingly large belly. From time to time, Toyohisa would come to negotiate with Yasuyuki and the blast furnace engineers in their white clothes about something or other and then leave again. And then giving her a sort of befuddled look, as if he were staring at something out of reach, he would mutter at Manyo's growing stomach, "You swell up more and more each time I see you."

It was around this time that the people of the ironworks learned that young madam Manyo was clairvoyant. The start of it all was a mysterious accident involving Toyohisa.

He and his fellow blast furnace workers, together with the engineers and the managers, had gathered at the plant and were working to repair the blast furnace and the summer weight loss problem. It was the early days of the hot season, so they were all dripping with sweat as they shouted at each other and worked the furnace. Some molten iron flowed out of the furnace and came into contact with some water, causing a small explosion. The manager squad ran first, followed by the engineers taking the opportunity to flee. Only the workers stayed to save the furnace. And then, a scattering spark or piece of iron hit Toyohisa's right eye.

Toyohisa thought he felt something warm, but he frantically kept working without realizing he was injured. Another worker noticed something running down his face, and Toyohisa himself became aware that his field of vision had abruptly changed. He was still standing in the same place, but his field of view had narrowed on the right, and he felt something warm melting and flowing down his right cheek.

It was Toyohisa's right eye. Syrupy, it melted and dribbled out, the crystal lens falling to the floor, glittering silver.

"Toyohisa!" a young worker cried out and instinctively reached out to catch the shining drops in his hands. There in his palms was Toyohisa's melted eyeball, squirming like a living creature.

Toyohisa, for his part, scolded the younger man. "Come on! Stay at your post!"

"But, Toyohisa, your eye! It's melting!"

"The furnace's more important. I still got my left eye. Another explosion is on the way."

"But—"

"We stop this thing even if it means our lives. I couldn't kill myself with a woman, but I'd do it for the blast furnace. I'd commit suicide with this one."

The young worker tossed the silver eyeball that had flown out of Toyohisa's head onto the floor with a splat and got back to work alongside his older colleague as he shouted orders. Everyone was stepping all over the place, all over the floor, and in the end, they lost track of just where Toyohisa's eyeball had been.

After it was all over, Toyohisa was carried out on the shoulders of the workers—weeping stoic men's tears, crying "Brother, brother"—and brought to the village hospital.

"Capital M told me to be careful about my right eye. Now that I'm thinking about it, she did tell me that. I plumb forgot." Muttering incoherently, Toyohisa repeated, "Capital M, Capital M."

The workers looked at each other. "The young madam told you that?"

"Yup. I don't believe in no superstitions, but, but, that Capital M, she ain't no regular person."

The workers at the furnace, young and old alike, had always adored their "Toyo" because of the way he worked with no double-dealing and because of his passion for the blast furnace. But from that day on, he became a unique presence at the factory.

The era of manly men harked back regretfully to a shining past, although it was slowly to make its departure from Benimidori. The provincial towns were always a little behind the cities but eventually did catch up with the postwar prosperity. When it came to things in decline, however, these visited the provinces before heading on to the cities. The workers of Benimidori, who had been held aloft by the continued dream of strong economic growth, began to have trouble believing in eternal prosperity a little sooner than the urbanites who continued to enjoy the good times.

Which is exactly why the misfortune and passion of young Toyohisa Hozumi, a man who lost an eye trying to save the blast furnace, captured the hearts of the working men of Benimidori. From then on, Toyohisa, hero of the blast furnace, supported the workers' spirits, and he was elected their representative whenever there was a negotiation or labor dispute with the management.

It was a summer day in the last month of her pregnancy when

Manyo first saw Toyohisa again after he had lost an eye in that unfortunate accident. His ruined right eye was already closed, as if becoming one with the skin around it, a kind of unremarkable wrinkle, with no eyelashes or anything. His left eye seemed a little sad. They ran into one another on the hill road, and Manyo involuntarily cried out softly at the one-eyed man carefully staring up at her. She approached him slowly and stared at his face.

As she looked at the damaged face, a warm feeling of intimacy welled up in her heart. This was part of the secret of Toyohisa's burgeoning popularity.

Toyohisa spoke first. "After you went to the trouble of telling me to be careful."

"Did it hurt?"

"Nah, didn't hurt none at all. I just felt something a bit hot. I kept on working without paying it no mind. I'm not a hero or anything, just an idiot."

"Oh." Manyo looked down at her feet. When her eyes fell on the paper he was clutching, Toyohisa thrust it out at her, almost as if he was asking if she wanted to take a look.

It was probably some labor dispute leaflet or something, but Manyo couldn't read it. She had never before hid the fact that she couldn't read from anyone, but for some reason, in front of Toyohisa, she felt ashamed of herself and quietly accepted it, instead of telling him she couldn't read it.

"Capital M, how…how'd you know this'd happen to me?" he asked with a strange look on his face, unaware of her mental struggle.

Fiddling with the paper she'd been handed, Manyo told him in a few words about how she was clairvoyant and about the summer long ago when she had seen a future with him older than he was then.

Toyohisa clearly looked like he both believed and didn't believe her. He had never been the type of man who believed in these sorts of mysteries. "You did, huh?" He kept his words brief, taking care not to hurt her. "And it was summer then too, you say?"

"Mm-hmm. I was still just ten. But I honestly never thought that a thing like that'd be the future. I didn't think you, all middle-aged then, could actually be a kid the same age as me living on the same steps."

"Well, we got a funny connection!" Toyohisa laughed.

"Mm-hmm, we do!"

He narrowed just the one eye now and stared at Manyo. Remarkably, there was no wind that day; it was a hot afternoon. The summer sun shone on them scorchingly. The luxurious green leaves were brilliant with the reflected light of the sun and dazzled the eye.

"Capital M. You were the only one who knew. You knew beforehand I'd end up like this. Weird feeling, never had anything like this happen before. I feel like you're special. It was the mountain people who took my mum off when she died when I was a kid. And you're a mountain girl. Gives me a weird feeling somehow..." His voice gradually trailed off.

The scorching summer sunlight burned them both.

Finally, it seemed like Toyohisa decided to try believing Manyo as a test. "Say, that middle-aged me you saw?" he asked brightly, in an about-face. "What was I doing?"

"Um, well...you were floating up in the sky. You seemed happy.

Like this, all soft and gentle. You were looking down at me, and our eyes met. And then you were all floaty again."

"Now what's that about?" Toyohisa laughed hard from his stomach. Tears popped up in his lone eye, and he slowly turned his back to Manyo as if to hide them.

The sun gradually grew darker as the leaves of the trees rustled gently in the wind.

Now, near the end of the summer of 1964, the year in which Toyohisa's right eye flowed out, fell to the floor of the ironworks, and disappeared, Manyo Akakuchiba gave birth for the first time.

Her belly swelled up so roundly that it surprised her mother-in-law, Tatsu; it was like an enormous water balloon. Whenever Manyo walked down the hall of the red mansion, the sound of water, the sloshing of amniotic fluid, echoed throughout the house. People said you could even sometimes hear the sound of water, like the wind howling, outside the mansion, up to the factory area, riding on the yamaoroshi wind. Each time, the workers would turn and look up at the mansion and remember that, now that you mentioned it, it was getting to be about time for the clairvoyant madam to give birth.

"Your stomach's so swelled up. What on earth could you have in there?"

The unopposed empress of the main family followed Manyo around in a dither. And wherever Tatsu went, the men and women of the branch families followed like the shit of a goldfish.

Sploosh sploosh. Over the last two months of her pregnancy, the sound of water could be heard everywhere.

Sploosh sploosh.

Sploosh sploosh.

The fetus came into the world one morning, accompanied by this exceptional splashing, birthed from Manyo's lady parts in the middle of a waterfall of amniotic fluid.

What kind of delivery was that, what kind of birthday, Manyo groaned as if having a nightmare when she recalled much later the day of her first child's birth. Because Manyo, when she pushed this baby out, a baby swimming in her stomach in a large pool of amniotic fluid—her stomach was swollen mostly with fluid, so the child itself was not especially large at two-point-eight kilograms—saw a terrible vision of the future. In terms of time, it was a long vision, five or so hours, a vision like a nightmare.

That morning, Manyo woke with the dawn and labor pains and roused her husband. "Honey, it's happening."

Flustered, Yoji went to call his mother. Her water was already starting to pour out as he ran down the long hallway, and the young couple's bedroom was transformed into a rank flood of water and blood. Then Tatsu came running and, seeing the state Manyo was in, shooed the men away and called the housekeepers in, which was when Manyo's long and terrifying vision of the future began.

The entire sad, dark life of the very child she was giving birth to flashed before her eyes. This birth, which should have been so full of hope, started with her seeing the field of view of the child she would soon give birth to through the deep red birth canal. Panicked, Manyo turned to Tatsu and cried out, "Mother! It's terrible! The baby's breech!"

"What? How do you know?"

"I saw it!"

If this daughter said she saw it, then Tatsu believed it, figured it was probably so. She reported those very words to the midwife she called up from the village.

"Breech? It hasn't come out yet. How could you know that, ma'am?"

"My daughter's clairvoyant!"

"Well, let's just take a look."

The vision continued of the breech child flying out of the birth canal, looking at its mother lying there exhausted, and then looking down as if inspecting its own body. Seeing the small genitals, Manyo unconsciously squeezed Tatsu's hand.

"Mother! It's a boy!"

"Goodness, so we have an heir, hmm? That said, you certainly do see everything, Manyo."

"He looks like you, Mother. A whole lot."

She saw her own self saying that in the vision to the child to whom she would give birth, so Manyo unthinkingly said the same thing to Tatsu. But soon enough, the vision gripped her so strongly, she couldn't say anything to anyone.

In the blink of an eye, her child had grown and started to walk. He went to school, he studied hard, he fell in love. The person he fell in love with was the boy in the seat next to him; in other words, this child was a homosexual right from birth, but no one knew, not his family, not his friends. Her son steadily grew bigger, a shadow in his heart. Occasionally, her own aging self would pass through his field of vision. The eyes her son saw her with were gentle. Apparently, he adored her as his mother, and Manyo felt a warmth in her heart.

The speed of the vision gradually eased and began to move at an easy pace. She was even able to hear things now. The voice that called out "Mama" was low, seemingly having changed at some point. His voice had changed, but Manyo herself was still in the middle of this first delivery, a very difficult labor, the son not actually having been born yet.

In the bedroom, now a peach sea of amniotic fluid, cold sweat poured down her face, and her mother-in-law gripped her hand as she panted heavily. The silhouette of her husband's long limbs as he paced in the hall outside, unable to relax, floated in the morning dew.

"Push, push," the midwife urged.

"Oh! It really is breech," the midwife whispered. The housekeepers boiled and brought water.

Her son was apparently a distracted man, Manyo thought, still seeing her vision. She worried about this one from the bottom of her heart. He didn't look both ways when he crossed the road. He put food in his mouth distractedly without looking at the expiration date. He appeared to be a serious man, always studying a textbook or with a document in one hand.

Halfway through, the vision changed subtly. He was apparently wearing glasses now. *Because you're always studying*, she thought, but at the same time, she was a little relieved that the son of an illiterate woman like her would be an excellent student. He went to high school, he went to university. Her son was very serious about his pursuit of knowledge and yet lived his everyday life so distractedly, falling in love once in a while.

Each time, he stayed quiet and swallowed his feelings. When a contagious disease eventually arrived from a foreign country, discrimination against homosexuals suddenly rose like a tidal wave. Cold eyes, everyone watching everyone in the locked-down provincial towns, shot through him countless times like an icy wind. Her son hadn't done anything wrong, but he lived in hiding. Sometimes, a revolt against society or hatred of an individual would erupt in him, and these sensations would crash over Manyo like a black wave, and she would cough violently. Her son lived in anger and rage.

And then, at a certain point, this stopped without warning.

Her son climbed the mountain. He was in love with the man walking in front of him. Her son's gaze wavered only once. Everything was over.

Manyo knew her son had died.

Even though he had yet to be born.

He had died abruptly.

Manyo despaired at this knowledge, and her tears fell in large drops. In the sea of amniotic fluid, as she writhed in agony, she cried for her child who had died—who *will have had* died—suddenly and prematurely. "Here he comes!" someone said, followed by the "Wah, wah!" of her son's crying. Manyo lost consciousness.

By the time she came back to herself, it was dusk of that day, and she learned from her husband sitting by her bed reading a book that Tatsu had named their son Namida, meaning "tear."

"Because you just cried so much."

"Uh-huh."

"Why'd you cry like that? Father and Mama are both delighted. You gave them a wonderful son to inherit the family name. And Father laughed that he looks like Mama."

"He did?" Manyo tried to get up but had no strength and so abandoned the idea. The vestiges of the terrible vision held her and wouldn't leave.

"You should rest," Yoji told her, unaware of this. "Just rest."

"I have to have a lot of kids," Manyo murmured.

"What?" Yoji asked in response, surprised. "Have a lot? Why?"

She said nothing and hiccupped. For a while he stroked his wife's rounded back, as if to comfort her.

The eldest son, Namida, born that day, was the person who would be my uncle. Because the character Tatsu had chosen for his name was not a standard one, the two standard characters of "Hata" were registered at town hall instead, but in the house, the name Tatsu had given him was used.

He was handsome and got good grades, and the branch families adored him as the young master of the main family, but unfortunately, just like in my grandmother's vision, he did die prematurely, not long after he turned twenty.

My grandmother had three children after that. "I closed my eyes reeeaal tight when I had 'em," she told me in her last years. "I didn't want to see. I didn't want to see anything that sad ever again." But as to whether or not she actually did see anything, only she knows for sure.

After this first delivery, a single change came over Manyo. She no longer smiled, no matter what happened. The fate of her beloved son scarred the heart of this mountain girl so deeply she never managed to recover from it. That time, for the first time, her power to see the future became a blade turned on Manyo herself in an unexpected form.

Two years later, the daughter of the main family, Manyo, was pregnant once again and gave birth to her problematic second child. But before I tell you that story, I must first tell you about Namida's childhood, the strange incident caused by the middle-aged housekeeper Masago, and the new breed of young people with their dark, festering eyes that rapidly began to occupy the country.

Namida's childhood didn't really stick in Manyo's memory. She saw pretty much all of it through his eyes during the five hours of the breech delivery, and this vision was likely etched much deeper in her brain than her recollections of the son who actually existed.

According to what the remaining older members of the branch families told me, Namida was a very good child who almost never raised his voice or made a fuss. They all had very nice things to say about him: he was serious and studied hard; it was perfect for a man like him to inherit the family name. He was a lot more put together than his father, Yoji; they wanted him to hurry up and find a good wife and inherit already; and so on and so forth.

There was just one point of concern, and that was his distracted nature. Or so said all of the older relatives. He was hit by cars three times while still in elementary school. "There's such a thing as bad luck, but even so, three times is a bit much, isn't it? I mean, getting hit by a car three times. The same child?"

When Namida was seven, he was walking along thinking and got hit by a three-wheeler in the middle of the road on the steps, which sent him soaring up into the sky. Fortunately, Toyohisa was passing by and plucked him from the sky, so the boy survived without any real injuries.

"You would've been in serious trouble if you'd slammed into the road like that," Toyohisa complained, excited and wiping away a cold sweat, before taking him back to the main house, clutching him in his arms rather than setting him down on the road again. "'Cause the master of the place went and made all the dirt roads asphalt. Sure is convenient, but you slam into that and one blow, you're out. Right, boy?"

Namida was a crybaby and often cried. Silent tears flowed from his eyes now too. He had had quite a shock being hit by the three-wheeler, and he apparently thought he was being kidnapped by this unknown one-eyed man. But when he saw his mother and the man talking with an intimate air, he finally stopped crying.

"Who are you, sir?"

"Me? I'm a worker down on the steps. And I'm a friend of your mom's. Right?"

"Oh. You're Mom's friend."

"You watch yourself around cars. I won't be there the next time one of them slams into you."

"Uh-huh."

But Namida was hit for the second time a week later.

For some reason, a car slammed into him once again as he was walking along the paved village road from the elementary school, a road with no traffic lights, no nothing. This time, he went to the hospital. Strangely, he was uninjured, but when the person who hit him, the wife of a young farmer, learned he was the heir to the Akakuchiba main family, the color drained from her face and she collapsed on the spot. Her husband and father-in-law came to the main house and scraped their foreheads against the floor and stayed like that for three hours, no matter how many times they were told that was enough, causing Yasuyuki and Tatsu also to suffer.

The third time was right around his graduation from elementary school, and this time, the cause of the accident was clear. Oblivious to the red light, Namida wandered across the street and bashed his head into the end of a dump truck, which had yanked its emergency brake. The driver and an official from the transport company came and apologized from the entryway, profusely enough to drive a person mad, and the entire family suffered.

Why would he get hit by cars when he was such a good boy he could give the graduation ceremony address? Yoji was frantic with each incident, running off to the hospital to make a fuss, but Manyo simply got a faraway look in her eyes and didn't say much of anything. The people in the branch families thought this strange, but it was probably because Manyo knew her son would live past twenty, no matter what happened.

Each time he was hit by a vehicle, Namida cried. And then he went to his mother and hugged her knees. "I was so scared," he said each time. And Manyo replied, "Your mom's here, you got nothing to worry about." Her voice was very gentle and affectionate. The people of the branch families recounted later how, unlike with her other children, Manyo always had a very polite attitude toward Namida, almost as if she were anxious about him. They thought it was because he might be her son, but he was still the heir to the main family. It probably wasn't that—or at least not that alone—but rather that Manyo was held captive by the future she had seen. A person fears the precious thing they are in the process of losing.

Not much about Namida's childhood stuck in people's memories apart from his good looks and how frequently he was hit by cars. Everyone simply quietly watched over him, expecting that this studious, good-natured Namida Akakuchiba would become a strong man worthy of inheriting the family headship. After all, the only one who knew about his future premature death was the clairvoyant madam, and the madam, naturally, endured those twenty years on her own, without telling anyone about her vision.

Quiet Namida only drew the surprised eyes of people when he was involved in his traffic accidents. This was also because an incomprehensible second child had been born, one who stole the spotlight ever since Namida could remember, and everyone focused their curious gazes and worried feelings on that child.

The heir, Namida, quiet, incompatible only with cars. Although he was a crybaby, he had stopped crying in front of people by the time he went to junior high school; from then on, he had probably cried by himself without saying anything to anyone. No one really remembers Namida now.

Rewinding back to 1964, the year Namida was born. The red heavens stayed as they had always been, but Benimidori below was swept up in the Olympic spirit, that symbol of postwar prosperity. The whole village was excited for the Tokyo Olympics, the first ever to be held in this country, and ever more households bought color televisions, riding the wave of strong economic growth. A grim air fell upon living rooms across the nation when a white person won the open category for men's judo. But the women's volleyball team were victorious in game after game, leading to the players being nicknamed the "Oriental Witches" and skyrocketing in popularity.

Meanwhile, the aura of moral decline shrouding the young people grew heavier for some reason. Among the youth of Benimidori, gaudy fashions—the electric guitar, the monkey, the Ivy Look—were in vogue. These kids were crazy about the Beatles, who came from the other side of the ocean, causing the adults of the village, who had come up with the postwar production and economy, to furrow their brows. Although they lived in the same region, even residing in the same houses in many cases, a rift appeared between the youth and the adults. Before anyone even realized it, they were no longer dreaming of the same future.

Sparked by the signing of the new US-Japan security treaty, the rebellion of these new youth spread like a flash fire, first hitting Tokyo and the big cities and then trickling down, strangely delayed, to the university students of the provincial towns, before turning into an antiwar movement against the war in Vietnam. These young people were all dark-skinned and wasting away, and they would leap into fierce discussions whenever they met. This prickly nature belonged only to them, the younger university students, a strange, dark hell of youth that those even slightly older or in a slightly different position could no longer share with them.

Toyohisa and his ilk were bewildered by the many fights they caused, these people who were not so different from them in age. "What do they even want to do anyway?" he asked Manyo. "What answer are they looking for? Huh, Capital M?" Manyo had no real answer to give, so she hummed in a *I dunno* kind of way.

The festering youth were at first faraway city people they saw on the TV news, but soon enough, they showed up in Benimidori, zigzagging down on the industry road, in what they called a "demonstration." The shrill voices of the young people began to be heard at Nishiki port, "Fight! Triumph! Fight! Triumph!" Trucks piled with containers of freshly caught seafood had a hard time reaching the market, and the fish spoiled and passed on to the next life.

Sick with youth, they rejected the current reality to try and grab hold of the future.

This was definitely the new generation's adolescence of depression. Toyohisa and his cohorts had struggled bravely forward, believing in the nation's postwar economy, but these young people burned with a black rage at politics. They were so completely different that you couldn't be faulted for wondering if they had been born in an entirely separate country.

Around this time, one male student, full of youthful vigor with a white beret as his trademark, was active leading the students of Tottori University. A pale, thin, and lanky twenty-year-old man was Hajime Tada. He was the first son born to the young couple who took in and raised Manyo, and the young couple, workers from the steps, had scrimped and saved for their oldest son to raise the tuition and send at least him to university. Hajime had especially good grades, but he threw himself into the tide of the times. "It's nothing but a bunch of elitists at university, living the good life off our tuition money." He tossed his textbooks to the floor at home. "It's dumb. I can't keep attending." When he was tossed out into the yard by an angry father, his thin body shook and he muttered, "You wouldn't understand, Dad." And he flew out of the house and went to live in the apartment of a female student. An air of decadence hanging around him, he got a cup of bukupuku tea at the jazz café in front of the station and talked politics and philosophy morning 'til night.

Hajime was far from good-looking, but he was strangely popular with women, and from time to time, he would tumble into a new woman's apartment before the night was up. Each time there was a zigzag demonstration, everyone shouting "Fight! Triumph! Fight! Triumph!", they would get into skirmishes with the riot police; ringleader Hajime was a nuisance to the Benimidori police. At first, of course, his parents would go to fetch him, but after a while, they stopped coming to bail him out.

The young couple most certainly did not intend to inconvenience Manyo, now a member of the Akakuchiba main family, but Toyohisa, who got on well with the husband at work, learned of the situation and whispered the news to her. Manyo slipped out from under the eyes of her husband, Yoji, and her mother-in-law, Tatsu, and went to get Hajime at the Benimidori police station under the cover of the night-time darkness. Hajime refused to be freed from the holding cell under the authority of the Akakuchiba main family, but Manyo could throw the weight of her big, tough body around when it counted and forcefully dragged her adopted brother out—"So now you don't listen to your big sister?"—to bring him back home to the young couple on the steps. This big sister, so close to him in age, had watched over Hajime since he was a baby, and he couldn't defy her. However, adjusting the beret dirtied in the holding cell, he said quietly, "You're bourgeois, sis. And I'm fighting social contradictions. What exactly are you fighting right now?"

The beret was stained with blood. His eyes were darkly stagnant, darker than the black smoke from the Akakuchiba Steelworks. Manyo was horrified that her little, tiny, unruly brat of a brother now had such a sad look in his eyes. When she delivered him to the lodging house on the steps, now an apartment building, the husband of the young couple came out. The look on his face was one of total exhaustion. Apparently, the little brothers and sisters were already sound asleep, and it was quiet inside the concrete lodging.

"Sorry about this, Manyo," he said, and she shook her head silently several times.

After he closed the door, she could hear Hajime's low voice. "I reject nation and family."

"Honestly," the wife of the young couple murmured. "You do what you want."

Staring at the closed front door, Manyo felt a chill run up her spine.

For the adults of that era, nation and family were essential in supporting oneself. But she had a feeling of foreboding that the future might be different. Perhaps this too was a vision. Unable to believe in the nation, not bothering to create families. Manyo shuddered with the ominous sense that such an era was on its way.

It was chilly all over the concrete apartment building. Shivering, Manyo returned home to the top of the steps.

The intellectual students continued to burn black black fires on the plains. Meanwhile, however, there were still many young people left behind by the developing economy who abandoned the farms and suffered in poverty. It was around this time that the country saw a string of crimes like the Yoshinobu kidnapping case, in which the perpetrator killed a child and hid the body in a temple and then took the ransom anyway; the Nagayama case, in which a poor young man shot and killed four people, including a security guard; and the 300 million yen robbery, the perpetrator of which still has not been caught to this day. The world was splitting at the seams. Outraged intellectuals. Industrial laborers getting rich. Farming villages staying poor. The changing capital, where more and more new buildings were going up for the Olympics, and the strangely unchanging provincial towns.

The world around Manyo and her people was transforming at a dizzying pace. All they could do was hold on tight to a world that was practically tumbling down a hill, heading who knew where, and try not to get thrown off as they lived their lives.

But to speak of the Akakuchiba main house in that period, the big issue, sandwiched between the joyous occasions of the birth of Namida and the birth of the second child—a girl—was the middle-aged house-keeper Masago "streaking" through the mansion repeatedly.

If you were to look at a picture from when she was young, Masago was a fairly attractive woman. Small build, thin waist like a willow tree, good doll-like face, sharp black eyes, long lashes. She had her black hair pulled back and wore the simple clothes of a housekeeper, half apron over her kimono, but her full breasts and buttocks and her half-parted lips came across as sensual. She was actually twenty-two or twenty-three in this photo, but she was already a little past thirty when Manyo married into the family. Manyo only remembered that she would suddenly feel eyes on her as she walked about the mansion, and the majority of times when she lifted her face, she would always find Masago there, hiding behind the main pillar, peeking out at her supposedly furtively. But although Masago was apparently intending to hide, about half of her would be protruding from the pillar, and the eyes she glared out with were surprisingly tenacious.

For about two years after Manyo married Yoji, that was all it was, and Manyo simply thought of her as that person who hides behind pillars. Everyone except the naive new wife knew right from the start that Masago was Yoji's you-know, so whenever Toyohisa or someone else was talking to Manyo and felt eyes on them, and then saw Yoji's you-know sticking out from behind a pillar when they turned around, they would get flustered and fumble.

In her later years, my grandmother told me how Masago seemed a little older than her actual age, as she related memory after memory. These drifted to the surface, hesitant, soaring sand castles crumbled after the waves have come and gone. Masago came to work at the Akakuchiba main house when she was seventeen, so the young master Yoji would have been thirteen or fourteen at the time. She was more beautiful, a flower in full bloom, and they came to spend their youth together, whether it was she who reached out to the young master or he to her. By the time Manyo arrived on the scene, several petals of this flower had started to change color and fall, but the woman was clinging to them fiercely.

Despite the fact that it was a remarkably cold year, from the fall to the winter of 1965, Masago streaked five times. The first time was in the morning. Stark naked, she sauntered by the Japanese-style room where the young couple were taking breakfast with their child. Startled, Manyo spurt miso soup like a broken water pipe. The young master, the key figure, was concentrating on removing the head from a *shishamo* fish—it was young, but he didn't want to eat the head—and so didn't even notice the unusual event passing down the hallway.

Immediately before this, Manyo, watching her husband tugging on the shishamo head, remembered the death she had seen long ago in a vision, Yoji's head going flying and leaving him dead, which saddened her and caused her to lose her appetite. But when she saw the middle-aged housekeeper strolling along naked, her appetite suddenly came racing back for some reason. Taking another serving of rice, she wondered just what exactly that had been about. She didn't quite understand it. She was certain it hadn't been a vision. The woman's naked body was so withered it was almost pitiable; a sight sad enough to make one sigh about how it was too bad, she was still something to look at when she was wearing clothes. The flesh of her stomach sagged, her full breasts drooped down like two baguettes, and her face was as expressionless as a Noh mask.

The second time Masago streaked was in the afternoon. Far on the other side of the backyard in front of the open doors of the reception hall where a guest sat, a naked woman went dancing from right to left, stunning both the guest and Yasuyuki there with him. This time, she was off in the distance, and both the visitor and the father-in-law incorrectly assumed the dancer was the young madam, who was said to be a strange one. But Manyo, although she was certainly a strange one, vehemently insisted that it was not her, rare tears filling her eyes. If she was getting that worked up, then she was probably telling the truth—this daughter might have been a weird one, but she was honest. But then who on earth was it, everyone wondered, until the naked Masago began doing things like sitting on the sofa in the parlor or climbing the dawn redwood in the garden and then, unable to get down, getting the gardener to put his ladder up so she could somehow scramble to the ground.

Finally, when she was found snuggled in the futon in the young couple's bedroom crying, the whole household threw their collective hands up, and Masago was sent to live with one of the branch families. This was apparently because Tatsu had decided that, all said and done, the woman had been the servant/mistress to her son the heir, and although they *could* send her packing, it wouldn't have been very compassionate to actually do so.

However, this slightly odd expression of love from the scorned Masago apparently stimulated the young master, and Yoji once again started visiting the woman who was now living with the branch family. His sweet new wife, Manyo, had recently gone through the ordeal of Namida's birth and changed completely, with a faint haze about her now that hadn't been there before, so perhaps this was also a factor. This was also right when Manyo was about to give birth to child number two, so it was the mother-in-law, rather than the husband, who stayed by her side and comforted her through days of unusually virulent morning sickness.

While she was unknowingly having her husband stolen from her by a middle-aged housekeeper with a penchant for nudity, in 1966, Manyo somehow managed to give birth to a hairy second child. This was her oldest daughter, Kemari Akakuchiba.

6. BAG AND SOLITUDE

That year was the Year of the Fire Horse in this country, which only comes once every sixty years. It was the year of the horse in the Chinese zodiac, but it was also fire in the system of Celestial Stems; the two overlapped in 1966. Horse and fire. Because both are powerful fire attributes, girl children born in this year were said to be restive horses with absurdly intense personalities. Girls who, above all else, would devour men. And for some reason, as if she had chosen the year on purpose, Manyo gave birth to a girl child.

This was also around the time that, after a series of pollution problems, the Diet finally tried to submit the "Basic Law for Environmental Pollution Control." Society began to take a closer look at the darker aspects of the country's prosperity. Demonstrators also stood in front of the Akakuchiba Steelworks to raise the question of the pollution problem. Yasuyuki began investigating a new European machine that would reduce the amount of black smoke, but the change wouldn't happen overnight.

In the meantime, the workers resolved to strike for wage increases; it was a tumultuous era. Standing between the labor union and the company was always Toyohisa. He was very active in trying to make the lives of the workers better, but given his desire to keep the blast furnace running, he maneuvered to somehow avoid a strike each time the threat was raised. The one time he couldn't stop the strike and the blast furnace was forced to shut down, he looked up at the blackened iron skyscraper and said nothing, tears flowing down his cheeks.

Throwing a backward glance at the crying Toyohisa, Tatsu, the god of fortune's double, came rolling out of the mansion. "What are men of iron doing stopping the fires?" she thundered in a high-pitched voice at the fresh-faced workers with their signs and megaphones and youthful vigor.

Her voice whirled like a tornado to echo throughout the factory lot, practically shredding the eardrums of the workers. The men let their placards fall, broke their megaphones, and began to make a strange sound; at the narrowed eyes of this round, fat woman burning with rage, even the sky grew cloudy and the wind blew softly as if afraid.

The labor dispute fizzled out, and the following morning, the tatara fires returned to the blast furnace.

"Toyo, don't cry. You'll be back to work tomorrow," Manyo comforted Toyohisa and his tears alone in a corner of the plant.

"I didn't want to stop for even a single day." He bit his lip. "It's sad, y'know, all this. Aah, about as sad as my mom's funeral."

"Toyo…" Manyo unthinkingly squeezed Toyo's hand, which was cold and clammy. They stayed like that for a while, not moving, but then Toyohisa finally pulled himself free of Manyo's hand and stood up.

"That said, the grande dame sure is something. I couldn't do it, and she just waltzes in and makes it happen," he muttered, slumping over. Tears still flowed from the one eye he had left. The deserted factory fell back into silence until only the dry sound of Toyohisa's footfalls remained.

When she got pregnant with her second child, Manyo started losing her hair for some reason, and her eyebrows also thinned out. The hair on her body steadily disappeared. When she was pregnant with Namida, her swollen belly had been full of amniotic fluid, which made an impressive sloshing sound, but her belly didn't swell out to quite such a state this time. The child in her stomach cried strangely: *unh ha ha ha.*

Manyo was terrified it might be a beast child or something. As her belly expanded, more of her hair fell out, and she knew she was growing paler with each passing day. And then she went into labor one night just when she was wondering what was happening to her. Yoji wasn't in the bedroom at the time, so Manyo crawled out to the hallway herself and yelled loudly for trustworthy Tatsu. "Moootheer!"

She yelled over and over and over again, and finally, from the very opposite side of the backyard in the mansion, from the very opposite end of the sloping corridor, she saw the female Ebisu come half running, half rolling along. In her wake, housekeepers opened fusuma sliding doors there, kicked in shoji paper doors here, and jumped into formation behind her, creating a parade of women, which finally arrived at the young couple's bedroom in the very deepest recesses of the mansion.

Manyo writhed in agony. Another difficult birth. She kept her eyes pressed so tightly shut for the entire five-hour delivery that Tatsu thought it strange.

"Why you got your eyes closed, hun?" Tatsu asked, and Manyo replied, "So that I don't look at what a kid doesn't want a parent to see."

Knowing too much creates obligations, Grandma added, when she told me the story in her later years.

Tatsu had the housekeepers boil more water, and when the midwife arrived, she said, with a serious face, "I don't know if it's breech this time or not. My daughter's got her eyes closed." After that, she simply held tight to Manyo's hand.

Unh ha ha ha. Unh ha ha ha.

Crying this strange cry, the child finally appeared headfirst, and everyone held their breathing, watching, as the child shot out suddenly and bounced once, twice, three times like a ball on the tatami-covered floor before finally stopping, as if it had calmed down a little. And then it opened its mouth wide and laughed. "Unh ha ha ha ha!"

It was smooth between the legs; it was a girl. She had a ferocious, excessively hairy face. This time, the baby's countenance was deeply sculpted, after Manyo's own. Born of Manyo and an Akakuchiba man, the child had a beautiful form and a powerful face, more so than other children. Given how different her bloodlines were, she was almost a sort of mixed-race child. This girl was a blackish color, with fine hair all over her body. She rolled herself and bounced fiercely, causing Tatsu to smile curiously.

"She's a lively one, hm? And hairy."

"Is she completely born, Mother?"

"She is. She's all the way out."

Manyo finally opened her eyes. When she grew accustomed to the dazzling lamplight, she opened her eyes all the way and stared at the second child she had given birth to.

The hairy baby scowled at her with a sharp glint in her eye, and Manyo cried out sharply before passing out. While she was unconscious, Tatsu, in good humor, named her Kemari, or "hairball."

"So this time it's a girl?" Yoji said happily when he finally returned.

About ten days after the birth, the hair covering this hairball of a baby all fell out, and her swarthy skin shone smoothly like a jewel. And Manyo's hair and eyebrows also started to gradually grow back.

This was the birth of Kemari Akakuchiba.

Of the many children Manyo gave birth to, Kemari was the most beautiful, but also the most willful. Kemari is mother to me, Manyo's granddaughter.

Because again, Tatsu did not use regular characters for the name, after a period of indecision, Yoji submitted "Mari" to the village office with characters meaning "thousands of miles," but in the mansion, she was always called Kemari.

The children born after her were first Kaban (bag) and Kodoku (solitude). Naturally, it was my great-grandmother Tatsu Akakuchiba who named them, and no one—not her husband, not her son, and not her daughter-in-law—could say a word against the grande dame's strange naming style. Only one person was willing to risk her life to oppose these names of Tatsu's, but we're not quite at that story yet.

That year marked the start of the final years of the last age of legend, and the births of children were interspersed with the deaths of the people close to them; a number of things rocked the Akakuchiba mansion up in the mountains, a house which leaned as if pushed hard by the finger of a giant. However, before I get to the births of the other siblings, I have to start with the story of the vision Manyo saw in the fall of 1968 when Kemari was two.

Kemari Akakuchiba was a wild horse. Once before she could even stand up, she cried sweetly, luring her concerned older brother, Namida, to her, and then bit down as hard as she could on his arm and refused to let go. The entire day, Namida quietly endured the little sister hanging from his arm until night fell and Kemari went to sleep, finally releasing him, when they took him to the hospital to have the bite treated.

Kemari either bit or kicked everything that approached her. Her mother was the only one she would completely submit to, but when she was beyond the reach of her mother's eyes, she would bite the butt of anyone who turned their back to her, even that of her father, Yoji, or kick people in the ear and nearly break their eardrum.

More than anything, Kemari loved things made of iron. From the time she was little, she would play with hammers and adzes, fiddle with nails—throwing them at people on occasion—and the housekeepers learned to stay hyper vigilant around the girl, not allowing their guard to drop for even a second. *She really is a Fire Horse girl.* Tatsu was admiring, but Yasuyuki was afraid and rarely approached the girl; he devoted all his energy to spoiling the obedient Namida.

That this Yasuyuki would die in six years, Manyo knew after seeing a vision one fall day. Thinking about it now, it was a very strange thing for people connected to the Akakuchibas, but Yasuyuki died an entirely normal death from illness.

The day of the vision, Yasuyuki was with guests when he called Manyo to the parlor.

"Yes, yes." She popped her face in the room, still holding Kemari.

Three government officials who had come from the central government office were sitting there with her father-in-law. Drinking the bukupuku tea Tatsu had set out for them, they looked up at Manyo, puzzled.

"Well, the madam certainly does have a rare look to her!"

"This girl, you see, didn't even know what the earth was until just recently."

Although he had been so unnerved in the moment, after a little time had passed, the story became one of Yasuyuki's favorites. It was not one of Manyo's, however.

"It wasn't just recently," she noted, disgruntled. "That was over five years ago, Father."

"See now? Very recently. My wife's also a strange one, but this girl takes the cake." With one hand, Yasuyuki shooed Manyo away, as if to say *That's enough now.*

A sullen look on her face, Manyo returned to the hallway, Kemari in her arms. And as she did, without warning, she came face to face with the dead, future Yasuyuki.

On one side of the hallway of the large house was a large Japanese-style room with the shoji doors left wide open, where a lone dressing table sat. The table was the only thing in the room, but the cloudy mirror on it was reflecting something else. She knew it was a vision, and she stopped where she was.

Manyo and her dark eyes were used to seeing dead people. She had already seen the worst possible vision, so her forever broken heart would not be hurt, no matter what this particular vision had in store for her.

Quietly entering the room, she calmed herself and sat in front of the mirror. Reflected there was a dead person quietly laid out on a futon. No one else was in the image, only this lone dead man, a blanket pulled up to his shoulders. His face was covered by a white cloth, so she couldn't tell who it was. *His head's on tight though, so it's probably not Yoji*, Manyo thought as she reached out a soft hand. Her swarthy arm went into the mirror, meeting with no resistance whatsoever, and she gently peeled back the cloth on the dead man's face.

It was Yasuyuki. "Ah!" Manyo cried. It was the very much alive man she had been speaking with moments earlier. The dead man's eyes popped open and looked over at her. She unconsciously drew her hand back.

"What?" the dead Yasuyuki muttered, in a voice that seemed to echo from the depths of the earth. "Is that the daughter who didn't know what the earth was?"

Manyo nodded.

"Why are you in the mirror?" His tone was puzzled, face unmoving, still fixed in the same expression.

"I could say the same to you, Father."

"Oh. Is this your clairvoyance then? And I suppose that given how big Kemari there is, you're in the past, hm? You found me from the past. Good. Good girl, Manyo. Daughter who didn't know what the earth was."

"Father?" The dead man was in a good mood, and the fear clutching her heart eased a little. She drew closer to the mirror. "Is it the future there?"

"Summer of '74. I die. I've been in bed since spring, really giving the family a lot of grief. Hey, Manyo, there where you are, it's before the oil shock, hm?"

"What?" Manyo questioned in response.

"Tell Yoji," the dead man said quickly, sounding panicked, the same frozen expression of death on his face. "I die in 1974. He has to take over as head of the Akakuchiba family. Got to have the proper succession. He has to hand the family name down to Namida. It's probably better if he's prepared. You have to make sure to tell Yoji. That I die."

"Father..."

"Tell him the oil shock's going to come a little before I die. Aah, he won't know what you're talking about if you just tell him that! A faraway Arabic country stops selling oil, and because of that, there's a worldwide shortage. We take an indirect hit, and we end up in that iron chill, big steelworks slump. I die in pretty difficult times. You tell him to get ready now. Got it? Understand?"

"All right, all right, I'll tell him." Manyo nodded over and over, and Yasuyuki, eyes wide open, stared hard at her. She was indebted to this father-in-law of hers in a variety of ways, so she lowered her eyes and murmured spontaneously, "Father, I...I haven't been the greatest daughter-in-law. I'm sorry."

She got no reply, and when she slowly raised her eyes, she saw that Yasuyuki had picked up the cloth and covered his own face back up. "Manyo," he said, in that voice that seemed to echo from the depths of the earth. "Don't you worry about it." He turned his face away abruptly and then was completely dead again.

The mirror shifted from this future summer bit by bit, and just when there was finally nothing reflected there anymore, even the dressing table itself disappeared somehow. There was absolutely nothing in the room.

Tumbling into the hallway, Manyo went looking for Yoji. She was in such a panic calling for her husband that one of the housekeepers took pity on her and went into the midst of the branch family to fetch Yoji from Masago. Yoji returned home, trembling with trepidation that his bride was rampaging after learning about his mistress. When he heard Manyo's story, the color drained from his face. "What's an oil shock?" he repeated over and over. She mumbled something about how the oil chills the iron, and at this, Yoji took his head in his hands and then holed up in his study, not emerging for three days and three nights after that.

When she peered in around midnight, Yoji was reading books, telephoning this person and that, and seemingly struggling with business details. He noticed Manyo and invited her into the study with a smile. "It's just because I've left everything about the business to Dad." He sat his wife down on his knee and played with her hair. "I always thought he would live a long, long time. But he only has six years left, huh?"

"Uh-huh, uh-huh."

"And I'm already thirty. I guess it's high time for this rich bum to do something," he murmured in a tone that didn't seem all that regretful before returning to flipping pages and cradling his head.

Yoji completely stopped visiting his mistress in the branch house, but this time, Masago did not run or dance around naked. Meaning, Masago had also just become pregnant with Yoji's child.

This child was his third child, born between Kemari and Kaban, and was recognized by the family without any real issue. And for certain reasons, the child terrified the people of the main family. But I'm getting a little ahead of myself.

In the lower plane of Benimidori at that time, pollution had started to be a real problem for a variety of reasons. The concrete apartments built at Yoji's insistence were constantly hazy from the smog, to the point where they weren't really visible from the top of the steps. Looking down from above, it was as if you were standing on a gray cloud; the overcast sky shone eerily. The apartments toward the tops of the buildings were hazy like a skyscraper hidden by clouds. The workers' homes were blanketed by clouds that made it too dark to go about their daily business during the day without the lights on. It was a world of difference from the old days when people looked up with longing at the paper lanterns glittering like the showcase lights of a tiered platform, the symbol of the strong economy. Asthma started to become prevalent among the children, and many of their worker fathers began to suffer from bronchitis. Older, retired workers collapsed from illness, and people began to whisper that workers make money, but they don't live long.

The mass production system needed for the mass consumption people dreamed about during and after the war gave rise to many work-related injuries and deaths, and it was no different in Benimidori. People died in accidents unthinkable in the era of craftsmen carrying out skilled manual labor—they were swallowed up and crushed in the huge machines—and the victim's bodies were too often scattered in pieces or flattened to the point where their own families were unable to identify them.

On the other hand, the world was beginning to take interest in the aggressive, avant-garde youth culture. The places where actual production took place remained sweaty and oil stained, and were increasingly left behind by showy modernity.

With nothing but their own bodies, the people fought, and when they woke up, the world around them was gray.

Still, the economy was strong as always, and everyone believed things would stay basically the same, that nothing would really change too much. Automobile production at Toyota Motor Company surged past three million vehicles, making their automobile output a force to reckon with at third globally. Steel, cement, textiles, and other industries followed suit and maintained already strong positions. Gross national product rose to second worldwide. The World's Fair was held in Osaka. After the Olympics, the World's Fair made faces shine. And the Akakuchiba Steelworks, as if trying to promise even greater prosperity, sent black smoke puffing up from its stacks every day and dyed the sky the color of coal.

It was at the end of the last of these prosperous days, on a cold winter morning, fluffy snowflakes swirling, that the housekeeper Masago gave birth to a girl.

With the branch family in such a commotion, Yoji too was restless and went out. No one told Manyo anything and no one from the mansion was sent, but Manyo climbed the tallest cypress tree in the backyard, narrowed her eyes, and looked down toward the red houses of the branch families in the distance. Perhaps her eyesight really was that good or maybe she was seeing a vision, but either way, Manyo saw the scene below quiiite well.

A woman with empty eyes was lying on a futon, Manyo recounted later. *There was just nooothing in those eyes. Next to her, the midwife was holding the woman's baby, showing it to her, but she didn't even make to glance at it.*

After giving birth to the girl, Masago no longer danced or ran; she simply stared endlessly up at the ceiling. But she stubbornly refused to let Tatsu name the child. The housekeepers gossiped later that she had been afraid that Tatsu would name her "Nude" or "Dancer." And before anyone knew it, Masago had walked down to the village office on the steps below, despite the fact that her recovery from the birth was so slow and poor, and named the child she had given birth to Momoyo, or "hundred nights."

It was probably a dig at Yoji's legal wife, Manyo, a way of saying the child was the product of a hundred nights spent together. The staff and the workers at the ironworks, their wives, and the people of the steps who had helped the day Manyo was married and pushed the bridal palanquin up with a heave and a ho were indignant at this slight, and loathed

Masago from that day on, noting she had no sense about how to be a concubine. But right from the start, Masago was not the type to fret over this kind of thing—if she was, she probably wouldn't have gone around dancing naked—and Manyo had married Yoji due to a strange twist of fate that was a liiiittle different from coming to be his wife because she loved him, so she didn't sink into jealousy the way people thought she would. At the very least, her appearance didn't change the way it had after the birth of her beloved son Namida. But Manyo did get just the tiniest bit glummer after that, more than the people who knew her well expected.

That morning, perhaps concerned about Manyo, who had climbed the cypress tree to look down on the child being born in the distance, Toyohisa came to visit. Behind the curtain of the increasingly intense flurry of snowflakes hiding the hill of the main road, Manyo could see him trudging up in the distance, like he was weaving through clouds.

In the middle of the hill, Toyohisa, who never stopped midway, stopped. Manyo realized he was having a coughing fit. And then he slowly started to walk again. He opened the gate to the backyard and, figuring that Manyo would be somewhere in this garden she loved, he craned his neck looking for her.

Something came over her. "Toyo!" she called out. Surprised, he tilted his head back, and from up in the branches of the cypress tree, she jumped down toward him like an out-of-season red leaf. "Toyo, catch me!"

"Whoa!" Toyohisa stretched both arms out, opened his remaining eye as far as it would go, and nimbly caught the falling Manyo. They stayed like that for a while. Then, after momentarily tightening his lean arms around her back, he slowly withdrew his hands.

Manyo stood alone with Toyohisa in the cold of the wintry, dead garden for a long time.

"Toyo, you came up real slow, hm?" she said.

"You could see that?" Toyohisa asked her, curious.

"Mm-hmm, clear as day."

"You got good eyes, huh? You really do."

"You take the trouble of walking up the hill when you should just fly up. After all, you're a flying man."

"Ha ha! You still thinking about that?" Toyohisa held his stomach and laughed. And then, he took a large mandarin orange from his pocket and handed it to her. "Someone gave me a bunch. You can have one."

"Thanks."

"How's things lately?"

"How's things . . . When you got two kids, it's busy. Although we got the servants, which does make it easier. When I was in the Tada house, there were a whole mountain of little brothers and sisters, and I used to take care of them. Guess I'm living in luxury now, huh?" she said and, still standing there, began to peel the orange. She popped a piece in her mouth; the orange was sweet.

A dry winter wind blew hollowly through the garden, and the damp snow that had piled up on the trees fell to the ground with a heavy sound.

She recalled the morning she met Toyohisa. How he laughed easily when he called her a mountain girl. Two eyes on his young, unlined, dazzling, smiling face. The young man burning with hope, full of pride. How many years had passed since then?

"Toyo, you don't got a family?" she asked abruptly. She was worried about Toyohisa and also uneasy about things changing.

"I don't."

"Me and you, we're twenty-five now. Getting to be time."

"I only got one eye now. No girl's gonna marry me."

"That don't matter. You're a good worker. You said yourself way back when, that's the most important thing for a man."

Toyohisa narrowed the one eye he had in a smile. They walked through the garden side by side and sat down on the edge of the large hallway. The breath they exhaled was white. In the wintry garden, only the orange peel Manyo had tossed aside shone a lively color.

"Me, I dunno." His eyes grew dark and he stared at the snow at his feet. "I think I just can't get my head away from that image of my mom dying. It's a thing having someone die on you like that. But I s'pose having a family wouldn't be a bad thing if it was with a sturdy woman."

"A sturdy woman? You say the strangest things." As she spoke, Manyo abruptly remembered the Goldfish taking a husband after losing her beautiful brother in the furisode kimono way back when.

She chose a sturdy man, the Goldfish did. For Manyo and her generation, sturdy men, sturdy women felt like they would struggle desperately to the death to crawl up a cliff, become covered in sweat and oil in that desperation.

And now, a weak woman had given birth to the child of her husband. The steps were shrouded in black smoke. Toyohisa had lost an eye and was just sitting next to Manyo like this. Five years later, the oil shock would come, and in that chaos, a very reliable man, Yasuyuki, would die of illness.

Manyo thought about the flow of time. The sun rose on a hundred nights, set on a thousand days.

And then at exactly that time, according to what the people of the branch family said later, the housekeeper Masago, staring up at the ceiling with empty eyes, finally held her child in her arms. As Tatsu, the women of the branch family, and the midwife looked on, holding their collective breath, the woman suddenly spit in the face of her child.

"Doesn't look like anyone! Not the young master, not the grande dame, doesn't look like any of them! I wanted to give birth to an Akakuchiba baby! What am I supposed to do with a baby who takes after me?" she yelled, and broke down in heaving sobs.

Masago pushed herself too far going to the village office two days later, submitting the child's name, and then making her way back home again, and she took to her bed after that. She never danced again, simply slept and woke and raised the child, but about eleven years after that, unable to wait until Momoyo was grown, she took ill and passed on to the other world. Her posthumous Buddhist name managed to incorporate the words "nude," "daybreak," and "dancing woman," and the old-timer housekeepers gossiped that having been given a name like that, Masago was sure to come and haunt them.

When she told me this story about Masago, my elderly grandmother grew the tiniest bit somber. I asked her why, and she murmured despondently, "Because I never felt so strongly I'd dance naked for want of a man. I've always felt obliged to her somehow. Strong woman like that."

After Masago's death, Momoyo was brought to the main house on Tatsu's orders and raised together with Namida, Kemari, Kaban, and Kodoku. Kaban told me later on that she was a reserved but rather wanton child.

"She was a good kid, but stubborn. She was always so annoyingly persistent, sullen, quiet, but she slept with each and every one of Kemari's men. Stealing men was in her blood. That's passed down, mother to daughter. Aah, what a terror."

Momoyo, the child of a hundred stolen nights with another woman's husband, a child whose own younger sister from a different mother would say had stealing men in her blood, and the Fire Horse Kemari, who became the heir to the main family when Namida passed on, would begin their battle some thirteen years later, but that is very much a story for later.

Roughly around the time of the man-stealing Momoyo's birth, the Beatles came to perform in Japan, the World's Fair ended, and the Asama-Sanso incident, perpetrated by young people with stagnant, dark, fierce eyes rocked the world. And while all this was happening, the end of the world the future dead man had foretold through the medium of the visionary mirror, the year of the oil shock came, and a storm of fear swept through Benimidori.

7. IMAGINE

The red heavens stayed as they had always been, but in Benimidori below, the wave of modernity was changing people's everyday lives and culture whether they liked it or not.

Going into the 1970s, the young people filling Benimidori were a generation that took on an excessively subdued attitude. Most likely, they were not fundamentally different from the youth of other generations, but rather than ranting loudly about their passions and dreams, they kept these close to their hearts; this was a generation that had learned how to play it cool. Listless young people formed circles here and there in the village, and busy adults in suits passed them as they slacked off and did nothing.

The oil shock came in the fall of 1973. The cause was the political situation in the Middle East, far, far from this country, so for the majority of people it was a bolt from the blue. They expected today to be like yesterday, and then the price of crude oil suddenly leapt up over twenty percent. Fearing shortages, people ran out to buy. Memories of postwar rationing and black-market rice raced back to life in the minds of the older people.

The reason for the worry that there might not be enough in the way of daily necessities was the production floor in each industry. Prices rose, and in the steel industry, the enormous slump known as the "iron chill" began. People started saying that business had just been too good up until then.

In Benimidori, just as the new year was rung in, the ever-reliable Yasuyuki fell ill. Toyohisa and the workers came running, but the heir, Yoji, living his days in a carefree fashion, was exceptionally calm and managed to weather the iron chill, making various reports to Yasuyuki at his bedside. The son became the captain of the enormous ship that supported the economy of Benimidori, aka the Akakuchiba Steelworks, and continued sailing smoothly across the ocean of modernity.

To speak of my grandmother, a little before this, she gave birth to her third child, Kaban. Figuring that once the oil shock hit, they wouldn't have any leeway for traveling or anything of the sort, Yoji took Manyo to the Tamatsukuri Onsen resort in the summer of '69. This was the first and last time the two of them went on a trip together. In the last month of her pregnancy, Manyo's belly protruded curiously squarely, and as a couple, they scratched their heads in puzzlement as to why it would be angular this time. But the girl she gave birth to was the most normal baby they had had.

Manyo went into labor at the resort inn and managed to get through the terribly difficult birth by herself, keeping her eyes shut tightly again.

In a panic, Yoji put the newly born child in their square travel bag, scooped up his wife, and hurried back to Benimidori to seek Tatsu's instructions. His mother held the child and, in very good humor, named her Kaban. And although this meant "bag," although it was likely not particularly appropriate as the name of a human being, although it was a regular word and not a character to be used in a name, no one in the main family could offer any opposition. After thoughtful consideration, Yoji delivered a name with the characters for "flower" and "disc" to the village office.

This second daughter strongly resembled Kemari, but she looked quite a bit more normal than Kemari. Perhaps because of this, she also lived a great deal longer than Kemari.

After that, my grandmother gave birth to her youngest child, a boy, in '75, and then as if satisfied, she had no more children. Manyo always watched her oldest son, Namida, from a bit of a distance. She dealt with Yasuyuki's death and the large-scale reform of the ironworks over the course of '74 to '75.

Just as in her vision of the future, Yasuyuki breathed his last due to illness in the summer of '74. To make sure the past and present were properly connected, Manyo hunted down a dressing table for the all-night vigil and placed it imposingly and conspicuously in the room. The people of the branch family watched Manyo, piqued, wondering what the young madam could possibly be doing, but she said nothing about why she was setting up the dresser there. Given that Tatsu didn't ask about it, the people of the branch family, while curious, could not very well ask, and so, circling her at a distance, they watched as the clairvoyant madam finally took a deep breath and stared at Yasuyuki's remains.

The large-scale reform of the ironworks was solemnly carried out by Yoji, to mark the boundary of Yasuyuki's death. The iron chill took the bloom from the formerly sought-after position of worker, and it started to change from its past glory. People began thinking that, rather than working on a three-shift system covered in sweat and oil, the shrewd choice was to work in an air-conditioned office in style. The sons of the workers didn't try to follow in their fathers' footsteps anymore. The workers weren't white-collar people in an office, but neither were they craftsmen carrying on a tradition. It was an occupation that bore no fruit, a shooting star born of the strong economic growth. Its luster faded in the fleeting days, and these workers, in uniforms rather than suits, began to be thought of as ancient man-shaped cogs to be used mechanically in the dim factory.

The iron chill only lent strength to this idea, and as young people stopped applying to work there, the average age of the workers rose. Production output shrunk, and they ended up with surplus personnel.

"Unless you see it with your own eyes and feel it on your own skin, you can't know the blast furnace," Toyohisa insisted as the representative for the workers, working on the front lines with the blast furnace, but he and Yoji were of different opinions.

The time for this theory of "heart" had passed; it was just annoying now to have the workers pointing out each and every little thing. More important to management was to bring in young, unthinking, coglike workers who knew to do their work efficiently with the framework laid out by the engineers.

"Toyo, we're letting people go. You need to trust the judgment of the machine more. These days, we can control the blast furnaces just fine remotely. And the engineers are there."

"No. You don't understand, sir. The blast furnace is alive."

The two butted heads, and Yoji increased labor intensity, reduced personnel, and introduced new machines as a countermeasure to the pollution problem. Older workers who couldn't adapt to the new environment were dismissed one after another in order of seniority. Soon, only the cold sound of the machines echoed within the factory, and the steady shouts of the workers disappeared.

It was air-conditioned inside the plant now, and the humidity, the demon behind the summer weight loss, was also controlled. No matter what the season, the temperature and humidity stayed constant. With nothing but their own bodies to bargain with, workers were made to get their driver's licenses and shifted to delivery work. Yoji explained that what was needed from the new generation of men working in this country was footwork, skills, and licenses.

"Toyo, it's important not to be too set in your ways. You need to be able to change jobs as you please. And you need a license. As long as you have a driver's license, even if you can't work here anymore, you'll be able to find another job. And if you get good with machines, your options really open up. Do you understand?"

"I don't. I don't understand what you're talking about, sir. I just can't trust this remote control or whatever you call it. I don't want to have anything to do with something like that."

"Well, you do what you want. The likes of a worker should keep his nose out of things. You don't understand anything, after all," Yoji said coldly and ended the conversation. Perhaps this also came from the faint, albeit ingrained jealousy of a man who had spoken more intimately with his own father when he was alive than Yoji had, the man's own son.

These words—"the likes of a worker"—coming from the mouth of the young president crossed a line. Toyohisa's expression changed, and he said nothing.

With that day as the boundary, the two would under no circumstances speak to each other again, even with Manyo's intercession. Both were stubborn men of the Showa era.

There was slightly less black smoke rising up from the ironworks. They kept production output down and tried to survive, slowly changing along with the times.

Manyo was frequently alone in the mansion. She was busy with the three children, and given the industry crisis they were facing, her husband locked himself up in the office and rarely returned home.

Feeling the pains of labor, she realized for the first time that their fourth child was in her belly. Her stomach hadn't swelled very much this time, and perhaps because this youngest child was the shy type even after being born, he didn't make too much of a fuss about being in her womb when he was a fetus.

It was New Year's Eve when she realized in a panic that she was going to have a baby in that parlor where she had discovered the globe and batted it around like a cat not long after she had married into the family. The room held a color TV now, so Manyo was watching the annual *Kohaku Uta Gassen* singing contest there, as she chatted with the children and the housekeepers over the traditional New Year's soba noodles.

"Mother!" she shouted, eyes shut tightly, and Tatsu came along as if rolling once again. Manyo was completely white and shaking like a leaf. Tatsu slapped the housekeepers on their bottoms, had them boil water, called the midwife, calmed down, and helped Manyo deliver.

This era saw a progressive shift to the nuclear family; newlyweds wanted a shiny new two-bedroom apartment or a little house in a residential area in the suburbs. The husband became a company man, and the wife and child were left alone, just the two of them, just the three of them in the shiny new house. Yoji had also become a workaholic and almost never looked back at his wife, who had become sort of hazy at some point, or his children.

Eyes closed, giving birth alone, Manyo fondly recalled the husband she had met in the distant past at the bukupuku tea shop, when he had treated her to a cup of tea. The Yoji who had, rather than drinking alcohol or buying women, simply been lazily reading a troublesome Western book as he drank tea like a schoolgirl. Long hair, arms too long like a shadow man. His thin voice reading the menu. And then the head that popped through the air in her vision.

That Yoji was long gone. The man at the office now, the one who never came home, was Yoji the businessman, a man Manyo didn't know. He never set foot on the actual production floor but simply had constant meetings morning and night with employees in suits in the air-conditioned office. Glad then sad then glad again at the calculated numbers, he fine-tuned his next plan for reform. People with health complaints because of the pollution filed a lawsuit, and his time began to be taken up by meetings with lawyers.

The reserved child the solitary Manyo gave birth to in the midst of all this, without even crying, was a boy.

Tatsu named this child Kodoku, "Solitude."

Thinking this name was a curse, Manyo hesitantly asked Tatsu about it. This was the first time since she had married into the family that she had given her opinion to her mother-in-law, albeit very tentatively.

Tatsu shook her head sadly. "A name doesn't decide fate," she murmured, staring at Manyo with small eyes. "This child's fate is such that the only name he could be given is Kodoku. It's already been decided that he'll have this name."

Manyo couldn't say anything else. She felt a little shiver of fear. *I have given birth to solitude from my belly.*

After wrestling with this child's name, Yoji delivered "Jiro" to the village office. However, in the bright red mansion, not a soul called him by that name.

Kodoku took after Namida. He was the more reserved of the brothers, but he had a graceful, beautiful face. He silently looked up at his mother. Finally opening her eyes and looking at the baby, Manyo unconsciously hugged the child as if to encourage him.

Tatsu notified the office of the sudden birth, and Yoji came back very late that night. His face was still young, so Manyo thought with relief, *He's not gonna die just yet.* He slept a little next to the baby, and when morning came, he went back to the office. Manyo's delivery was also announced to the branch families in the morning. Manyo heard what sounded like a woman howling from the direction of the branch houses on the hill below, and she said later that she thought it had probably been Masago, but she didn't seem certain. *Or maybe they were keeping a dog,* she added, cocking her head to one side, so I don't know what the truth of the matter was. In any case, on New Year's Day 1975, a very quiet, sad boy was born into the world, almost tumbling into the final year of the age of legend in Benimidori.

And then, the age quickly proclaimed its end, this age of the legend of Manyo Akakuchiba, the abandoned child taken as a daughter by Tatsu, empress of the Akakuchiba main family, a hostage to the ancient gods. A wind blew down through the provinces of Hoki in the southern part of Tottori Prefecture and Izumo in the eastern part of neighboring Shimane Prefecture—strange lands of legend in modern times, old-style regions trapped in the mountains—upending them and changing everything. The tourists who swarmed to the region seeking mystery and legend could no longer see any ancient signs of the old provincial culture and clime so unique to Izumo. The end of this land came quietly in the seventies, until finally, it seemed that both Tottori and Shimane were simply two more far-flung regions among the prefectures of Japan. If any mystery remained, it was in the person of Manyo Akakuchiba, who continued to live peacefully there as a clairvoyant. Perhaps some other elderly people like her are scattered about Benimidori, but at the very least, I don't get any sense of them.

In this last year of legend, Manyo climbed the mountain with an old friend. I should actually be long done with the story of this era, but

I'd like to finish by noting one final memory of Manyo's mixing dream and reality.

Manyo's friend, the Goldfish, aka Midori Kurobishi, had left everything to do with Kurobishi Shipbuilders to her Rikidozan-lookalike husband so that she could spend her own days carefree and well dressed. She had three children and then shut it down. "If there are too many, they get to fighting," she said. She also faithfully headed over to the Benimidori Chamber of Commerce and Industry three times a week to learn flamenco. Clad in gold and black, she made her castanets sing with passion. Manyo dodged each time Midori invited her to come along, but one day, Midori came to greet her with a solemn face. "It's not about flamenco today."

"What's wrong?"

"Climb the mountain?"

Midori seemed excessively clear-headed as she yanked Manyo by the hand. She said something had caught her eye in this area when she was looking at an aerial photo someone from the government had taken to make a map.

"Something caught your eye?"

"It was a black and white photo, so I couldn't really tell what it was. But I'm sure I saw something—looked like a bunch of square boxes. Maybe I was just seeing things, though. 'Cause I've been forever thinkin' about my brother so much."

"Square...boxes."

"You remember, stray cat? That night? That morning?" The Goldfish popped her eyes way out and looked back at her, and Manyo—having set out walking in a kimono and zori dress sandals, leaving the children in their room—managed a nod.

"How could I forget?"

"Me too. The two of us picking up my brother's body. It was all over the place. And I was like this, carryin' his head, still warm. His black hair with the gold combs. And then pulling on his arms. Right? His legs were so heavy, took both of us to carry them. Right, Manyo?"

"Right. We put your beautiful brother in a square box. Took everything we had, and then we fell asleep right there, the two of us." Manyo remembered how that night, the box had at some point disappeared without a trace, and in its place lay a single wild rose on her own lap.

Nowadays, even if a family did have a suicide, no one burned tokonen grass. You didn't see purple smoke snaking its way straight up to the heavens, thin like a rope. Were they still up there in the mountains? Or had they gone off somewhere far away? No doubt like a black wind. Manyo's parents. The outlanders.

Manyo steadily climbed in the direction the Goldfish indicated. It was autumn, and the mountain grew quite cool when night fell. She didn't know if they'd be able to get back home even if they ran all the way, but for some reason, the woman, no longer young, felt an inexplicable urge forward, and her feet did not stop.

"Who cares if we make it back home again?"

Manyo thought about it. The mother who raised her had said that the way a woman can repay a kindness was to have a lot of children. She had already given birth to four, which meant, if you counted his mistress's child, Yoji had five children. She had given him advance warning of the oil shock, a worthwhile deed since the Akakuchiba Steelworks had managed to avoid going under and pull through to that day. *The job of the clairvoyant madam's over now*, she thought. Her only unfinished business was her real parents. The outlanders and everything about them was a mystery that could not be solved.

The Goldfish was silent, pointed at the mountain, and walked on. At some point, the two started holding hands, something they hadn't even done as children, and sang as they climbed. Up an animal trail. Through bamboo groves. The Goldfish sang to Manyo an English song she had never heard before.

The Goldfish turned her pop eyes on Manyo as she sang so very earnestly, and a strange feeling came over Manyo. "What's that song?" she asked.

"It's John Lennon."

"Is it popular?"

"The young people at our shipyard sing it. They showed me a picture. The man who sings it is all pasty-faced."

"That so?"

"He kinda looks like my brother. All soft. Say, my brother was soft too, right?"

Manyo remembered the beautiful feminine man with the hem of the furisode kimono flipped up. She nodded and murmured that he was.

The pair walked for three days and three nights through the mountains, pressing forward, never losing their way somehow, even at night. When dawn broke, exhausted, they dozed a little in a ravine, but they would wake spontaneously together with the rising morning sun and continue their trek deeper and deeper into the mountains. When they came across a river, they drank the water as if bathing in it. They plucked and ate fruit from the trees. They moved forward, plunging straight ahead without a map, just like the mountain people.

Late at night on the third day, they dozed in a valley. When dawn broke, the Goldfish violently shook Manyo awake. "Stray cat! Stray cat!"

"What, bulldog?"

"It's here. This is it. Where my brother is."

Manyo slowly opened her eyes and saw that scattered around the ravine, pale purple in the morning light, were dozens, maybe hundreds of square wooden boxes, damp with morning dew. Wild roses were in full bloom out of season all over the valley, and dotted among them were the boxes. The women's hands could not pry out the tightly hammered nails, but one box had nails loose enough for them to pull the lid off. Combining their strength, they opened the box to find stuffed in there a beautiful woman in an old kimono with a splash pattern who had turned to grave wax. The eyelashes on her closed eyes were long, and straw rope was still wrapped around her neck; her thighs and shins had been broken so that she fit the box neatly. *Kanei Era Year 5* was written on the inside in black ink.

Manyo and the Goldfish were dumbfounded; the woman looked like she might be alive even now. *So the corpses here stay as they are forever, not rotting, not turning to bone?* Manyo wondered. A cold morning wind then blew down through the valley, and the second it hit the open box, the woman's skin and eyes and everything turned to dust and danced up with the gust, reducing her to an ancient corpse and leaving behind nothing but gaping cavernous eyes and wonderful black hair.

"Brother!" the Goldfish shouted, still frozen in place. Her voice rang out in the ravine and came back as an empty echo. She shouted even louder, "Brother! Brother!"

"Mother! Father!" Manyo yelled. After all this time, the sorrow of being abandoned suddenly attacked her heart there in the morning haze of the valley. "Mother! Father!"

"Brother! I'm here!"

Salty tears flowed. The two embraced and shouted endlessly.

"Father!"

"Brother!"

There was no answering voice, only the countless boxes. The wild roses swayed in the wind, the morning haze grew thicker, and finally the ominous boxes of the valley and the field of flowers grew faint in the purple fog and disappeared to parts unknown.

Sobbing, Manyo and the Goldfish joined hands and walked down the mountain. They brought their voices together to awkwardly sing the English-language song.

"Imajeen all za peepul!"

"Peepul!"

Manyo's voice lagged a little behind the Goldfish's from time to time. They held hands and continued to walk as if part of a parade. These two old women—no longer young, their jobs one as the wife, the other as the heir daughter complete—cried as they drank the water trickling from rocks, plucked and ate the fruit of trees, and kept pushing ahead, their feet red with blood blisters.

"Wonder where they went," Manyo murmured, not actually asking the Goldfish. "Those people like the wind who left me. Wonder where they went."

"Probably deeper into the mountains," the Goldfish said, wiping her tears away. "World's gettin' smaller, after all. Middle of the mountains, it's probably no big secret darkness no more. But the Chugoku Mountains are a haunted place. If you go way, way deep, you won't show up in them aerial photos. Us village people can't get there either. Those ancient Hoki woods are still there in the real depths of the mountains. I'm sure they went down deep, in those depths. So's they could stay the same."

"Then I really won't get to see them."

"You're a child of the village now. Let's go home to Tatsu's."

"Uh-huh."

"My brother's spirit, he's all quiet, surrounded by flowers and wind in that valley. I had three kids 'cause I wanted to give birth to my beautiful brother, but not one of them looks a bit like him. But it's fine. My brother's a man of wind and roses now. Imajeen all za peepul!"

"Peepul!"

They started crying wet tears again, continued marching, and returned to the village three days later.

The people there had been running around in confusion, looking for the young madams of the Akakuchiba Steelworks and the Kurobishi Shipbuilders who had disappeared so suddenly, like the wind, and failed to return home for such a long time. But they avoided further problems by saying that they had gotten lost on the mountain road. They then returned to the mother-in-law like a female Ebisu and the husband like a new Rikidozan and carefully raised their respective children to adulthood without ever speaking of the mountain or the boxes again. Manyo saw visions every so often, and Midori danced the flamenco each week.

This was in 1975, the fall when they were thirty-two, Manyo Akakuchiba and Midori Kurobishi, both past their prime already.

And this is where the story of the age of the last legend in Benimidori, of the twenty-three year period from 1953 to 1975, of the births of the boys and girls of clairvoyance and steel and wind, ends.

And then ten years later, in the winter of 1984, I—Toko Akakuchiba, daughter of Kemari, unworthy granddaughter of Manyo—was born.

PART TWO

THE AGE OF THE ENORMOUS AND THE EMPTY

1979–1998: KEMARI AKAKUCHIBA

Kemari Akakuchiba was a spitfire and a woman of steel, but she had one enemy she could not beat: the dead. Kemari was a tough girl who lived to fight, but every so often, in a curious twist, she would have her feet knocked out from under her by some dead person. The first was the housekeeper Masago, who fell ill and died that summer in 1979 when Kemari was twelve.

Taken in by a branch family in the middle of the steps and living in a detached residence on their property, Masago and her somber and sullen daughter, Momoyo, spent their days quietly in the dim gloom, not even knowing how to enjoy themselves. There was, however, one thing at least which excited them involving the eldest daughter of the main family, Kemari.

Masago at this time was in her late forties, bits of gray mixed into the black hair of her tight bun, and not much given to paying any particular attention to her appearance. Grumbling and grousing, she would take her daughter by the hand, come out to the hill road of the steps, and stare silently. At ten, Momoyo was two years younger than Kemari and had the same gloomy face as her mother. Her long hair hung braided down her back. As evening drew near, Momoyo would tilt toward the horizon a face too pale, too devoid of color for a child, and stare at the hill road of the steps with her mother to watch the intrepid Kemari who invariably passed their way when dusk came.

That spring, Kemari of the main family had started junior high at Benimidori Public Junior High. This was at the height of delinquent culture, and hot-blooded Kemari, who had been born covered in hair in the year of the Fire Horse, immediately began hurling abuse at the older students, even though she was nothing more than a snot-nosed grade seven, and raced her bicycle, and later a motorcycle for which she did not have a license, up and down the roads of the village alongside her friends. With her mother's solid, big body, sharp eyes, and a slim, well-shaped nose, she was powerfully beautiful. In the manner of a true delinquent, her glossy black hair was tied back in a ponytail with a bright red ribbon. Her gloomy-faced, illegitimate younger sister, Momoyo, watched tire-lessly, endlessly fascinated, as Kemari tore up the hill road of the steps.

Each time, Masago would give her daughter's shoulder a shake and mutter, "That's your big sister. But your big sister gets to be raised all careful and precious by the main Akakuchiba family. Pitiful, ain't it, you and your mom all alone in a branch family guesthouse. You really are a pitiful child." Her mother's words blanketed Momoyo like a curse. Kemari, of course, could hear none of this; she revved the engine, and the wind erased all other sound. "I slept with her daddy a hundred times, a thousand times even, to have you. A hundred nights, a thousand nights…All that and here you are. Pitiful."

Masago deeply despised Kemari, who had been born a little sooner than her own daughter, and would unfailingly stand rooted to the hill road like a ghost, glaring at Kemari. The target of those spiteful eyes would occasionally notice her and ask a son of some branch family or someone, "Why does that old woman stand there? She's always standing there by herself."

The son would invariably hem and haw, but the truth was, he felt a curious discomfort at Kemari's *by herself*. Masago was never by herself; Momoyo was always in tow. This mysterious blind spot became known to all at the family meeting after Masago's death to madness, which had surprised the people of the Akakuchiba family.

Masago's death came in the summer of Kemari's first year of junior high. Kemari was climbing the hill road on her motorbike, *sans* license and with modded air horns blaring as always, when Masago jumped out in front of her, completely naked, her first nude dance in over a decade. The pugnacious delinquent was shocked—she was still a child, after all—and as she swerved to avoid Masago, she turned the wrong way and went soaring through the air, bike and all.

"Kemari!" the throaty voice of her delinquent friend cried.

Kemari's bike spun a complete 360 degrees in the air, made contact with the hill road, bounced once, and survived unscathed.

Seeing this, Masago dropped to her hands and knees and began to wail. Her mind had already half set out on its journey to the next world. Momoyo came flying from the branch family house, tears streaking her gloomy face, and dragged her naked mother away. Her cheeks burned reddish black with shame. "I'm sorry, sister," she whispered, in a voice like a mosquito buzzing, but even now Kemari took no notice of Momoyo.

Her big, black eyes simply gaped at Masago. "Why don't you just die already?" The naked middle-aged woman turned around to spew her venom, and Kemari simply snorted in laughter.

"Boring as hell. Save your naked butt for your man, old woman."

Her friend was right there, so Kemari was talking her usual tough talk, but she had actually gotten whiplash from the impact of the landing, and for a while after that, she would be stuck with a ridiculous plaster cast around her neck. For a style-conscious middle-school student so proud of her punk ponytail, this was a cross to bear, but she couldn't actually complain about it.

From that day forward, Masago took to her bed in the branch family guesthouse where she came down with a high fever and breathed her last, still grumbling her resentment against the main family.

A quiet funeral was held by the branch family, and of the main family, only the grande dame, Tatsu, was in attendance. And then in the evening of that day, the red light of the setting sun blanketing the sky, Tatsu took Momoyo by the hand and returned to the main house. When they passed through its gates, Momoyo dropped her eyes to the ground and snickered.

It was Kaban, Momoyo's younger sister by a year, who remembered Momoyo's soft chuckling. She said she felt a shiver run up her spine and thought, *A monster child's come through our door.* Yoji didn't even glance at this monster of an illegitimate daughter, perhaps out of consideration for his wife, Manyo, but Tatsu called Manyo over and ordered her, in a tone that brooked no argument, "You'll be raising her."

"Uh-huh." Manyo nodded with the same somehow sad, distant eyes as always. And then she shifted her gaze away from Momoyo to stare hard at the back of her oldest son, Namida, passing by in the hallway at that moment.

Namida turned, noticed his mother, and narrowed his eyes in a smile. Time quietly stopped for the mother and son gazing at each other, a scene repeated almost daily in the mansion.

The other people in the main family always found their eyes on the wild horse of an oldest daughter Kemari, but the young madam Manyo's gaze always quietly chased after Namida alone. He was studying for the high school entrance exams and had just started attending a tutoring school with the aim of attending the top academic school in Tottori Prefecture, formerly an Imperial university preparatory school in the old prewar system. The stand-up collar of his uniform shone black. Manyo kept staring.

The people of the main family had been brought together in the reception hall, and the children were seated next to each other. Only Kemari was late, having said something nonsensical like "I got a rally." Still there in body but not in spirit, Manyo took Momoyo by the hand and led her into the reception hall. Yoji was a bit fidgety.

In a gentle voice, Manyo announced that these were her siblings and they'd all be living together from that day on. Namida nodded and said nothing, but he had his beloved mother's feelings at heart, and he glared fiercely at his father, Yoji, who was busy pretending not to know anything about anything. Kaban was afraid of the gloomy girl and how she hung her head, grinning.

"She honestly seemed so ecstatic, so delighted at finally being a member of the main family. I half thought she cursed her mother and killed her or something. Hmm, well, I suppose that's not possible, but still," Kaban recounted later, as an adult. "Anyway, Momoyo just loved Kemari. They were sisters, so it was weird, but she was basically Kemari's fan. I mean, she used to just watch and watch her out there on the steps, and she was so embarrassed when Kemari saw her mom naked. And then they end up living together under the same roof! I just know she was overjoyed that day."

However, putting a damper on Momoyo's happiness was none other than Kemari Akakuchiba herself. When this unconventional girl finally returned home, late for the family meeting because of her rally or some such, in a terrible state—on top of the cast for whiplash, her body was covered in scratches and cuts, and there were even scribbles in permanent marker on her face, begging the question of what was she doing and where—she simply muttered, "I won." And then she poked Kodoku, the smallest and youngest sibling, tucked away in a corner of the reception hall. "Of course," she bragged, and Kodoku shrank even further into himself.

At this time, her younger brother was still in kindergarten and shy to boot, the most indoorsy of a family that didn't leave the house much. More than anything, he feared his older sister Kemari, but she felt a deep love for this quiet, fearful brother. She poked and tickled him and he dodged her for a while, before Kemari, covered in cuts, still wearing her school uniform, moved briskly and assuredly to stand before Momoyo.

The family, knowing the volatility of the girl's temperament, held their breath in anticipation. Her father, Yoji, even gave up his pretense of aloofness and half rose to his feet. Things had gotten a little complicated because of Masago's death, but in his own way he probably had a soft spot for Momoyo, who did share his blood.

But Kemari didn't look at the younger girl; she simply kept moving. Momoyo lifted her face and her gloomy expression eased slightly. "Kemari, my sister," she said, in a voice so sweet it was surprising that such a melancholic girl could produce it.

Kemari showed no reaction, making everyone wonder if she had even heard Momoyo. Then, in a move that surprised the family as one, she turned her backside to the wicker chair where Momoyo was seated and plopped herself down.

Momoyo leapt up like a cornered cat and fled the chair, tumbling wretchedly to the floor. She then looked up in mute amazement at her cut-up older sister, sitting comfortably on the wicker chair she herself had occupied until mere moments earlier.

"Did someone say something?" Kemari asked her mother, mystified. A shiver ran up the collective spines of the main family, and they looked back and forth between the two girls.

Leaning back in the wicker chair, legs outstretched, Kemari was torn up from fighting, but she was large in stature and held herself like a queen, a beauty that naturally shone. Momoyo on the floor had a gloomy, pale face and looked like a skinny, dirty stray cat. Heaven and earth. Light and dark.

The girl on the ground bit her lip so hard she drew blood and stared up at her sister. The people of the main family, filled with trepidation, watched. Even when Manyo pointed with a "See there," Kemari's gaze wandered through the air.

Kemari Akakuchiba's eyes were unable to see Momoyo, her younger half sister.

When exactly had it started? No one could say, even as they ran back through their memories of Kemari's childhood. Manyo cocked her head, while Kaban commented, wonderingly, "Just how *did* it happen…"

Kemari's eyes did not register the younger half sister. She was apparently convinced that when Masago was still alive, she had stood out on the road by herself. Perhaps it was that Kemari, standing in the light, could not see Momoyo in the darkness. Or perhaps Masago had done something bad to her when she was a baby and had built a wall in her heart. The people of the main family trembled apprehensively as they came up with one hypothesis and then another, but the truth of the matter was never known.

Kemari sat in the wicker chair and cocked her head innocently. "What're we talking about?"

Momoyo said nothing and looked up at the main family's dazzling Fire Horse daughter. Eventually, a suspicious light took up residence in her eyes. The deep affection she held for her older sister twisted and distorted inside her. With Momoyo as her instrument, Masago's resentment continued to trail after Kemari.

At any rate, this was the fateful first encounter between the sisters from different mothers, Kemari and Momoyo Akakuchiba.

The Akakuchiba Steelworks continued to reign over the village of Benimidori from the heavens, an enormous warship voyaging the great deep, even as it came up against the oil shock and the iron chill stemming from it, the pollution problem, and the many other changing tides of the times. The mansion at the top of the steps was splendid and dazzling, as always, but rapid changes came to the lives of the people in the world below as modernization continued its steady march forward.

Way back when, in the Benimidori where Manyo and her husband Yoji had spent their youth, the main drag in front of the train station had been the town's shining star. The arcade street stretched out in front of you as you exited the station, the vegetable and fish market set up shop in the morning, and in the afternoon, it was busy with people shopping. Restaurants clustered around the opposite end of the arcade, and you could eat Western style or Chinese or anything you wanted there. A five-story department store popped up there as well, and it was every child's dream to eat the children's lunch on the top floor and look out from the roof at the scene below.

However, the iron chill was a turning point, and this station-front area, the best district in town, slid into decline with alarming rapidity. Young couples started leaving the apartment buildings in town and on the steps to secure mortgages on detached houses with yards in the new residential suburbs. Previously, life in apartment buildings, complete with the three modern miracles of washing machine, television, refrigerator, had been the be-all and end-all, but to these young couples dreaming of their own houses built on their own land, apartment buildings were old and stank of poverty. Plus, in the suburbs, you didn't have to worry as much about the pollution from the steelworks, and if you had your own car too, the commute was a breeze.

As the car class grew in the suburbs, the station area turned bleak and desolate before anyone even realized it. Like a movie on fast forward, the town was gray in an instant. The markets stopped happening, and the arcade shops shut their doors one after the other. Their sons grew up to be besuited office workers instead of taking over the family business. This was back when people still believed in the lifetime employment system for office workers and the security of a pension after retirement. These people were also essentially unfazed at the mortgages that would take a lifetime to pay off.

The car class also began to frequent the large volume sellers in the suburbs, with their ample parking. Branch offices of businesses with head offices in the capital began to pop up regionally. Nationwide, no matter where you went, you'd find the same stores, the same kind of people coming to them to buy the same products; this was the start of a new era. The money these provincial consumers spent began to flow like a deluge to the businesses in the cities.

In this way, the car class escaped to the suburbs, and the station-front area, with nothing to hold it up, fell further and further into decline, leaving nothing but gray ruins. The days passed as they always had for the Akakuchibas up in the heavens, but in Benimidori down below, a new era came surging through like a tidal wave, and the village had no choice but to change.

It was in the middle of this surging wave that the Fire Horse daughter of the main family, Kemari Akakuchiba, age thirteen, lived out the days of her adolescence.

For most of each day, the former shopping district of the station front, abandoned ruin that it was, was largely devoid of people. Only the gray faces of the poor still remained. And teenaged students.

The junior high and high schools they attended were near this old shopping district. For these students, who commuted to school by bus or by bike, going all the way out to the stores in the suburbs that the adults used was no easy feat. For this reason, the station area was crawling with students, but since they spent hardly any money, the stores did not profit, leading to the curious ruin of the arcade. Toward the end, around 1980, the dingy shopping street became a den of delinquent boys. Adults and serious students alike feared the area and would under no circumstances set foot in it. The street was the dark, cavelike stage for their theater of conflict, an old neighborhood with no adults, where conventional wisdom and common sense meant nothing. In point of fact, it was into this arcade that Kemari, in junior high now, set foot and fell in with a bad crowd, her parents unaware.

"Kemmy, let's go to the disco. I don't even care what happens tomorrow. We gotta have fun now. Let's just go nuts dancing at Miss Chicago tonight."

During summer break of her first year of junior high, Kemari made one close friend, a girl named Choko Hozumi. She was the niece of Toyohisa Hozumi, the Akakuchiba Steelworks worker who was still single even then. The child of the Hozumis, a family proud of their steelworking heritage, she was quite attractive and got extremely good grades. Choko herself didn't know it, but right around that time, her father had gone and bowed his head before his older brother Toyohisa, who was still single and working.

"A black kite like me went and had a hawk like Choko. I want to send her to university. Will you help out if she makes it that far?"

So Toyohisa set up a savings account in Choko's name and began to save up for his niece's tuition. But all this was done without the girl's knowledge.

Choko Hozumi, known simply as Chocco, sat next to Kemari in class. Their classmates were afraid of the delinquent Kemari with her ponytail, her too-long uniform skirt, and the fighting spirit of her red ribbon and kept their distance, but Chocco was dauntless, actively engaging Kemari. She yanked on her ponytail, chatted with her, and invited her to hang out after school.

Chocco was a slender, cute girl with the bob cut fashionable with girls then and large, drooping eyes. She also had a preppy air to her, with stickers of male pop stars plastered on her perfectly flattened school bag, and she was tremendously popular with the delinquent boys. She was, so to speak, the school star.

When summer vacation came, Chocco became the mascot for the Iron Angels, the bellicose biker gang Kemari put together comprised of grade seven girls, and from then on, she was always perched neatly on the back of Kemari's bike, air horns blaring as they raced through the village and flew along the national highway hugging the sea. And yet

Chocco's grades did not drop. She was a strange girl with two faces, two sides of the same coin.

It was summer break when Chocco came to invite Kemari to the disco Miss Chicago in Yoimachi Alley. Kemari was scarfing down watermelon on the veranda and looking out at the brilliant red flowers in the backyard of the Akakuchiba house when an unfamiliar girl's voice announced gloomily, "Someone's here to see you, Kemari." It was probably Momoyo.

Kemari figured it was a new housekeeper and paid her no mind. "Coming!" she called as she stood up and threw the watermelon rind into the backyard. She heard a cheerful voice from the entryway. "Kemmyyyyy!"

"Who's that girl?" It was the gloomy voice of a girl she couldn't see.

"Prob'ly Chocco." Kemari sounded annoyed.

"Who's Chocco?"

"My homegirl."

"…homegirl. What's that?"

"A friend you care about more than anyone else."

"Oh," the gloomy voice murmured softly, sadly, and there was no further follow-up.

Who knew how many times they had already gone to Miss Chicago that summer? Kemari had only just dipped her toes in delinquent culture, and she thought it was the adult world. Full of something like love, something like friendship, something like fighting—excitement, in other words. The real adults could try and stop her all they wanted, but it was futile.

Going out into the entryway, she saw Chocco waiting for her, cigarette hanging out of her mouth, dressed to the nines in the casually conservative and very feminine style popular with teenagers then. Manyo and Toyohisa passed by in whispered conversation about something. Manyo, seeing his niece smoking, reached out a long, sturdy arm, snatched the menthol cigarette from Chocco's lips, and cupped it in her hand before Toyohisa had the chance to lift his eyes. She unfolded her fingers before Chocco's face, and the girl gulped and opened her eyes wide.

The cigarette had disappeared.

"Cooool, Mrs. Akakuchiba. How'd you do that? What did you do?"

Chocco got excited and made a fuss, and Toyohisa, on the verge of yelling at her, lost steam and said nothing.

Manyo let out a sigh of relief. Her friend Midori Kurobishi, who had been working on her flamenco skills, had also become obsessed with magic classes as of late. Manyo had basically been forced to learn this little trick with a "Well, if you insist," but it did come in handy from time to time, which surprised her deep down.

"Girls shouldn't be smoking, all right? You'll regret it when you have kids."

"Tch, I get it. I mean, my uncle's already glaring at me there," Chocco said, as if the whole thing bored her. But the second Manyo and Toyohisa left, she stuck her tongue out at them and lit a second cigarette.

For kids of that period, smoking was the soul of rebellion, the opposite of innocence. Even as she coughed and teared up at the smoke, Chocco mumbled around the cigarette dangling from her lips, "Let's go. We gotta dance."

"Yup." Kemari nodded, in her ponytail and red track suit. They headed down the hill road of the steps and stopped at one of the lodging houses along the way.

The steps, where in the old days little bungalows with gardens had stood with paper lanterns dazzling the eye when night fell, were now completely transformed, lined with concrete apartment buildings. The number of people living in the once-popular apartments in this area had dropped, and the cracked concrete had sunk into a lifeless gray. Chocco's place was also on the bottom floor of one of these, but the building Kemari frequented was a corner of the edifice where the Tada offspring lived.

"Hey," Kemari said, familiarly, and the black lump squatting in the motorbike parking of the building lifted its face. A man just past twenty or so, with long hair and a slender physique.

Shinobu Tada. When he was still active, he had been the first leader of the Red and White Camellia Kings, the biker gang controlling the Chugoku region, but he had retired a little before he turned twenty and now ran Red and White Camellia Princess, a shop specializing in weapons made from Akakuchiba Steelworks steel on the first floor of a mixed-use building in Yoimachi Alley. For the delinquents of Benimidori, he was like an older brother, worthy of respect.

Chocco blathered on about how cool Shinobu was, but Kemari was afraid of this man, so she always used polite language with him.

"Hey, Kemari. How's yer mom?"

"She's good. Just before we came, she was holding a lit cigarette in her bare hand."

"Ha ha ha! That's really something."

Shinobu Tada might have been a mere resident of the steps, but his parents were the Tadas, the young couple that had taken in and raised abandoned Manyo. As the youngest child, Shinobu was also nothing more than the cute baby brother Manyo had taken care of right up until she went to marry into the family in the heavens. After she became the young madam, both she and her adopted family stepped back, so they didn't see each other very often, but Manyo still felt a strong connection to the kindhearted young couple and their children as her family.

Shinobu also held Manyo's daughter Kemari in respect for a particular reason. Delinquents measured people by only two rulers: how good you were in a fight and how manly you were. In a decidedly unwomanly way, Fire Horse Kemari was absurdly good in a fight, but she was also kindhearted after a fashion, keeping an eye out for her friends. Maybe because she was the daughter of the Akakuchiba Steelworks, she took to steel weapons like a fish to water, and she remained undefeated against ever-increasing numbers of girl delinquents.

To begin with, Kemari and the majority of the girls in her grade were born in the year of the Fire Horse. Not a single quiet-natured one among them, they were tough girls who'd just as soon hit you as look at you. And they started to come together around Kemari. At the same time, other tough girls born in the same year at different schools, in different prefectures were, in fact, rising up as one and would someday be part of a national boom in girl biker gangs, known as "Lady's." But this would all come a little later, after they had made their high school debuts. In any case, the grade seven Fire Horses gave themselves up to the impulses that bubbled up from within them, and a distinctly unfeminine, brazen war cry thundered from each town. And the girl that most impressed Shinobu Tada as being the strongest in Benimidori was Manyo's daughter Kemari.

"I fixed your bike."

"Thanks, brother."

"You should hang out at the weapons shop sometimes."

"'Kay." Kemari bowed her head. Chocco giggled excitedly and nudged Kemari. It was funny to see her friend nervous around Shinobu.

Chocco got on behind her, and horns blaring, they raced down the hill road of the steps.

"This is fun, Kemmy."

"Yeah?"

"Uh-huh."

Chocco's laugh as she clung to her back was contagious, and Kemari smiled a little too.

"As long as I have fun right now, I don't care if I die tomorrow. I mean, we're young and all!"

Choko Hozumi was a star at school as a top student; she got on well with the boys, who thought she was cute; and after school and on summer vacation, she raced around the national highway, breaking speed limits, as the gang mascot. She was a strange girl, chameleon-like, ephemeral and brash, the kind likely to live to a hundred, and yet equally likely to die abruptly and unexpectedly.

With Chocco behind her, Kemari raced through Benimidori.

"This is fun, Kemmy."

"'Cause it's me and you."

"Ah, you're killing me."

They stopped in Yoimachi Alley and went into the only disco in the neighborhood.

Stylish older guys stood on the steps. The young girls were hungry and gorged on all-you-can-eat soba noodles and spicy stir-fried shrimp, not paying any mind to the fact that the noodles were cold and dry. Then Chocco lit a cigarette and sat back. When they could no longer hold out against the intense music and the flood of lights, they slipped out onto the dark floor and danced until they were drenched in sweat. Exerting themselves on full stomachs like they were, their sides started to hurt.

"Ow ow ow! My stomach hurts."

"Me too, Kemmy."

"So what? It's both of us?"

"Aha ha ha! We're, like, total idiots!"

They laughed as they danced. Miss Chicago was more of a hangout for preppy boys and girls rather than punks like Kemari. The night was flashy and gaudy with no gang fight brewing; there was none of that sense of urgency that a fight would start soon. Chocco and her cuteness fit in perfectly at the crazy Miss Chicago.

After dancing till dawn, they went outside, followed by several of the preppy high school boys, one of whom placed a hand on Chocco's shoulder and forcefully invited her for a drive. Kemari's iron fist whistled through the air, and the high school boys were down on their hands and knees, clutching their solar plexuses and vomiting.

"You don't get to talk like that to the mascot of the Iron Angels. Take a look in the mirror, potatoheads, and try again."

Chocco squealed in high-pitched laughter, like it was all a game. They leapt onto Kemari's bike, passed down the national highway from Yoimachi Alley again, and climbed the hill road of the steps, Chocco laughing the whole time, like she was having a fit.

"Ah, that was fun! I don't care if I die right now."

"What're you talking about? We're gonna live to be a hundred, Chocco. We got a lot more fun ahead of us!"

"Hee hee! Glory days, huh, Kemmy?"

The bike shook, the engine roared, and the pair climbed the steps.

While her daughter was off enjoying the adolescence so typical of the times, her mother, Manyo, was learning all about the customs of the main house from grande dame Tatsu while she raised her children. Her days as the young madam were very busy ones.

The color of pain in her eyes growing deeper with the passing years, Manyo continued to chase after her eldest son, Namida. Yoji, who had recently gotten a separate bedroom and who was rarely seen in the main house while the sun was still up, still watched his wife very closely, once muttering, "You look at Namida like a girl in unrequited love."

"Do I?"

"You never—" He swallowed the words that would come next and fell silent, but most likely, he had been about to say, *You never looked at me that way.* Manyo cocked her head to the side and regarded her husband. He also got a faraway look in his eyes and stared absently at her.

Between them, a hollow that only the couple knew of had been born. They relied on each other, but something empty had begun to open up right in the middle of them.

All the while, Manyo yearned for Namida and continued to stare at him, but she also seemed to find various things about Kemari interesting, things she would mention—sometimes surprised, sometimes curious—to the girl's younger sister, Kaban. Manyo was most likely worried about how her daughter had become a juvenile delinquent and turned so violent, but what she found stranger than all of that was, in fact, Kemari's taste in men.

Starting around this time, Manyo was constantly tilting her head to one side, puzzled, and murmuring, "That girl's perversion's just never gonna straighten out."

Perhaps being a beautiful girl by nature was a negative in fate's tally. Kemari's selection of men was, always without the slightest hesitation, entirely perverse. She liked exceedingly ugly men, and throughout her life, she fell in love only with men with twisted faces, covered in pimples, with diamond-shaped chins and eyes like soybeans, the kind of men women loathed.

This perversion of Kemari's started when she was too little to remember; she would cling excessively to workers whose faces were burned or stiff from accidents at the steelworks factory. Once she started junior high, Kemari began flirting with men, supposing herself to be an adult at that point, but the first of these, Takeshi Nojima, was again a boy who was exceedingly ugly, although he did have fairly good prospects.

Takeshi Nojima was a delinquent, and the *soban*—leader of all gang leaders—at Benimidori Junior High.

This period around 1980 when Kemari was in junior high was when the "strong man" distilled in fiction took over the young people of Benimidori. The youth of this generation, coming after the obvious manliness and wealth their parents' generation so desperately worked toward, changed this sought-after goal into a sort of fiction, and it was in this strange form that it lived on in the culture. In junior high and high school, there was one boy known as the soban, who everyone had decided was, without a doubt, the strongest of all of them. These boys weren't actually invincible, but rather, their friends had collectively, unconsciously, created this story. Complicit awareness. Dry boys living through familiar stories.

This tendency in fact started around the time the prime minister— in a way, the country's soban—Kakuei Tanaka started to lose his own standing due to the Lockheed bribery scandal. Almost every day, the TV news and the papers were full of live coverage of the big man's downfall, a massive tree being felled. The adults of the village no doubt had their own thoughts on the various happenings of the time, but the children, they began feverishly creating their very own tale of enormity.

The children saw each other's blood, each other's tears, momentarily sliding past something glittering like friendship. They looked up to the soban at school, and then they went home to read the story of the delinquent's struggle in gutsy sports manga full of baseball or boxing.

Benimidori Junior High School was made up of a gymnasium, a little schoolyard, an old gray school building, and a new pink building hurriedly built to house an increasing number of students, with a third-floor walkway to connect the two. All the windows in the old building were cracked, and on the exterior walls of the gym, where the entrance ceremony was held, bizarre bits like "Nice to meetcha!", "Wild Angels," and "Crimson Lotus Special Attack Squad" had been spray-painted in red. The fiction the children had created was leaking out into the real world, and school violence started to become a serious social problem. The story of the strong man was finally having an impact on society, whether anyone liked it or not.

The soban was chosen in the spring from the new grade nines. Custom had it that the delinquents would line up in a row, in mimicry of the yakuza ceremony to name a new successor, in the third-floor walkway of Benimidori Junior High and swear their allegiance to the new king. Takeshi Nojima, the new king selected that spring, was much smaller than the boy who had been the soban until the previous year; instead of size, he had a tense and somehow nimble-looking build. If the previous year's soban was a sumo wrestler, then Nojima was a boxer. His eyes were sharp too. He rose to victory in the blood-spattered midnight fight theater, and his hand didn't even flinch over the brakes when they played chicken on their bikes. Even on the verge of falling into the dark, stormy Sea of Japan spreading out below the cliff, he raced coolly ahead toward death. Naturally, if this strong figure was seared into the minds of the other boys, then it was so much more so in the hearts of the delinquent girls watching as they hung from their boyfriends' arms. But these girls liked pretty boys, so they didn't have the slightest interest in Takeshi Nojima as a member of the opposite sex, although they did hold a curious reverence for him, perhaps aided by that exceedingly ugly face. *The king this year's perfect*, they all agreed.

And the first person Kemari ever loved was this exceedingly ugly, outstandingly brave Takeshi Nojima.

Takeshi had an unhappy upbringing. Around the time he became a delinquent, when he started junior high school, was right around the time his father, who had hit the bottle hard after losing his wife to illness, had brought home a drifter he knew from Yoimachi Alley and made her his new wife. Men and women drifting in from the cities, all with their own special circumstances, would sporadically show up in the bar district of Yoimachi, and this woman was one of them. The majority of these people were from the Osaka area and seriously in debt, and so in this bar district in a small village on the Sea of Japan side, there was always a need for a certain number of touts and hostesses who could handle the Osaka dialect.

Takeshi took his mother's mortuary tablet and left home, turning to the older brother presence of Shinobu Tada, the former head of the Red and White Camellia Kings. Shinobu was not anywhere close to a blood relation, but something welled up inside him at the sight of this boy standing in his entryway in the dead of night, leather-jacketed and pompadoured, clutching his mother's mortuary tablet. Acknowledging the absurdity of it, Shinobu took him in, and ever since, Takeshi Nojima had been pounding molten steel and making weapons at Shinobu Tada's, while spending his days outside immersed in fighting. When night came, he went to sleep in the 4.5-square-meter room on the second floor of the weapons shop.

Kemari fell in love. She began trembling all over the instant their eyes met. But when her good friend Chocco learned of this love, she laughed in big guffaws.

"Falling in love with a guy! Kemmy, you sure are a boring girl."

"I-I am?"

"I'm not falling in love with any guy. I'm gonna make him fall for me. Then I'll be all 'Nyah nyah nyah!'"

The two thirteen-year-olds rolled around laughing for nearly an hour, sticking their tongues out at each other. After that, Kemari was a regular visitor at the Red and White Camellia Princess where she got to know Takeshi until the two of them eventually ended up openly dating.

Takeshi, owner of an exceedingly ugly face, and Kemari, a beauty who could only shine, would seem to have been all wrong together, but they were in fact a fairly well-matched couple, a surprise to the other students at school when they saw them together, and a self-evident truth for their delinquent friends.

These two shouldered the wounded beast of the bloodthirsty fiction, the destiny of the boys and girls born to these times, the agitation of youth that needed to be acted out by someone chosen by the era. When Kemari and Takeshi got together, this air of fiction was immediately amplified.

"I thought when I took him in, I wouldn't let the girls get all crazy around him, but I can't really say anything if it's Kemari, now can I?" Takeshi's guardian, big brother Shinobu, grinned wryly and teased.

"I mean, they're both trying to be the strongest. And Chugoku's a big place, y'know."

At this big brother's suggestion, Kemari started to dream a magnificent dream, an impossible dream. To first make the Iron Angels—the girl gang she ruled over, still only thirteen—into the top motorcycle gang in the prefecture, and then on to control the entire Chugoku region. For Kemari, born and raised at the foot of the Chugoku Mountains, the only world she could truly grasp as being real was, in other words, Chugoku. The indeed grandiose notion of becoming number one in the world transfixed her.

"I wanna be the strongest, Takeshi." She was passionate as she told her boyfriend about this dream. "We'll make these mountains roar our names."

Incidentally, although Takeshi, two grades ahead of Kemari, was the soban, a renowned punk, deep in his heart, he had tucked away a secret, soft, romantic spot. He loved beautiful things. Well-formed sharp-edged weapons. Red flowers blooming in a field. A girl's long, glossy black hair. The words coming out of Kemari's mouth were the fierce, unwomanly words of someone in the very center of delinquent culture, but Takeshi held his tongue, fascinated by the deeply chiseled, sculpted beauty of Kemari's face. Her words were not just words, but music. The ugly boy stared with awe at the visage of the wild younger girl while that glittering summer came to an end and fall descended on them. Decaying leaves dyed red danced down from the heavens.

As Takeshi devoted himself to fighting, Kemari ruled over an ever-increasing number of Iron Angels companions and raced along the national highways with them. As usual, behind her rode the mascot Choko Hozumi.

"Go faster! Faster, Kemmy!" Chocco was always laughing. "So fast that we can never come back to this world!" Her excited voice reached Kemari's ears, without being drowned out by the roar of the machine below them.

This punk Kemari was also shy and didn't really talk much with her family about love and the like. She was also embarrassed to speak with her friends, so the most she could do was whisper to her good friend Chocco. But during the fall of grade eight, when she was building her name as a delinquent, she did manage to catch hold of her older brother, Namida, and talk to him a little about love.

He was in high school then, attending the best academic school in the prefecture, and he was always in his high-collared uniform and carrying a textbook or reference book tucked under his arm. With his graceful face and his school cap, her older brother was in every way different from Kemari. These siblings had not made anything resembling conversation for a long time, even when passing each other in the mansion. Kemari was jealous of the way Kaban, still in elementary school, would get to ride around carefree on Namida's back.

However, one day after school, when Kemari was flirting with Takeshi as they slipped through the arcade to walk in front of the station, she ran into her big brother. Namida had taken off his high-collared jacket and was in nothing but a T-shirt, hair disheveled and, remarkably, without a textbook in hand. She was just thinking how he seemed totally different from the mansion when she noticed he wasn't alone, but with a friend. The friend had similarly removed his jacket and was also in high school, leisurely strolling along next to her brother. He was tall with a decent face, the sort girls squealed over.

When he met Kemari's eyes, Namida stopped moving as if surprised. But then he started to smile, and Kemari relaxed.

"Namidaaa!" she called out to him.

"Hey, Kemari. What, you on a date?"

"Yeah."

Kemari—who you could tell at a glance was a delinquent, with her red-ribboned ponytail, school uniform skirt with the hem let way down, and flat school bag complete with iron plate—was arm in arm with Takeshi, outfitted in his pompadour and the baggy pants favored by the punks. Kemari thought her scholarly older brother might be uncomfortable with delinquents like her, but Namida casually introduced her to his friend, "This is my little sister."

"She's pretty cute."

"Thanks. I think so too."

Namida and his friend waved and went on their way.

After that, Kemari often saw them together here and there around town. "That's Sanjo," Namida told her. "We promised to go to the same university, so we're studying together."

At any rate, ever since running into him in town that day, Kemari found herself able to talk to Namida easily in the mansion as well.

"Namida, you in love?"

One morning that fall. Kemari asked him the abrupt question over breakfast, and Kaban, sitting beside her, spat out her clam miso soup.

Manyo was stunned and picked up a cloth to wipe off Kaban's face and blouse.

Having finished eating, Namida stood up and left the room with Kemari. "I am," as they walked.

"Heh heh. Me too."

Secretly trailing behind Kemari as she walked down the hall chatting amicably with her older brother was the invisible girl. Despite the fact that there should have been no one behind them, they could hear the dark sound of steady footfalls. Most likely, this was also the half sister, Momoyo. She was uninterested in Namida, and Namida, for his part, perhaps out of consideration for his mother, carefully kept his distance.

"That boy from the other day?"

"Yeah. Name's Takeshi."

"He's got really clear eyes, huh?"

"Oh! You could tell?"

"Uh-huh. Still, that's some face."

"I like that part too."

The wind blew and several red leaves fluttered to the earth from the trees in the garden.

"Kemari. You ever think about where that love's gonna go?" Namida asked his sister as they walked down the hall. His face was pale with an ephemeral quality surprising for a boy of sixteen.

"Where it'll go? Nah, not really."

"You don't? Hm, I guess it's still too soon for you. I mean, you've only just started. Your life of love, I mean."

He's surprisingly snotty, Kemari thought. Just as she was musing, *Guess you don't know unless you talk to him*, Namida stopping moving.

"When you're in love, you stop having a future, y'know. Time should just stop."

"What d'you mean?"

"Nothing. Just keep this between us." He fell silent.

Feeling eyes on her back, Kemari looked over her shoulder, where she saw Manyo staring their way from the opposite end of the hall. She realized her mother's eyes were not turned on her, but rather on her brother alone. Why would she be looking at him like that? That morning, like so many other days in the mansion, Manyo stared at Namida, and Momoyo at Kemari.

Namida turned as well and grinned at their mother.

This day when she was in grade eight was the lone time Kemari and Namida discussed love. After that, Namida kept matters of the heart a secret, and Kemari was for some reason or other bothered by his air of secrecy, but she was also hesitant to intrude and too young, so she quickly forgot and didn't ask him anything else.

It would be much, much later that she would regret not talking with him more at this time.

2. VIRGIN PINK

In this way—racing around on her bike with her friends, roaring her battle cry, modded horns blaring—Kemari's junior high days slipped by in no time at all. She couldn't ride during the heavy snow in winter, but when summer or spring break came, Kemari and her girlfriends would blithely scale the Chugoku Mountains and run down the "Lady's" of the high schools of Hiroshima and Okayama as if they were military commanders from the Warring States era.

The adults turned a blind eye to it, but the gossip network of children is tremendous indeed, and Kemari became a legendary delinquent in the Chugoku region at that time, so much so that anyone in junior or senior high who didn't know her name was assumed to be living under a rock. Meanwhile, the heroic saga of her boyfriend Takeshi and his fighting prowess, along with talk of how cute her mascot Chocco was, also rippled through this world. Racing along the national highway of Benimidori after school, going on campaigns on the other side of the mountains on holidays, Kemari's might knew no bounds.

From time to time, she was taken into custody. Suspensions from school, house arrest—they were everyday occurrences. Each time, Yoji would get angry and grill Manyo about her supervision of and responsibility for their daughter. Manyo would bow her head to her husband and to her mother-in-law, Tatsu. And then she would go and get Kemari from the Benimidori police station. The black ponytail, now down to Kemari's waist, would bristle, and she would rage against even the police. The officers, hesitant because she was a girl, would be unable to subdue her, but Manyo would only have to bark, "Really! Idiot child!" and she would be instantly calm.

Being scolded by the incredibly quiet woman who was her mother always made Kemari sad. Manyo would jab her in the head, thump her on the back, and finally yank on her ear, and she would leave the Benimidori police station pathetically muttering "Ow ow ow" as she started to walk.

To Manyo, her daughter's wild ways were beyond mysterious. When she was that age, essentially all she had been doing was looking after the little brothers and sisters in the lodging house on the steps. What on earth was this behavior of Kemari's, this lashing out from deep inside like a wounded beast?

This was the era when nationwide, in-school violence and the slip into delinquency for junior and senior high students was considered a real problem. Manyo bowed her head to the man from the Hozumi family who had similarly come for Chocco and complained about this situation to him, without thinking. The man was hesitant since he was, after all, speaking with the young madam of the Akakuchiba main family, and simply bowed his head with a "It's just as you say, ma'am." But the next day, Toyohisa came by the main house unexpectedly and waved from the backyard at Manyo walking down the hallway.

"Toyo."

"Seems you had a bit of trouble again yesterday."

"We really did. Just listen to this, Toyo."

Manyo prepared some bukupuku tea on the veranda and sat down with Toyohisa. She was gradually beginning to feel a worry and a panic about her daughter that this was perhaps no time for the girl to be fooling around. Toyohisa didn't have any children of his own and loved his niece very much, although he had never told her that, and he sat himself down with a "hup," irritation rising to his face.

"Strange business, hm, Capital M? Being young."

"It really is, Toyo."

"You remember? Listen. There was that time that Tada kid, Hajime, kicked up all that fuss. I wondered back then too just what those kids were even up to. We weren't so different in age, but I couldn't get my head 'round it at all."

"There was that too, wasn't there." Manyo nodded, recalling this incident smack in the middle of the era that saw the Akakuchiba Steelworks pollution problem and the wildfire of the student movement.

Hajime Tada had had eyes darker than the black smoke in those days, but after a while, he took a break from university to travel across the American continent with a trumpet in one hand before coming back and graduating without incident. He now worked at a fisheries research institute in neighboring Shimane Prefecture and had a wife and children. Once the agitation of his youth had passed, he was curiously rejuvenated and was now an indulgent middle-aged man with good color in his cheeks; only his trademark white beret remained the same.

"Little Hajime was so excitable back then." Manyo grabbed a bean from her tea.

"But, y'know, this is still different from that. Dunno what it is though. No clue."

The youth of that slightly earlier time had wrestled with politics and burned brightly with the ideology of making a better society, but at some point, before they knew it, that era had passed, and the young people who existed now had holes inside them.

Kemari and her generation had no ideology, nor any awareness of society. Unable to even see the real world they were so uninterested in, they instead painted their own fictional world over the real. Delinquent culture was the shared illusion of the young. This culture did champion ideals like building a nation and superior fighting skills, but as to what they were fighting for, why they were riding—the heart of it was nothing but a hole. And this was exactly why the young people burned. They burned because there was nothing.

However, this sort of thing was, to the adults, unfathomable. Manyo and Toyohisa couldn't stop themselves from wondering what would happen if the girls were to get in an accident and hurt themselves, and their faces grew grim. The girls cast contemptuous looks at these two with their worried looks, and the empty sound of modded horns trumpeting along the road on the steps echoed out that day as well.

Over the course of her three years of junior high, Kemari gained dominance over all of Hiroshima and Okayama. The Fire Horse girls rose up as one and ran wild in villages and towns everywhere, but there wasn't a sister anywhere in the mountains at least who could take on Kemari Akakuchiba. With Shimane and Yamaguchi left as a later exercise, Kemari's middle school days began to draw to a close.

Meanwhile, the invisible younger sister, Momoyo, started at the same Benimidori Junior High School. She was very staid with her braid and serious in her school uniform, exactly as prescribed by school regulations, and there were very few within the school who had any idea she was Kemari's little sister.

Momoyo was thirteen when she stole her first man. That is to say, for Momoyo, to live was to steal men, a trait she had inherited from her mother. In the shadow of Kemari burning with her military campaigns, Momoyo approached Takeshi Nojima, shining with a dark light.

Takeshi displayed a stubborn machismo in his promises with other boys, but he could be rather sloppy when it came to girls. One night, walking along a path through the rice fields, cigarette hanging from his lips, Takeshi noticed the junior high girl who kept following him silently. When he turned around, he saw a mischievous light in the girl's eyes, an awareness of complicity. Wondering *What's up with her*, he gave her hand a yank and the girl grinned. He became entangled with her, and they fell in the dry paddy before the planted rice, a bullfrog croaking throatily as he became a sacrifice to Momoyo's thieving.

After that, Momoyo would come up, trailing along behind him and grinning just when he was about to forget the whole thing. At first, he was simply fooling around, but Takeshi seemed to gradually become captivated by the girl's gloomy air. She had a passive femininity, as it were, that Kemari, bone dry and exceedingly indifferent, did not.

When he was tangled up with the somber and sullen Momoyo, he was walking through town at night, and he ran right into Kemari just once, as she was coming out of the weapons shop, Red and White Camellia Princess. But mysteriously, although he was leaping out of his skin, Kemari simply raised an indifferent hand to him, said, "Hey, Takeshi," and kept on walking. He didn't know Momoyo was her younger sister or that Kemari couldn't see her, so he was surprised and also a little hurt.

When Kemari was graduating from junior high, Takeshi was going into grade twelve and starting to think about retiring from the delinquent life. In this unique subculture, boys and girls grew up fast. The norm was to retire once you hit eighteen and become an adult. If you let it drag on and just kept racing around pretending you were still young, you were inviting serious scorn and condescension. He began to put a little distance between himself and Kemari. And as he grew older, the longing for beauty also began to grow distant in the heart of ugly Takeshi.

To speak of Kemari's younger sister Kaban at this time, she was a slightly preppy girl, obsessed with TV music programs. She would soon be starting junior high, and in her childlike way, she was starting to pay attention to her appearance.

On TV, one adorable "idol" after another made her debut, singing songs about love in wonderful costumes. Kaban memorized the dances and practiced them over and over. And then she would grab hold of her little brother, Kodoku, and put on one-woman shows with him as sole audience member.

Scouts often came through the provincial towns holding auditions for new talent. Unbeknownst to her family, Kaban would take her own picture and enter these idol contests. Although not on the level of her older sister, she was still a fairly pretty girl with big, beautiful eyes, but perhaps because of her young age, she would almost always be eliminated before she could get to the actual audition stage. Still, she didn't give up and kept entering every contest she could. When she occasionally did qualify to take part in a preliminary regional audition, she would leave the house without telling her parents, big bag in hand, only to be captured by one of Manyo's subordinates at the audition venue.

"Stupid Mom! Why does she have to ruin everything?"

Again, although not on the level of her older sister, Kaban had a fairly fierce disposition, and she would swing the big bag around violently in the entrance to the venue. Manyo would then calmly discuss the situation with her forcibly returned daughter.

"You're still in elementary school. When you get to be more grown-up, you can take responsibility for yourself and do whatever you'd like. Okay?"

Kaban glared at her mother, tears springing up in her eyes. At a time when her own appearance was the only thing that interested her, Kaban unjustifiably resented, albeit ever so slightly, this woman who had not been kind enough to make her as beautiful as her older sister. *If I had just been born beautiful like Kemari, for sure I'd be an idol.*

Kaban was more attached to the preppy Choko Hozumi than she was to Kemari. "Chocco's so stylish," she would say. With Kemari, however, she would get cheeky—"Punk! You...bear girl!"—and get a punch from her sister, "The hell!"

The oldest, Namida, was just about to start grade twelve. He was also studying for the university entrance exams and had his uniform collar properly up, school cap on his head, as he walked down the hallway of the mansion with sorrowful eyes and a textbook in one hand. Kemari occasionally caught glimpses of this stiff brother, but she couldn't forget how he had looked when she ran into him in town with his friend, their collars unfastened, hair mussed, laughing as they walked, relaxed and having fun. She cocked her head as she wondered which was the real him. Namida, meeting his sister's eyes, would always smile in a quiet way; his face was unexpectedly ephemeral and pale.

For the junior and senior high students of this time, the delinquency movement—the in-school violence and the like—was only half the story. The majority of students were also squarely in the midst of the spartan battle known as the entrance exam war. The strong men, the workers of Benimidori charged with the reconstruction after the war, were starting to feel the futility of labor. They dreamed of the stability of a detached house out in the suburbs bought with a home loan; they dreamed, in other words, of something permanent. They wanted their own children at least to rise through the ranks in the new education meritocracy and gain a higher social standing than themselves.

Private cram schools were the main battlegrounds for the exam war in Benimidori. The majority of students began attending cram school after cram school in grade eight or nine. There, they were taught that the child in the seat next to them was not their friend, but their rival. They memorized facts, took mock exams, and were divided up in each class by their scores. The children determined their worth numerically. Several cram schools opened up in the mixed-use buildings by the station, and when evening fell, the children were sucked into them, columns of battle-scarred soldiers.

One day, when Kemari and her friends were racing around town, horns trumpeting, they peeked into a cram school half as a laugh, and as they hung from the window, they saw a familiar face. Alice band neatly holding back the bob cut that was always carefully blown out, fresh-faced and makeup-free, their mascot Chocco ran a pen over the pages of her notebook.

Startled, Kemari let go of the window and fell to the ground. "Kemari!" At the cry from one of her friends, Chocco looked up and noticed them hanging there. She cocked her head slightly and giggled.

And then exam warrior Chocco was getting a ride home from cram school on the back of Kemari's bike. "Kemmy, we're already fifteen, y'know. Time's moving way too fast, right?" she said, as they raced along the national highway.

"Still fifteen!" Kemari shouted back.

"Already fifteen!" Chocco yelled.

"Guess so."

"Once junior high's over, I'm done with being bad. I decided I'm doing things right. I feel like I wanna see just how far I can go."

"How far where?"

"In this stupid world, Kemmy."

Choko Hozumi was an excellent student, boasting the top marks at Benimidori Junior High, smart right from the start with seemingly no need to go to cram school. The teachers gave her due respect for this, but Chocco's ambition was far greater than what those teachers envisioned for her.

"Which is why it'll be goodbye soon, Kemmy."

"Goodbye? Why? I mean, your grades and mine aren't even in the same universe, so we'll for sure be at different high schools. But we can still keep hanging out like this. We're still fifteen."

"Already fifteen. And the thing is, okay? I decided this year's the end of being bad. I'm gonna get serious in high school, and when I grow up, I'll save the bad stuff for just the nights. I'm gonna live well, and live long. Which is why it'll be goodbye soon."

Her words pierced deep into Kemari's heart. She let Chocco off in the middle of the steps, waved with a "See ya," and stayed staring at her best friend's back as she climbed the stairs of her apartment building and grew distant. Then she went home, barged into her little brother's room, and gave him a tight hug from behind while he was reading manga. Kodoku trembled like a hunter attacked by a bear. Kemari would never dream of showing a glum face to anyone else in her family, but starting around this time, she would come and hang out in Kodoku's room whenever anything happened.

"Kodoku, hang out with your big sister."

"Nooo, I'm reading manga right now."

Paying no mind to the little boy curled up in a ball in one corner of the room, Kemari pulled a manga from the shelf and started reading herself.

A *shojo* manga about adorable love and friendship with flowers and lace decorating each page, the farthest thing imaginable from Kemari's style. Kodoku was more interested in this type of comic than the stories of blood and gore. He would use up his allowance to line his book-shelves with these manga, and then Kemari would come along and read them. "Pfft!" she complained. "This is for babies." And yet she would occasionally sniffle rather loudly. Kodoku and Kemari might have been in the same room, but they never talked, they just read manga, so it was impossible to say if they were close or just the opposite. Everyone in their family wondered at this strange relationship. *Those two get along, don't they? Wonder why…*

In this slightly melancholic fashion, Kemari's last year of junior high passed. She took the high school entrance exam for a school with the lowest pass rate of all the public schools, a place where no matter how great the baby boom for that year had been, the application rate was on the level of seventy percent. In other words, it was a den of delinquency. She easily made it in, and almost all of her friends followed suit. Chocco, with very nearly the top mark of all the test takers, passed with flying colors the exam for the academic school Namida attended, the former Imperial university preparatory school, and announced her retirement as mascot at the Iron Angels meeting after the graduation ceremony.

"Goodbye, everyone. I'm retiring from delinquency. Now I'm going to go to Todai itself, the University of Tokyo, become a diplomat, and when I'm a grown-up woman, right? Just at night, I'm gonna go on the wild woman prowl."

The girls burst out laughing and shouted their encouragement at Chocco. "You go, Chocco!" "Goodbye! Stay strong!" "You'll never be wild. Try for slightly excited. Hee hee hee!" These delinquents all looked scary, but they were kindhearted girls, so they hugged her and pressed their cheeks together, and were sorry to see her go. Only Kemari turned her back to Chocco, sullenly angry.

"You go wherever the hell you want. Nothing to do with me, someone like you."

"Kemmy…" Noticing the shaking of the large back clad in the modified sailor uniform, Chocco drew in her outstretched arms. "Goodbye, it was fun. I'll never forget all the times we rode together. I mean, that was our youth, after all." She slowly turned her back to the Iron Angels, threw out her chest, and walked away. The cherry blossom petals danced and scattered in the air around her.

Kemari didn't make a move to turn around; a teardrop fell heavily at her feet.

After that, the now mascotless Iron Angels rode around trumpeting their horns like they always had. And Kemari Akakuchiba rode through this spring of her fifteenth year, a year that would never come again, alone on her bike, lighter now. Flurries of cherry blossom petals blanketed the national highway.

Namida said something about this, didn't he? Kemari abruptly remembered her older brother's words. *Time should just stop.* His pale, unexpectedly ephemeral face as he murmured it. *If time stopped, then I could just keep riding around forever with my best friend, the girl I love,* she thought. But youth is beautiful precisely because it does pass.

That spring break, Kemari rode with her friends, rode alone, and gave herself over to the impulses welling up inside her body, raging throughout Tottori like a red storm. And when evening came, she'd barge into her little brother's bedroom and read those melancholic shojo manga.

Her boyfriend Takeshi too, speaking of him, they had grown apart before she knew it. Perhaps because of her rough personality or because of her outstanding beauty, Kemari never suspected her partners of cheating on her or having a change of heart.

And then the day she started high school came along. The entrance ceremony honestly made her mother Manyo's head hurt, and was a sign of the ups and downs to come.

Takeshi Nojima was in grade twelve at the high school Kemari was starting at and still ruled as soban as he had in junior high. Kemari's introduction to high school, a den of delinquents and fashion victims, was marked by trepidation at the arrival of either the soban's girlfriend on the part of the older male students, or of the leader of those brazen junior high girls on the part of the older female students.

Kemari slipped weapons into her school bag, defended her uniformed back with an iron plate, hid razor blades between her fingers, and went to face the entrance ceremony. She cursed out the older girls lying in wait at the school gates, totally ignored the older boys setting off firecrackers in the middle of the ceremony, and when she was ambushed on her way home, got into a fight in the schoolyard.

This was a battle among the girls, and the older boys just watched, cigarettes dangling from mouths. "Your girl's crazy strong. Damn," one of them said to Takeshi, around the time the Asadaame candy tin was full of crushed butts.

"Yeah." Takeshi nodded, there in body but not in spirit.

Now in grade twelve, Takeshi had at some point been gutted by the man-stealing eighth-grader, Momoyo. His heart was far from Kemari. The couple was connected by the shared ideal of delinquent culture, but Takeshi's heart was privately in the process of pulling away from that as well.

For Takeshi, who was turning eighteen that year, it was getting to be time to spread his wings in the adult world at last. Having spent his days as a top fighter, he made friends with a punk on the boxing team and became obsessed with the sport. He started going to the sole gym in town and dreamed of applying for pro status. But this was a practical dream and a worldview that didn't fit too well in the world of fiction that was delinquent culture. He said nothing to Kemari about any of it.

And so, the boy in Kemari's first romance began to end their relationship with her completely unaware.

Even after she started high school, Kemari continued her campaigns, gaining control over Shimane during summer vacation of grade ten. She was constantly in an ill temper and always raging. She drove in her usual dangerous fashion, but strangely, never got into accidents.

Just once, in town, she ran into Choko Hozumi, who graduation day had separated from her.

On her way home one day—for once not riding her bike but instead wandering along the tree-lined street by herself—a group of girls came along, giggling noisily. She heard their laughter like the ringing of bells. Black hair neat, skirts right around knee-length. *Pretty serious. These girls are uptight*, Kemari noted to herself. The girls also noticed her, and they whispered among themselves, "Gross, a juvie." Trying not to meet her eyes, they moved toward the enormous cherry blossom trees, avoiding Kemari as they approached. *Pfft!* she sniffed scornfully.

She glanced over as they were passing each other and saw that the girl second from the right had big, beautiful, drooping eyes and straight black hair. She was tilting her head slightly and laughing gracefully. Choko Hozumi. Her neat blazer and the virginal pink of her unmade-up cheeks were dazzling.

The newly neat Choko Hozumi grew distant without meeting the eyes of Kemari in her too-long sailor skirt, red ribbon on her ponytail.

"Todai. Diplomat. Only at night. Wild woman."

Singing a nonsense verse, Kemari ran as fast as she could along the tree-lined road, and the genius girls stopped, startled. "Ugh, what was *that?*" they whispered at each other and started walking again.

"When does youth end anyway?" she asked Kaban, who was in the middle of practicing idol dance moves on the veranda.

"Don't talk like an old lady, sis," her younger sister responded, relatively scathingly.

Kemari sighed and tossed her school bag out into the garden. The leather bag and the steel plate it held fell with a heavy crunch onto the gravel of the garden. On a whim, Kemari started copying her sister's dance routine.

"See? You put one hand out like this and you sing, 'You.' You take that arm, spin it around up behind your head and sing, 'I miss you.' You're holding the mic with this hand. Hey! You're pretty good at this!"

Manyo watched enthralled from the garden as these sisters who looked so much alike danced alongside each other. "You know," she said later. "When she was being cute, she was just a regular girl. But that was the only time I saw her like that."

Now then, to speak of this younger sister Kaban, she had just become a junior high student, her long-awaited dream finally coming true. Preppy and coquettish by nature, Kaban hated the standard-issue backpack and yellow hat that were *de rigeur* in elementary school, so she was ecstatic at making the jump into the new world of sailor uniforms, leather shoes, and white socks. At the thought of finally starting junior high, immersing herself in style, making loads of preppy friends, and being made much of by the boys, she practically floated to the entrance ceremony—until being plunged to the depths of hell by her older sister Kemari.

There was, after all, simply no way the delinquents of Benimidori Junior High could just leave their leader's younger sister be, not when she looked so much like Kemari. The boy who had been selected as that year's king went around to the grade seven classroom to greet the new kids, fresh lines shaved out of his hair. As he walked down the hall, he shouted a familiar "hey" at her, and when she went to pick her things up, a delinquent she didn't know gave her a hand. Which is why the boys didn't go for her at all. She might have been cute, but the environment around her was too terrifying.

On her third day of school, her half sister, Momoyo, popped her head into her classroom. Her relief at finding this staid older sister, braided hair and perfectly regulation uniform, was transient as Momoyo yanked on her hand and pulled her out into the hallway. "Let your big sister show you around the school." And then: "Behind that gym there, Kemari used to squat down and smoke. I saw her." "That hole there, our sister kicked that spot and made it. I saw it." "This lawn here, okay…" Momoyo was delighted to impart all this knowledge quite loudly, so the fact that Kemari was her older sister became even more widely known at school.

Strangely, the delinquents treated Momoyo, the sister Kemari did not see, with silent contempt, but they seemed to think Kaban was all right and were hyperattentive. Kaban kept going to school, basically fed up with the whole enterprise already, getting dragged away by Momoyo from time to time and forced to listen to stories about Kemari.

"Honestly, I was surprised she had spent so much time just watching Kemari," Kaban told me later, exasperated. "From behind a pillar, from the passageway, everywhere. She watched her every single day. Like a stalker. Weird, hm? I mean, her own sister."

Once she got comfortable with her, Momoyo—whose name was written "hundred nights"—confessed all sorts of things to Kaban in her melancholic voice. "I slept with Nojima. We slept together a hundred times."

"Kemari'll kill you."

"She will not."

Once summer break was over, Kemari switched boyfriends, leaving Takeshi Nojima for a new boy. This one too was a delinquent with an exceedingly ugly countenance; within the prefecture, he was called Demon Yamanaka.

"I slept with Yamanaka," Momoyo whispered in the shade of the trees in the schoolyard, in the fall of that year.

"She's gonna kill you..."

"She won't. And I slept with him a hundred times."

Back then, Kaban didn't know what to do with Momoyo.

"Anyway, she was pretty gloomy. I know we're related and everything, but there was something mysterious about her. That habit of hers, when she opened her mouth, it was all slept with him, didn't sleep with him. Honestly, we should've just thrown her in with Kemari and split the difference."

Throughout grade seven and eight, while she was making these Herculean efforts at school, Kaban continued to work with the unswerving aim of becoming an idol singer at home. In the evening, she clung to the TV, never missing an episode of the music show popular at the time. She would record the show on cassette and listen to it over and over to learn the songs. For the dancing, she would stare with eyes like dinner plates at the videos she made and memorize every move. And she never failed to enter an idol contest; she burned with the passion of her dream.

The youngest, Kodoku, was still very much a child and totally absorbed in his children's network. Kemari and Kaban were completely oblivious to this development, but right around that time, the family computer came onto the market, and elementary school children couldn't get enough of it. Kodoku was one of those many thrilled children, and he pestered his grandmother Tatsu to buy him one. He played video games every night at home and then talked about them every day with his friends at school.

Although Tatsu was still the grande dame of the main family and the object of much fear and awe, she utterly spoiled the quietly obedient youngest child, even as half of her watched harshly and intently over Namida, the oldest. While Kemari immersed herself in delinquent culture and Kaban focused on becoming an idol, Kodoku entered the world of video games and left behind the desolate reality of the outside world. But all of these were the childish ways of living in the age of fiction.

In addition to the rise of video games, the occult exploded in popularity at schools across the land. Stories like the slit-mouth woman (known to attack children with scissors) and Hanako of the toilet (knock on the stall door three times, say her name, and she appears), along with the *kokkuri* divination game, spread through the country in the blink of an eye via the children's word-of-mouth network. In the classroom, excited children everywhere chattered about the Himalayan yeti, the Loch Ness monster, the secret of the Nazca Lines. Turning on the TV, you were greeted with specials on unidentified flying objects and aliens. Kodoku dared to get into a channel war with Kaban—who wanted, of course, to watch idol shows—because of one such program and was sent flying into the backyard with a sharp "Quit it!" Tatsu later gave Kaban the scolding of her life for hitting Kodoku.

He was still in elementary school, but Kodoku had given up. One of the children's many fads was Nostradamus's prophecies. According to this prophet from the Middle Ages, the world was going to end in the seventh month of 1999. A meteor would come crashing down. An ice age like that which brought about the extinction of the dinosaurs would begin. Nuclear war would break out. Enthusiastically discussing the various hypotheses, Kodoku came to this feeling of resignation. He counted off on his fingers how old he would be then. Twenty-four. When he thought about everything ending while he was still so young, he lost all interest in doing anything. His father Yoji rebuked him as he was lolling about, ignoring his homework.

"Whatever," Kodoku retorted. "Homework when I'm just gonna die at twenty-four?"

His father sent him flying with a slap to the cheek.

Sulking, humming a song that wasn't quite a whistle, Kodoku kicked at rocks and walked along the steps. "This is dumb. Everything is dumb." The heart of an elementary student who had given up too soon. Reddish-black fall leaves drifted past his clear small profile.

"Hey, Kodoku!" Whizzing by on her bike, Kemari slipped a hand around her brother's hips and kept racing along the hill road. Kodoku was also faint-hearted, and he let out a scream and called for his grandmother Tatsu.

At this time, Namida was in grade twelve. He got top grades and his teachers gave him their stamp of approval. They said he could get into any public university, but it seemed that the eldest Akakuchiba son wouldn't be allowed to leave Tottori. The heir to the main family, the heavens of Benimidori even then, narrowed his search down to Tottori University and decided to take just their entrance exam.

Kemari asked him about it at supper, and Namida smiled warmly. "I'll be with my friends. Staying in the area actually works out best for me."

"Hmm, I guess…"

Manyo said nothing, she simply stared at Namida, black eyes sad, years of suffering etched into them. Her eldest soon looked at her and grinned.

The year ended without incident, and Kemari started grade eleven. Namida breezed into Tottori University and exchanged the high collar of his high school uniform for the open collars of casual shirts paired with jeans.

The eldest son of the Akakuchiba main family, he was also quite popular with the girls at the junior college, whose more stylish elements began frequenting the house, asking after Namida. Namida seemed annoyed by them and never came out, so they mostly fell to Kemari, who handled them somewhat roughly—"You got some business with my brother, sister?"—and the junior college girls always fled, scattering like baby spiders, though they would creep back before too long.

At university, Namida joined the decidedly unglamorous hiking club and would go walking with his friends on days off school up in the Chugoku Mountains. Tatsu would hand Namida the boxed lunch she had gotten a housekeeper to make and see him off as he left.

"That boy really is a serious one. Not a word of romance."

She was likely comparing him with her own son, Yoji, at that age. Tatsu still reigned over the mansion as the grande dame of the main family, but she was gradually yielding authority to Manyo, beginning with the more trivial things. By this time, it was essentially Manyo giving all the orders to the servants. While Manyo was busy running the house, Tatsu was the one who received Midori Kurobishi when she occasionally came by; they would roll about with laughter as they chatted about magic and rakugo and all sorts of things. While Midori, in her usual gilded splendor, clutched her stomach and laughed with the grande dame, every so often, she would see out of the corner of her eye Manyo passing by in the hallway.

"She really is pretty busy," she would say, and Tatsu would nod.

"She is. Once I'm gone, that girl'll be running the whole show round here." That said, Tatsu had good color in her cheeks, and roundly fat as she was, she didn't look to be going anywhere anytime soon.

Momoyo was, as always, focused on her man stealing, but she was also facing the high school entrance exam. When Manyo called her aside and asked her if she had academic aspirations, she said in a gloomy voice that she wanted to get into a trade. Asked whether she'd like to go on to university, she sullenly, silently shook her head. Manyo recounted with a sigh later how that could have been the hesitance of an illegitimate child, but either way, Momoyo had stubbornly set her sights on a commercial high school in the region. Manyo managed to grab hold of busy Yoji to discuss it, but he said he would leave the matter to her, so she had a bit of trouble with the whole thing. However, Momoyo did not change her mind and, in the end, narrowed her choices down to a single commercial high school and took their entrance exam.

The direction of the wind was also changing slightly. The Fire Horse high school girls born in '66, who had been developing their delinquent culture and running wild all over the country, exploded into a "Lady's" fad; a magazine catering to the subculture was even founded. As the region's most famous delinquent, Kemari Akakuchiba could be seen posing heroically in every issue, representing Chugoku, shouting her battle cry and swinging a steel pipe or racing through the rice fields, banner flapping behind her. More and more girls became Lady's, and the battles between them grew correspondingly fiercer. In the schools, however, the fashion was quite the reverse, as the next era was ushered in.

The general student population dove even deeper into the exam wars. The person in the seat next to you wasn't a friend, she was a enemy to be kicked down; getting good grades and "winning" in the education-oriented society was still considered more important than anything else. The parents who had bought their detached houses on loan put the rest of their money into their children's education. And it wasn't only the boys; girls were also pouring their energy into studying. Not long after this, the Equal Employment Opportunities Law was enacted, and several years after that, the world of politics saw the number of female Diet members in the opposition jump sharply, a movement called, among other names, the "Madonna Sensation." Girls were still very much fumbling their way forward, but they also won victories in the exam wars and started to believe that if they got an advanced education, they too could become winners, supporting the central pillars of society. Whenever

Kemari noticed these steady changes in the world around her, she would remember her now-distant, once-close friend Choko Hozumi.

Brilliant Chocco, aiming to attend the best academic institution in the country so that she could become a diplomat. Adorable Chocco, boasting about how she would live well in this stupid world. Just remembering it, Kemari couldn't help feeling that her friend's face back then hadn't been triumphant or burning with hope, but that her eyes had rather been curiously awake, like ice, sad.

This was also when serious children began to crack with increasing frequency, as if unable to endure the heavy pressure of the education-oriented society. Incredibly quiet children attacked their parents like beasts, swinging bats or other weapons. Others abruptly jumped from buildings. A bizarre stress with no outlet proliferated in the world of children.

And with this, the schools began to transform once again. The era of flashy in-school violence announced its gradual end, and in its place, an era of vicious bullying arrived, in which the children descended upon the weakest among them. They stopped baring their fangs at the adults, turning instead to the black game of killing each other's spirits.

Kodoku suddenly stopped going to school. Tatsu realized that he was pretending to leave and then coming back through the backyard to hide in his room, and went to scold him. Manyo also took the opportunity to reprimand her son. His face drained of color, and he burst into silent tears.

He said nothing to his grandmother or his mother, not confessing what the problem was even when his older brother, Namida, was brought in. When night fell and Kemari came home, covered in blood and swinging a chain, she heard the whole story from her mother. She kicked in the sliding fusuma doors of the room where Kodoku had holed up and went inside. Her younger brother was scared and hid in the closet, but his eyes glittered like a cat's in the darkness as he glared up at his sister.

"Kodoku, kids are picking on you, yeah?" Kemari tossed aside the chain and peeked into the closet.

"Yeah."

"Teacher know?"

"Sh-sh-sh-sh—" Kodoku heaved with sobs. "Sh-she said if you get picked on, it's your fault too," he said finally and wrapped his arms tightly around his large sister, covered in blood and looking down at him. He felt a mysterious sense of security, as if he were hugging a large hairy dog.

Hugging her little brother back, Kemari clenched her teeth tightly. "As if! That's just an excuse the grown-ups make. Any teacher saying stuff like that's human garbage."

"R-r-r-r-really, Kemmy?"

"Really. I wouldn't lie to you. Kodoku, you can't give adults like that the time of day. Pfft! As usual, teachers are stupid old people."

When Kemari told them what was happening, Tatsu and Manyo weren't able to fully grasp the situation at first. Manyo had had some unpleasant experiences being bullied by Midori Kurobishi's subordinates, but through the various twists and turns of life, she was now good friends with that little ringleader. The adults clearly thought the bullying with Kodoku was on this kind of level, and Kemari said hesitantly, in a small voice, "Mom, could you lick a toilet? Could you take your underpants off in the classroom in front of everybody? There's girls there too, you know."

Manyo understood. Tatsu, who adored Kodoku beyond measure, shed tears and began to sob. It was the first time in her life that Manyo had seen this mother-in-law, the nothing-other-than-unflappable woman of the heavens, shedding tears. But the grande dame was indeed getting older, and perhaps she was just more easily moved now. Because the malice that would attack the treasures that were her grandchildren, unlike her children, unlike her daughter-in-law, wounded Tatsu deeply.

At her mother-in-law's tears, Manyo suddenly became stronger. She pulled her hair back in a severe bun and, wearing a red kimono with a black *obi* belt, went to call on the elementary school. Kodoku's teacher was a still-young woman just out of university and oozed with visible fear at the visit from the young madam of the main family, but she still came out with the principal and the year-head teacher to tell her that there was actually no bullying going on, that the children were just having problems getting along, and that their policy was for the teachers not to interfere. Manyo sensed an air of self-protection and gave them a dangerous look, one strongly reminiscent of hardened Kemari.

"Could you lick a toilet? Could you take off your underpants right here? Do you think this is okay because it's a child? You might do well to remember when you were a child. You wouldn't have been fine with any of that, would you?"

After that, the school side apparently put the effort in, but the black wave assaulting the classroom like the heaving sea of the times was beyond adult comprehension.

Kodoku stopped going to school. He locked himself in his room at the mansion, played video games, read manga, and when night fell, sobbed soundlessly. When he was crying, Kemari would come out of nowhere, flop down on the floor, and read manga. Kodoku talked about this later, albeit in very few words. "It was like I had a big dog beside me, like I could relax then. When Kemari was with me."

Around the end of that year, a single boy slipped through the backyard glittering with snow to visit Kodoku. "Heeey," he called quietly, in a voice like an owl hooting. The boy had been Kodoku's classmate until the previous year and also liked video games. They had talked a lot when they were in the same class. And so, one kindred spirit then another began to come together at the mansion.

Kodoku—whose name was written "solitude"—had lost school, but he hadn't lost his friends. When evening came, the boys with shy eyes so much like Kodoku's gathered to play video games together. Kemari stopped popping in then, instead strolling down the hallway sometimes and roughly tossing through the gap in the sliding door paper bags stuffed with candy she had apparently gotten from gambling at pachinko.

"Nygaah!"

"Ow!"

The boys were surprised at first, but they gradually grew used to the assaults and starting saying things like "Still nothing? Where is the scary sister's candy attack?"

A time of solitude and frustration for the broken children. And there was one other person caught up in the black wave of the era: Kemari's best friend, who was quite estranged at that point, Choko Hozumi.

She got the call from Shinobu Tada, the owner of the Red and White Camellia Princess weapons shop, at the end of that winter. Kemari was in grade eleven, famous with an established reputation in the Lady's world. Her long, waist-length ponytail swinging, she raced around the Chugoku region like the wind. Her fans were legion; any number of girls boasted they would gladly die for her.

Kemari was appropriately unnerved at the call from Shinobu after all this time. He had knocked up a girl working in a dumpling store in Yoimachi Alley who had retired from the gang life two years earlier and had taken responsibility like a man, so he had a family at that point. He also helped out with the childrearing, and the long-haired child was in red overalls playing in the weapons shop. Kemari was somehow not very good with the child and tended to stay away from the weapons shop.

Unsettled, she rode her motorcycle down to Yoimachi Alley, where for some reason, in front of the building, the boy she had broken up with, Takeshi Nojima, was skipping rope with a stoic face. He spun the rope with astonishing speed, endlessly jumping. Tense to begin with, she tightened up even further, her beauty taking on a bizarre sculptural element. As she watched dumbfounded, Takeshi lifted his ugly face and noticed her.

"Been a while," he said as he jumped.

"W-what are you doing?"

"Jumping rope," he replied briefly.

Baffled since she had no idea he wanted to be a professional boxer, she nonetheless said, "K-keep at it," and went into the weapons shop.

The instant she stepped into the Camellia Princess with its steel weapons dangling everywhere, Shinobu's child, hair down its back, began to clamber over her. Muttering "Owowow," Kemari looked around for Shinobu.

He was sitting at the register in the back. A little fuller with meat on his bones, he nonetheless had the same fierce eyes as ever, like they could cut right through you if you simply met his gaze. A chill ran up Kemari's spine.

"Heeey," she said, quietly. "Long time no see."

"'Sup. Been a while. Heard about all your heroic deeds."

"No big deal."

The child scrambled around her, drool dribbling from its mouth. She was very close to ripping the child off herself when Shinobu noticed and set the child on his own lap.

"But...something up, brother? You wanting to meet right away, some kind of problem?"

"Mmm...Lots of handy stuff these days, huh, Kemari? Like answering machines."

"Huh? Answering machines?" Kemari asked in response.

Home-use phones had started to move from the black rotary dial telephone to a new push-button style complete with answering machine. The public phone company was privatized in this era, becoming NTT, and service improved in leaps and bounds. Soon, so-called "telephone clubs"—phone sex with strangers that occasionally led to real sex—came into fashion. As did the "message dial" service, which allowed people to communicate with strangers and exchange information by calling a specified number and leaving a message. Message dial evolved into the premium rate telephone number service "dial Q2" and then expanded into services like pagers. Computer communication services were on the verge of beginning. New tools like these were coming into the world to permit anonymous connections between strangers with the same objectives. The first step toward all of it was likely the answering machine, which simply recorded a message.

But Kemari and her ilk were unfamiliar with this new culture. She cocked her head to one side. "Yeah, guess those are handy," she muttered.

Shinobu remained grim. "Kids jump at this kind of thing, you know. But I guess kids using it with other kids, adults with other adults, absolutely no problem with that, right?"

"Uh-huh."

"But lately, there's an idiot around here hooking up kids with adults."

"Uh-huh…"

"You sure are thick, Kemari…I'm talking about prostitution."

The cigarette dropped from her lips, and she looked at him, stunned. He kept staring, grim.

"Huh? Prostitution? No way. This's got nothing to do with the Lady's, right? I'm in charge around here, and we got a ban on hooking and huffing. I run a straightedge team."

"I'm totally aware that your gang's nothing but idiots who race and fight, and maybe shoplift sometimes. Look, Kemari, the world out there, it's slowly changing, you know? And the people you'd least expect are popping up and taking over. It's frustrating. The time when your regular bad guy would do regular bad guy things is pretty much over. Take a look at Takeshi. He's all serious now."

"What are you talking about, Shinobu?"

"The people coming to check out the weapons here. It hasn't been real delinquent kids since last year maybe. I see more and more normal, boring kids. The ones pulling the phone into their rooms and using the answering machine for prostitution aren't the punk girls and their messed-up families." Shinobu twisted a corner of his mouth up.

And then, as if it hurt him to do so, he barked the name of a certain high school. Kemari kept the cry in her throat from leaping out. It was the prefecture's most prestigious high school, the old university prep school her older brother went to.

The memory of the genius girls she had passed on the tree-lined street back when she had just started high school returned to life in the back of her mind. Cherry cheeks and dazzling black hair that had never seen a package of dye. Virginal pink girls, eyes lowered, bleeding contempt and fear at Kemari's appearance.

"No way."

"They use this new tool, the answering machine, for anonymity, right? Then they hook up with old dudes, name a high price, and sell themselves. No mistake. And I know who they are too. People talk to each other in Yoimachi. Lately, we got a lot of girls coming from southeast Asia to make some money, but we only got a fixed number of johns down here, so they have to scramble for them. The adults of this town aren't about to let a bunch of amateur high school girls steal their money."

"But...there has to be some adult making it all happen. Shinobu, those milk-scented, virginal pinks don't have that kind of head on their shoulders. They're just kids. They don't know nothing about anything except studying."

"Kemari."

"Some dirty adult's gotta be in charge and taking a cut," Kemari said, almost spitting, and Shinobu shook his head.

He gave a piece of candy to the child, who was getting restless. "It's not an adult. It's one of those virgin pinks in charge of the whole operation. This is the scary part of all this...Look, I've told you this much, you have to have figured it out. Why I went out of my way to call you. The head of the Iron Angels...she's not your responsibility, but you can't run away from this either!"

Shinobu raised his voice, and Kemari was stunned. Although her instincts in this underworld were generally sharp, she had absolutely no idea what he was talking about.

"The rookie who rode behind you." Shinobu sounded irritated. "The one who was always cracking jokes, laughing too loud. Get it?"

"Chocco?" Kemari's eyes flew open.

He looked at her for just a moment with something like pity before continuing. "First, someone at that school realizes before anyone else that there's a risky way to use the new phone technology. She lures in her classmates, takes them along on a pretty profitable adventure. I asked around, looks like this sort of thing's starting to happen all over the country. And it's a fact that it's spreading from the capital bit by bit out to the rest of us. These virgin pinks, as you call them, they're worn down by the overheated exam wars. Gradually ruining themselves on their own. Their parents don't know. Their friends don't know. But everywhere else, the one in charge of the whole mess is an actual adult. Pretty young princesses taken in by the bad, bad man. And the princesses don't even realize the bad man's skimming from the top, they're just excited about the adventure. This town alone, though, is different. Grade eleven, class E, national cultural studies course genius, Choko Hozumi. Top of her class, also very hot. The entrance curve at that school's seventy-eight, which is about right. So I started to check her out, figuring something was up there. And it turns out, she's managed to slip in with these milk-scented princesses at this famous school, but she was originally a punk, the Iron Angels mascot. And once I heard that, I remembered seeing her, Kemari. She was always on the back of your bike, cute little Chocco. And now she's way past the grown-ups in Yoimachi. She's putting these amateurs, these pretty little bitches into circulation one after another."

He shot a glance at her. "Get it? Look. Yoimachi belongs to the adults in Yoimachi. Tell Chocco. Tell her to get the hell out right now." His expression was scary, like he was a completely different person, and he glared at her.

"Chocco's..." Kemari groaned. "I can't believe it. Chocco's not like that—"

"Don't be soft, Kemari. Face facts!" he shouted, and she swallowed her words. "Back in middle school, she totally took girls down to make her place in this world, didn't she? And the Iron Angels had her back, so she strutted around like she owned the place, did whatever she wanted in the shadows. She's not just cute. She's a sneaky little bitch, a black widow." He practically spat the words and then turned his back to her.

Face drained of all color, Kemari staggered out of the Red and White Camellia Princess.

Takeshi was still skipping rope. Sweat sparkled and scattered and fell, drops of moonlight on the asphalt.

Crescent moon hanging hazily in the night sky, Kemari straddled her bike and rode quietly through Yoimachi. For the first time in her life, she rode silently, not revving the engine, alone, a funeral procession on the national highway.

The children were starting to break. Child ate child, and adult men ate little girls. Kemari had the thought, for the first time, that all the riding, the fighting, it was all meaningless. Tears fell and didn't stop.

Up. Up. Up to the top of the steps. To more happiness for everyone. She ran up the road soundlessly to return to the mansion, where she stood alone, frozen, in the backyard.

A grown woman now, Kemari stood rooted to the spot, oceans of tears pouring from her eyes, and finally shouted up at the night sky.

"This suuuuucks!"

Manyo, who happened to be walking down the hallway, jumped and let out a short shriek.

"Chocco, you stupid idiot!"

Kodoku took refuge in the closet, just in case. Kaban was in the process of running away for the *nth* time, so was not in the mansion that night. Surprised by Kemari's cry, the birds in the garden, which had only just returned from the north, took off all together noisily into the sky. The lingering snow fell with a whump from the pine tree. The moonlight shone dimly on motionless Kemari.

In the Akakuchiba household, a variety of invisible powers were slowly being ceded by the grande dame to the young madam.

Even after her husband, Yasuyuki, fell ill and died, Tatsu had remained hale and hearty, enjoying a long life. Her pale body grew increasingly fat, which seemed like a sort of good omen, to the point where employees at the steelworks cherished the aging Tatsu and felt that even laying eyes on her was a blessing in and of itself. She grew more and more to resemble the god of fortune, Lord Ebisu.

Meanwhile, although the young madam Manyo had a sort of haziness to her ever since she'd given birth to Namida, around this time she began to lose weight as if she were being absorbed into Tatsu and came to look more and more settled than the older woman. Midori Kurobishi—nicknamed the Goldfish, also referred to by Kemari somewhat in fear as the "flamenco granny"—continued to frequently stop by for tea with her old friend. At the request of no one, she would gather Manyo's children before her and dance the flamenco in her black dress, tabi socks sounding against the tatami-matted floor. As a child, Kemari had been deeply afraid of Midori's face painted white with a slash of red, but as she grew up, she began to make fun of her—"Act your age, granny!", "monster flamenco," etc.—and would receive two thumps on the head for her efforts, one from Manyo, one from Midori.

The people of the mansion were afraid of the savage daughter

Kemari, but Midori was indeed the older and the wiser, and she would dole out the thumps on the head unafraid and lecture Kemari like it was an everyday thing.

"You can't keep worrying your mother like this. And quit dressing so weird."

Kemari, naturally, protested at being rebuked for her appearance by a woman in a black flamenco dress and golden high heels. "Who's the weird one here? Pfft!"

As for the Akakuchiba Steelworks, they managed to get through some difficult times through a reduction in scale and a management policy that expanded the areas of operation. They rehired the ancient tatara ironworking craftsmen, anticipating the wave of consumers in that era that burned excessively hot for luxury goods, and began supplying the department stores of the cities with high-end knives under the Akakuchiba Shirushi label. They also branched out into the manufacture of automotive parts and TV cathode-ray tubes, shifting bit by bit to diversified operations. None of the younger employees knew that Yoji, many years before, had been a high-class slacker who lost himself in Western books as he sipped tea in the bukupuku tea shop.

With the changes at the steelworks, the hero of the blast furnace, Toyohisa Hozumi, gradually lost influence. In the increasingly automated plant, the very idea of "worker" was wavering like a fire starting to go out. Even so, Toyohisa went into work every day without fail. He was still single. And ever since that day long ago when he caught Namida after he was hit by a three-wheeler, he had been particularly fond of Manyo's eldest son. At every opportunity, he would tell the old story—"And I caught him like this. Aah, that was such a close one"—and embarrass Namida.

For the people of the main family, Namida was, as always, the brilliant scholar attending the national university in the region, and while they expected great things of him as the heir, he was also a fairly unobtrusive boy who didn't make any great waves. Instead, their attention stayed squarely focused on the child immediately after him, Kemari.

Momoyo started at the commercial high school, where she learned the abacus and bookkeeping, and began to prepare for the working world. Kaban was preppy as always, tossing back permed hair and fooling around with her friends. She was preparing for the entrance exams, eyes on a private high school the preppy aspired to. She was attracted to the idea of being able to attend in street clothing rather than a uniform and the luxury of being stylish.

And the youngest, Kodoku, shut himself up in his room and lived in fear of nuclear weapons.

According to what he later told me, the Cold War between the two military powers of the US and the Soviet Union continued in the shadow of postwar prosperity. The balance of nuclear powers temporarily eased tensions, but with the Soviet invasion of Afghanistan, the Cold War was reignited and accelerated by the possession of nuclear weapons. "All they have to do is press the button and the world ends," it was whispered, very plausibly.

If the east pressed the button, radar would detect it, and the west's nuclear weapons would automatically launch high into the sky. The radar would detect this too, and the east would send even more missiles flying. Lethal radioactive fallout would come raining down, "nuclear winter" would arrive, and the world would be destroyed.

It was truly an absurd situation, but it was also obvious that no one could stop it. The only ones who could change things were the people in authority, but for the children, those people, that change, was something beyond reach; they were far from authority, far from politics.

The world ends.

One morning, suddenly.

With a dazzling light.

No matter how hard you worked, how much you wished for peace, your prayers would go unanswered. You might have had a future, hope, love, and it would all abruptly return to nothing.

When he thought about all this, Kodoku felt that everything was increasingly futile. "It's all stupid, all of it," he muttered and rolled over on his side on the tatami in his room. As he stared up at the ceiling, he became irrationally anxious. Resignation came, too soon for a child, to take root in his heart. And so he continued to live in his room in the depths of the mansion, drifting in a world that might at any moment be abruptly cut short by some power he couldn't see.

And outside the mansion, Kemari, shaking uncharacteristically, was heading out to see her best friend.

The famed high school sat solidly in the middle of the business district, an area of town with a great deal of foot traffic. It had been there since the old days, so the campus was expansive with three separate schoolyards alone; the baseball, soccer, and track and field teams got to practice after school, each team on their own field. Academic, athletic. Study with exercise elevates the soul and makes a virtuous person.

Kemari leaned back against the front gates of this straitlaced high school and waited for her former best friend Choko Hozumi to come out.

The girls walking through the front gates laughing and chatting were surprised by Kemari and her red-ribboned ponytail, which so clearly marked her as a delinquent, and hurried away in a cloud of whispered shrieks. Eventually, illuminated by the red evening sun, a conspicuously black, truly obsidian shadow approached, swaying. The silhouette was deeply uncanny, the physical sensation of black smoke rising, the unpleasant smell of the asphalt. The shadow stopped when Kemari lifted her head.

Tidy loafers with white knee socks neatly folded over three times, down to the ankle. The blazer of her uniform had been very carefully ironed. Kemari knew her before her eyes reached the face. Chocco.

"Hey. Long time."

"Is that . . . you, Kemari?"

Chocco's face was, as always, cutely innocent, the perfect mascot. Her eyes, slightly drooping, were big and beautiful and damp, her cheeks a light pink. And yet her shadow was an ominous jet black. A pillbug moving slowly atop the asphalt stepped into this shadow and instantly rolled up into a ball and stopped moving.

Kemari got annoyed looking at this shadow. "I gotta talk to you." Roughly.

"Okay. I'll listen."

Both were girls of few words. Kemari threw a leg over her bike, and

Chocco jumped on behind her. The students around them stopped and stared, stunned.

"What? Hozumi?"

"That's Hozumi, in the grade above. What is she…?"

Chocco wrapped her arms around Kemari's back and squeezed. When they started out, she heaved a hiccuping sob.

"Don't cry!" Kemari yelled, angrily. "You're getting me wet!"

"It's just, Kemmy," Chocco said, sobbing like rain punctuated by lightning strikes. "We used to have so much fun, huh? You were my glory days."

"They're not over yet. We're only seventeen, aren't we?"

"Already seventeen."

"Christ, this again?"

They went into a hamburger shop that had come from the capital, in front of the station. It smelled like the other side of the ocean, like America. They ordered hamburgers and fries, and while Kemari ate, Chocco left most of hers. "I'll get fat."

"How're things?" Kemari asked, since she didn't actually know what to say. Chocco spat with laughter. "How're things" was what her father, Yoji, always asked Kemari and the other children, scratching his head as if troubled, on those somewhat rare occasions when he ran into them in the mansion.

Still laughing, Chocco raised her face. Her eyes were sober. *Pretty different from the Chocco I know*, Kemari thought. *She's prob'ly been through a ton of shit. Eyes on Todai, gonna be a diplomat, cool grown-up lady who's only bad at night, that's gotta be a tough road.*

"Things? Well, studying's awful. Once you get into grade eleven, the course gets split into arts and science, and then halfway through grade eleven, it splits again into national and private. Your major changes depending on what university you're sitting for, and everyone switches classrooms for every class. In English and math, we're ranked, and the ranks are pretty fluid since we have mock tests each month."

"I have literally no idea what you're talking about."

"You don't need to." Chocco whirled her straw around, stirring up the milkshake that was beginning to melt. "But a girl who's ugly and a genius has, like, zero value. So horrible. So you gotta be cute. Blow out your hair, paint your lips, nails too. Right?"

"Uh-huh…"

"Kemmy, you know that feeling where a girl just wants to ruin herself?"

Kemari leaned forward and stared at her friend, eyes fierce, beast-like. Chocco's were cloudy, her mouth twisting up lazily.

"That's why you came, isn't it?"

"Uh-huh." She nodded briefly, and Chocco grinned broadly.

"Found me out, huh? And here I figured I could keep going for longer, better."

"Chocco, you're not doing anywhere close to good, seriously. They found you out right away, and all the grown-ups in Yoimachi are super mad about this high school kid who's not even trying to hide her little operation. That town's already carved up into territories. You've seen the Asian girls there lately, right? You're messing with their turf."

"What's gonna happen to me?"

"It won't be any big deal. Just pull out now."

Chocco snorted. A vulgar gesture, unbecoming to such a cute girl. "Kemmy, you don't get it. How we feel."

"If you just wanna ruin yourself, you don't need to try so hard. The world's not just about school."

"It's only school. Our obligation," Chocco said and bit her lip hard. Then she hung her head, smiled, and laughed in a curious way. A somehow rough laugh the old Chocco had never had. "The kids at my school, they're good at studying, but they're dense. They're stressed, they're curious, so when you invite them on an adventure, they all just come running. 'Cause they're hungry for a self who's dangerous, who their parents don't know. I made a bundle."

"Chocco..."

"Kemmy, can't you protect me? We can split the cash right down the middle. I'm not scared of the grown-ups of Yoimachi Alley, as long as you got my back."

"There's no way. Me hanging out, just kids marking their turf."

"Come on."

"Anyway, get it together. Girls eating girls, how's that gonna help anything? There's nothing good happening anywhere. And you said you're gonna go to Todai, be a diplomat. So does being a strong woman mean copying all the bad stuff guys do? That's not how it works. Chocco, that's totally not how it works."

Chocco's face grew pale. She got to her feet roughly, and her chair fell to the floor behind her, making a huge noise. She threw her melted shake at Kemari's face and ran out of the hamburger shop.

"Hold up, Chocco!" Face dripping with milkshake, Kemari chased after her. "I don't want it to end like this. Let's keep talking!" Long ponytail and red ribbon fluttering, she gave chase after the surprisingly swift Chocco racing through the business district. She found a peddler woman, borrowed a bitter melon, and threw it like a boomerang, hitting her friend squarely in the head, and the girl went down.

Kemari ran to her side, lifted her into her arms, and gently called to her, "Hey, Chocco."

Chocco was unconscious, but after Kemari shook her roughly, she finally opened her eyes. A trail of tears ran slowly down her cheeks. "We had so much fun back then, Kemmy. I wanted it to go on forever. I really did."

"Nothing's over yet. Some time's passed, but we can get it back, okay? Chocco, open your eyes already."

"I'm done. Until I disappear if I don't do things right."

That day was the last time Kemari looked on the face of her good friend Choko Hozumi.

The summer they were in grade twelve, the front pages of every national newspaper reported that the police had busted a prostitution ring comprised of girls attending a prestigious school in the San'in region. At the start of it all, the adults brushed it off as delinquents and fashion victims who never obeyed school rules anyway, but when they heard that the girls involved were all serious, unassuming, and excellent students, they were dumbstruck. Arrested or taken into custody were a dozen girls, all in grade twelve, between the ages of seventeen and eighteen. The principal offender, Girl A, did not engage directly in prostitution herself, but instead used the phone set up in her bedroom to bring in customers, whom she then introduced to her classmates, taking a broker's fee for her services.

The juvenile division of the Benimidori Police was left cradling their collective heads in their hands, the incident far surpassing their understanding of the division they worked in. The supposedly obedient teacher's pets were starting to break. With the black winds of rumor swirling around, Choko Hozumi's family was no longer able to remain in the provincial town and, forced to escape to the city, they took their belongings and fled to Osaka. Her uncle Toyohisa alone remained and mediated between the family and his niece. Choko was expelled along with the other girls and then sent to reform school.

None of her family and friends tried to see her. For the brilliant, adorable, and dutiful "Girl A," this was an unfamiliar place. The majority of her old friends turned their backs on her, but the evening she was sent to the reform school, quiet Lady's arrived on their motorcycles and completely surrounded the car she was in, like a funeral procession. The reform school was on the other side of the Chugoku Mountains in the depths of Hiroshima. The gang girls did not race their engines or turn on their lights or even speak, but simply crossed the prefectural border to see Girl A off to Hiroshima. At the sight of them, this silent cavalry, the adults trembled, not understanding the meaning of it.

When the car slipped through the gates of the Hiroshima reform school and grew distant, all at once, the Lady's flashed their lights, raced their engines, trumpeted their modded air horns, and generally made a fuss. "Goodbye!" "Goodbye!" "Goodbye!" You could hear their cute voices calling out. "Chocco!" "Chocco!" "Chocco-bear!"

And then Choko Hozumi disappeared from Tottori.

The year Chocco disappeared, Momoyo was in exceedingly high spirits, Kaban told me later.

"She'd roam about the mansion, humming little songs. She was normally such a gloomy person, so it was actually fairly unsettling. Maybe she was a bit happy that Kemari's friend was gone. I don't know."

As always, Momoyo continued to stare passionately at Kemari from the shadows of pillars, from the tops of joists, from the undersides of desks.

"You'd think she would've gotten sick of it in good time, but she never did. So strange. I even suspected that she cursed Chocco so she couldn't be with Kemari anymore. But I suppose that's not too likely."

As always, Kemari led her Iron Angels and ran wild. But her heart was heavy now, quite the opposite of Momoyo's good humor, and she sighed and lay around on the veranda. From time to time, Toyohisa approach her there. His precious niece was in serious trouble, and he had aged remarkably, but when he talked with Kemari about the girl, his heart got a little lighter.

It was right around this time Kemari met a mysterious Filipina.

Fall came, heavy clouds collected over the San'in region, and they were subjected to a long spell of rain. As she flew through Yoimachi Alley on her bike, her tire slipped in a puddle and she fell hard, for the first time in her life. The ground rose up to meet her, and the bike flew off, wheels spinning. She saw herself reflected in the clear puddle, but although Kemari herself was silent, the Kemari in the puddle opened her mouth.

"You okay? You dead? Hey?" The girl spoke with a curious intonation.

As Kemari lifted her eyes from the puddle, she saw a young Filipina wearing her face standing there without an umbrella. The Filipina stared at Kemari, also surprised.

More and more women were coming to Yoimachi Alley from Southeast Asia to earn money, women who were later called "japayuki." You often saw them when night fell, walking briskly, skin the same color, eyes dark. This Filipina, who seemed about Kemari's age, had features very like Kemari's. She was tall and solidly built, her skin was dark, and she had a deeply chiseled face set with black eyes. Only her hair was different, frizzy with curls, hanging down to her waist.

Kemari herself looked like her mother, Manyo. Her distinct face should have been that of those mountain people who had crossed the oceans to come to Japan in distant ancient times and now lived in hiding in the depths of the Chugoku Mountains, a face that spoke of a bloodline in southeast Asia.

Perhaps getting the scent of the same land from each other, separated by an eternity and the vast expanse of the ocean, the two put their faces together and stared at each other for a long time. It was like looking into a mirror. Finally, Kemari stood and went to pick up her fallen bike. The Filipina helped her. Both were quite strong, and they easily got the bike up again. The rain had grown heavier, so Kemari handed her own folding umbrella to the Filipina. She slowly revved the engine and looked back over her shoulder as she pulled away from the woman from another country with her own features. The Filipina also had a strange look in her eyes, almost a regret at parting, and stayed to watch as Kemari's bike grew distant.

This woman's name was Aira. And not too much time would pass before the mirror-image Filipina and the heartbroken Kemari met again.

During the few months left before graduation, Kemari was very quiet. Her older brother, who normally didn't pay much attention to the family, was worried about her; he was even seen walking around the mansion, calling to her. "Kemari? You here? You good?" In other words, she was so depressed even her family could tell. Whenever Namida went hiking on a day off school, he brought rocks from the dry river beds or wildflowers home with him and handed them to her with a "Here, you can have these." He was a handsome boy who got good grades and had a gentle nature, but as Kemari would secretly whisper to Kaban, "The thing is, he doesn't get girls at all." However, for all that, she would decorate her room with the rocks and bunches of plain flowers she received from him, seemingly genuinely pleased by them.

In this final year of high school, Kemari ruled over her Iron Angels, going beyond prefectural boundaries to cut through Shimane already under her control and attack the formidable enemy of Yamaguchi Prefecture. When she destroyed the Lady's of Yamaguchi through three hungry days of battle, they zigzagged their motorcycles along the national highway, singing the trilling song of their horns, to return home.

It was just getting to be time for the snow to fall. Snow in the San'in region is very wet and heavy, and locked in by this dense blanket, Kemari and the delinquent girls grew quiet. Instead, it was Kaban kicking up a fuss in the mansion. She was advancing, for the first time, to the San'in region audition round of an idol contest. She was already in grade nine and had saved up a fair bit of her allowance. She argued and fought with Manyo, but her mother did not budge an inch until Namida stepped in on Kaban's side. "I'll take her." He had a soft spot somehow for his little sisters.

So during winter break, Kaban, with her brother, crossed the Chugoku Mountains and made the trip to Hiroshima. Onstage, she sang and danced and bowed her head with a polite "Thank you very much," but in the end, she lost by a very narrow margin. She hung her head in disappointment. On the way back to Tottori in the car driven by Namida, they passed a group of motorcycles, quiet for some reason, with the flag of the Iron Angels flapping. Kaban had been crying in the passenger seat the whole time at the pain of losing the contest, but noticing the strange air of the group they passed, she clung to the window and stared out at them.

"Is that Kemari...?"

At the head of the group sliding down from up in the mountains, lights off in the thickening darkness, was her older sister. Kaban shuddered at the look on her face, illuminated for an instant by the headlights of Namida's car. Her face was expressionless, skin pale like a corpse, ponytail and red ribbon fluttering.

"I mean, that ribbon looked like blood. Just remembering it now gives me chills," Kaban later related.

Behind Kemari, groups of delinquent girls stretched out in columns, dressed in tracksuits and padded kimonos, girls who in other words looked as though they had flown from their houses without bothering to change their clothes. All their faces were white like phantoms. In the darkness of the night, large, heavy snowflakes dancing here and there, the girls glided by them toward Hiroshima, a ghostly cavalry. No engines revving, headlamps off, no belligerent war cries. Shuddering, Kaban turned her head back and back to watch them as long as possible as she returned to Tottori in Namida's car.

It was late by the time they arrived at the Akakuchiba mansion, and Manyo sat heavily in the entryway, waiting. "I didn't make it!" Kaban reported, and her eyes blurred again with regretful tears.

"You didn't?"

"Why didn't you make me more beautiful, Mom?"

"What are you talking about? You got plenty. A woman should live based on what she's got." Manyo brushed aside Kaban's complaints and made no move to get up from the entryway step.

Unshouldering her bag, Kaban realized her mother wasn't just waiting for her, but also Kemari, who had gone out somewhere. "What's going on with Kemari? We passed her earlier in the car."

"In the car? Whereabouts?"

"When we were still in Hiroshima."

"That so? I s'pose that means she's off to Hiroshima then," Manyo murmured quietly. "Have to ask Toyo in the morning."

Kaban was about to ask what she meant when she heard the sound of a car coming in through the gate, which was followed by her father,

Yoji, stepping into the entryway. He saw his wife and daughter sitting there and was surprised. "What are you doing?"

"Oh, well…"

"Welcome home, Dad."

Yoji looked tired as he nodded. "Don't sit around here, it's cold. Go on inside. You'll catch cold," he told Kaban, and she nodded and stood up.

When Kaban popped her head into the kitchen just past noon the next day, she found Kemari sitting vacantly on a chair, having apparently come home without Kaban noticing. Kaban started to say something to her but then swallowed her voice. As it had been the previous evening when they passed her on the national highway in Hiroshima, and her sister's face was so pale, she could almost believe it wasn't her sister sitting there. She had a dangerous look to her, as if she had accidentally been possessed by the dead.

"Kemari?"

"Ah, Kaban."

Even her voice, so throaty and powerful until the previous day, was different. A crease sprang up between Kaban's eyebrows, and she peered at her sister. "What's wrong?"

"Y'know, Kaban, I know when youth ends."

"When?"

"When you say a goodbye that can never be undone," Kemari said simply and then twisted her head to the side. Lighting a cigarette, she stared up at the ceiling with eyes that seemed to have seen the land of the dead.

Kemari Akakuchiba was a spitfire and a woman of steel, but every so often in her life, in a curious twist, she would have her feet knocked out from under her by some dead person. And this was the case here, as well. The dead person in question was Choko Hozumi. The previous morning, Chocco had died in the Hiroshima reform school. They said she passed on because of a cold that took a sharp turn for the worse in her frigid room. They also said she hung herself with her stockings; the cause of death wasn't clear. But the fact that she had abruptly left this world was.

When they learned of Chocco's death, the girls of the Iron Angels crossed the Chugoku Mountains, surrounded the Hiroshima reform school, revved their engines, turned on their headlights, cried out in voices that were not quite voices, and sent off Chocco's spirit, perhaps leaving with the dawn.

Together with the morning light, the Iron Angels once again ran down the national highway, horns blaring, and passed back over the mountains to return to Tottori, a young funeral procession. The dazzling light shone mercilessly on their pale faces, all without expression, as if possessed by the dead.

After that night, Kemari seemed resigned, no longer filled with the fire that had burned so brightly for fighting and riding. But she still had responsibilities as the head of the Lady's gang Iron Angels, which she had built to an enormous size with her own hands and was positioned to take over as the ruler of the entire Chugoku region at long last. And Kemari took her responsibilities very seriously.

In the winter of grade twelve, she continued to fight, face still pale, still haunted by her dead. Before she graduated, she needed to gain total domination of the region. The final, decisive battle took place in a parking garage in a corner of the abandoned shopping street. Remnants of enemy factions lingered in her own Tottori Prefecture, but Kemari brandished her steel weapons from the Akakuchiba Steelworks and took them down one after another, these tough girls also born in the year of the Fire Horse. Each time her steel chain whistled through the air, three girls fell, and two dropped unconscious to the ground when she threw an iron pipe. Kemari also took her fair share of blows and was soon covered in blood, but she didn't feel any pain or suffering. It was as if all sensations in her had gone somewhere far away. The dead person inside her no doubt carried them off.

Fighting like wild beasts, the girls eventually all fell, and that night, Kemari cemented her position on the throne of Chugoku's Iron Angels. She turned toward her ecstatic companions, announced her resignation, and ceded leadership to a senior member. The girls of the gang were thrown into a panic, but Kemari had made her decision.

"It's the right time."

"Kemari…"

"I'm not on fire anymore. Tonight's my final flash."

The senior girls saw the exhaustion and sadness in Kemari's eyes, a look they had never seen before, and reluctantly accepted her resignation.

The retirement ceremony for Kemari the following month was showy. A photographer from the motorcycle magazine had come running from the capital and captured the perfect shot of Lady's riding along the national highway. News of Kemari's retirement spread through the delinquents' nationwide word-of-mouth network, and from Monbetsu in the north to Hikojima in the south, they cheered the legendary delinquent as she bowed out. Kemari stepped back from the front lines, still a hero. She relinquished her treasured bike to the girl who had become the second leader of the gang and walked home alone on the highway.

Climbing the hill street of the steps, she saw Shinobu Tada in the motorcycle parking of the apartment building. He stood up slowly and bowed respectfully and wordlessly. She smiled faintly and kept walking up the hill.

For a while, her family didn't notice that she had finally retired from the motorcycle gang life. They finally found out when Kaban came across a magazine article and brought it home; then the entire family heaved a sigh of relief.

"I won't have to do the little shrine pilgrimage anymore to pray she doesn't hurt herself," Manyo let slip at the breakfast table.

Only Tatsu nodded with a "True, true." No one else in the family had known that Manyo was doing any kind of prayer pilgrimage, and so they stared dumbfounded. And then on behalf of the entire family, Namida nudged Kemari's head with his elbow.

"Ow ow!" Kemari looked down, embarrassed, and then shut up and let him nudge her. Getting caught up in the moment, Kaban took a jab at Kemari and got a real punch back.

For about a year after that, Kemari didn't really go out.

Perhaps spent after her retirement, she didn't appear to be attending school in any real way either, despite the fact that she was so close to graduating. She undid the red ribbon which had long been her trade-mark and stopped wearing her hair up in a ponytail. She grew out the fringe, that former bamboo shade over her forehead, and switched to a straight, one-length hairstyle.

She gave up all of her delinquent street clothes—embroidered satin jackets, long, tight skirts, glittering sandals—and started wearing adult fashions, jackets with shoulder pads over tight miniskirts paired with high heels. She drew on her eyebrows, painted her lips bright red, and carefully did her eye shadow. Kemari became a surprisingly beautiful adult woman.

"It was like she turned into this fashion plate. I thought it kind of sucked." This from Kaban who had been so staunchly and vocally in the fashion victim camp at that time.

Kemari occasionally poked her head in at the disco Miss Chicago, but she really only ate some yakisoba in fond memory of days past; she never stayed and danced until dawn. Seeing her, the delinquent high school girls would get flustered and come to pay their respects to Akakuchiba, their legendary Lady's older sister. Kemari would laugh coolly and say something along the lines of "I'm retired now. Just relax, all of you."

Her lover, Demon Yamanaka, was already a rookie yakuza member in Yoimachi Alley at the time, but he and Kemari appeared to have broken things off long ago. Which meant that the man-stealing Momoyo was for a while left with nothing to do.

During this period, when Kemari seemed to have lost her nerve, the only one who knew what she was doing in secret was her little brother

Kodoku. Once again occupying his room without permission, Kemari reached for the shojo manga she read sometimes, whatever she could lay her hands on as always. "Huh, so they got a submission corner," Kaban heard her murmuring as she passed by in the hallway, but she apparently didn't think too much of it. Kemari got her driver's license, went to one of the big stores for the car class out in the suburbs—driving safely the whole way—and bought a mountain of art supplies. She then spread these out in Kodoku's room and started doing some kind of something.

It was a year later, in 1985, that the nerveless Kemari was reborn like a phoenix, and in the showy style of a bird of paradise to boot. I'm her daughter and even I don't know what she was thinking, but a year later, Kemari found an unexpected occupation.

Japan was also experiencing the beginning of a bubble economy. Although Kemari and the other delinquent boys and girls ran wild and brilliant through their teens, once they graduated from those ranks, they quickly became adults as if some evil spirit had been exorcised from them. The boys found work in the region, one becoming a mechanic, another a contractor, and still another studying and going on to become an ambulance attendant. The girls got pregnant one after another, married their boyfriends, and became stay-at-home moms. The approaching bubble was wholly unconnected with these once-delinquent girls and boys. The ones made to dance were the diligent eager beavers in the delinquents' shadow, pushed into delinquent culture themselves.

Now in university, they bought cars, dressed in style, and reeked of the capital. The disco stopped being a place to lazily eat yakisoba where middle schoolers showed off their moves on the floor, giggling and screeching, and became somewhere adults hung out, a stage where the spotlight shone on the female university students and office workers. The late-blooming eager beaver Fire Horse girls ruled over the disco nights of the capital in their tight dresses.

Companies pushed outside of their main fields of business, going into debt to do so. Land prices went up, and land sharks started maneuvering behind the scenes. The general population also bought condos on loan and wore expensive designer clothing. University graduates were in great demand in industry, but that was in the capital. The people in the San'in region simply watched all this through that convenience of civilization, the television. The village of Benimidori did not change in any noticeable way.

Kemari didn't pop her head up to so much as glance at the late-blooming, university-debuting Fire Horses. Once in a while, she would go hang out in Yoimachi Alley. She seemed to have started dating an exceedingly ugly university boy she met there, but everything besides that was shrouded in mystery. The boy had come from another prefecture to go to university and knew nothing of Kemari's terrible legend. He apparently thought she was nothing more than a kind of pretty girl with long hair and red lips, and he dated her without giving the matter too much thought.

Other than the very occasional outings with this boy, Kemari was locked up in her room day and night, drawing something. "Roses are so hard to draw," Kaban happened to overhear her muttering, but she had no idea what that meant. Then, on the order of about once a month, Kemari would walk down the hill road of the steps to the post office and post a large, square envelope. Other than that, she only went out to wander the town or stayed home and read manga on the floor, which eventually, naturally, led to her family wondering.

"Too much energy's a problem, but too quiet's pretty scary," Manyo grumbled. And just as she was hesitantly starting to discuss with her mother-in-law, Tatsu, about maybe going and saying all those prayers again, a single change came upon them.

A strange man came from Tokyo to visit Kemari.

Mid-twenties. Italian suit, gold watch. He had long, lean legs, and with every step he took, his gleaming leather shoes made a stylish sound on the asphalt. His shoulder-length hair was dyed brown, and he had the neatly attractive face of someone accustomed to the softer things in life. In other words, shrouded in the air of a disco night in the capital, he was not the type of man ever seen in this country town.

From the instant he alighted on the Daibenimidori Station plat-form, the man drew attention. Walking down the large street in front of the station, the young men and women coming out of the shops stared at his back. As did the older men and older women. And children and adults. The man, heedless of the countless eyes glued to his back, con-tinued to walk, map in one hand. He looked up at the hill road of the steps and frowned slightly, but slowly began to climb it.

Residents poked their heads out of the apartment buildings of the steps. "Who *is* that man?" they whispered to each other excitedly.

"How far's he gonna go up?"

"Climbing like that, he'll hit the Akakuchiba mansion."

Unusual for fall, the yamaoroshi wind swept violently downward, mixed with fallen red leaves, and pushed up against the man. For an instant, the feet in the gleaming leather shoes threatened to lift up and fly off, but the man dropped his hips to glue himself to the earth. Perhaps he had unexpected backbone. The yamaoroshi gusted against him again and again, but the man braced himself and kept climbing.

In front of the Akakuchiba mansion, the man stopped.

A girl with long, disheveled hair stood in front of the gates. She wore a red kimono, and her narrow eyes focused intently to stare at the man.

"Oh! Are you Kemari Akakuchiba?" he asked, thinking this the tiniest bit creepy.

The girl hesitated for just a moment and then nodded silently. The man whipped his business card out and bowed his head. "It's a pleasure to meet you."

The card was sharp, like it could cut through skin, embossed with the name of a publisher. The man's name was Tamotsu Soho. He was an editor with a shojo manga magazine.

"Kemari, the manga you submitted to us made it to the final round, but unfortunately didn't make the cut in the end. The artist judge didn't like it. But I felt it was interesting. A bit weird for a romance manga, but still. Which is why I thought I'd come and meet with you."

Soho spoke fairly quickly, and the girl opened her eyes wide in surprise. *Creepy face*, he thought as he began walking alongside her.

"Naturally, I've spoken with the editor-in-chief as well. So let's talk. This is also my first time nurturing new talent, but I really think you can do it."

He stepped into the entryway with her. A surprisingly impressive mansion. *I get it, she comes from a rich family,* he thought as he took off his shoes, and the girl abruptly squeezed his hand tightly. Dragged along, he walked down the polished hallway and entered the parlor. The girl played with the globe and stared at Soho.

He started to feel uncomfortable. "Would you be interested in drawing something else, not the work you submitted? You don't have to do romance stories just because it's shojo manga. And I feel like your views on love won't really go over well. So, what kind of…" As he went on, he felt a sense of pressure like an invisible hand pushing on his eyeballs, and Soho closed his eyes. And once he closed them, he didn't open them again. "So how…about we make…a good manga…together…" Soho fainted.

How much time passed then?

Someone was shaking him roughly, and he slowly returned to consciousness. There was an unpleasant weight on his shoulders as if he had gone and taken a swim in the Sai no Kawara river, where the souls of dead children go. When he opened his eyes, he realized it was already pitch black outside, despite the fact it had been morning when he arrived. There was a girl's face in front of him.

A girl who didn't resemble the earlier girl in the slightest, all sharp features and dark skin. Her long hair was in the fashionable one-length style, hanging down to her waist, and her lipstick was bright red. She was wearing a body-hugging dress with a chain belt, and large hoops dangled from her ears. She was gorgeous, the kind of woman you don't even see in the capital very much. She had lowered the thickly drawn ends of her eyebrows and was shaking Soho.

"Who are you? And why are you sleeping here? You Kaban's boy-friend or something?"

"Kaban…?" *Kaban* meant "bag," and Soho's head started to hurt again at the bizarreness of the words "bag's boyfriend" alone. He closed his eyes. This time, he was able to open them up again right away.

"What are you doing?" The girl poked him roughly. "Still, you got style. And you're way older than Kaban."

"Older than bag…?" Soho managed to get up somehow and spoke to the strange girl. "My name is Tamotsu Soho, and I came to see little Kemari Akakuchiba."

"If you're looking for little Kemari, I'm her."

"What?" Soho asked in response, quickly followed by "That girl before?" He explained that she had long hair, wore a red kimono, and was in her late teens or so, but the real Kemari Akakuchiba simply cocked her head to one side.

"There's no girl like that in this house. The housekeepers are older, and I only have one little sister, but she looks like me."

"But I know she brought me here. Holding tight with her cold hands."

"Cold hands…? Oh hey, maybe it was Masago."

"Who's that?"

"A housekeeper we used to have, my dad's lover. But she died ages ago. She was pretty famous for her naked dancing. Weird lady. Look at you, Soho! No one around here's seen Masago's ghost and you're hold-ing her hand!"

He started to lose consciousness again.

Frighteningly enough for Soho, every time he came to the house after that, "Masago's ghost," as Kemari would have it, was standing at the gates of the mansion where she would take Soho's hand and stare at him with dark eyes. Sometimes the girl was in a kimono; other times, she was dressed in the utterly normal navy blazer, plaid skirt, and sneakers that were the favorites of the modern high school girl; occasionally she was even in a high school uniform. However, whenever Soho would oh-so-timidly inquire about her, Kemari would, without fail, wonder curiously, "There's no one like that in this house. So weird. You know my sister Kaban, right? And then there's my mom and my grandma. And there's five housekeepers, but they're older. So bizarre."

At any rate, on this day, Soho repeated anew his editor spiel to the real Kemari Akakuchiba. The piece she had submitted to the shojo manga magazine was a love story depicting two girls vying for the love of one boy. It had ultimately been rejected, but the young editor/serious manga reader sensed some new potential in the crude, funky work. His editor-in-chief had twisted his head around with a "You do? In this?" but thought it about time for Soho to try his hand at cultivating a new talent rather than just handling the manga artists passed down to him by veteran editors. Which was why Soho had come all the way from distant Tokyo to what seemed like the end of the world, the western part of Tottori Prefecture.

"Seriously? I can't make my debut with that story?" Kemari said, displeased.

Face to face with the cheeky youth, Soho sensed something promising in her unworldly, overly self-confident attitude. "There's no way. It's a weird story."

"Weird."

"So here's the thing. Isn't there anything else you want to draw? Something other than a love story."

"Something I wanna draw, huh?" Kemari brushed back her long hair and started to think, with a bit of a yawn.

Soho was gradually overwhelmed by Kemari's very non-newbie attitude and her seemingly farsighted dark eyes. She did not seem like a girl of nineteen in any way, no doubt because of the spirit of resignation in her brought about too soon by her long years of fighting and the end of those years. But the man who had come from the capital on the eve of the bubble knew none of this.

"The thing is, Soho, I don't read, and I have, like, no education. And I mean, my friends, they're all from the *zoku.*"

"Zoku?"

"Ha ha! Bosozoku gangs. Until last year, I was one of them, riding around on my motorcycle, just racing and racing. Made my family worry loads. My mom even went and prayed all over the place every morning without telling any of us. But that's all over now. Last year, a really good friend of mine died far away, right?"

"Was it an accident?"

"Nah … They nabbed her and she died in the can. Such an idiot. I just wanna forget all about her already. Seriously." Kemari slowly brought a menthol cigarette to her lips and reached for a lighter. Without a moment's delay, Soho had his own out and was lighting her cigarette. "Thanks," she said in a low voice, nodding at him.

"Was it hard for you?"

"Yeah, I guess it was. But it's not something you can forget just like that or anything. All that time with her, that was my youth. But that's over now."

Her premature resignation, out of place in a girl so young, wafted up to the ceiling with the smoke from her cigarette. Soho's eyes glittered as he took Kemari's hand.

"The hell. All of a sudden," Kemari said, annoyed.

"Kemari, you, that's it. You should draw that."

"Huh?"

"Manga's drawn for young readers, after all. So a manga artist should draw their own youth. That time, it's yours alone. What do you think about drawing it?"

"But the stuff I did's totally not typical shojo manga. It's pretty messed up."

"Turning it into shojo manga is my job. Leave it to me. I'll shape the stories that come out of you into the perfect shojo."

"You sure are weird, Soho," the amateur Kemari sneered.

Soho had a premonition then. This collaboration would be a huge gamble, but he had ambition. He dreamed of creating a hit comic with his own hands and leaping to the top of the industry, he told her passionately.

"Oh, that so," Kemari replied. And then she began to scribble out a storyboard in her notebook. As she drew in pencil a picture with a ponytail swinging swordlike up against the background of a blue sky, an elementary school kid, roundly fat like the god of fortune Ebisu, came walking down the hallway.

"What're you doing, sis?"

"Drawing manga."

"Again? You never go out, you just lock yourself up in the house. But you still do your makeup. You're really weird lately."

"Kodoku, hun, truth is, I'm a manga artist now. So y'know, buy my books."

"Really? Wow! That's so cool!"

Kemari glanced back at Soho and gave him something approaching a smile for the first time since they met, having kept a sober look on her face until that point. When she smiled, she looked disarmingly young and helpless.

"You saying that, Kodoku, that means a whole lot. I'm gonna give it my best."

"Yeah...But, look, from now on, draw in your own room."

"Ha ha! Got it."

The round kid disappeared down the hall. Smiling, Kemari ran her pen over the page.

The storyboard she drew and showed him then was fairly rough, filled with intensity and violence, blood and impulse, and a too-peculiar worldview that would not fit in the framework of shojo manga. Reading it, Soho patiently guided her through each and every page.

"You drew too much in this scene. If you hold back a little, your idea's going to be better communicated to the girls."

"Here should be longer—do this scene with a two-page spread."

"The setting should be more specialized. Be more daring, draw what you want. But make the heroine an average girl. Otherwise, female readers won't follow you. She needs to be much more average."

Processed through Soho's careful sense of balance, Kemari's work—rough, violent, and somehow angular—became surprisingly refined and turned into a manga appropriate for junior and senior high school girls to read, while still being compelling in a way that hadn't been seen before. Soho left the other manga artists he was responsible for to fend for themselves and stayed at the Akakuchiba house for five days completing the storyboard in a near trance. Then, pushed along by the yamaoroshi, he ran down the hill road of the steps, nearly flying.

"My goodness, what a handsome man," the wife half of the Tada couple, the people who had raised Manyo, murmured excitedly when she happened to pass him. Soho called out in a friendly voice to this graceful older woman and got directions to a place with a copier.

In a corner of the supermarket, he made a copy of the manuscript at ten yen per page, hunted down a post office, and sent the copy to the publisher in Tokyo. He ran back to the mansion and roused Kemari, collapsed on the sofa, asleep with her mouth open, and began to go over the details of the story.

His editor-in-chief called, and they decided to publish it as a one-shot story. He said they could serialize the work if the reader survey results were good, and Soho kicked awake Kemari, who had again collapsed into sleep on the floor, and had her ink the one-shot piece. When she was finished, they started to discuss the serialization.

"Um, who is that man who's been here the last while?" Manyo peeked into the parlor somewhat concerned. Namida suggested that it might be Kemari's boyfriend, and Manyo lifted a stunned face to her son. "It can't be," she said, shaking her head back and forth. "Kemari falling for such a good-looking man as that."

And so, Kemari Akakuchiba's debut work, *Iron Angels!*, depicting love and friendship and fighting amongst the "Lady's" bosozoku gangs, was published in the manga magazine, which was when her family learned that she had somehow become a shojo manga artist. Before they even had the time to be surprised by this, word came from Tokyo that her first outing had been number one in the reader survey. Kemari and Soho hugged each other and shook hands heartily with both hands.

Immediately after this, the magazine decided to begin serialization of the epic Lady's manga *The Scroll of the Benimidori Lady's Battle: Iron Angels!*, a work that shone brilliantly in the world of shojo manga from the mid 1980s to the end of the 1990s. It was the start of a long-term serialization that would continue for over twelve years and become Kemari's personal battlefield.

Soho holed up in the parlor and talked with her day and night. A total beginner who didn't know left from right, Kemari often got confused, lost confidence, and occasionally proffered frustrated tears. Soho chastised her and gave unerring advice. In the incredibly vast ocean of the manga industry, Kemari and her partner jumped aboard the tiny boat *Iron Angels!* and set sail somehow.

Around this time, Kemari and Soho moved into a stereotypical honeymoon period, a sweet season of harmony between a young manga artist and an editor at the top of his game. Energies perfectly matched, they alone made all the decisions. Negotiations for secondary use, merchandise, and the like were all left to Soho, and Soho's authority within the publishing company grew rapidly. Kemari had the deference and thirst one would expect from someone new to the industry, and she absorbed everything with surprising docility and flexibility.

Finally, after six months or so, Kemari got the hang of it. She started anticipating the feedback Soho would likely give her. Weekly serialization is brutal, and she was always chased by deadlines, so much so that she was soon reluctant to spare even the time to talk with Soho; instead she would often simply decide on her own and keep moving ahead with the drawing.

In the beginning especially, Soho was constantly shuttling between Tokyo and Tottori, but when *Iron Angels!* became a smash hit, he stepped down from working with other manga artists to become the dedicated editor for Kemari Akakuchiba. As the need for him to advise her grew less, their relationship changed subtly. Before she made her debut, Soho was the boss, and their relationship was like superior and subordinate, big brother and little sister.

However, the two became equals soon enough, and then as if the ground were shifting, author Kemari ended up on the boss side of the equation, with Soho managing the whole thing. His job became waiting around for her to finish the manuscripts and taking them from her. The seed of the tale Soho had found grew inside Kemari and began to pour out like a muddy stream. At the same time, the inevitable D-Day approached when the royalties of Kemari, a new manga artist, would surpass the salary of Soho, an employee of a major publisher.

They both had modestly fumbled their way along with this manga, only to have it surpass every hope they held for it in their hearts to become a smash hit. The magazine's sell-through immediately jumped to over eighty percent. At this time, the weekly shojo manga magazine itself was in an era of decline—the idea of switching to a biweekly format had even gained traction at a meeting—but the tide turned thanks to the appearance of Kemari. Weekly sales of just under two hundred thousand copies soared to seven hundred thousand. This popularity was a phenomenon in and of itself, a tsunami that Kemari wasn't able to fully handle.

For some strange reason, serious girls with glasses and black hair and absolutely nothing in common with delinquent culture were reading *Iron Angels!* in their rooms, talking about it in class, and Kemari was immediately hoisted up as the darling of their generation. Reporters from the capital descended on Tottori to talk to the young star. In Kemari's twentieth year, the year after serialization began, the first book collecting the chapters serialized in the magazine was published and reprinted in huge numbers.

When she was paraded around the country on a signing tour, the real ladies of the Iron Angels appeared from out of the blue and surrounded the van Kemari was traveling in, banners flying, rolling on bright red motorcycles, leaning out of car windows, damaged brown hair fluttering in the summer wind. How much of it was manga? How much of it was real? The lines were blurred with this Lady's escort, punks straight out of the manga, and the next generation of bespectacled girls who were Kemari's readers squealed with delight. Each signing venue was circled by endlessly moving Lady's. Based in the village of Benimidori, with a general membership of more than a thousand girls, the Iron Angels never once spoke to the now respectably employed Kemari, but simply silently escorted her from Hokkaido in the north to Kyushu in the south. The country at this time had entered the era of the ostentatious bubble economy, and delinquent culture was already quickly becoming a thing of the past, with fewer and fewer people around to carry on the traditions. The currently serving female delinquents gathered around Kemari as if it were their last hurrah.

Time passed. Kemari cemented her reputation as a best-selling manga artist. Every time she toured the country, there were fewer Lady's in her escort. Their ranks became full of gaps, missing teeth from a comb, as one after another, the girls became adults and transformed into the good wives and mothers of the towns. They left the escort group and gradually joined the lines of bespectacled girls at the signings. They held children with hair growing long down their backs, got Kemari's signature, shook her hand, and went home. The memory that they had once been soldiers smoldered deep in the depths of their hearts alone. Like the burning of phantom tatara flames.

Kemari did the signing tours with a smile on her face, and the handsome man Soho was right there with her. The girls shrieked at the beautiful manga artist and the gorgeous editor standing by her side and took pictures of the pair with disposable cameras. For their part, Soho and Kemari both turned unclouded smiles toward the cameras. But the honeymoon between the manga artist and the editor was already approaching its end.

D-Day had long since come, and they gradually had less and less to say to each other when no one else was around. Soho's standing in the editorial division had shot up dramatically, but no matter how many hit works he might produce, he was still an employee of the company, and his salary didn't change much. The gold from the mine went first to the publisher, and then to Kemari Akakuchiba.

Iron Angels! was published under the name of the manga artist Kemari, but in truth, it was the work of Kemari and Soho. There was a trust between manga artist and editor, a friendship between man and woman, and a bond like monkey and trainer. But they both lost sight of each other's heart, and once they had lost that, there was no going back.

Kemari was buried in work. The power structure had flipped, and now that Soho was left simply standing around waiting for the manuscript, constantly being by the side of the manga artist he had nurtured and set free into the world—the manga artist who had at some point become this enormous something—was a man's prison. But this was business for Soho, and he had a responsibility to Kemari to see through what he had started. *If only Kemari Akakuchiba were a man*, he caught himself thinking. Back in the office, he was the editor in charge of *Iron Angels!*, powerful enough to make grown men weep, but before the manga artist, he felt like he was nobody at all. Kemari, supported by the manga, soldiered on without breaking. Soho, pushed to the edge by the manga, broke.

One day, when he was descending the hill road of the steps, heading to the post office, the manuscript Kemari had drawn in hand, the yamaoroshi blew down over him and the pages danced up into the sky. Looking up at them, Soho's mind went blank. If he ran to gather them up, he could get them all. But Soho did not run. He did not gather them up. In the end, he just stood there and looked up at the gray Tottori sky, as if he had no energy left. The muddy stream had changed Soho and it had changed Kemari. Utterly exhausted, he couldn't even produce tears.

"I lost the manuscript," he told her when he returned to the mansion, and Kemari went insane with rage. The two looked hard at each other for the first time in a long time.

The eyes of the editor who had nurtured her were dull. Kemari could see that they no longer held love, expectation, or even the will to try and fight her. In Soho's eyes, there was, for some reason, scorn. In Kemari, Soho simply saw money, power. Kemari bit her lip. Not heeding her assistants crying for her to stop, she slapped Soho's cheek hard. Still, Soho said nothing.

"Apologize. Get down on your knees and apologize to me."

Without a word, Soho got down on his knees and pressed his forehead to the tatami-matted floor. The nurturer and the nurtured.

"That's enough," Kemari muttered and went back to her studio. "We'll redo it." Together with her assistants and without sleep for a full three days, she finished the pages and silently handed them to Soho. From that point on, they stopped speaking to each other altogether, all the while living under the same roof and working on the same manga series.

Kemari decided that she would take half a day off every week, on Monday evening. During this time, rather than going out somewhere for a change of pace, she would almost always sit on the veranda and stare out at the backyard. When the one-eyed worker Toyohisa would come to visit, she would call out to him, things like "If you're looking for Mom, she's in the parlor," and sometimes, he would stand and chat with her.

The now grown-up Kemari would often talk with her mother's friend, the stubborn worker at loggerheads with her father. Kemari was also a stubborn girl and was, in fact, afraid of change.

Toyohisa and Kemari frequently talked about the girl they had lost. She had been Toyohisa's niece, and he was ashamed of the way Choko had died. He was an old-fashioned man, so it hit him especially hard.

"People just talk about all the bad things. She might have gotten a little strange once she started high school, but she was a good kid back in the day. But they're out there saying she was rotten right from the get-go."

"Let them. Uncle, all that matters is that we loved her. They'll be onto some other gossip pretty quick. But love, that's forever, y'know?"

"Miss Kemari, you saying that means a lot." Toyohisa sniffled loudly.

Toyohisa hadn't changed at all, in very much the same way as his beloved blast furnace, which remained as it was even as the times changed. Her mother, Manyo, was often with him. Her father, Yoji, as usual, had basically all his time taken up by the company and didn't have much to do with the household. He of course knew that his oldest daughter, Kemari, had become a manga artist, but instead of particularly objecting or voicing an opinion, he left everything family-related to his mother, Tatsu, and his wife, Manyo.

Kemari was scared of change, but that summer when she was twenty and selling like crazy, she ended up facing a very big change indeed, a bolt from the blue. The summer of 1986.

At last, the difficult summer her mother, Manyo, had foreseen descended upon the Akakuchiba main family.

My uncle, Namida Akakuchiba, was turning twenty-two that year. He was about to graduate with top marks from the regional national university, and everyone at the Akakuchiba Steelworks felt reassured at the thought that this brilliant son would one day be taking over for his father. In any case, the four other children were Kemari, the deeply delinquent girl turned manga artist no one could figure out; the eternally gloomy man-stealing Momoyo, who did nothing but sleep with men; Kaban, the flashy high school girl focused exclusively on fun; and Kodoku, still in elementary school and hiding in his room. Everyone trusted Namida, and Yoji of course had started to passionately teach him about business administration. And then it happened, with no advance warning, at this critical moment when Namida was about to take up his position as heir.

On summer break, he went hiking with some friends from school, heading high up in the Chugoku Mountains, upstream of the Hino River. The group was all singing loudly together when they realized they could no longer hear one of their voices, but Namida had already disappeared from the mountain path. His friends said he had probably slipped and fallen into the Hino River, but none of them had seen it. By the time they realized their chorus was short one voice, he was gone. Almost as if this world had been a temporary stop all along, he simply vanished from the mountain path.

His friends cocked their heads, hearing or maybe not hearing the sound of water splashing in the distance, far downstream. "Heeey! Namida!" they shouted. "Akakuchibaaaaa!" They raced back and forth along the mountain path. Determining that he had, in fact, disappeared, they descended from the mountains and notified the police. One friend was half crazed and tried to go off the cliff after him, but his friends cried out "Sanjo!" and used force to stop him. Search parties later scoured the mountains, but Namida had disappeared without a trace, as if he had evaporated from this world.

At the Akakuchiba house, Yoji was unable to concentrate on work; Momoyo took a break from her diligent, devotional man-stealing; and Kemari completely dropped her weekly serialization, went to pieces, and hurtled through the mountains, praying at every shrine or temple she came across.

"Namida! Namida!" She ran along the mountain paths like a madwoman, her cries echoing throughout the range.

The people of the branch families shared in the work and also walked through the mountains looking for Namida. Could the oldest son, the central pillar of the main family, really simply vanish as if carried away by the wind? While the people of the mansion went out and over the mountains and ran around calling Namida's name, his mother, Manyo, alone locked herself up in her room and did nothing.

The aged and well-fattened Tatsu Akakuchiba came over to where she was sitting quietly like a statue, placed a hand on her knee, and said, "It's okay. Manyo, it's okay."

At that moment, Manyo broke the silence she had kept over the twenty-two years since the night she had had the vision of Namida's death. She fell prostrate across Tatsu's plump knees and wailed inconsolably, in a way no one had ever seen before. Like the morning she had given birth to Namida. "Mother, I-I knew! I knew it'd turn out like this. I'm sorry I didn't say nothin'. Everyone expected so much from him!"

"It's okay. Ever since I picked you to be his wife, I had an idea one of the children you bore would be carried away in the mountains. You're the child of mountain people, after all."

"But I...I knew..."

Shoulders shaking, Manyo lifted her head and stretched out the index finger of her right hand. And then she pointed out at the backyard. "Namida'll come home in the morning," she murmured, pointing to the small brook flowing through the garden, where she had often stood frozen, by herself, since she came to the Akakuchiba house. "Just his empty body's coming home. I knew. I knew it all. I'm clairvoyant."

At Manyo's words, Tatsu went out into the backyard and stared at the brook. The water was clear, trickling down over the rocks from the mountains, the plants in it swaying gently. She took a deep breath and called for Kemari in a voice like thunder. At the sound of the grande dame's voice, which practically echoed through the town below, it seemed that even the wind stopped and the mountains shuddered.

Returning to the house covered in dirt, barefoot, hair completely disheveled, Kemari stood in the garden, and Tatsu pointed at the brook. "Look there. Got it?"

The younger woman sensed that something was strange and nodded wordlessly. Then she sat down on the veranda and stayed there a long time staring at the dark brook, even as day turned to night and the owl hooted. Face bare, covered in dirt, eyes bloodshot, Kemari clutched her knees to her chest, and the night wind gently caressed her. She continued to stare at the brook, barely blinking, much less sleeping. Eventually, dawn began to break.

Namida was repatriated. He flowed slowly down the stream and returned to the mansion, cold now. It was exactly as Manyo had seen in her vision.

Namida's body floated lightly in the narrow stream. In this little brook running with the water of the Hino River, the drowned boy had flowed and drifted and finally arrived. A faint, gentle smile was plastered on his pale face.

Kemari stood up quietly and, disturbing the gravel of the crimson lotus, ran over to him. Plunging into the brook with bare feet, she lifted her brother's body with her strong arms. "Namida, Namida…" The slight smile glued to his face was the same gentle one he would give her when their eyes met when he was still alive. "Namida, Namida…" Shaking, Kemari stepped out of the brook and, soaking wet, staggered through the halls of the mansion. "Namida, Namida…" She dripped water, her long hair was covered in mud, and her arms cradled the older brother who was so heavy in death.

Tatsu called out to the girl lurching down the hallway in the morning mist, and Kemari turned and saw a halo around her. She was stunned, and for the first time, she felt like she could rely on this grandmother before her. "What are we gonna do, Grandma? What are we gonna do?" she repeated helplessly, and Tatsu nodded slowly. Kemari dropped her older brother, fell to her knees on the spot, and began to sob, the howls of a wounded beast. Manyo, coming out of her room, opened her eyes wide and stared at her son's body in the hall.

Manyo's hair turned silver overnight. That long, wonderfully black hair that Kemari had inherited was gone. From the roots right down to the tips, the hair that twisted down to her waist and covered her dark body became the color of snow as it first begins to fall.

Three generations of the main family's women—Tatsu, Manyo, and Kemari—sat stunned around the corpse of the ever-reliable eldest son, cold now and yet still smiling faintly. Sensing the change in the air, the family and the people of the branch families began to gather.

Yoji was shocked by the sudden death of his son, but when night fell he noticed Manyo, tremendously quiet with eyes that looked like she had given up, and went over to her.

"Did you...know? Did you...see this?"

Manyo nodded slowly. "I knew."

"Why didn't you tell me?" For the first time since he married her, Yoji slapped Manyo. She hung her head and stayed still. For a while, he too stood rooted to the spot. And then he asked his wife in a terrifyingly quiet voice, "When am I going to die?"

She was silent.

"Just as much as you know. Tell me. The reason Akakuchiba Steelworks has held on this long is because I knew about my father's death. Manyo, you're clairvoyant. I've been running things with the idea that I'm going to live a long time, but I don't actually know that."

Manyo looked at her husband. He had grown older, to the point where there was no longer any real difference in the aged face that had died when the head went flying in her vision so long ago. She knew he was very close to the age when he would die. She prostrated herself before her husband and told him that it wasn't far off. Yoji bit his lip so hard it bled.

Kemari was a young woman who knew nothing other than fighting and manga, and they couldn't expect much from her younger sisters, either. And the baby of the family was still in elementary school. Yoji paced, and for the first time in his life, got lost in the labyrinthine hallways of the mansion. Perhaps he was shaken by the news of his death. Or perhaps it wasn't Yoji who was shaken, but the Akakuchiba mansion itself now with no one to inherit it.

After wandering hopelessly lost through the labyrinth for five hours before finally arriving at the night-long vigil over the body, Yoji grabbed Kemari's wrist as she clutched the coffin and wept. Soho held her other wrist tightly. That week's chapter for the manga magazine had already been canceled due to the "sudden illness of the author." Which meant that they wouldn't be able to cancel the following week for the author to "do research" or something. This shojo manga magazine was managing to hold on because of the popularity of *Iron Angels!* If Kemari wasn't in the next issue either, sales would plummet and heads would roll. Soho still wasn't speaking to Kemari, but he held firmly onto the cash-cow manga artist he had brought up in this world.

When Yoji pulled Kemari up, handsome Soho was dragged along and dangled at her side. Unaware that anyone at all was holding onto her, Kemari cried out her older brother's name and wept.

"Kemari, have you ever done what your father's told you?" Yoji yelled.

"No."

"And have I ever bowed my head to you, my daughter?"

"You haven't," Kemari replied, weeping.

"Will you do something for me now?"

"All right."

"Get married."

"Got it."

"What do you mean, 'Got it'?" Soho roared. "I need you to stay single another ten years at least, or we are in some serious trouble!"

Yoji stared hard enough at Soho's smoothly beautiful face to burn a hole in it. Soho didn't flinch but simply glared back. Kemari hung her head, arms stretched between them like the baby in the Judgment of Solomon. Her face was, again, curiously void of expression, as if she were possessed by the pale corpse.

That night, a strange tension ran through the siblings. Everyone in the family knew their mother was clairvoyant. They guessed that their father telling Kemari to get married now that their older brother was dead meant that their father's death was also not far off. In which case, the family had to bring in a man who measured up to their father as an adopted son to protect itself. The duty of women born into the old families was to stay in the shadows and ensure they kept the family safe.

Kemari was a delinquent, but she also had a strong sense of responsibility. From the moment of her older brother Namida's premature death, she bore the burden of two different responsibilities: To continue writing the smash hit manga *Iron Angels!* And, as eldest daughter of an old family, to protect the Akakuchibas. These duties settled onto the solidly broad shoulders of the barely twenty-year-old woman.

Kemari was a woman whose life was changed by the dead every so often. This was also one of those times.

At the vigil, Soho alone was unaware of the circumstances surrounding Yoji's request. To him, Kemari was just a manga artist. He feared his cash cow being taken from him, snatched away. At any rate, although he may have occupied a place in the mansion as the editor "attached to Akakuchiba," he was poorly informed about the inner workings of the family. To the point where even then, he was convinced that Momoyo sitting there at the vigil was, in fact, the ghost of a housekeeper, and he tried his best to avoid her eyes. He knew nothing of the true nature of the strange tension reverberating through the family.

Seeing Kemari so easily consent without even asking whom she would be marrying, he nearly ripped his own head off and roared a sad battle cry, before running—practically falling—down the hill road of the steps and rushing into the two-story wooden NTT building. A telegram to the publisher in Tokyo was typed out, and the information flew toward the capital, glittering in the night sky.

KEMARI AKAKUCHIBA SUDDEN MARRIAGE STOP CANT STOP
STOP SOHO

Soho's head rolled.

The next day, the morning of the funeral, another handsome man came from the east, clad in an Italian suit and looking very much like Soho. His business card, sharp like it could cut through skin, was embossed with the name Akira Togane. Togane attended the funeral and said his greetings to Kemari. He asked whom she would be marrying, and she said, "Dunno." Through their investigation, the publisher already knew that Kemari was dating an exceedingly ugly university student from the area who was the same age as she was. However, when he mentioned the name of this student, Kemari answered, as if mystified, "Prob'ly not him."

Togane, less passionate about manga than Soho but more astute in general, managed to grasp the basic situation by nightfall. Kemari would take a husband for the sake of the company, and that meant the marriage wouldn't interfere with her work. She missed just the one week of serialization, and after her brother's funeral, she went back to drawing manga. Tears dripped down her face and Togane wiped them away. He also got her more assistants. He made arrangements for an army of gorgeous manga artist reserve troops to be called in from the capital, and they came running. The army, seven girls strong, was permanently stationed in Kemari's studio in the depths of the Akakuchiba house, where they drew backgrounds and pasted tone.

Kemari continued to draw. The tears she shed were wiped away by her new editor. Weekly serialization is brutal. The love or lack thereof for any series is made cruelly clear through the weekly readers' survey postcards, and anything dropping even slightly in popularity gets cut. The passion of the readers had made Kemari a star, and it was also this invisible power that brooked no interruption and forced her to keep moving. The vein of gold Soho had discovered was mined by Kemari's own hands, and the muddy stream continued to flow. The passion of the readers grew. Before anyone knew it, she had become the main attraction, supporting the entire editorial division. They could no longer allow the flow to stop if they could at all avoid it.

Kemari continued to draw. Tears crawled down her cheeks and were wiped away by the hand of the stranger Togane.

And then without a moment's pause after her older brother's funeral, a husband for Kemari was selected.

It was Tatsu who decided on Kemari's husband. Yoji selected as candidates a number of promising young men working at the Akakuchiba Steelworks and went to discuss them with his mother. From the pile, Tatsu selected one photo without so much as a glance at the other photographs and personal histories. "This one." As for Manyo, she seemed to have seen Tatsu choosing this man in advance, as she knew about it already and readily consented before Yoji got the chance to say anything.

Wincing at the choking body odor of the girls filling the room, Yoji went into Kemari's studio to tell her about this development. "Got it," she said, without lifting her head. Togane accepted the personal history of her husband-to-be on her behalf and tossed it on the desk.

However, that evening, as she continued to draw her manga, Kemari murmured, "Ah!" She had just realized that she hadn't told her lover she was getting married. Naturally, speaking with him directly made the most sense, but she didn't have time for that. Kemari was in such a cruel spot that the printers would shriek in complaint if her hand stopped moving for even a moment.

She abruptly remembered that woman's face. The large eyes and dark skin so like her own. That body with the big frame, the sturdy physique. The face of the Filipina whose name she didn't know, the one she had run into in a rainy Yoimachi Alley.

At once, still inking with her right hand, she picked up the phone with her left and called Shinobu. He had had three more children after that first one and so had plenty of kids to watch out for at that point. Perhaps he was run ragged by these children, since instead of Shinobu, the person who answered the phone was Kemari's first boyfriend, Takeshi Nojima.

Takeshi had finally managed to get professionally certified and tended the shop during the day, while devoting all his energies to boxing at night. Kemari told him about the Filipina, and he laughed. "Seriously? And here I was happy to hear from you after all this time. C'mon, what is this even about?"

But Shinobu in the distance replied in a loud voice, "I know her! That's Aira." According to Shinobu, he had mistaken the Filipina for Kemari and gotten to know her after talking to her a few times in Yoimachi.

Kemari, right hand inking, used her left hand to call the club where Aira worked, and the woman herself answered.

"My name's Kemari. Remember me? We met in Yoimachi Alley a couple years ago."

"Kemari?"

"You helped me pick my motorcycle up."

"Ohh. You lent me an umbrella, yes?"

It had been only two years earlier, but Kemari felt like this meeting had happened ten years ago. She'd forgotten about the umbrella part.

"I still have the umbrella, you know," Aira said, and laughed lightly on the other end of the line.

Aira was a year older than Kemari, twenty-one. According to Shinobu, she had gotten sick and was currently off active duty, but in debt, so she was answering the phone at the club. Shinobu neatly arranged things with Yoimachi, and the next day, Aira came to the Akakuchiba mansion.

She still strongly resembled Kemari, but Manyo didn't notice for some reason when she welcomed her in the entryway. The two women looked so much alike that the housekeepers thought Kemari had gone and gotten a perm at the hairdresser, but Manyo alone was oblivious to the resemblance. "Kemari, you have a guest!" She took Aira by the hand and showed her to the interior room.

Perhaps finding the older woman's rippling silver hair remarkable, Aira reached a hand out to stroke it. Manyo turned around slowly and looked at Aira with eyes that had sunk sharply after Namida's death.

"It turned silver overnight."

"It's very pretty."

"Hmm. Maybe because it's a sad color."

Aira's frizzy black hair hung down her back. She had big, beautiful eyes like pieces of obsidian in her dark skin, and she had drawn on garishly bright red lipstick. Long, smooth legs stretched out from hot-pants. Kemari dragged herself out of her studio and raised a hand. Aira also waved, as if embarrassed.

Standing together, they really did have the same features. They had likely inherited the blood from the same region and been born in two different places, separated and kept distant by the ocean. But one was the daughter of a wealthy family, while the other was ill in a foreign country. A curious empathy and opposition rose up in the two women.

"So you bought me, huh?" Standing in front of Kemari, Aira twisted her lips up sardonically.

"I did. Money, money, money."

"So what am I supposed to do, Kemari with the money?"

"Pretend to be me. Relax. Get better."

Aira snorted, "Pfft!" She looked at Kemari's mess of a studio, and then she stared at Kemari herself, who no matter how you looked at it, was clearly not getting enough sleep, her skin rough, eyes blood-shot. "Oh, I'll relax. Enough for you too, Kemari," she said, and Kemari smiled just a little.

From then on, Aira was Kemari Akakuchiba's body double and began appearing in public instead of Kemari, who continued to draw her manga in the depths of the mansion. Waves of reporters came crashing down on Kemari Akakuchiba, *the* shojo artist of the era, for interviews and other stories, to the point where she couldn't actually get any work done. So Aira would meet the TV crews and the magazine interviewers and say whatever she felt like saying. Her Japanese pronun-ciation was fairly accented, and she hadn't been given any instructions or done any homework for the role on her own, so her body double act was all over the place. But this curious Kemari was accepted, and the number of requests for interviews grew ever larger. The real Kemari left all of these interviews, the publisher's brilliant parties, and any and all public appearances to Aira.

Aira's first job—breaking up with the university student—went off without any real trouble. She met with the boy without really understanding the task at hand, but the student had already been gutted by the man-stealing Momoyo, so he nodded perfunctorily at Aira's words, accepted the break-up with a quick "I understand," and went home.

Kemari's wedding was fast approaching, and Aira had nothing to do, so she lolled around in the studio. "So who are you going to marry?" she asked Kemari.

The other girl lifted her head and replied, as if troubled, "I dunno."

"There's a picture here." The editor Togane, looking just as exhausted as the manga artist, pointed at the personal history. For some reason, Momoyo's fingerprints were all over it.

Aira looked at the photo. "He looks pretty average," she informed Kemari. Getting no response, she looked up to find that Kemari had fallen asleep, still sitting with pen in hand.

Togane shook her awake. Remembering Namida again, she started to sniffle, and the editor wiped her face roughly. Desks were lined up in the studio in an organized fashion, with several girls working wordlessly to assist Kemari. Aira quietly left and returned to the small, comfortable room she had been given.

The day of the wedding came. Pen still in hand, Kemari had her hair and makeup done, lipstick applied, and white dress put on before she finally stood up. "It's done! Look! Togane, take it!" Togane accepted the pages from her and ran to the post office. He sent the manuscript and then collapsed from exhaustion on the spot in the post office. He was carried off in an ambulance, and Kemari faced the moment of her marriage in the mansion to the distant wailing of the sirens whisking away her handsome editor.

To speak of the key element, the groom, he was, at that time, vacillating on the hill road of the steps, so terrified and nervous he was ready to simply run away. Hearing the ominous sirens off in the distance fanned the flames of his unease for no good reason.

The groom's name was Yoshio. He was twenty-seven and originally from a steel family on the steps; his father was a worker. When his father had been transferred from steel production to delivery work, which came with a pay cut, Yoshio started delivering papers to earn his high school tuition. After graduation, he paid his own way through the top educational institution in Tokyo before returning to his provincial home in Benimidori. He had finally finished paying back his student loans by working at the Akakuchiba Steelworks.

Yoji appreciated his serious working style and his sharp mind, and had just given Yoshio a managerial position despite his young age. And then one day, he had invited Yoshio to the bukupuku tea shop on the steps below, and just as he was sitting down, wondering what this unusual meeting was all about, Yoji had begun sounding him out about marrying into the family. That had been a mere ten days earlier.

As a mere worker, it was an unfathomable step up in the world, and at first, when he thought about how much easier his life would be made by his new siblings, he was beside himself with joy, but when he thought about it carefully, the Akakuchiba daughter in question was probably Kemari and her not-so-clean sheet. Commuting to the Akakuchiba Steelworks from his apartment on the steps, Yoshio had nearly been run over countless times by Kemari's motorcycle during her delinquent days, not to mention the times he had been surrounded by her friends and ridiculed. He prayed that it was the younger sister Kaban, but when he thought this through, he realized Kaban still hadn't graduated from high school, so he figured it probably wouldn't be her. He ever-so-timidly went to check with the president and learned that his proposed partner was, indeed, Kemari.

Unable to refuse at that point, Yoshio had hurried to consult with his family and cry with his friends, and before he knew it, it was the day of the wedding itself. In the end, his parents made him take along a wedding wardrobe and chest of drawers, both made out of paulownia wood, for his marriage into another family. So Yoshio resigned himself, and that morning, despite his disquiet at the ominous sirens, he continued to climb the hill road of the steps.

In general, he was an excellent employee and a solid manager, but he wasn't the type to burn with ambition. He was a man who, Yoji had determined, had sufficient talent to safely manage the company and hand it off to the next generation. Before his wedding, as well, he wore that same serious face and climbed the hill road of the steps, shaking all the while.

When he finally reached the Akakuchiba main house, Yoji and

Manyo were standing there in formal wear in the garden. With more legs and arms than he knew what to do with, Yoji was almost the perfect picture of a shadow at night, and Manyo stood next to him, long silver hair fluttering. "You made it," she said, and Yoshio silently bowed his head. Kemari wearily appeared, wearing her white dress. Of course, it was not her body double attending the wedding ceremony, but the woman herself.

The Akakuchiba main family was still not entirely over the shock of the loss of their eldest son, and everyone had a curiously distracted look on their faces. Kemari wore a white veil and was given a cute bouquet to hold. Yoshio could hear her muttering, "This look sucks." He didn't understand what she meant and was afraid to stand next to her; his knees began to shake without his consent. As he stood by her side, he felt a strangely tense aura around her. Two auras, in fact, particular to someone responsible for generations, intertwined and emanated from his bride. The impression was one of brilliance and, running counter to this, death.

That night, Yoshio sat still in the gloom of their sleeping quarters staring at the wall, until finally, after midnight, Kemari dragged herself in. Outside, he could hear the short cries of the girls bustling about, running in and out of the studio.

"Mr. Togane collapsed."

"What'll we do without an editor?"

"Sensei gave us the next storyboard already, so get together materials for the backgrounds first."

"What about Sensei?"

"Wedding night!"

"Ohh, right!"

Kemari, long hair pulled back, no makeup on, stood there like a ghost, a totally different person from the woman in the gorgeous dress that afternoon. Her face and body were both exhausted, and he could see an impatience that was surprising in a woman of twenty. Bloodshot eyes in dark, rough skin. Yoshio regretted once again this marriage and was filled with the desire to flee back to his family on the steps. But then he noticed her hesitation, as if facing a small, scared animal and unsure about what to do, and he stared up at her.

She seemed to get some of her good humor back and flashed him a smile. Her face was transformed; she was unexpectedly childish and helpless. Yoshio suddenly lost his fear of this Fire Horse girl. For some reason, his new wife appeared pitiable. He remembered that she had just lost her brother, also seven years older than her, as she stretched out a solid arm and roughly yanked on his slender hand.

"What a hassle. Take off your obi."

"What?"

"Undress yourself."

Kemari scratched her head and dragged him after her, so that he almost fell into the futon. He felt a shudder of fear run down his back, and there, for the first time, he truly understood that he hadn't just gotten married, he had been taken into the main Akakuchiba family, which had ruled over the heavens of the village of Benimidori since time immemorial. In a vague sense, there were no men, no women there. It was the blood connection that ruled.

And there too, on the floor on their wedding night, there was no woman. Yoshio felt there was simply a will in the darkness. Finally, a warmth covered him, not the body of a woman, but rather the will of the blood that possessed the mansion. This, which had embraced Manyo in the past, enveloped Yoshio that night.

Kemari leaned on him and silently, wordlessly wept. As the tears fell from her cheeks, Yoshio abruptly felt that he loved this large, powerful, exhausted, beautiful woman. He gently stretched out slender hands to take his wife in his arms, and Kemari in the depths of the darkness smiled so faintly it was hard to call it a smile at all.

After that, she commuted to the marriage chamber enthusiastically, trying to get pregnant. Outside, he could always hear the hurried voices of the girls.

"Inking's done, start erasing."

"Where's Sensei?"

"The new editor's here."

The new editor was called Watanuki, this one another handsome man in his mid-twenties or so who also wore expensive suits. He picked up with the serialization of the manga, and the dirty stream of gold poured into the mansion and flowed off somewhere.

At any rate, Kemari and Yoshio, forced into marriage abruptly due to Namida's passing, managed in their own way to develop the bonds of a married couple and accept each other.

Now then, the year after the year after that, a member of the Akakuchiba main family set out for the capital.

Momoyo, who had graduated one step ahead of her and found a job in the region, tried to stop her—"Please stay"—but Kaban was stubborn and insisted that she wanted to go to a junior college in Tokyo. The eldest daughter Kemari had taken her husband, and everyone was satisfied with the new son and the fairly good head that sat on his shoulders, so the family somehow found it in them to hear Kaban's plea. Manyo was opposed, but Kemari took her sister's side at the family meeting.

"Let her play for two years at least. Otherwise, she won't settle down, not a girl like Kaban. Right, Yoshio?"

Yoshio, who was facing the water, cleared his throat. The company was a different story, but at the family meetings, he held back and didn't speak too much. But Kemari had stood her husband up and spoken to him, and since Kemari held him up, Kaban and Kodoku, in their own ways, also started to acknowledge Yoshio as having power in the family.

Kaban had turned eighteen and given up on becoming an idol. Instead, she had begun to think she'd like to be an actress. Saying she was off to chase her dream, she started life at junior college, alone in Tokyo. The single student of the time was moving from the traditional apartment or boardinghouse to the small but stylish residence called a one-room condo. Instead of the old seven-square-meter tatami room with a Japanese-style toilet, a nine-square-meter room with laminate flooring and a plastic "unit bath" was the in thing.

Right around the time when Kaban went to Tokyo, bubble culture was blossoming. Every night, Kaban went to dance, scantily clad, at the disco. The nights of the female university students were brilliant and bawdy. Kaban and her preppy friends became sophisticates in no time flat and lived through the nights, surrounded by expensive presents, dazzling darkness, and sweet whispers.

"Tokyo's so much fun! I want to stay here forever."

Kaban went to acting school and got the occasional audition. The results were not what she wanted, but she forgot everything in the delights of the night.

Just when Kaban was getting into house music and dancing, crazed, in whatever spotlight was available, her younger brother, Kodoku, was finally getting the chance to live his life out from under the shadow of nuclear weapons.

According to this youngest child, what followed was the conclusion of the Cold War. Given that he had lived through his elementary school days in fear of the specter of nuclear winter and the outbreak of the Third World War, the end of the Cold War was an extremely surprising turn.

Kodoku watched the Berlin Wall separating East and West Germany come down on TV. The youth of the nations freely scaled the wall and were not gunned down by the border patrol; they shouted fierce cries and took the wall down, a call for peace. You could even buy chunks of the Wall. Kodoku was very surprised. The Soviet Union was gone, and Russia was a country of its own again. The system of one-party rule by the people's party collapsed, other political powers were born, and the world changed at a dizzying pace.

Kodoku had started junior high, but he only went the first three days before, of course, going back to refusing to attend. When the school called his father, Yoji, he said Kodoku was aiming to take the high school equivalency test and was studying at home. Kodoku was strong-willed; perhaps he took after his older sister Kemari. He studied by correspondence, got good grades, and his father begrudgingly allowed it.

The year 1989 began with the death of Emperor Hirohito, a rather significant change. People were shocked by the new Imperial year, the fact that their years would no longer be preceded by "Showa," and quietly digested the notion that an era was truly ending. The line for the Imperial register was long indeed, and news of the emperor's death was all over TV and the newspapers. A sadness and sense of loss multiplied and spread. Several dark weeks passed as if a heavy black blanket had been placed over the entire nation.

It was decided that the new Imperial era—and the years within it—would be called "Heisei." Little by little, people seemed to finally settle down again. Time was relentless in its march and many things changed, but still, the earth kept turning as it had done up to that point. When spring came and the warm sun poured down over this earth, the Akakuchiba main family in the heavens of Benimidori was rocked yet again.

Tatsu Akakuchiba, who had long reigned as the grande dame, finally fell.

While small of stature, Tatsu was quite fat and practically rolled as she raced about the mansion, but that spring, walking down the hallway to her grandson's room, she slipped and fell. The multicolored *konpeito* candies she had been planning to give to Kodoku scattered magnificently across the floor, and Tatsu called for Manyo in a thin voice.

The housekeepers came, but she would not allow them to touch her, instead continuing to call for the strange daughter-in-law she herself had selected. Manyo had just gone out to do the shopping, and it took a fair while for her to return, but Tatsu lay on her back in the hallway the whole time, groaning in the middle of the scattered candies, and allowed neither the housekeepers nor her son, Yoji, who heard about the commotion and came home, nor the family heir, Kemari, to touch her person. When Manyo finally returned laden with shopping bags, the elderly woman announced in an anxious, thin voice, "I hurt myself. Carry me to my room." Manyo tossed aside the bags and rushed to her mother-in-law's side.

This mother-in-law had, until that point, been in good health and roundly fat, so much so that standing alongside her daughter-in-law, whose hair had turned silver and whose eyes were dull, the two women didn't appear that different in age. Manyo easily lifted Tatsu with her solid mountain girl arms and carried her to her room. The doctor came to examine her and announced that she had broken her leg. From then on, Tatsu was confined to bed, and Manyo was constantly by her side, tending to her. Almost overnight, the body that had been such a fat ball became small and thin, and as her flesh fell away, her face did indeed come to resemble her son Yoji's. Only Manyo was allowed into Tatsu's room, but just once, Kemari stood sluggishly by the door and called out to her mother.

"So this is finally it," Kemari said, stroking her mother's unkempt hair as she came out of Tatsu's room.

"What do you mean, it?"

Kemari pointed at her own stomach with a look of irritation. She and her husband had made a baby. When Manyo went into her room to announce the news, Tatsu said in a thin voice that she wanted to see Kemari.

Going inside, Kemari saw how shrunken her grandmother's body was on the futon. She almost yelped but was quick to swallow the cry.

Tatsu was small and pale, a mere girl now. Her eyes, wider and bigger now because of the lost weight, crinkled as she smiled. "So you got one on the way?"

"Yeah, finally. And they said for a week anyway, my manga can take a break."

"Tough times for a baby to come into."

"All times are tough, Grandma. I mean, they're tough in their own way, y'know?"

"Heh heh heh. You're such a fearless girl." Tatsu narrowed her eyes and looked up at Kemari. Then she tenderly stroked the stomach that was starting to swell slightly. The sun went down, and the sound of the wind brushing up against the leaves of the trees came from the garden.

When later asked about this year, 1989, I make a point of replying that it was the year of the Tsutomu Miyazaki murders. That way, most adults simply stop with "Mm-hmm." It was also the period when people started noticing all the new religious movements, like with the rise of Aum Shinrikyo. Those who had grown up in the age of fiction became adults, and the world started to see some very strange crimes, as if fiction were bleeding into reality.

This was the sort of year in which I was given life. Yes, in other words, at this time, Kemari Akakuchiba was pregnant with me, Toko Akakuchiba.

In the fall of that year, the slimmed-down grande dame Tatsu peacefully breathed her last and fell asleep forever. The people of the branch families and many of the villagers of Benimidori came to the funeral service. The younger of them, seeing Tatsu's form in the casket, wrinkled and yet pale and slender like a girl, stared in amazement, almost unable to tell who it was, but the older ones smiled—"Goodness, she's back to her old little self, isn't she?"—while wiping away tears.

As the grande dame, Tatsu had had more power over the Akakuchiba main family than her husband, but in the end, she returned to what she had been before she got married and departed on her trip. Funeral palanquin swinging, she descended the hill road of the steps slowly. A flute player, an old man playing the conch, and a drummer assembled, and they sent Tatsu off merrily and joyfully. Because it had been a peaceful death, her people buried her warmly with smiles on their faces.

On the way down to the bottom of the steps, the funeral palanquin rocked heavily from side to side, just once, although there was no wind. "Oh, Mother," Manyo murmured.

Among the villagers gathered there were the Tadas, the couple who had raised Manyo. The husband suffered from rheumatism and was in a wheelchair, slowly pushed by the wife, since his joints were hurting that day. They clapped their hands together as they faced Tatsu; they had the sameness of expression and gesture characteristic of those who have spent long years in each other's company. Eventually, the Tada couple were surrounded by their sons and grandchildren, and the truly large family returned to their apartment building on the steps, in a trail of small groups.

Manyo watched them go, her long, now-silver hair fluttering in the autumn wind. The Tada wife looked back once and smiled at her.

Manyo dipped her head slightly. The mother who had raised her had grown old, but there was still something young about her, and when she smiled, there was a kindness to it.

When, in this way, the grande dame Tatsu finally left the mansion and moved on to the next world, people began to refer to Manyo as the grande dame. She had been running the entire house ever since Tatsu collapsed, so she wasn't particularly confused by it, but Kemari was, as people began to call her the young madam. She was drawing her manga, as usual, and she left everything else to her body double, Aira. She was essentially the same as she was at twenty, when she locked herself up forever to focus on her manga. So even though the people around her called her the young madam, she was still largely unaware of the doings inside the mansion.

And then, that winter, Kemari felt the pains of labor and called her mother. Her mother took her by the hand, and the midwife came running. In her studio, Kemari, in a cold sweat, face haggard, continued to give instructions to her assistants. Manyo felt how strangely untroubled this Kemari was, in diametric opposition to her own suffering when she gave birth to her children. It wasn't the sort of thing you'd expect from a woman about to give birth for the first time.

But the truth was that at precisely that moment, in another room in the mansion, the Filipina Aira, born with the exact same features as Kemari, was writhing in agony, almost as if she had undertaken the challenge of labor on Kemari's behalf. She had been done in by a shrimp dish she had made, trying to reproduce the flavors of her homeland. "My stomach hurts!" she cried.

Kodoku passed by Aira crawling from her room to the hallway and had no choice but to look after her until morning. He tried to call for someone, but all the women of the mansion, from the grande dame to the housekeepers in training, were completely preoccupied with Kemari's labor.

Right around the time Aira was groaning incoherently about how the shrimp was bad, Kemari, looking sad, brought a girl into the world, right there in the studio. Perhaps thanks to her other self, Aira, it went surprisingly smoothly for a first birth.

"You did it," Manyo announced in the morning light, and Kemari heaved a sigh of relief.

"I did it," she murmured.

Wholly unbecoming the daughter of Kemari and the niece of Namida, I was born in the most normal of ways. I came out wailing the sob of the newly born, and I stopped crying when Manyo held me.

"I did it. I did it. Ah, thank god," my mother, Kemari, said, a single, small teardrop falling.

Yoshio, permitted to be in audience, came into the room and, somewhat hesitantly, took me in his arms. And then Kemari named me Toko, using the characters for "eyes" and "child," and sent in the notification to the town hall. "'Cause your eyes are so big and beautiful, they make an impression," she told me when I grew up, but I believe my mother was lying.

The truth is, I should have been given a different name. Tatsu, who would be my great-grandmother, had decided on it while she was still alive. It was a little while later that Kemari named her baby Toko and submitted the notification. When Manyo went into Tatsu's room and carefully cleaned it out, cradling each of her mother-in-law's possessions with love, she discovered a half sheet of paper. On it was written large in Tatsu's round handwriting, "Jiyu."

Freedom.

That was the name my great-grandmother had wanted to give me. I really should be Jiyu Akakuchiba. I still grumble and complain about this even now to my uncle Kodoku. And each time I do, I go off by myself for a while and think about freedom.

What is freedom? For those of us living in the modern age, what on earth does that mean? What is freedom for a woman?

What, what, what?

When I'm thinking like this, circling round and round, I'm an unhappy girl, just a little. I resent my mother with a painful ache. She would have never told anyone, but maybe the truth is, she named me Toko because of the similarity to Choko. I've thought this might be it for a long, long time.

Not long after I was born, the bubble burst.

Stock and land prices plummeted, and bank loans became uncollectable. People playing around with risky ventures went bankrupt one after another, and people who had only dipped a toe into projects like buying and selling land outside of their core businesses found themselves in the rather difficult situation of having to dissolve their central concerns and instantly found themselves out on the streets. University students, having difficulty securing work, became members of the reluctantly underemployed group known as "freeters" in large numbers.

Although the provincial towns saw almost none of the blessings of the bubble, for some reason, the aftermath of the bubble's collapse slammed into the small towns and villages like a storm. "Black below," aka Kurobishi Shipbuilders, plunged into bankruptcy, an enormous tree falling. The people of Benimidori were shocked. Kurobishi Shipbuilders had washed its hands of the shipbuilding business and was shifting to construction, but under the influence of the bubble, it had also taken out loans to engage in real estate speculation, and the company was submerged by the tsunami of plummeting land prices.

The Rikidozan-double who was the Kurobishi son-in-law collapsed from overwork and breathed his last in no time at all. Midori Kurobishi went round to each of her independent children, but living together didn't work out well, and she ended up on the Akakuchibas' front step with her third child, who was still in high school. This third child was a girl called Yukari. Yukari got excellent grades and ended up being cared for by the Akakuchiba main family until she graduated from university. She herself insisted that she would work to earn the money for her tuition, but Yoshio, having been through that particular hardship himself, was fiercely opposed. "That's no life for a girl." Normally, he deferred to Yoji and almost never offered his opinion at family gatherings, but in this alone, he was firm. Kemari was also in agreement with him, and the matter was passed at a family meeting.

Yukari lived with her mother, Midori, in the mansion until she graduated, but after that, she struck out on her own. She became a career woman working for the Chugoku Electric Power Company and went round and round the Chugoku region, transferred for work to Okayama, Hiroshima, Yamaguchi. She proposed that her mother come live with her, but Midori hated the idea of living anywhere other than the village of Benimidori where she was born and raised. With Manyo's intercession, mother and child both accepted that they would live apart, which is how Midori came to stay on at the Akakuchiba house even after that, spending her days learning flamenco.

The collapse of the bubble wasn't so much that it cut down the Akakuchiba Steelworks as well, which had been, at best, steadily pushing ahead, but even still, the wind was definitely strong enough to rip off a few leaves and branches. In the spring of 1992, when the enormous warship was rocking and shaking, trying to ride out the wild waves of the aftermath of the bubble's collapse, the Akakuchiba Steelworks was abruptly faced with a frontal attack.

The weather that day was apparently very good, right from the morning. Because they knew the time of their parting was near, Manyo and Yoji passed each and every day in harmony. They were once again sleeping in the same bedroom, and they talked about this and that all night long. Yoji spoke and Manyo responded in just the right ways.

Yoji also started walking around with Western books again. Carving out ten minutes in the morning and ten minutes in the evening, he read the books as if devouring them. The majority were novels from overseas in the original language. Almost as if he had remembered his pride from when he was an upper-class idler in the past, he would mutter a single line of a novel in fluent English and bring a cup of bukupuku tea to his lips.

One day that spring, Yoji rented a traditional banquet carriage on a train to entertain business clients. Inside, they were seated on expensive floor chairs, and the group passed over the Chugoku Mountains, traveling to Okayama, on the JR Benimidori line, while being served tempura and meals featuring mountain delicacies, which they enjoyed with local sake as they looked out at the cherry blossoms.

Yoji left in high spirits. *I'll be home later*, he informed Manyo, told his adopted son Yoshio a few things, and glanced into the studio where Kemari was working, as if worried. And then he looked out on the back-yard for a while.

It was after noon. The train was about to go over the Amanobe Bridge, which was scattered with cherry blossom petals and stretched across a deep ultramarine ravine halfway through the Chugoku mountains, when—for a mere instant—a surprisingly powerful yamaoroshi blew. The banquet carriage flew lightly up into the sky, and a warning bell sounded as the train shook violently, as if informing its passengers that it would keep ascending into the sky. And then when the wind died down, the vehicle tumbled head over heels amidst the scattering blossoms into the deep, dark valley far below the bridge.

The president of the Akakuchiba Steelworks, Yoji Akakuchiba, was sliced up by a piece of steel buckling falling from the ceiling as the carriage fell, and just as in his wife's vision, his head went flying and he died abruptly.

It took a very long time indeed to pull up the train from the bottom where it had landed, and a helicopter from a TV station in the capital even came to cover the event, circling all around the mountains. But the people of the Akakuchiba family knew that when they did bring it up, the president would have already lost his life.

The following morning, Toyohisa set Manyo in the passenger seat and drove the jeep at full speed over the mountain roads to the scene of the accident. The bridge, looking like thin wire soaring up above the ravine, reflected the morning light, and in the valley far below, they could see a lump of steel, a mere shadow of its former train self. The carriage was crushed, and pieces of it coiled about like ferocious black snakes. "Aah," Manyo murmured.

Toyohisa looked down into the ravine. "Sir! Hey, sir!" he cried in a small voice. He got no reply. "Young master! Heey! Master! Hey..." He dropped to his knees and crouched there. From behind, his body looked very small. He was almost an entirely different person from that young man of twenty who had been so clear and full of self-confidence.

"Heeey. Master..." Toyohisa began sobbing like a child. "Young master. Master..."

Above their heads, the news helicopter circled and roared.

In this way, Yoji Akakuchiba met his sudden death this spring when the rough waves of the bubble's collapse eddied and swirled. In a way, it was a death very much like that of his father, Yasuyuki, who had so long ago collapsed and died when the wave of the oil shock came along.

For a time, quite a fuss was made over the fact that riding in the fallen train had been the president of a major local company and the father of the famous manga artist. Aira undertook the interviews on Kemari's behalf, but as usual, she didn't understand the circumstances, so she simply gave whatever answers she felt like, and before long, the requests stopped coming. The son who had married into the family, Yoshio, was made the new captain of the Akakuchiba Steelworks ship, and once again, the company managed to make it through a difficult situation. Yoshio understood his own role only too well.

Remarkably, Kemari came out from her studio and bowed deeply before her husband. "Yoshio, please take care of us." He couldn't help thinking again that this wife who earned vast fortunes was still somehow a pitiable little girl. He nodded firmly, trying to reassure her, and stroked his wife's head gently, softly.

Under Yoshio's leadership, a new system was put in place at the company, and the enormous warship slowly began to change course under its new captain. Yoshio decided to abandon steel production, which was always in the red, and make the other manufacturing the company's main business.

That season, when it was made known that the fires of the blast furnace would go out at the end of the year, the one-eyed worker, Toyohisa Hozumi, was already knocking on fifty's door. Rather than fighting back, he simply muttered, "That so?" The death of his beloved niece, Namida's accidental death, and the death of Yoji, whom he had been at odds with, had aged Toyohisa a great deal, and he no longer talked much. And like many others at the plant, he would sometimes feel pain when he coughed.

"Toyo, that said, little Yoshio's still young. Stay with him, watch out for him," Manyo implored, but Toyohisa smiled wryly and shook his head.

"I can't be in a place where there's no blast furnace, Capital M. I'm a steel man."

Steel production wasn't booming the way it had been in the postwar period of strong economic growth, but even so, there were many plants left all over the country that were just managing to scrape by. Toyohisa listed a few factory names. Manyo had lost her reliable mother-in-law, her eldest son, her husband, and now even Toyohisa was going to leave her; she fell prostrate on the tatami and wept, lamenting the season of the setting sun.

In winter that year, the large snowflakes danced down. And at year's end, under Yoshio's orders, the fires of the blast furnace were put out. The Akakuchiba Steelworks blast furnace was a jet-black tower high in the sky. The blaze of the crimson lotus of molten iron burned, the black dragon of smoke puffed up every day. The familiar springs of steel. The bright postwar future. The steel fires that had made it through the oil shock and the iron chill, supporting so many, were now finally extinguished.

The blast furnace, cold now, soared eerily in the sky. It was a sinister black, a hole cut with scissors in the winter sky, with its mix of snow and rain.

One night, Manyo, sensing someone's presence, opened her eyes and found a letter by her head. Written in delicate, fine-lined characters was "Madam Manyo."

It was a farewell letter from Toyohisa. She hurried out into the hallway and sent her eyes flying out into the backyard; she felt she could see a slim back receding in the nighttime garden swirling with fat snowflakes. The letter apparently just said that he was going far away. Now that the red tatara flames had been put out, the Akakuchiba Steelworks was likely an empty place with no use for a steel man like Toyohisa. She had felt close to him ever since she saw him in her vision when she was a child all those years earlier, and his parting was exceedingly difficult for Manyo; she took to her bed for a while after that. All she had left was her friend from the old days, nicknamed the Goldfish, whom she had taken into the mansion, Midori Kurobishi.

Midori devoted herself to caring for Manyo. She sat by her bed and did magic tricks, sang songs from foreign lands, and combed out her silver hair every day. When night fell, they talked about the valley of the wild roses deep in the mountains they had arrived at in the long-distant past. Neither of them remembered anymore that path that wasn't actually a path, and they felt as though they would never reach that place again.

"Be nice to go there again, hm?"

"'Cause my brother's there an' all."

"But, y'know, I feel like we can once we die."

"Gotta be together, Manyo. No fun to go by yourself."

Receiving word of her father's death, Kaban, the playgirl in the capital, made her homecoming. In the aftermath of the bubble, the disco nights of the city had stopped being much fun. Everyone was stingy and talking about money, which put a damper on the entire proceedings. Her dream of becoming an actress was, of course, far off. Although she had occasionally taken the stage with a small theater group and managed to get bit parts on TV, her big chance still had not come along, and she was getting a little fed up with the capital. At her father's death, Kaban washed her hands of big city life and came home, single suitcase in hand. And then, she hung around the main family house for a while, taking care of me in place of her very busy older sister.

In the end, Akakuchiba Steelworks somehow managed to make it through the economic collapse. Yoshio's staff cutbacks and downsizing helped, but a large part of it was the eldest daughter, Kemari, who earned millions, pouring all of her royalties into the company.

Iron Angels! continued to sell through printing after printing. Once it was made into an evening anime program, everyone who wasn't already reading it, whether children or adults, started to. The enormous sums transferred to her bank account by her publisher and the royalties generated by things like the anime and merchandise went through her and poured into the Akakuchiba Steelworks, a golden river. Quite simply, an enormous, empty act.

Best-seller Kemari was always flat broke. But without time to use her earnings and no hobbies to speak of anyway, she continued to draw her manga as always. That was all there was. However, perhaps this, in the end, was what supported Kemari Akakuchiba as a manga artist.

In the singular world of shojo manga, where young artists saw large sums of money come rolling in, staying current over the long term was a thorny path, but Kemari somehow managed to survive for more than twelve years. Many young shojo manga artists came out with hit works at the same time she did, or even after she did, and each time one of them appeared, the industry clamored, "Here's a rival to Kemari Akakuchiba!" But these girls got hold of the big money, suffered mentally, and in only a few years—or even more short-term, a few months—disappeared from the industry.

In this world, the strong ones were those who needed to earn money and those who dreamed of getting rich quick. People paying back some kind of debt to their parents or with many mouths to feed lasted longer than the plain old hard workers. The same went for those who were disgusting in their fierce obsessions with money. The unsophisticated young people were bewildered by the large sums of money; their spirits were easily broken.

Streaking through the industry like comets, the promising new-comers swaggered along, dressed up for meetings like birds of paradise, all insolent and audacious, but they were unable to keep drawing, or unable to maintain their popularity if they could draw, and in a mere six months, inevitably, their faces would change into tragic masks at the burden they carried on their young shoulders. They would get unusually fat or slim down like a mummy. Pale and drawn out, they cried that they couldn't draw anymore and disappeared one after another into some secret hell. Once they disappeared, they never came back.

Even those who did manage to survive and stick around leveled up as they aged and vanished from the world of shojo manga in a few years. They moved from battlefield to battlefield, from that genre called "Young Adult" to the even older demographic of women's manga, and shifted from the brutality of weekly serialization to monthly or even bimonthly, holding on to just enough work so they could do it while raising their children or what have you.

However, Kemari Akakuchiba had absolutely nothing to do with this moving through the ranks. Her battlefield remained, as always, the weekly serialization. The characters in *Iron Angels!*, who had been in junior high at the start of the series, were around this time in high school; they had finally conquered Shimane and were setting their sights on unifying the whole of the Chugoku region. The girl mascot, seemingly modeled after Chocco, had dark eyes and was straying off course—the scent of death grew stronger around her. The manga traced reality. Single-minded, Kemari was recreating her own youth in the story. The golden river flowed into the Akakuchiba Steelworks and continued to prop it up.

Kemari left the childrearing to her mother, Manyo, occasionally asking her younger sister Kaban to babysit, and devoted herself to drawing her manga. I was raised by Manyo. At night, I sometimes cried, missing my mother, but when I climbed out of my grandmother's futon and went to her studio, a man in a suit who seemed to be the editor—from time to time, a different person would be switched in abruptly, but each of them was inevitably handsome—would stop me. He would pick me up and say, "Don't want to get in your mommy's way, do we?" before bringing me back to Manyo's bedroom. A child seeking her mother is in the way for adults, I suppose.

I was very lonely. Once in a while, I would find my mother walking down the hallway during the day and race over to her, but she would only stroke my head perfunctorily and return, muttering, to her studio.

It seemed like there was nothing in my mother's head besides the work she had to do. There was no room for the child she should have been raising or the family she should have been creating. She was eternally the tireless and stubborn twenty-year-old girl, burning with dreams. She never changed, no matter how old she got.

You could definitely say that this was because of how busy she was, but I suspect the truth was that she was maybe one of those women of that generation who found it hard to love the child she had given birth to. Taking in Chocco's death that day long ago, Kemari was aware that her own youth had ended, but that didn't mean she turned into a proper adult right away. I think my mother never actually managed to become that proper adult. She had been chased from the children's world of fiction, but unable to step into adulthood, her spirit wandered in that state between death and rebirth, a heavy blanket over the entire mansion.

Kemari selected and dated ugly boys, but didn't maintain any kind of relationship. She was married, but didn't create anything resembling a family with her husband; she didn't take responsibility and raise the child she bore. All she could do was draw manga. Kemari the manga artist ruled over the Akakuchiba house like a giant phantom, but the real Kemari, my mother, was a hollow woman ... This is something I resent. Because I wanted my mother to love me. Because I didn't want to be ignored like a piece of furniture.

At any rate, I'm sure that during this era, there were plenty of women besides Kemari who were capable but unable to live in the real world. The future Manyo had seen in the distant, distant past, when the notion that having and raising children was a woman's happiness was no longer self-evident, had long since come.

However, despite the fact that Kemari was unable to be an adult, she did have that sense of responsibility as the oldest daughter of an old family that she had to at least take care of the family.

Raised by my grandmother Manyo, ever since I can remember, I pestered her for stories about the past. More than any fairy tale, more than any children's story, I loved the tales of the old village of Benimidori Manyo would tell me in her sleepy voice. When I got a little older and I caught sight of my mother resting on the veranda during breaks from work, I would of course ask for old stories from her too. She found it annoying at first, but she came to see that sharing her childhood memories with her young daughter sharpened them, which was useful for drawing her manga, and so although she refused to raise me, she would sometimes make the time to tell me her stories. In this way, I slowly grew up, frolicking in the pasts of my grandmother and mother.

It was around the time I was five when Tamotsu Soho suddenly returned to the mansion. The instant I saw him, I knew he was the editor who had come climbing up the hill road of the steps, who appeared near the end of my mother's stories of the old days. At that point, we were already on the sixth handsome man "attached to Akakuchiba"— Yabukawa, who was, in fact, glued to my mother. For some reason, all the beautiful male editors collapsed as they accepted my mother's manuscripts as if the Fire Horse girl were sucking the life out of them.

"Soho, huh?" My mother, not the least bit surprised, didn't even lift her head at Soho's abrupt homecoming after an absence of eight years. "Been a while. What's up?"

"Hide me," Soho said, and then my mother was surprised, and here finally, she lifted her head to look at him. Soho was now working at a different midsize publisher and, naturally, still editing manga. He was very good at his job and was employed as the assistant editor-in-chief of a manga magazine. However, the week before, he had lost somewhere a hundred pages of the original manuscript of a certain big-shot manga artist.

"Again?"

"Aah..."

"Look for them, Soho."

"No, I did. They're nowhere. If I go back, they'll kill me. And I..."

"What?"

"I don't want this job anymore. I'm sick of it."

The life of a manga editor wasn't as short as that of an artist, but there were more than a few who burnt out and disappeared from the industry. The ones who didn't disappear got promoted and ended up in management, but either way, it was rare for someone to stay on the front line of expression for long. Soho had changed again and had a much fuller face now; he was not the handsome man he once had been. Furrowing her brow, my mother consented to his request.

"What the hell am I gonna do with you..."

Soho had given everything he had to producing her debut work, and to Kemari—who passed through this world revering duty—he could have been seen as a sort of benefactor. Back then, their contempt for each other grew too great, and they hadn't been able to ride out the wild waves of their smash hit. In their hearts, they pressed their hands together; in their heads, they sneered. Remembering that period, Kemari couldn't help feeling she owed Soho a huge debt.

So in addition to Midori Kurobishi, another curious person, this one going by the name of Tamotsu Soho, settled into the house like a boarder. Soon enough, a search party came from the big-shot manga artist looking for him, but just this once, Kemari herself came out instead of her body double, Aira, swung her steel weapon for the first time in a long time, and forcibly chased him off.

"I'll kill you!"

It was an absurd threat, but this single phrase shut the mouth of Soho's pursuer. After that, Soho stayed on, hanging out with Kodoku and playing video games, or grabbing little me and flaunting his vast erudition. Given how long he had been working as an editor, his knowledge was naturally correspondingly comprehensive. Soho's learning stretched out great distances like the night, from Iceland in the north to South Africa in the south. But this was the same Soho who was convinced still that Momoyo was the ghost of a housekeeper. And since no one had told him about the beautiful body double, Aira, he was also convinced that one of the two manga artists was a doppelganger, and he was afraid of her.

There was also apparently a time when her husband, Yoshio, suspected that Soho was his wife's lover, but everyone in the family knew that this was not the case. Because the man-stealing Momoyo didn't lay a single finger on Soho. She often came and went from Yoshio's bedroom, but she showed not the slightest interest in Soho, and Soho too slipped around avoiding the ghost, so it was all very clear to the eyes of the family.

Momoyo, after graduating from high school, moved around from job to job, working in accounting at the Benimidori Chamber of Commerce and Industry, the Japan Travel Bureau, and an automotive shop, among others. She never settled down in any one place; she would change jobs before a year was even up. Not marrying, not falling in love, having no friends. Until the winter of her twenty-ninth year in 1998, she lived for the sole purpose of sleeping with Kemari's men.

The battle between man-stealing Momoyo and Fire Horse Kemari kept on going. Kemari was as blind as ever to her half sister, and Momoyo was as single-minded as ever in her succession of sins. Kemari felt a love like sudden flames once in this time, an affair that lasted from '97 until the following year. The young man from the rice shop who regularly came to the house, an ugly man as was her wont. When it started, a tension raced through the family. Although Yoshio had no time to watch his wife while he inched the company along through stormy seas, the women came together to gossip surreptitiously.

"Here we go again. That girl's libido won't fix itself," one murmured, and Kaban, who at that time was still kicking around the mansion, twisted up lips painted bright red and nodded.

"It really won't. Not when it's that bad."

"Mm-hmm."

"Kemari's perversion, Momoyo's obsession, they'll never get over them. It'll just keep going until one of them dies."

"But I do wonder why Kemari can't see Momoyo."

Kemari came along down the hallway in front of the two women whispering together, and Momoyo passed her on quick feet. Kemari walked straight ahead without hesitation, as if she had no idea Momoyo was there, and Momoyo silently gave way.

The conceit of being the eldest child, born from the belly of the legal wife, made Kemari glow in the mansion unawares. Momoyo was the shadow. Every night, wherever Kemari was, the lights would shine noticeably brightly, but it was the opposite wherever Momoyo was. No matter what a shadow might do, it can't be seen from inside the light.

Kemari was truly smitten with the young man from the rice shop, and so, in the blink of an eye, he was taken from her by the invisible woman. The young man also had a wife and child, but he immediately lost his head over Momoyo. Kemari was half crazed. But when the wife of the young man came along, baby in arms, and complained to her about her younger sister Momoyo, Kemari had no idea what she was talking about. The wife was frothing at the mouth with anger, and Kemari ran around the house.

"Come out, Momoyo or whoever you are! Get your ass out here!" she shouted, but Momoyo fled from the angered older girl and inexplicably climbed the beech tree in the backyard to hide there. Eyes like sharpened swords, Kemari ran through the labyrinthine hallways of the mansion, the collar of her kimono exposed. Manyo and Kaban tried to hold her back, explaining that Momoyo was there, that she had always been there. They were both crying. *She looks like this and this, she's been in our house since she was ten, see, that time, this time. She's been in that room there.*

Kemari didn't believe it. She whirled her head around and brushed her hair back. "There's no way I wouldn't have seen her if she was here. There's no way she's invisible to me. There's no such thing as invisible."

Tears scattered on her bared, dark skin. The mother and two

daughters hugged each other and wept, wailing. "She's here. She's here. Momoyo is," the mother said, and the younger sister wept, "Momoyo took Nojima from you and Yamanaka. She's always all Kemari, Kemari all the time. All she sees is you."

Kaban said she didn't know which of them she was crying for. To her, they were both her older sisters, related by blood. They both seemed equally foolish, and she was sad about both of them.

"Come out, Momoyo! Come out, Momoyo! Come out, Momoyo!" Kemari chanted like a Buddhist prayer. "If you're here, then show yourself and tell me why you steal my boyfriends. If you got something to say, then say it!"

At the commotion in the Akakuchiba house, the wife of the young man was frightened and went home, leaving behind Kemari, running through the labyrinth even after night fell, searching for her younger sister—"Momoyoooo! Momoyoooo!"—her face the spitting image of the *hannya* Noh mask of a woman driven mad with jealousy. In one hand, she held an iron axe, blood flowed from her eyes, red like rivers of molten iron, and she raced along the smooth hallways. The blaze of her maddening jealousy had the solid weight of a malice Kemari had never displayed before, casual as she had always been with men. But she had lost her youth while she had been so utterly focused on her work and had gotten older before she knew it, so perhaps it was exactly because it was this time in her life that she suddenly went mad. Weeping, Manyo and Kaban chased after her as she ran around with the axe.

She stopped unexpectedly, eyes shining red. When they looked in the direction Kemari was facing, in the distant darkness of the backyard, something heavy fell to the earth with a thud as if the blood-red gaze had shot it down.

Kemari took a deep breath. Then she brandished the axe and raced down into the garden, a red wind.

"I found you, Momoyooo!"

The thing that had fallen into the pond fled wordlessly. In the gloom, Kemari alone was surefooted as she ran; Manyo and Kaban said they could only follow the small footsteps the girl left behind in the dark garden with their eyes. They heard the slam of the door to the backyard closing, and Momoyo disappeared. She didn't return to the house after that, and when they found her the next morning, she was completely different.

The nets of the fishermen at the port at Nishiki caught a woman who appeared to have thrown herself in, both feet bound. Her hands were hooked, as if clutching something, and this was because she had tried to drag along the young man from the rice shop in a forced lovers' suicide. On the verge of being pulled into the water, the young man had escaped and his strength gave out in the rice shop storeroom, where he stayed shivering and shaking until morning. The suicide note Momoyo had left was in his hand. Delivered to the mansion, the shaky characters of the note read, "We die together." Yoshio read this out loud in a trembling voice, and Manyo went white as a sheet and fainted.

Once Momoyo had died, accidentally alone, Kemari quieted as if her demons had been exorcised. On the day of the funeral, Kemari picked up the photo of the dead girl amidst the white flowers and cocked her head. "So this is Momoyo? This is really Momoyo?" she asked uncertainly.

From the mouth of every family member came the question, *You really never saw her?* Kemari tilted her head to one side. "No," she said. "Where the hell was she all this time?" Peering into the coffin, she saw the unfamiliar woman lying there silently. The dark eyes that had stared at her older sister from the shadows of pillars, from the tops of joists, from the undersides of desks were now shut tightly and reflected nothing at all.

She could see Momoyo now that she was a corpse. Kemari cocked her head like a child and peered at the dead face, puzzled. "You're Momoyo? You're Momoyo?"

And then again, Kemari's face was pale and ominous, as if possessed accidentally by the dead person.

This was in 1998, and the world was approaching the end of the century. The Akakuchiba Steelworks was stable somehow through downsizing, and Kemari continued to draw her manga as usual. The story, serialized for over ten years, filled more than forty volumes. Readers all over the country wept at the scene when the mascot based on Chocco died. They were already on the tenth handsome male editor, Hashibami. Also in the house besides the family were Midori Kurobishi, the body double Aira, and the erudite Soho.

At a family meeting, talk of Kaban marrying into one of the branch families came up. Kaban, already in her late twenties, murmured, "S'pose it's getting to be that time." The branch family son was also someone she had known since childhood, and Kaban's attitude was easy: "If it's him, then I guess it's okay."

That year, I, Toko Akakuchiba, was only nine years old. I had no idea whatsoever about Kemari's fit of madness since I was sleeping or something that night, but I remember Momoyo's funeral very well.

Just maybe, maybe…I think the real truth of it was that my mother had actually been able to see her little sister Momoyo. Although we'll never know now. Either way, a clairvoyant woman was a natural dreamer, and a manga artist woman was a natural liar. The old stories my grandmother and my mother told me were their own subjective tales and nothing more. What bothers me now is that short, one-off story originally submitted to the contest by my mother, before she poured more than twelve years of her life into the serialization of *Iron Angels!* That genuine piece of shojo manga, depicting the clash of the protagonist and her rival in love, the pages scattered with rose petals that were too cute for Kemari Akakuchiba. However, since no one could say it was well done, even as empty flattery, and it was also a losing entry, it was never published in the magazine. No one ever had the chance to see it, but there was a copy quietly tucked away in a drawer in my mother's studio, which I found and read.

The truth is, the rival in love in it has exactly the same features, the same way of speaking, everything, as her younger sister Momoyo Akakuchiba. The similarity is so great that Kemari really couldn't get away with saying she couldn't see Momoyo.

She *could* see her. She *could* see her. She could see *her*. By ignoring her, the Fire Horse Kemari had perhaps bullied and killed the man-stealing Momoyo…

That said, I can't press Kemari for answers and ask her about her true intentions, not anymore. The summer of that same year, 1998, Kemari went on another trip. The final chapter of the long serialization of *Iron Angels!*, which had gone on for over twelve years, was taken up with the protagonist's retirement from the gang through a final, deciding battle in an abandoned parking garage. When she finished drawing the manuscript, my mother smiled at me; I had been amusing myself by helping her. "Toko, thanks." She stood up, and as she headed toward the futon spread out in the nap room next door, she said, in a small voice, "Chocco's here, so I guess that means I'm going?"

Her tone was light. Unlike her usual persona, the difficult, bestselling manga artist, she sounded carefree, like she was enjoying herself, somehow strangely girlish. Applying the tone, something I had learned to do by watching, I offered some vague reply, before suddenly becoming aware of something and lifting my head.

"Mom...?" I opened the sliding doors and went into the nap room.

Kemari had collapsed on the futon and was already dead. I went to help her up, but she was leadenly heavy, like a dead animal, and my child's hands had nowhere near the strength needed to lift her. I ran out into the hallway, calling for someone, anyone, and Soho came running. Tumbling into the room, he stared down at my fallen mother. "Hey. Kemmy." His voice was curiously dry and cold. The family then gathered, and her husband, Yoshio, was called home from the office.

The tenth beautiful man editor, Hashibami, dashed in, snatched up the manuscript of the final chapter laid out on the desk, and pasted the last of the tone in. He raced to the post office, sent the manuscript of the final chapter, and then flew over to the wooden NTT building to send a telegram.

KEMARI AKAKUCHIBA SUDDEN TRIP STOP CANT STOP STOP HASHIBAMI

The telegram turned into light, flew off into the night sky, and arrived at the publisher in Tokyo.

Maybe Choko Hozumi really did come for her. And in the end, my mother never did become an adult. No longer a child, but unable to grow up, like so many other girls of her generation. Kemari struggled between death and rebirth for this short time, those ten years; she suffered, she drifted not knowing her path, and then she left on her trip on a night in the summer of the thirty-second year of that rare fighter and manga artist, Fire Horse Kemari Akakuchiba.

And here, I end the tale of the age of the enormous and the empty, encompassing youth and loss and the battle between a set of sisters. I, Toko Akakuchiba, was nine.

I do think that's a bit early to be separated from your mother.

PART THREE

MURDERER

2000–FUTURE: TOKO AKAKUCHIBA

1. WILD ROSE

And in this way, we finally arrive here, the present. Your storyteller, Toko Akakuchiba, has no new tales of her own to recount. Really, not even one.

I am Manyo's unworthy granddaughter. Aah, honestly. I'd die so I could apologize to her, but I'd prefer to keep living.

After I was separated from my mother by death at age nine, my aging grandmother raised me in this old family, which had fallen back into silence and sadness. With the switch to the manufacturing business, my father changed the name of Akakuchiba Steelworks to Red Dead Leaf, Inc.—basically the characters of our last name translated into English—and kept things on course there. The enormous, ancient warship continued its journey, navigating those rough waters.

The royalties earned by my mother, that unparalleled shojo manga artist, all went at every turn to help the company, even after she was gone.

Without fail, a scene from my mother's manga appeared in the company newsletter distributed each month, where it was noted that she had been the company president's wife. Automation continued apace; the amount of manual work was ever on the decline, as was the number of employees, down to who knew what fraction of the company's heyday. Even so, however, the steelworks continued to give the young people of Benimidori precious employment opportunities.

The Akakuchiba mansion fell into disrepair, and most of the inner rooms were no longer used. The number of housekeepers also decreased at the same time. The gardeners grew old and died one after another, and because no new gardener was hired to replace them, the wonderful backyard that my grandmother had so loved became ridiculously overgrown, burning red in autumn like an ancient tatara forest. At the start of the 2000s, the years of my adolescence, five of us lived in the mansion: me, my grandmother Manyo, my uncle Kodoku, and the boarders Midori Kurobishi and Tamotsu Soho. My father came home late at night and left again early in the morning, so he was a shadowy nonentity; you never knew if he was there or not.

The bright red mansion, former ruler over Benimidori, the town's distant heavens, had over the course of the years absorbed the air of modernity without anyone noticing it and now appeared to be a perfectly normal house in the mountains. Except that sometimes, even though there was no wind, the roof shook and the red trees in the backyard writhed. This happened when my grandmother showed herself. Perhaps because of her efforts to maintain the house, the wrinkles carved into her face were too deep for her relative youth. When the large, silent

Manyo walked down the hallways, hem of her red kimono flapping, long silver hair swinging, the woods would stir, and for the slightest of instants, the mansion seemed to regain its air of mystery from the age of legend. Manyo was still the grande dame of the Akakuchiba main family, and everyone took her existence in and of itself as the anchor for their own spirits.

Kaban was in the main house for a long time, staking her claim on the high-class slacker role her father had once occupied, but in her late twenties, she married the son of a branch family, a boy she had known since childhood. She had four children who usually kept her quite busy at the branch house, but lately, she seemed to leave all of that to the housekeepers to ascend the hill road on days when the weather was nice, coming back to the main house for tea before returning to her married home. When she found me, she would point out into the garden, biting into a manju bun, and reminisce fondly.

"See? That beech tree there? That's where Momoyo went and hid. Then she fell out into the pond below it and ran away," she informed me. "And then she said something about 'we die together,' and she died by herself. Now that I'm thinking about it, not long after that, Kemari died too, hm."

The Filipina Aira, Kemari's body double, disappeared unexpectedly after my mother's death, all of which was a long time ago. Life in the Akakuchiba main house was unhurried, with a curious lineup of people, an erratic pseudo family brought together by happenstance, not your usual nuclear family.

I attended the local public junior high school before going on to an entirely normal, coed high school. As one might expect from my name, made up of the characters for "eyes" and "child" as it is, my eyes were fairly big and attractive, but I had neither my mother's arresting beauty nor Manyo's power. I was, in other words, a regular girl. Which is perhaps exactly why I was drawn to the tales of the Akakuchiba women, my grandmother and my mother. They had a glittering past, a history; they were my roots. Me, nothing more than a normal, young girl. When I thought about them, I felt a certain worth in myself too.

Ours was a family with many deaths, so there was quite the commotion at the household altar pretty much every morning when my grandmother Manyo lit the incense. Pictures of my great-grandfather and grandmother Yasuyuki and Tatsu; my grandfather Yoji; my uncle Namida; my mother, Kemari; and my aunt Momoyo adorned the wall. When Manyo prayed, calling out the names of the dead in order, the Goldfish granny Midori Kurobishi next to her would also call out the names of her own parents, husband, and brother. The smoke of the incense shimmered purple like the smoke of the tokonen grass in the distant days recounted in the stories and hung in the air of the house. Coughing, I would run down the smooth hallways—"Okay, I'm off!"—and leave for school. Manyo would interject a small "See you later" into her prayer.

I would step outside, the scent of incense still clinging to me as I started down the hill road, looking down at the depopulated apartment buildings of the steps, in such decline that they were already essentially ruins. The enormous blast furnace, fires put out long ago, rose up darkly in the hazily gray sky. The town administration had talked to us about pulling it down because it was getting old, but I knew that my father had no idea how to broach the subject while my grandmother was still alive.

The clairvoyant madam of the Akakuchibas, aka my grandmother Manyo, passed away soon after I turned twenty, and with that, my father finally proceeded with the demolition of the blast furnace to transform the old plant site into a vacant lot, but I'm getting a little ahead of myself here. First, we should talk about when my grandmother was still alive, when I was in high school.

My uncle Kodoku was a little over thirty. Once he passed the high school equivalency exam, he attended a regional university and then locked himself up in the house again after graduation. Later, at my father's suggestion, he got a job at Red Dead Leaf. He wasn't particularly passionate about the work, however, and spent his days off locked up in his room, as always, immersed in his video games. Having been a misanthrope since junior high, he was definitely not one to initiate any kind of human contact, but he was really very fond of me as his niece.

Normally, he was reserved and so inconspicuous in the mansion that it was almost eerie, but during the Western Tottori Earthquake that hit the region in 2000, he bravely volunteered his body without the slightest hesitation, to protect me in the backyard, and was seriously injured by a falling metasequoia, which broke his leg. He worried excessively about me, the daughter of his prematurely dead older sister Kemari, and tried to shelter me from everything. For my part, as a child, I was deeply attached to this weird, kindhearted uncle, and on rainy days, I would hang out for hours in his room, just as my mother had in days past.

As for the freeloader Tamotsu Soho, he shamelessly continued to live in the Akakuchiba house, despite the fact that the manga artist who had been his connection to the family was dead. He was in his mid-forties, but he seemed to have no interest in working. Once, he turned on the TV and they were explaining what these NEETs—young people not in education, employment, or training—were about exactly. "Oh! That's me!" He laughed lightheartedly.

"Tamo, a NEET's someone who holes up in their own house. You're in someone else's house," I told him cheekily.

He nodded, looking serious. "That's true."

Soho's erudition even then spanned vast distances. When he talked, he naturally drew on this extensive knowledge, so to my child's mind, he was a fascinating old man.

"Did you know, Toko? In pre-Meiji Japan, when they were translating the English word 'love,' there was no perfect fit for it in Japanese. In other words, the concept of romantic love itself didn't exist. Our current fickle love fad came from the West."

"Oh, I knew that."

"You did? Well, how about this? There's a tribe in Micronesia that doesn't have a word for sadness."

"Huh. I didn't know that."

"The closest word they have is 'fago,' but it means something like when you see someone suffering, you empathize, you suffer with them. There's no word to express the pain in your own heart. No need for it. Those are some pretty nice people, right? I mean, just think about it, Toko. They have this concept of being distressed about someone else's sadness, but they have no way to be sad about their own sadness. Even though we humans are basically obsessed with our own sadness, y'know? I mean, we have this tendency to think everything's fine as long as *we're* okay."

"Yeah…"

"And I heard about a tribe in Africa where the women marry each other. They make their kids with a close male relative of their partner, see? And then the women live together. Pretty surprising, right? Don't you breathe a little easier at the fact that the common sense of the world we live in is not common sense everywhere you go?"

As I grew up, I realized that in Soho's erudition was inevitably a longing for some other cultural sphere that did not exist for him. Although he was a handsome man with a higher education, he had stopped working in his mid-thirties and had been devoting himself to the life of a high-class slacker ever since, but he still seemed to have some of that curious proactive spirit so particular to the generation who had known the bubble. I can't help but think that his knowledge was backed by the conviction that his train would most certainly arrive at some life better than the one he was living now, in some culture more satisfying than this one. This was a quality my generation lacked. We had almost no understanding of such a feeling. I simply drifted my way to adulthood, in this country where everything was already over.

And so, we come back to my story.

After starting high school, I joined the brass band, which I had also been in in junior high. I didn't inherit the wonderful physique of my grandmother or my mother—I was a very small girl—but despite this,

I played a surprisingly large trumpet. I would blow with my entire body and sound would come out of it.

Because of depopulation and the declining birth rate, there were fewer students at the prefectural Benimidori High School, and they were overly passionate about extracurricular activities. After school, the members of the baseball team, the soccer team, and the track and field team shouted and raced around the schoolyard, while the band played inside the school building. The white curtains fluttered in the breeze, and when we peered out the windows, the Chugoku Mountains soared lush and green off in the distance, endless rice fields spreading out before them. The scent of earth filled our noses. Around the time that we band members packed it in and walked home, laughing together, the baseball team were the only ones still there, running around the field, dirt-covered uniforms illuminated by the setting sun.

I—no, none of us average high school students had any real ambition. We were often lectured at length by our homeroom teacher on this very subject. About how we should be fired up with what we wanted to be and impossible dreams while we were young, how we should be burning with a sense of righteousness and trying to change the world, how we should live like fire. "You kids are missing what it means to be young." What *does* it mean to be young? I suppose apathy and depression in and of themselves are not the disease that is youth.

The path ahead of us was broad; there were so many things we had to do. An uneasy season, riding in a small boat shrouded in mist. That's how I felt about my adolescence. Which is exactly why I wanted to be kind to those classmates who happened to be riding in that same small boat with me. We took care of each other, we worked together to at least enjoy our lives at that moment. Frame of mind was everything. We got a good hold on the mood of the place and let ourselves get carried away in conversation with each other so that we wouldn't float off. After getting excited with our friends, we were a little tired. What we really wanted was to talk; what we couldn't manage to get out of our mouths was the hazy, heavy feeling writhing around in the depths of our hearts.

There was just one thing that did spark fire in us. Anything related to love. On this subject alone, we were allowed to burn without bounds, we agreed silently among ourselves. My classmates fell in love, broke up, and then found their next boyfriend. And me, to speak of Toko, when I was in grade eleven, I fell into the most garden variety of romances.

Yutaka Tada was in my class. We went to different junior highs, so I only learned of his existence in high school. His father, a police officer at the local Benimidori police box, was one of the children of the Tada couple who had taken in and raised Manyo. Yutaka was on the baseball team, and before I even knew it, my eyes started chasing after him, around the second term of grade ten, whenever I cut across the schoolyard on my way home from band practice.

He had relatively clean-cut features and was popular with the girls. After his grade twelve teammates retired to focus on university entrance exams, he became the team's best player. When Yutaka swung the bat, the white ball danced up into the evening sky, flying endlessly, farther and higher, until it disappeared. I stopped and followed it with my eyes. So far, so high...it was dazzling, a longing in me. Ours was an age when people did not often get so hot, but that didn't mean we hated the passionate people of our generation. Rather, we simply cheered them on, those people with the special passion and talent to accomplish the things we ourselves couldn't. The ambitionless tend not to get particularly jealous of the ambition of other people.

Yutaka was always hot and sweating. Back then, he was one of the cool kids with a particular brilliance that attracted the eye, so I became the target of envy for the other girls when we started going out. The summer of grade twelve was all about the qualifying tournament for the big Koshien national baseball tournament, and the brass band went out to the prefectural stadium in the fierce heat every day to play our encouragement. My trumpet glittered gold against the summer sky. Yutaka hit several home runs in a row, and thanks to him, in a remarkable turn, in this last summer of high school, Benimidori High ended up going to Koshien. The whole village was thrilled, and a bus to Koshien was chartered. Yutaka was the town hero.

"You just have to do what you can," Yutaka said that summer, a small smile coming to his face as we strolled along the arcade street in front of the station on what could hardly be called a date.

The arcade street had essentially been a ruin during my mother's youth, but now, many small shops catering to younger people had opened up, and although progress was modest, the area was starting to get its former vibrancy back. Played out here time and again was the story of the young person who had gone to the capital in the days of the bubble only to lose their youth with the passage of time, and their job and assets with the recession, and inevitably return to the region to start a business. At any rate, they made enough money to keep open the previously closed shutters of the family shop, and most importantly, since they didn't have to pay rent, they were able to turn their hobbies into jobs. We young people didn't have much in the way of allowances, so no great sums of money were dropped here, but the arcade street was the perfect lazy date spot, a bit of wandering through shops full of accessories and clothes, having a cup of tea when you got cold. That this place had once been the den of delinquent girls and boys was the long distant past.

"Because you can't do what you can't do, even if you try to force yourself. I think that's the only way I can shine."

"Cool as a cucumber, eh, Yutaka?"

"Nah, I'm still fighting the pressure. The mayor's really laying it on us. And your dad's even paying attention; he brought rice and sake over." A sad smile rose up to his lips as he spoke, not quite the stuff of heroes.

We walked along lazily, and local high school students and female junior high students in particular squealed as they surrounded Yutaka. They made a big fuss—"You can do it, we're rooting for you"—and then glared glancingly at me by his side. We didn't hate those with special abilities, but we were intensely jealous of the people who received their favor. I often found weird things in my shoe locker around that time. Most of it was garbage or lumps of dirt. But I wasn't full of myself or anything because Yutaka was famous. I mean, I was me; the fact that I was a regular girl hadn't changed one bit.

That summer, the people of Benimidori got on a chartered bus and headed east. East. East. We crossed the prefectural border and kept racing along until we reached Koshien Stadium. We cheered our team on with everything we had; the band played until we collapsed, and the adults yelled their hearts out. But Benimidori High lost in the second round. Despondent, I fell asleep on the bus, and when I came to again, the sun had set completely. We finally got back to the village in the middle of the night, burned by the sun, drenched in sweat. And then, the summer was over.

Looking back on it now, I feel like my youth was so utterly ordinary. I met Yutaka, worked hard in band, had fun with my friends. My grandmother was always waiting for me when I got home. Depopulation had definitely eaten away at the village. I live in the modern age and I have no passion. Perhaps I grew colder bit by bit after that day when the tatara flames, which had been with the Akakuchibas from ancient times, were snuffed out. The extinguished fire of the blast furnace. Those ferocious flames. The glittering future. Days past.

When I graduated from high school, I went on to a junior college in the region. I studied half-heartedly; I worked part-time at a crepe shop in front of the station; I had quiet fun with my friends. When we were nineteen, Yutaka and I fought over something stupid and broke up, but we got back together again after about six months. We had both tried dating other people, both decided that our original partner was better after all, and both come back to each other. I'm not what you'd call a particularly self-confident woman, so I was concerned about how I would stack up now that Yutaka had dated other girls. The way he was in bed had changed subtly, which secretly hurt me very deeply. After he graduated from high school, he got a job with a company in the area, but he quit that job when we broke up and had started working for a different company by the time we got back together.

Yutaka's father was a police officer, and he lived with his wife and son in a two-bedroom wooden bungalow behind the residential police box. Yutaka wanted to move out on his own, but when he thought about how much money he was making, he realized he could either live by himself or have a car. He decided on the car, and on our days off, we often went driving together. We met frequently at the old love hotel The Chateau along the national highway, always in the same light blue room with the round bed, so I gradually started to feel like we were living there.

I loved Yutaka, but that feeling isn't particularly worth discussing here. As often happens, a woman simply becomes fond of a certain man. We sometimes talked about love, but we were both of the same opinion. There was no such thing as a soul mate. We women and men simply choose a partner we run into and happen to get along with, and then we stick together. If the circumstances were different, perhaps we would have paired ourselves off with someone else. And that's fine. We had chosen each other and were together now; we were satisfied with that.

From grade eleven to twelve, Yutaka was famous. He had a lifetime's worth of being in the spotlight, but when he left baseball, he abruptly became a regular person. He seemed to understand this in his head, but it still mystified him in his heart. My affection was unrelated to his fame; I liked him for who he was, but maybe I wasn't able to communicate that feeling very well. Maybe I would have been able to if he had been just a friend. Sometimes, things don't come out the way you want them to precisely because the conversation's between a woman and a man.

"If I was gone, you'd still be able to go on living and everything, right?"

"Yeah, I guess so ... I think I'd get through it somehow."

"Right? Although if I lost you, I'd die."

"Liar."

"Yeah, I'm a big fat liar, Toko."

We'd have cool conversations as we sang karaoke at the love hotel with the doubtful name mashing English and French together or report to each other the trifling incidents that had happened when we were apart, hanging out in a laid-back, lazy sort of way.

Yutaka didn't seem to really grasp that he was a grown man, that he was no longer the hero of the baseball team. He would leave for work in the morning, come home at night, go for drives with his lover on his days off. He was worlds away from the rough masculinity my grandfather had shown Manyo, and he steadily grew calmer and more distant from that masculinity. His carriage was supple, and he was always gentle and kind, almost to the point where he was no different from my female friends.

And that's about all there is to tell about us.

Something on the level of an incident happened when we were a little over twenty, involving the death of my grandmother and a flying person. It was a mysterious episode, strangely upsetting to our would-be tranquil spirits.

After I graduated from junior college, I got a job at one of the local businesses with the intention of building up some work experience, but it was boring and I soon quit. Lazing about the house, I felt fenced in even though I had nothing but free time; it was that kind of life. People kept saying that the economy, which had been in a recession since the collapse of the bubble, was recovering bit by bit, but the number of people who were stuck at home unemployed remained constant. A lot of my friends actually worked part-time jobs but couldn't get anything full time, and some of the ones that did land in a good place after graduating from a four-year university soon wanted to leave those jobs. I was surrounded by young, high-class slackers. No matter what we did, it was impossible for us to take professional pride in our work, to fight each day and feel like hard work was worth it. The world had moved forward higher and ever higher and then flipped around so that, like Midori's older brother who had slipped and fallen to the very bottom of the steps way back when, we were all now slapping down against the ground.

With no great ambition, I also didn't really have any desire to spend wads of cash on anything, so I wasn't particularly interested in earning money or in going out all the time. I was robbed of even my sense of self; the thought of being in the world, of being someone never crossed my mind. I was loath to bow my head or nod along at things I didn't agree with. And then—how to put it—the oppressiveness of the days as I grew into adulthood. I remembered anew that my name was supposed to have been "Jiyu," I was supposed to have been "Freedom," and I would agonize over it. Was I free in the end, simply loafing around like I was, never having to worry about where my next meal would come from? What is freedom for us? What on earth is freedom for a woman?

I was lying around the house, wrestling with these questions, when my grandmother Manyo called me. Filled with trepidation that she was going to lecture me, I headed toward the living room where she was

sitting casually, bukupuku tea set out before her. Her dark skin was a
little thicker and wrinkled now, and the long hair that had in the past
gleamed ebony was completely silver, but sitting there like that Manyo
still had a real aura of power, and I saw my grandmother once again as
the woman they called the clairvoyant madam of the Akakuchibas. She
was wearing a kimono the color of decaying leaves, obi belt loosely tied,
and just as she had in her girlhood, rather than tying her long hair up,
she let it hang loose down her back. When I sat down next to her and
began to drink the tea, she narrowed her sharp, large eyes and stared at
the face of her unworthy granddaughter.

"How you been lately?"

"Um, the usual."

"That so?"

I speared a bean from my tea and popped it in my mouth. "I dunno,"
I said, munching on it. "It's like I can't find anything I want to do. No,
more than that? It's like I totally can't even find the passion I need to
figure out what I want to do. You know what I mean, Grandma?"

"That's a problem, hmm," Manyo replied, unhurriedly, rather than
going on about how I was spoiled or how nice it was that I had such a
luxury, like the majority of adults did.

As I drank my tea, I remembered something Manyo had told me
ages ago. About the Manyo who had replied "I got enough" when Midori
Kurobishi taunted her for being an uncivilized country girl. A penni-
less, illiterate stray. And yet she was satisfied—poor of spirit as I was, I
couldn't help but find this Manyo unfathomable.

I was convinced "I don't got enough." The thought "I'm not satisfied with this" ran through my head just about every day. But I could also hear another voice admonishing me, "This is fine. You can't live your life with outsized expectations." The "it's not enough" was a shriek in my heart, while the admonishing "this is fine" was the voice of the times I lived in. That's what it felt like. I was so anxious I wanted to scream out loud. But what would I scream?

And surrounding my ill-defined anxiety and dissatisfaction was the still air of the depopulated village. I was at a loss for how to express all this, but I felt at ease next to my grandmother, so I said nothing in the end and just drank my tea. My grandmother looked up at the peaks of the Chugoku Mountains off in the distance beyond the backyard that I could see through the open veranda doors.

"I s'pose they forgot." Her voice sounded a little sad.

"Huh? Forgot what?" I asked.

"Me." Manyo smiled.

"Who did?"

"The mountain people."

"They couldn't have just forgotten you and left you behind," I said, with a force partially fueled by shock, and her eyes clouded over sadly. Her face staring off at the distant mountains weakened slightly, tinged with a dark shadow that seemed out of character for my normally stout-hearted grandmother.

"Perhaps not."

"Yeah, definitely not."

"Then I wonder why they did leave me there."

I tried to say something in response, but I was at a loss for words.

This older woman was my grandmother, but she was also an abandoned little girl. A deep affection for her welled up in me. *I love my grandmother*, I thought. We stayed silent like this, the two of us, sipping our tea, until Midori came down the hallway and instead of passing by, added herself to our number. With my grandmother, I had another cup of tea as I watched Midori's magic tricks, and the three of us spent a leisurely afternoon together.

This was the last day I drank tea and chatted with my grandmother Manyo Akakuchiba. Right around this time, Red Dead Leaf had been instructed by the town administration to take down the blast furnace and turn the area into an empty lot, so everyone at the company was incredibly busy. The administration and some citizens' groups were singling out the ancient blast furnace as an earthquake hazard prone to collapse. But demolishing it required time and effort, and most of all, money. My father and Kodoku were fairly discouraged and rarely came home from the office. When they did, they clapped their hands together as if in prayer at the large figure of my grandmother, silver hair shining, walking in the backyard or passing by in the hallway. The clairvoyant madam, her presence was even then the rock on which our hearts rested.

However, during this time when we still all relied on her like this, a few days after our chat over tea, Manyo began to rush about, cleaning her room and organizing her kimono.

Passing by, I stopped and asked, "Grandma, what's wrong?"

"It's getting to be time for me to die, so I'm cleaning up," she said dreamily.

I stood there gaping, and feeling my eyes on her, my grandmother slowly lifted her face. The red evening light coming through the transom illuminated the wrinkles in her dark skin. She wasn't the sort of person to kid about something like that, but I tried to convince myself it was a joke anyway. Because losing my grandmother was so terrible I couldn't even imagine it. I laughed it off.

"That's still a long way away. And we all still need you and everything. I mean, c'mon, Grandma—"

"I'm going to die tomorrow morning," she murmured, again as if talking in her sleep, perhaps without even hearing me. A chill raced up my spine. It abruptly occurred to me that what Manyo was saying was true. The thought made me nervous, and I spent the whole night going back and forth between our rooms. I felt like if I told someone, they'd laugh at me and say she was just teasing me, but I couldn't forget that chill going up my spine.

Halfway through the night, the light in her room went out. I squatted down in the hallway and looked at the pale moon shining in the night sky high above the backyard. Maybe my grandmother really was going to die. For me, having lost my mother and been raised as the unworthy only child of the main family, Manyo, more than anyone or anything, was my heart's anchor. My model for how to live as a woman of the main family, how to support the house from the shadows, was none other than shining, silver, large Manyo. I was still young, a nobody, a dull girl who had absolutely no idea how to live. *If Grandma dies*, I thought, and just that was enough to blur my vision. I wiped away the tears that spilled out with the back of my hand and heaved with silent sobs.

After about an hour like this, I sat there vacantly. And then when I couldn't stand it anymore, I licked my index finger to wet it and poked a hole in the paper of the sliding door. Peering into the room, I saw Manyo sitting at her dressing table with her back to me. Although she was supposedly an adult, that back looked unusually small. The mirror of her dressing table reflected her face etched with wrinkles, but her eyes weren't looking my way. They were open wide, seeing something. *Maybe the future.* I was uneasy at the thought. Manyo had continued to see the future all this time, even now. And that night too, she looked as though she were trying to see something that was invisible to everyone else.

"…didn't know."

I heard a low voice. I perked my ears up.

"It was just, I was embarrassed…didn't say nothing."

Who on earth was she talking to? I felt bad for spying on her and quietly pulled my face away from the door. I went back to my own room. An hour or so passed, I got anxious again, and I set out down the hallway so that my feet didn't make any noise. I felt like the backyard had taken on a sinister darkness that went beyond the dark of night. A single dried, reddish-black leaf fell gently, floating down to my feet despite the lack of wind.

I quietly peeked in through the hole I had made in the door earlier. And then I swallowed my breath.

Manyo was lying on her back on her futon, eyes firmly closed. The silver hair that reached down to her waist was spread out on the futon like an enormous glittering fan. *It's like the fan of a god*, I thought. Wrinkles were carved into her swarthy skin, and a long suffering you couldn't see when her eyes were open drifted across her face. It occurred to me that Manyo wasn't sleeping, but had in fact collapsed, and so I murmured, "Grandma," and opened the sliding door. A strong wind blew, and the garden shuddered. I lifted her heavy, large body into my arms, and Manyo groaned. It was a low, short moan like that of an animal. I shrieked and called for my father.

My father, who was at the back door having returned from the office at precisely that moment, came running down the hallway. But Midori Kurobishi coming from within the house was faster. Kodoku also woke up, and the doctor was called. I clung tightly to Midori's rugged body and cried myself hoarse.

"Grandma, Grandma!" Half crazed. "It's too soon. I'm such a mess—you can't leave me like this. The Akakuchiba family still needs its clairvoyant madam."

I felt that if Manyo died, the house would be swept away by the times, felled like an enormous tree. Just like the "black below," Kurobishi Shipbuilders had collapsed with the bubble. I had to keep calling her back for as long as I had a voice, and so I continued to cry for Manyo. Midori was also frightened and added her shrill voice to mine.

Kodoku roused the branch families, and Kaban hurried up to the house, frantic. Finally, when the people of the branch families thronged into the mansion and made a commotion, I sat and shook in one corner of the room.

Manyo was still with us until dawn. Especially at the beginning, people crowded into the room where my grandmother slept, but they gradually moved to other rooms and began praying or simply staring at the tatami-mat floor. Midori, torn between the restraint of someone who wasn't a relative and her desire to be by Manyo's side, crouched like an aging black guard dog on the threshold between the room and the hallway, hanging her head, eyes popping. And then, she nodded off to sleep, still crouched there. I gently placed my robe over her shoulders.

Dawn came, bringing a moment when the only people left in the room were me sitting in the corner, Midori drowsing on the threshold, and my grandmother on her futon, a gap in the comings and goings of the many visitors in the house. As if sensing this, my grandmother suddenly opened her eyes.

"Toko, Toko," she called. I crawled over from my corner and hurried to Manyo's bedside.

"What is it, Grandma?" Trembling.

"I want to see a wild rose. Toko, go pick me a wild rose from the yard."

I hurried to my feet, went across the hallway, and jumped down into the backyard in my bare feet. I raced through the wild garden, which burned a fiery bright red, found a bush of wild roses, tore some off, and, clutching the flowery bundle with both hands, returned to my grandmother. I knew she was dying. My grandmother, the woman who was still almost part of the house itself. I braced myself for it. But I was still rocked by it. I flew into the room carrying the roses, tripped on Midori's legs, and fell. Midori didn't wake up. Bunches of roses gently encircled my grandmother's long silver hair spread out on the futon, red roses on the silver fan.

Manyo opened her eyes and called my name. "Toko, Toko."

"I'm here. What is it, Grandma?"

"Thanks, Toko. You're a good girl," she said to her unworthy grand-daughter. *Am I really such a good girl?* I thought as tears came to my eyes, so I said nothing and crawled back to her side. A single wild rose sat lightly next to her face.

"You're the one who's the good person, Grandma. Way better than me. I mean, you're the clairvoyant madam. I think you're amazing."

"I'm not a good person."

"Of course you are. I don't know what I'll do if you leave me. I'll be the only woman in the main family. And I can't be like you, Grandma. I'm scared of you leaving me all alone."

Manyo slowly moved her head to look at me with a strange, troubled expression. Her eyes seemed to want to say, *That's a surprising way of thinking.* She slowly opened dry lips, so I brought my ear closer to her mouth.

"Toko. I know you'll be okay."

"But I'm telling you, I won't."

"You really are a worrier. Aren't you, Toko? But, well, me, I haven't been a good person."

"Grandma, that's—"

"You're the only one I've told this." Closing her eyes slowly, Manyo forced a weak voice out. "Way back, I killed someone. No one knows, though."

"What?"

"But it wasn't out of hate..."

Those were her last words.

From the corner of one of her closed eyes, a single tear flowed. She took a breath in and didn't breathe it out; Manyo left the land of the living.

My grandmother, abandoned as a child, growing into a woman who married into the main family, becoming in the end a presence that was almost the Akakuchiba house itself. The bright red soul of Manyo Akakuchiba abruptly disappeared before me, her granddaughter.

I was floored. In the room buried in wild roses, I sat quietly with Manyo's corpse for five minutes, or maybe ten. The silence pained me. Eventually, I could produce sound again, so I called for my father in a small voice.

"Dad, Dad." My voice was so thin, it surprised even me and reached no one. It gradually grew louder. "Dad! Come here!"

Midori's eyes flew open. She looked at me and cried out, and tears started pouring from her pop eyes.

My father came running from across the hall. The doctor also came, checked her pulse, and announced that she had passed. At Kaban's instruction, the wives of the branch families dragged my floored self out into the hallway. A white cloth was placed over Manyo's face. The old men of the branch families clapped their hands together. "Amitabha have mercy, Amitabha have mercy," they murmured, invoking the name of the Buddha. "The clairvoyant madam has finally passed on. Thank you so much. You've worked so hard all this time for the sake of the Akakuchiba main family. Hmm, Manyo?" Everyone nodded and clapped their hands together at her withered body, the life in it having flown off.

"Amitabha have mercy, Amitabha have mercy."

"Amitabha have mercy, Amitabha have mercy."

"Amitabha have mercy, Amitabha have mercy."

All of my relatives attributed my ghostly countenance to the shock of the family heir at the death of the grandmother who had raised her in place of her own mother. And of course, they were not mistaken. The women of the branch families comforted me with things like, "You gotta be strong now too" and "You're your grandmother's girl, so it must be hard for you, but she died a peaceful death."

Manyo's final words gradually came back to life in my ears.

Way back, I killed someone.

No one knows, though.

Still completely stunned, I retreated bit by bit down the hallway. I put distance between myself and the corpse of my beloved grandmother, the woman I'd held in such high esteem for so long. I slid down the hallway.

But it wasn't out of hate…

Two hours of me sitting in the hallway passed. Before I knew it, it was fully morning. I finally stood up and ran down the hall, the grown-ups preparing for the wake in the corner of my eye. Clouds rose up from the bundles of incense Midori Kurobishi was burning as she chanted. Purple smoke coiling around me, I tumbled out of the gates of the Akakuchiba house and looked down on the apartment buildings, those near ruins. And then I took out my cell phone and called Yutaka, crying.

"Toko?" he answered in a mumbly voice that sounded like he was eating something. "What's up, first thing in the morning? You're a NEET. Isn't it a little early for you?"

"Grandma died."

"What?"

"She murdered someone."

"Huh? Which is it?"

"Both. I don't know. What am I going to do…" I started sobbing and leaned back against the old stone gates. My voice shook when I spoke. "No one knows. I'm the only one. That Grandma killed someone a long time ago."

"Killed? Who?"

"I don't know. I don't know."

Trembling with fear, I looked back at the house. Now that it was no longer inhabited by the clairvoyant madam, the Akakuchiba mansion looked a little old and slanted. The autumn leaves burning darkly like the tatara flames grew incredibly thick, fire lapping up against the house from the backyard.

I heaved a sob. The world I thought I understood had abruptly begun to crumble under my feet with a whine. Tears spilled from my eyes.

How could my grandmother be a murderer?

2. WHOM DID SHE MURDER?

Yutaka Tada got in his Corolla II and raced over to the house. Bathed in the morning light, the light blue car came up the deserted hill road of the steps and stopped abruptly in front of me where I had broken down crying. The driver's side window came down, and his fair-skinned face, tan faded, approaching adulthood, peered out at me.

"Toko?" Yutaka said. "I just stopped by before heading to work. I can't stay long."

As choked up as I was, I still managed somehow to explain what had happened at dawn. Yutaka in his suit looked at his watch several times—"I have to go into the office for a minute at least, but I'll be back soon"—and he trundled off back down the hill road.

I went into the mansion and stared vacantly at the adults busy getting ready for the wake. My cell phone rang, and Kaban glanced back at me.

"Friends at a time like this? Turn it off," she grumbled. "Honestly, kids these days..."

Running out into the hall, I answered the phone. It was Yutaka. Apparently, he had arrived at work, punched his time card, and then sat at his desk for a mere five minutes before announcing that he was going out to make the rounds. He came as far as the gates, stopping his Corolla in the same place as before. He took his suit jacket off and hung it on a hanger in the backseat. "Get in," he told me, and I went around to the passenger side. My tears had finally stopped.

I put my hand on the door when something suddenly nagged at me. I looked back at the mansion. My uncle Kodoku was standing in the garden, looking absently at the ground at his feet. The two of us were close, so I wanted to say something to him. But I felt like this of all things was something I could never tell him. For Kodoku, Manyo was his beloved mother, and beyond that, although he had kept on aging physically all the way into his mid-thirties, emotionally, he was still unusually young and sensitive. Having passed twenty and become a "young woman," I had at that time long caught up with Kodoku in this department and would no doubt surpass him. I loved my solitary uncle very much, but I also held him in a sort of contempt as a man, as an adult. I was convinced I couldn't rely on him.

I sat down in the passenger seat, and the Corolla started out slowly. Yutaka gave me a can of cold coffee.

"Drink it."

"Uh-huh ... Thanks."

"If we drive around town, someone from work'll find out there's a girl riding next to me. We'll go out by the sea."

"Yeah."

We drove unhurriedly down the national expressway, turning onto a sandy coastal road off the industrial highway along the Sea of Japan that had fallen out of regular use. The pine forest stretched out endlessly, and there was no sign of anyone on the beach, out of season as it was. The Sea of Japan was gray, wild waves crashing violently again and again.

We got out of the car and sat down next to each other on the chilly sand of the beach. The sea and the sky were dyed their usual smoky color.

"You okay?"

"Yeah...no."

I shook my head. I had been in chaos this whole time. I couldn't bear the fact that my grandmother was gone. It was a pain—as if part of my own self had been pinched off and also whisked away to the realm of the dead—and a fear.

Grandma, I cried in my heart. *Grandma. Grandma. Don't go yet. Don't leave me all alone.* I was anxious and sad, and my confusion even greater.

The ominous voice came back to life again.

Way back, I killed someone.

I shook my head hard. *It can't be true*, I thought. Recalling the figure of the grandmother I knew, Manyo Akakuchiba, as we stared out at the sea, I could see only the gentle and kind clairvoyant madam, the woman who lived not for herself, but rather for the Akakuchiba family she married into. Where on earth had those last words of hers come from? Had my grandmother actually been telling me that she killed someone?

The faces of the many dead who had left the mansion crowded into my mind. Namida, Tatsu, Yoji, Momoyo, and Kemari...None of them appeared to have been killed by Manyo, and they all seemed to be glaring reproachfully at the face of this pathetic grandchild. "There's no way, there's no way." I looked up at Yutaka next to me. He was watching over me with a very worried expression.

He looked like he couldn't quite figure out what, if anything, he should say. We had come this far together without ever really talking with each other about anything too serious. Nor did we talk with our families, our lovers, our friends. Maybe not even with ourselves. We fled from society, from strife, and with only a half-baked resignation, we had somehow, in the blink of an eye, made it into our twenties. We weren't qualified to be human beings.

Neither Yutaka nor I knew what to say now. He seemed so hurt, looking at me with the saddest eyes, and I had the sudden realization, *Oh! This is probably fago.* That word the tribe in Micronesia uses. That feeling of being sad yourself because of someone else's sadness. At that moment, Yutaka was in a state of fago. It seemed like a kind, woolly thing.

"I can't believe my grandma could've killed someone or anything like that, but if it is true, I think she must've had a reason."

"Yeah...you're right." Yutaka nodded. "I mean, she doesn't seem like someone who'd do something so irrational. She's weird, but she's the sort of person who only does things that make sense to her. She's someone you can trust like that."

"Yeah."

"So then there should've been some something that made sense, if only just to her, like she had to kill them."

"I don't know. But I want to know. Still, to understand whatever the reason was, I have to figure out who she killed and when."

"Yeah. That's tough."

We fell silent then and stared at the ocean.

From time to time, waves reared up in the smoky sea. Yutaka looked at his watch and made a face like it was about time for us to be getting back. I stood up first and brushed away the sand sticking to my skirt. He bent over to help me, and I glanced at him out of the corner of my eye.

He didn't yet look good in a suit. The fit wasn't quite right. It didn't look at home on his body; it looked as if he had been only recently wearing a high school uniform. Overall, he was slender, with an air of adulthood starting to curl up around him. I was also thinner than I had been in high school, and I had the feeling that I was coming into my adult body. The kinds of clothing that looked good on me had also changed. Although the two of us were supposedly gradually turning into full-fledged grown-ups, I knew our feet were not yet on the ground, that we were still drifting.

Returning to the car, Yutaka said, "Once I get off work tonight, I'll call you."

I nodded and got into the passenger seat. "Sorry for making you worry." I rolled down the window of the moving Corolla. The cool autumn wind ruffled my hair.

"Go ahead. Make me worry all you want."

"Hmm?"

"I want to help, I want you to need me. I'm a man and all . . . Although that said, I'm not all that much use."

His voice was a little dark, so I glanced over at him. The same quiet face as always. Losing confidence in himself little by little, making compromises in his now regular-person self one day, but unable to follow through the next. Shaken by the passing days, that young, anguished, gentle face.

"I do need you."

"Really?"

"Yeah, really."

"Before . . . this morning. When you called. Because you were crying, right? For a second, I was like, I gotta step up. I mean, I'm a man."

"For a second?"

"Yeah. But maybe it's in me a bit still now."

"Huh."

The Corolla picked up speed. The mid-morning industrial road was empty. A truck piled high with Styrofoam seafood boxes overtook the car at an incredible speed, and Yutaka stepped on the accelerator, ready for a fight. It turned into a high-speed chase with the truck. I let out a little cry. This was dangerous. It was unusual for Yutaka to be reckless, and the whole thing surprised me, just a little.

When I returned to the house, preparations for the wake were ongoing. The people of Benimidori came together here: the women went into the kitchen, while the men wandered about aimlessly inside. I passed by a young man with a conch. An older man was telling him not to let it get blown away, even if the yamaoroshi blew, and the younger man nodded with a serious face as he clutched the conch. The elders of the village had gathered in the reception hall and were chatting animatedly, sharing their memories of the clairvoyant madam. The descendants of the Tadas, who had taken in and raised Manyo, were urged toward good seats, and sake was handed around as they told the stories of Manyo's single days that they had heard from their parents. Drinking proceeded apace in front of the reception hall's fusuma doors and the painting of the large school of bright red snapper swimming in the Sea of Japan, as men with faces as red as those snappers chattered on and on with joyous zeal about their memories of the clairvoyant madam.

Instead of an early death from sickness or an accident, Manyo's passing had come after a long life in service of the main family, so there was absolutely no gloom that night or at the funeral the next day. I was asked countless times about her cleaning her own room the afternoon of the day she collapsed, and each time, the older relatives looked at each other admiringly. "Clairvoyant right up to the very end. That woman even knew when she was going to die." And then they all chattered about the past again. *That time too, she was the only one who knew the future. Oh, and remember that other time.*

Only Midori Kurobishi was downcast, locking herself up in her room and silently burning incense. When night fell, the elderly wife of the Tada couple came, brought by her sons and daughters. The husband had passed away from illness two years earlier, but the wife was still as fit as a fiddle even now at nearly ninety. Alongside her eldest son, Hajime, who had just reached retirement age at the fisheries research institute, she clapped her hands together over Manyo's corpse. After a while, she moved away from her children and sat down alone in the hallway. I approached her from behind and heard her murmuring in a small voice, even though there was no one there.

"Must've been so rough, hmm? You worked hard, did you? I was always clapping my hands together down there and praying for you." She was talking as if the silver-haired, big-boned Manyo was right there next to her, and a chill ran up my spine. Hearing my footfalls, the Tada wife looked over her shoulder, and her face wrinkled up into a smile when she saw me rooted to the spot there. I bowed lightly and sat hesitantly beside her. And then she told me bits and pieces of Manyo's childhood.

The weather the next morning, the day of the funeral, was lovely. The dark, fiery leaves covering the trees shuddered in the autumn wind and danced up into the sky all at once, just like sparks, as the funeral palanquin carrying the coffin of Manyo Akakuchiba passed through the gates of the main house. I opened my eyes wide and stared. Now that it had left, the bright red spirit of my grandmother would never return to the mansion. Just as she had come rocked in the bridal palanquin up the hill road of the steps that faraway day, Manyo now left the mansion forever in her funeral palanquin.

Goodbye, Manyo.

I felt as though the mansion lurched into an incline, howling, pushed by the wind. The last woman to marry into the family, watching over the final glory of the Akakuchiba house, saving it from the shadows. The red autumn leaves were shaken again by the wind, a large number of them dancing up and then falling back down onto the road like tears. And the funeral palanquin slowly descended the hill road among these fluttering, falling leaves.

Men clad in old costumes came along at some point bearing instruments. They blew the conch, shook the bells, hit the gong, and danced around the palanquin. There was no yamaoroshi this morning, and so the conch was not blown away, the flute was not broken, and the funeral palanquin bearing Manyo very calmly descended the hill road of the steps, taking until afternoon to reach its destination. We relatives walking behind it gradually grew less tense and followed leisurely, talking about Manyo as we did. I walked in between Kodoku and my father. When we reached the very bottom of the hill, I felt as though I were being called by something and quickly whirled my head around.

The bright red house on the distant peak, as if thrust into the surface of the mountain. Nearly all the fiery leaves encircling it had, in these few hours, fallen to the ground, and the garden was dark. The hill road was covered in the decaying leaves, which turned it the color of the tatara, a river of molten iron. The mansion sank dimly into the shadows, looking as if it had been cut loose of the land of the living without a word. *Ah*, I sighed. Was the Akakuchiba family coming to an end at last? With no one left to inherit the power of the house, this thing without real form but definitely in existence, had this place Manyo had inherited and watched over stopped breathing with her death?

Trembling with fear, I unconsciously reached for my father's hand. He stared at me as if to ask what was wrong. Following my gaze, he looked up toward the mansion, but the change in it seemed not to be reflected in his eyes. "Same huge old house as always," he murmured, so I nodded emptily. Yes, it was a big house. Even now. The form that was visible, at least.

What I was afraid of was this, that although I was the only woman now that my grandmother and my mother were gone, I—the heir to this big house—would be able to do nothing despite the fact that I needed to inherit its power. From ancestors long, long ago, this house had been kept safe and the bloodline had carried on, all the way down to me here and now. But I, the last one born, was unable to connect with the future in any real way. Wasn't I ruining this precious something that had continued all this time? Wasn't I the guileless desolater of all this history? Ah, that's the last thing I wanted to be.

I looked up at the mansion, sunk in darkness even though it was still daytime, and shook with fear.

Manyo's funeral lasted until evening, and it was well into the night when, finally, the conch finished playing, the large choir of Buddhist sutras had been chanted, and the people of the town were done dancing. I dawdled and loitered fearful of returning to the mansion enveloped in darkness. For the trip home, the whole family piled into a car and ascended the hill together. I didn't want to get out, perplexing both my father and my uncle. I did eventually step out of the car to stand before the gates. "I'll take care of things properly, so please let me in," I murmured.

Take care? Of what, exactly?

I felt like this was how the house responded. The corners of my mouth trembled. "I'll try to live my life properly. As best as I can."

This time, it seemed the house had no reply. I hung my head, and still entirely lacking in confidence, I slipped through the gates. My father and my uncle were far ahead and looking back at me strangely.

"What are you doing? Come on. You're just tired," my father said.

The men can't see anything, they can't feel anything, I thought, which was funny to me somehow. I wondered all over again what exactly had happened in this house, supported all this time by women in the shadows, just who had been killed by the clairvoyant madam. After stepping through the gates, I was halfway to the entryway when the branches, nude now having dropped their leaves, moved sharply, skeletal, and caressed my cheek gently, despite the fact that there was no wind. Perhaps to encourage me. Perhaps to taunt me.

I caught up with my father and my uncle and stood between them. I looked at each of their thoroughly exhausted faces in turn. "It's so empty without Grandma here."

"It is."

"You're right."

They both nodded. Behind us, the skeletal branches made a curious dry clacking sound.

That night, I huddled in my room alone and thought about the lives of my mother and grandmother. I made some bukupuku tea, and as I drank it, I opened my notebook and jotted some things down.

My grandmother and my mother often let me hear their stories. I knew all about that long ago day when my grandmother saw the flying man, about the Shimane National Safety Forces man who died when the carbine exploded, about the time the Goldfish, aka Midori Kurobishi, yanked on my grandmother's hair and pulled out a clump, almost as if they were episodes from my own life. I had vivid, clear memories of the pain and surprise, as if she and I had experienced them together. And my mother, I knew her very well. How she was a violent woman. How that romantic perversion of hers played out over and over again. How she spent her youth with what kind of friends. How she fought life as a manga artist. I knew it all so well, as if I had had front-row seats to the movie.

But since the time of these stories, a hundred nights had seen their dawns, a thousand days their dusks. A long, very long time had passed, many people had become part of the mansion, and a great number of them had, in the end, died. And the majority of them had died in mysterious ways. Exactly who had my grandmother killed, and why?

I finished my bukupuku tea, clutched my ballpoint pen, and wrote everything I could remember about my grandmother's life in the notebook. Around the time night was giving way to day, I had finally gotten to the part where she went to get married. I dove into my bed and slept. Whatever else I might be, I was young and unemployed, so I had plenty of stamina and time. I got up in the morning and started writing again. And then, that entire week, I stayed holed up in my room, writing about my grandmother. Next, I started putting my mother's story on the page. It took a very, very long time. After that, based on my own memories, I extracted the army of the dead connected with my grandmother to the extent of my own knowledge.

I got out a new notebook and wrote "Murderer" on the first page. And then doubting and believing in equal measure, I added a question mark. Then I wrote Manyo's name: "Manyo Akakuchiba," "Sanka," "clairvoyant."

Then I wrote "Dead." There were likely some that I hadn't gotten, but I wrote down the dead that I knew at that point in order of age.

Murderer?

Manyo Akakuchiba   —Sanka, clairvoyant

Dead

Around 1953?   Manyo, age 10
Person with carbine, gun exploded, vision

1960   Manyo, age 17
Midori Kurobishi's older brother, train suicide, vision

1974   Manyo, age 31
Yasuyuki Akakuchiba (father-in-law), illness, vision

1979   Manyo, age 36
Masago (husband's lover), illness

1984   Manyo, age 41
Choko Hozumi (daughter's friend), unknown

1986   Manyo, age 43
Namida Akakuchiba (eldest son), accidental fall (?), vision

1989   Manyo, age 46
Tatsu Akakuchiba (mother-in-law), old age

1992   Manyo, age 49

Yoji Akakuchiba (husband), train accident, vision

1998   Manyo, age 55

Momoyo Akakuchiba (the lover's child), attempted double suicide

1998   Manyo, age 55

Kemari Akakuchiba (daughter), overwork (?)

My fingers shook as I wrote. She couldn't possibly have killed the carbine person, and Midori's older brother and the housekeeper Masago were people so far in the past they didn't seem real to me. But Namida was my uncle, and my mother had married my father because of his sudden death, which is how I came to be born. The number of dead connected with my own existence increased over the following years. If any of them really had been murdered, the victim in it was definitely my business too. The memory of the unfortunate Momoyo's funeral remained crystal clear within me, and my hand shook a great deal when I wrote the last name, "Kemari Akakuchiba."

There's no way my mother was murdered, I thought, feeling a chill. After all, I had seen her die myself. I would never forget that night. "I'm going," she murmured, went into the next room, and closed the sliding doors. When I hurriedly opened them, she had collapsed on the futon and wasn't breathing. I yelled for someone and everyone came running, but they weren't in time. She was still young, but she died from over-work. I would never forget that night.

I had listened to my grandmother's old stories as if they were distant legends, but as they approached the present, I began to keenly feel that no, they weren't. They weren't legends—all these things had really happened. I stared at the page and thought about it.

I want to know what happened.

I might have been an unworthy grandchild, but even so, I was the daughter of this house, the heir. Although I was unemployed and lying around the house like this in the middle of the day despite being already twenty-two. Although I had absolutely no sense at all within myself of being connected with anything in the future. Although I was the very picture of an apathetic youth. Although.

I also felt that there was inside me something like the pride of the daughter of a house. I also felt like there wasn't. Just as I resolved to figure out what really happened in the Akakuchiba house, my cell phone rang. Put off by the idiotic ringtone, I read the email that had arrived. It was from Yutaka. He was apparently worried about me. After making a promise to meet on the weekend, I abandoned my notebook and fell into bed. Yes, my determination and desire to do something didn't last. Sloth and distractedness had seeped deep into my young, unemployed spirit.

I fell into a light, lazy sleep and dreamed of Manyo. Tears of blood poured from her large eyes, rivers of molten iron, and she raced around the smooth hallways of the mansion, brandishing an iron axe. The collar of her kimono was open and her long hair fell in waves...No, it wasn't Manyo, it was Kemari. It was the memory of the night Kemari cursed Momoyo. I rolled over in my sleep. The next morning, Momoyo was dead. She had failed to force her lover into a suicide pact and had died alone. Oh. In the memory, both women seemed equally foolish. And of course, I was too. I cried when I woke up. So many times, the blood of its women had rained down in this house. The blood of the women who held it up. And now the only woman left was pathetic Toko Akakuchiba.

When I woke up on the weekend, it was already nearly ten o'clock. I hurriedly crawled out of bed and washed my face. I had promised to meet Yutaka, so I changed and made myself presentable before going to the family altar. Midori Kurobishi was already there, burning great plumes of incense, and I sat down next to her, coughing intermittently in the purple smoke.

The pictures of the dead hanging on the wall looked down on me all together. I got the sense that voices, ripples inaudible to the living, were saying all kinds of things, and I dipped my head. I didn't get the feeling they were saying anything particularly good. On behalf of the dead, Midori Kurobishi started my day with a lecture in a hoarse voice. "Y'know, Manyo'll be worried sick if you don't stop lazing around and get it together." I replied with equivocal uh-huhs and closed my eyes. I felt her leave the room. When I opened my eyes again after a while, I was alone at the smoke-filled altar. I looked up at the photos and stared at the faces of my ancestors one by one.

The one I was most drawn to was the photo of my inexplicably graceful and refined uncle Namida. But I felt like the one I most strongly resembled was my grandfather Yoji. His face was oval-shaped and sharply defined, but somehow naive. The photos of Kemari and Momoyo hung next to each other, friendly. Momoyo's eyes were upturned, and it looked

as though she were staring hard at Kemari to the left. Kemari was feign-
ing ignorance and facing straight ahead.

Casually, I began opening the various drawers and things of the
altar. Inside the biggest drawer, which held sticks of incense, I found
something tucked away. I unrolled the piece of paper, and an envelope
with "Madam Manyo" written on it in quick strokes fell out. A letter. But
why would she keep it in a place like this rather than in her own room?
I wondered as I surreptitiously opened it.

I unfolded the lone page it contained and dropped it in the next
instant with a yelp. I felt a cold breath against the nape of my neck. A
terror, a shock like the page had cut a finger off.

The page read simply, "We die together." Momoyo's suicide note.
The woman of a hundred nights who failed at her lover's suicide and
died alone. Wondering what it was doing here, I looked up at the wall
of photos. I got the sense that sad-looking Momoyo and her upturned
eyes were secretly smiling. The photo of Kemari hanging next to her was
a little crooked, knocked askew by a wind blowing in from the veranda.

I returned the page to the envelope and tucked the whole thing back
into the depths of the drawer. So many pasts surrounded me, trying
to come back to life. Memories of the dead, hearts starting to pound
vigorously. I was no longer able to think of anything but Manyo's and
Kemari's stories. I left the altar and ran down the hall, patting down
my clothes, now steeped with the scent of incense. My phone started
to ring. Yutaka. I went to grab my bag and head out, and bumped into
Kodoku along the way. He looked at me as if dazzled. "Oh, you're going
on a date?"

"But, I mean, don't you wonder how much of it is actually true?"

"Huh?"

I was talking with Yutaka about my grandmother and my mother as we drove along the coastal highway. With one hand on the wheel, he narrowed his eyes and made this slightly skeptical comment when I told him I was writing down the names of the dead in a notebook and thinking about them in the process.

"But, Yutaka, my grandma might've been weird, but she was honest. She wouldn't lie."

"Yeah, I know that. But."

Our route took us slowly down the coast and then shifted back up to the mountains where we could look down on the ocean from up high as we slowly descended again. The view was nice, but it was a road we had been down a million times, so we were pretty much used to it, and neither of us were really bothering to look out at the scene.

Driving us down the same old highway, Yutaka cocked his head. "It just feels more like a dream, like it's some kind of story. I mean, look, I think you basically just tell all the good parts when you get old, and you're telling your grandkids about when you were young. Like, when I get old, I'll probably exaggerate a little when I'm telling my grandkids about Koshien or when I met you. So you know."

"That's just you."

"Come on. My point is, we don't know how far we can trust Manyo's stories. Like the one about how the Kurobishi heir was hit by a train and died. Is that really true?"

"*I* think it is."

"Don't get offended. I'm just trying to look at this from a different angle. We've got this boy brain—girl brain difference here, we should use it."

He parked the Corolla at a restaurant along the coast. We got a table near the window, and he ordered the chicken doria while I got the seafood spaghetti. I took my notebook from my bag and handed it to Yutaka, who flipped through it with a serious look on his face.

After a while, our food came.

"The past is tough, huh?" Yutaka nodded as he started to eat. "Like, I mean, do you really know how Masago and Yasuyuki died? It'd be great if they still had their records at the hospital or something, but it's been thirty years."

"Yeah. Right." I nodded with him, winding spaghetti onto my fork. "Even if those records are gone, maybe the doctor from back then's still alive."

"Oh yeah. Maybe."

"I'll try finding him. I mean, I've got nothing else to do."

"Hmm. It'd take some guts, but maybe you could try asking Midori about the whole thing about her brother being hit by a freight train."

"Oh yeah. Although I'd need to work up the nerve to do it."

We left the restaurant and set out again. Yutaka said it would probably be better to avoid suppertime, and I nodded, "Yeah, I guess." We decided to go back to the Akakuchiba house right away to see Midori Kurobishi. She had gone to her flamenco lesson and wasn't home, so we sat down on the veranda facing the backyard and waited for her to get back. Yutaka was surprised at how early the leaves had fallen that year; autumn had only just begun. An infinity of naked, skeletal branches shuddered in the wind and looked down on us.

Kodoku passed by in the hallway and smiled when he saw us. His smile, when seen close up, was scary, like his cheeks were spasming, but Yutaka was used to it and bowed lightly with a smile of his own. Spitting words out machine-gun style, Kodoku began peppering Yutaka with questions about his job now, his salary, everything. Flustered, Yutaka was managing to hold his own and stammer out some kind of answer to the various inquiries when Soho came along from the opposite side. Kodoku joined him and they went off down the hallway together, chattering about something or other. Their voices grew distant, and just when we could no longer hear them, Midori came to take their place. She was wearing her black satin flamenco dress adorned with gold embroidery and humming to herself, seemingly in a good mood.

With Yutaka there next to me, I was able to see my own house fresh, objectively, with an outsider's eyes. *What a weird family*, I thought. There were a lot of high-class slackers in the house then, myself included. We weren't related by blood, but we continued to live our strange little lives together. All of us were all over the place. Now that I was thinking about it, we hardly sat down at the dinner table all at the same time anymore; we ate what we wanted when we wanted. We were more like friendly roommates than a family. Was this progress? No, it couldn't be. Maybe it was the collapse of the family.

"Oh ho! If it isn't Yutaka Tada!"

Midori had gotten quite near before she noticed Yutaka. He was a little scared of this gilded and gaudy old woman who had brought some color to the cheering section at Koshien, but he very politely bowed his head in greeting. Midori had been a huge fan during his high school baseball days, a remarkably passionate groupie, and a smile now spread across her face. She slipped her hand into her pocket and pulled out several thousand-yen bills. Yutaka was quick to refuse—"I'm an adult now, but thank you"—but Midori kept pushing, so that in the end, he took two of the thousands. I couldn't suppress my laughter at this little back and forth.

"Midori, sweetie, there's something I wanted to ask you," I said, and she looked my way, pop eyed.

"'Course. What? Need some love advice?"

"Not by any stretch of the imagination. That's not it."

Midori's peeled and popped eyes got even bigger as she looked down on me. I felt a sudden chill and shivered.

The three of us moved single file to the room in the mansion given to Midori, a fairly large one of about thirty square meters. It was filled with primary colors—all glittering dance clothes, posters of dancers, lamé high heels—and just walking in made me a little dizzy. Yutaka was relaxed and found a clear spot on the floor to sit down before broaching the subject of our investigation with Midori.

"We wanted to ask you about something, Midori. Toko says she always used to get Manyo to tell her stories about her past."

"Hoh. Mm, well, you an' Manyo were close, hmm, Toko? Grandkids are different from your kids. They're just so cute they turn you stupid."

I felt like what she was saying was rude somehow, but I stayed quiet for the time being.

"So anyway, when Toko was telling me some of these stories, there was one thing that kind of bugged me. Um, it's about your older brother. He was supposed to have been held prisoner in Siberia and never managed to make it home. He should have inherited Kurobishi Shipbuilders. It's about him…"

The smile vanished from Midori Kurobishi's face. Just as a sad, shadowed expression appeared to replace it, a single tear spilled from those peeled and popped eyes. Yutaka fumbled around for a handkerchief while I pulled out tissues.

Midori nodded. "So what did Manyo tell you?"

"Oh, well…that he was hit by a freight train."

"Mmm, that he was. That's what happened. But it was so long ago now." She then stood up and, after turning her room upside down looking for it, finally found a picture of her brother to show us. It was an old monochrome photo, so it was hard to tell, but he seemed to be a slender man with a fairly attractive face. "He was such a beautiful man. And I was so happy when he came back from Siberia. But his head, things weren't quite right up there. All soft in the noggin, he just wandered all over the place. And one night, I was right there with him when he jumped in front of a train. Ended up all in bits and pieces."

"So then, your family…"

"No. My parents knew. We hid the fact he'd come back from the neighbors, but that night, he was gone, and the next morning, there was such a commotion. They were all talkin', a national freight train hit somebody. And then big brother didn't come home after that. I'm sure my parents caught on. Everyone heard about how there was blood on the train car, and the train definitely looked like it had hit and killed someone, but they couldn't find the body, no matter how hard they looked. They even wrote it up in the papers. But I kept my mouth shut, and Manyo didn't say nothin' neither. And the grown-ups o'course would never even dream two little girls'd clean up the body. It ended up staying a mystery. Aah, I remember it like it was yesterday." Midori narrowed her eyes. Exhaled once. "Aah, ever since then, me and Manyo've been friends, y'know."

Yutaka and I exchanged a look.

We left Midori's room, and I poked Yutaka as we walked down the hallway. "See? Grandma's story *was* true."

"Yeah, guess so."

"Where's my 'sorry for doubting you'?"

"I'm sorry. Please forgive me. I love you."

I blushed. Red-faced, I nudged his back. "You don't have to go that far."

"Ha ha ha! But, the thing is." He cocked his head to one side. "Manyo's stories might have been true, but you heard nothing about a murder in any of them. So if she wasn't lying to you, there has to be some part, some truth she didn't tell you. Like, she told you about Midori's older brother, but why did she leave out the part about how it was in the papers and everyone was talking about it?"

"No, well, that's—" I started and then stopped myself. How was my grandmother supposed to check the papers when she was illiterate? Of course, if people had been talking about it, she should've caught wind of it, but Manyo in her single days didn't really have any friends, and her social sphere would've been pretty small.

But then I remembered that Manyo had sometimes wanted to hide the fact that she couldn't read, depending on who she was with. She spoke freely about it with Yoji, who became her husband, but for some reason, she hid it from the worker Toyohisa. And even though I was her grandchild, I couldn't decide whether she would have been fine with Yutaka knowing or if it would have embarrassed her, so I decided not to say anything.

Indifferent to me and my silence, Yutaka kept talking, passionately. "So, like, when Manyo was telling her precious grandchild her stories, maybe she intentionally left stuff out. Like she was hiding the fact that she killed someone. Or maybe she wanted to forget it herself."

"R-right."

"Like, in the story about Midori's brother, maybe it wasn't an accident. Maybe he died because of Manyo, and she just left that bit out on purpose."

"I don't know if that's it. I mean, he was totally unconnected to my grandma. And she was at home asleep when it happened. It was Midori who saw him get hit by the train."

"Yeah, that's true. I was just thinking out loud. I'm sorry. I love you." Yutaka laughed lightly.

We headed back down the hill in the car to the library. We just barely made it before they closed, and we got the librarian to show us the old newspapers. She was kind of sexy, older than us, around thirty. We told her we were looking for articles on old accidents, and she got really into it, digging through all the archives, searching with us.

"Hee hee. You're like a pair of detectives or something. Even though you're so young."

"Um, there was an article about this accident my grandmother used to talk about, and I ended up wanting to know more about it."

"Uh-huh, I get that. I love my grandparents' stories too, you know. It's weird, right? They're about things that really happened here, but they sound like legends or something. I wonder why that is... Oh, here we go!"

I brought the newspaper article to my face and read it, the smell so particular to old newspapers wafting up to my nose.

And there it was. A report on an incident in 1960 in which a body supposedly hit by a freight train disappeared. It was apparently quite the topic of conversation at the time. And while we were at it, we also found that the accident with the Shimane prefectural National Safety Forces in 1952 had happened. A young man of nineteen from the region who had joined the National Safety Forces met his accidental death due to an exploding carbine.

"By the way, how much faith do you put in these kinds of stories about the past?" Yutaka asked the librarian.

"Hmm." She cocked her head to one side. "I think they usually involve a little exaggeration, and maybe some bits imagined later mixed in." The librarian's cloudy eyes grew distant, dreamy.

When we left, the librarian handed us her business card, saying we should feel free to use the library whenever we needed to look anything up. Yutaka took the card from her and put it in his wallet.

"I don't think Manyo killed either of them, though," I said from the passenger seat on the way home.

"Yeah." Yutaka nodded. He drove me home again, letting me out at the gates at the top of the steps.

"See you." I waved a hand, and he waved back.

I went back to my room and opened my notebook after changing my clothes. I drew a firm line in pen through the first two dead on the list: "person with carbine" and "Midori Kurobishi's older brother."

Eight remained.

The new week started, and things got busy outside. I was wandering around with a mug of milk in one hand, staring out at the backyard with sleepy eyes, when in a rare occurrence, I came across my father. He looked pressed for time in his suit, headed toward the entryway.

"'Morning, Dad."

"Oh, Toko. Kicking back as usual, I see. That reminds me." My father looked back at me as he pulled his shoes on. Through the open door, I could see a car stopped by the gates and the driver waiting next to it. My father was apparently as busy as ever. "You know that the administration told us to turn the plant site into a vacant lot, but we only just managed to get a rough idea of the capital involved. So we can get on with it finally. It's going to get pretty noisy down there. You probably won't be able to stand it, hanging out here during the day. You'd be better off going out somewhere."

"Oh, you're finally doing it." I nodded as I drank my milk.

"I'm sure it's going to be a pain for you to have to invent some reason to go out every day. I've got it! Why don't you take the opportunity to get a job?"

"No thanks."

"Well then, how about we get you married?"

"No. Thanks."

I put on some sandals and went outside with my father. We stopped and looked up at the smoky sky. For a while, we were silent.

"Hey, Dad? I guess it must've been hard for you to tell Grandma about the blast furnace."

"Mm-hmm. But you know, it reached its limit a long time ago," my father said. "Steel can't keep the company afloat. And everything goes to pot when it's not used. Plus, if you just leave some old thing like this as it is and there's an accident, you got a real problem on your hands. So you have to worry about it collapsing. Or turning into some kind of hotbed of criminal activity, as they say. Town hall's really been on us about it, from the perspective of structural integrity and crime prevention. It was quite a stroke of luck it didn't come down on us during that earthquake back in the year 2000."

"Seems like it's going to be a lot of work to take it down."

"Well, compared with putting it up, I'm sure it'll be just a blip," my father said, a little sadly. "Everything's like that, after all. Starting something, continuing something, that's the really hard part," he said and started walking. The driver reverentially opened the back door. My father waved at me and got in.

That week, I put some real effort into the project, running all over Benimidori. I chased down information on the whereabouts of the doctor and nurses who used to work at the university hospital. It was a small town, after all; it didn't take much to find out where anyone was. "Oh, if that's who you're after, then…" I popped in at the seniors' association where I got more than a few looks because I was young.

"Mr. Yasuyuki of the main family, mm-hmm," said the old woman who had been a nurse, with a distant look, as she pushed tea cake on me. "I remember him veerrry well. It was such a shame. Getting sick and dying like that. But he fought so hard. Right up to the end, he was giving instructions about this and that for the company. And oh yes, the son, Yoji? Mr. Yasuyuki called him right to his bedside, and they talked and talked."

"Wow."

"Don't know too much about Masago, though. You, you must know muuuch better than me. Come now, she was *the* dancing naked housekeeper."

Another old woman came over in a wheelchair and started chuckling. "Oh, Masago! Such a funny one. But just terrible the way she died. Stark raving mad."

"Oh really?"

"She didn't seem too sweet on that sullen little girl of hers either. I just know she had her heart set on being the lady of the main family. And if it had been some little princess from somewhere who married him, she would've given up, to be sure, but instead he took to wife some worker's girl from the steps, and a stray to boot. And she just couldn't stand that. Got weaker and weaker over the years, finally gets pneumonia or some such, gets a fever, and then she up and dies. Her hands were all angry, like this."

The old woman crooked the fingers of both hands into hooks and made a scary face, peeling her eyelids back. I shuddered. Her hands looked exactly like when my aunt Kaban told me about Masago's daughter, Momoyo, dying. So did mother and daughter both die with the same hook hands?

"Um. What about my great-grandmother Tatsu?"

"Oh, Mrs. Tatsu was old age. She died a peaceful death," another old woman chimed in, having come over after hearing my voice.

On my way home, I brooded over all of this as the bus shook under me. I took out my notebook and drew lines through "Yasuyuki Akakuchiba" and "Tatsu Akakuchiba" with my pen. I hesitated about whether to draw one through "Masago" too and started thinking harder about it.

Masago died of pneumonia, but after listening to those old women, it wasn't a stretch to say that it had actually all started with her fixating on the peasant Manyo marrying into the Akakuchiba family, an obsession that only grew until she died. I had the sudden thought that maybe Manyo's heart ached at the idea that she had essentially killed Masago. My grandmother could be overly serious sometimes.

In a small town, people get tangled up with each other; there's no way around it. It's impossible not to have something to do with each other, and sometimes, some of those connections might end up being someone's death. But how much of it is simple misfortune and how much is murder? I felt like it was Masago herself who caused her death, that it wasn't my grandmother's fault. And my grandmother should have understood that too.

Eventually, I decided to draw a light line through Masago's name too. Five of the names were gone. Five were left.

Just as I was arriving home, my friend sent me an email. I got annoyed with the whole enterprise, threw my notebook into my room, and decided to go out to karaoke with my friend. I needed a change of pace to clear my head.

Around the middle of that week, I woke up in the morning and went out to stand on the veranda like I always did, staring out at the backyard as I drank milk. Seemingly one step away from winter now that all the leaves had scattered early, the chilly garden sprawled before me. A little sad at the thought that I would have to say goodbye to the blast furnace soon, I stepped outside and turned toward the factory site, soon to disappear from this world.

Carved out of the surface of the mountain, the vast plant was deserted, sunk into a gray gloom. Cracks shot through the asphalt everywhere I looked; the place was run down. Towering up from the center of it all, the blast furnace was the dry greenish-black of iron, and although it was man-made, it instilled in me a strangely worshipful feeling.

My spirit trembled as I approached it. Something like fear rose up in me. But as I drew nearer step by step, my eyes started to see that it was, after all, an ancient and scarred structure, and I gradually began to think of practical things. *If there's another big earthquake, this tower could be really dangerous. I mean, it's really old.* Worrying like this, I finally came to stand in front of it. I stretched out my hand to touch the blast furnace gently.

In the distant past, this enormous iron-colored chimney had pierced Manyo's consciousness at the time she'd become a wife, still puffing its black smoke. It was damp to the touch. The smell of iron hung in the air like blood. There was scaffolding for climbing up the side like the kind you see on bathhouse chimneys, which made the whole thing feel a bit like a joke. I grabbed on with both hands and started up. After I had gone about two meters, I abruptly looked back and stopped, dizzy at the unexpected height. The ground seemed to shimmer for a moment.

"Hey! Toko!" I heard someone call. I looked off in the distance, and there was Kodoku in his suit. He was with people in work wear and other men in suits. He waved his hand in a downward direction several times, as if to say "get down." I hurriedly jumped to the ground.

"That's dangerous." He came over and poked me in the head. "And, aah, your hands are filthy."

"I'm sorry. You working?"

"Yeah. Meeting on the construction work. Although the work won't be done until spring prob'ly. We won't be able to do anything after it starts to snow." Kodoku started going around the plant site, explaining whatever needed to be explained. I watched for a while as he moved away.

Nearly twenty years had already passed since the closing of the steel plant. Long ago, long, long ago, our ancestors crossed the ocean, bringing the primitive tatara technology with them, to come to this land.

They made a tatara shop and set down roots here. And once they did, they lived and died all that time in this region, connected to iron, even as the technology developed and demand waxed and waned.

I remembered the old worker who had, in the distant past, been deemed the hero of the steelworks. Naturally, I didn't remember his face. Just his name. The worker Toyohisa had lived alongside the new technology in the period when the ancient tatara plant was transformed into a Western-style steelworks, and he was proud of his connection with it. That new steel plant, modernized by my great-grandfather Yasuyuki. Once my grandfather Yoji was appointed president, he made it even newer, introducing technology to automate it. It was a never-ending battle with the ever-changing economy of this country, and likely also a son's holy war against the lone, young, no-name worker who had taken up the obsessions of his father, once the boss of the entire operation. And the adopted son, Yoshio—my father—was the son of a worker from the steps, but he saw which way the wind was blowing and gave up on iron entirely, shifting to manufacturing, and the ancient blast furnace was cut loose from the enormous battleship.

Yoshio stopped the tatara flames, and the worker Toyohisa walked away from the cold blast furnace and went off somewhere. Toyohisa's father, too, a long time ago, had been a tatara worker stubbornly clinging to the ancient tatara plant, the flames of which had been stopped because of the appearance of the blast furnace. These men, in their respective eras and their respective iron industries, and the strong women who had stood in the shadows. Tumultuous days illuminated by the tatara flames.

Lost in thought as I looked up at the blast furnace, I could hear,

from off in the distance, Kodoku's voice imparting whatever information was carried to me by the autumn wind. Kodoku was working. He
was in charge of tearing down the steel plant at Red Dead Leaf. I felt like
it was only fitting that the job go to him as the youngest child, and then
I was sad again. I kicked a pebble at my feet and started slowly walking
back to the house.

3. THE MAN WALKING IN FRONT

The following weekend, I went out with Yutaka. He emailed me like he always did, and as we drove along, we talked about what we should do that day. It was unpleasantly chilly, as if autumn had come to an end without my noticing it; an almost wintry, wet wind blew. We got the idea of going to see a movie, so our first stop was the cinema. After the film ended, we came back outside and strolled down the arcade street.

Back when we were in high school, we used to hang out in this area all the time, on dates, seeing friends. Students are basically stuck walking or biking, so the area in town where they can hang out is necessarily limited. When I was still in school, there were already tons of cheap stores, clothing shops, and cafés around here geared toward students, but it seemed like there were even more of them these days. Its past as a den of delinquents a distant paradise, the area was inundated with cute shops targeting girls. We chatted with a few of the people you'd call the owners of said shops, and of course, they were all of my mother's generation; middle-aged people who had experienced the bubble. The scent of the capital lingering on them in their stylish clothes, they packed their shops with imported furniture and random objects the local shops didn't carry. We went into one of these, a snug little place no more than twenty square meters large that was a café during the day and a bar at night. Yutaka's guy friends had recommended it, saying it was a pretty good place for a date.

The owner was a man in his late forties with a mustache, and an air of refinement somehow reminiscent of the capital wafted around him. He was probably one of those people who had spent their youth in the capital and then returned to the region. We sat down at a table toward the back, and when I ordered tea, he stared hard at my face for some reason. To myself, I wondered what his problem was, but he didn't say anything that would shed any light on it. He simply returned to the counter and brought our drinks after a little while. He stared at my face again, but still, he said nothing.

I put some sugar in my tea. "Toko, are you still thinking about that thing?" Yutaka said as I stirred it.

"You mean my grandma, right?" I took a sip. "I'm still trying to figure it out. I mean, I don't have a job, so I've got the time."

"You get anywhere?"

I took the notebook out of my bag. Showing him the list of the dead with the five names left on it, I explained how the nurses had said they definitely died of some illness. Yutaka drank his coffee and pondered the new information. "The other day, with the librarian," he said quietly, as he pointed at Choko Hozumi's name. "You know, at the library."

"Oh, uh-huh." I nodded, remembering the woman. "She was having fun, huh? Like a detective."

"I got her card, right? And it's just sort of an unusual name." Yutaka took her business card out of his wallet. The name of the library and the contact information. And then, right in the middle, "Yasuyo Hozumi." We looked at each other.

"Maybe a relative?"

"Maybe. You said Choko Hozumi's immediate family ran away to Osaka, but her relatives probably stayed behind, right? And it's a small town. I think she's probably a relative. I mean, all you have to do is throw a rock and you hit a cousin. Heh! Pretty romantic environment." Yutaka's tone turned sarcastic.

"Honestly, Yutaka."

We tried calling the library right then and there, but it was apparently closed that day and we got no answer. Yutaka said, "I'll go and ask on a day it's open." He was much quieter than usual, and when Yutaka was quiet, it meant he was grumpy. When something bad happened at work, he always dragged it into the weekend and got like this, sort of apathetic and taking it out on me to a certain degree. I pretended not to notice, but I was worried that something was bothering him.

That evening, at our usual love hotel, The Chateau, Yutaka was still lost in thought, flipping through my notebook with excessive enthusiasm. I sat on the edge of the round bed and went to turn on the TV.

"Don't move. The springs are super noisy."

The old bed did in fact creak, but I got kind of huffy about it. "Well, it's not like I have anything else to do."

"I'm thinking about the stuff with your family right now."

On the way home, the Corolla, with Yutaka behind the wheel, slid down the embankment and got stuck at an angle, halfway into the dry river bed. I called the Japan Automobile Federation on my cell, while Yutaka sat on the ground, resting his chin in one hand while he threw pebbles into the river with the other. I thought it was weird, so I asked, "What's wrong?"

He shook his head. "Nothing."

"Really."

"Why do people even work anyway?"

"Isn't it to put food on the table?"

"Like, in this whole country, I wonder how many people my age are proud of what they do. Maybe they're all just hating their jobs and doing them anyway. Maybe you have to keep going with things you hate. Is that what it means to be strong if you're a man? If it does, then I am totally not a strong man."

"You hit a ton of home runs, didn't you?"

Yutaka threw another rock. "That was a long time ago. Back then, right? I know I sound like an old person right now, but still. Back then, I thought I just had to do everything I could. So I didn't even think about quitting practice, no matter how hard it got. But now that I think about it, I really liked baseball. I liked it more than anything. And that's why I could take an objective look at my own abilities. That's why I was so on fire to try and do whatever I could. I get it now, now that I'm a grown-up."

"Yutaka…"

"Right now, with work, doing whatever I can, I can't get into it. I don't like it. But there's nothing I can do about it, is there? Because I'm a grown-up now."

"Hmm…"

Yutaka's voice grew quiet, like he was telling secrets. "Is being strong out in the world the same as being strong as a man?"

"They're different." Here alone, I was emphatic. "I'm sure they're different."

If only I could have given him some useful advice at that moment. But unlike him, I wasn't out there in the world trying, so I knew before I even said anything that whatever I came up with would be nothing more than empty words. The former brilliant home run machine Yutaka Tada finally started sniffling and burst out crying. I sat there quietly and held his hand, not knowing what else to do.

"Quit your job. If it's that awful."

"I can't do that either. Unh! I can't. Hng! I-I have to be a strong man."

"In the world? Who cares about that? You should just be you, that's enough. The people who love you will always be with you. Right?"

"I can't do that either. It's not that. Toko. Unh!"

JAF arrived, and the sky blue Corolla II was rescued without further incident. Since Yutaka was sobbing, I ended up having to settle the bill.

Still crying, Yutaka set his hands on the wheel, and we climbed the hill road of the steps to bring me home. At the gates, I watched the Corolla II disappear, zigzagging dangerously, while I wondered what being strong as a man even meant. When I went into the mansion, surrounded by the dead garden, I caught a glimpse of the glittering hem of the Goldfish, aka Midori Kurobishi, in her black and gold costume walking down a distant hallway. Kodoku's large bag lay on the floor in the entryway. Soho traipsed by, hand plunged into a bag of potato chips. I didn't feel like I could count on any of these adults, and I sighed.

Night fell, and I felt my father, Yoshio, finally come home. Weekends, holidays, none of them mattered in the slightest; my father went to work. And then when he came home, he would slip in through the back door without making a sound. Now that his father-in-law, his mother-in-law, and his wife were no longer in this world, he was supposedly the strongest member of the Akakuchiba main family, and yet he was the same reserved person he'd always been. I popped my head out the back door.

"What's this?" My father was at first surprised, and then he smiled, pleased. "A welcome party? I'd have settled for the cat, but my daughter, well, that does put a smile on my face."

He had apparently had a little to drink. I took his briefcase and brought a smile onto my tired face. "Long day, huh, Dad?"

"Oh, the usual. I'm glad to see you, though. This is a rare treat."

"Hey, Dad?" I trailed after him down the hallway, as my small-statured father moved forward in short, toddling steps. When I was with him, the mansion took on a deeply peaceful air, and I almost started to believe that it was impossible that these hallways had really held an axe-wielding Kemari running about half crazed or a housekeeper mad about dancing in the nude. Which was exactly why I loved him.

"Um, what does it mean to be a strong man?"

"I s'pose that'd be a man who protects what he loves," my father said without hesitation, albeit in a slightly alcohol-slurred voice.

I was at a loss for words. "He would protect the things he loves?" I parroted back, making the question sound formal for some reason.

"Mm-hmm."

"What about a man who's strong out in the world? I mean, like you, Dad."

"Your dad's a weak one. Didn't you know? The truth is, I'm the adopted son."

So he was drunk. "I know," I said, a little exasperated. "I'm your daughter. That's not what I meant. Like, you're the president and stuff. You have a lot of money and stuff. Like, you're an important person, you have a title."

"No idea about all that," he said, in a half-hearted sort of way, maybe getting annoyed now.

Kodoku, perhaps hearing our voices, came out into the hallway in his pajamas and started walking behind us. "What's wrong?" he asked me in a small voice. "You're not thinking of dumping Yutaka, are you?"

"N-no! I'm just asking."

"Speaking of protecting what you love, remember that heroic man who saved you from the metasequoia during the earthquake? That was me, you know."

"Oh! I forgot! C'mon, Kodoku. You always bring that up."

Remembering Yutaka's tears, I felt like crying, although it was kind of a bit late for that. In my grandmother's old stories, the strong men in Benimidori were tough and worked hard. According to my grandmother, it was the blood and sweat of these laborers that brought about the postwar recovery. In my mother's stories, a strong man was the delinquent boy in fashion at the time, a skilled fighter. Proving your bravery and spending all your time fighting, the strength of the flesh, that was their way of life. Then came the golden wave of the bubble, but that era of overstuffed wallets was gone almost before it started.

Exactly what kind of person was the strong man of the present age?

Thinking about the crying Yutaka, my soul ached. Fago. Fago had slipped into my heart as well. Biting my lip, I tugged on my father's crooked tie. "Maybe I'll get a job."

My father was surprised. "What?"

Kodoku's eyes also flew open. He stared at me. "What's up, Toko? All of a sudden like this. I thought you were the lazybones of the house."

"Meh, nothing's up." I was embarrassed, plus I knew my follow-up thought would sound like I didn't really take the world seriously, like I was spoiled, and I couldn't bring myself to say it to either my father or Kodoku. But I just wanted to share some of the same hardships as home-run machine Yutaka, whom I loved. I thought about men, and I got this feeling like I couldn't stand it anymore.

The season rapidly descended into winter. Winter in the San'in region was cold. Fat snowflakes, sticky in a way that was particular to humid regions, fell, and the heavy, half-melted snow piled up densely on the ground. I didn't see much of Yutaka in this time when the first tiny flakes of snow of the winter were beginning to flutter down from the sky. I didn't hear anything from him, and it was hard for me to reach out.

In the two weeks or so I didn't see him, the snow started, the sky became even smokier, and I went to something like a job interview. At a company that had just started operations in the area, a general call center.

The building was essentially a one-story factory on an enormous empty lot in the suburbs, and when I went inside, I saw it was packed with booths. Filling the entire building were orderly rows of steel desks topped with displays, where men and women my age in suits were endlessly answering phones. Under contract with a variety of large companies in the cities, the call center's only business was to act as a telephone support center. The contracts were quite diverse, everything from repair requests for electrical appliances, to explaining stock trading losses, to computer technical support.

For the first three days, I received training in how to be an operator, and I was made to repeat the same words over and over again as my slight dialect was polished into standard Japanese. "You young people learn so fast," my instructor told me. "When we hire housewives for part-time work, they really get stuck here." Which made me feel a little less anxious. At the call center, you got to work in a suit and eat lunch in a stylish café with a terrace on breaks, so it was like a little taste of the capital. The pay was also slightly better than other businesses in the area, so it was a popular job with young people. When I went outside after work in the evening, the Chugoku Mountains soared up in the distance, and it was strange to suddenly be in the splendor of nature. I started working five days a week, morning until evening, and my body quickly grew accustomed to the tight skirt of my suit and the low heels.

I didn't hear much from Yutaka. With no plans for a date on the weekend, I decided to go hang out with friends or walk around town by myself and kill time. I didn't have a car when I was on my own, so I took the bus into town and then wandered around the arcade street. When my feet got tired, I went into the small shop that was a café during the day and a bar at night that I had gone to with Yutaka that time. It was already evening, and the place had just switched over to bar time.

I took a seat at one corner of the counter and ordered a cocktail. The mustached owner again looked at my face doubtfully, like he was struggling to remember something. I couldn't relax there somehow, and I left the place after having just the one drink.

The tiny snowflakes kept falling, and around the time I was starting to realize that it was really winter, I got a call from Yutaka. From the sound of his voice, he seemed to have gotten back some of his usual cheer. "Toko, how's work?"

"I just started, so I don't really know. How about you?"

"Mm." He didn't answer. Instead, he started talking about Yasuyo Hozumi, the subject of our conversation the other day. "I called the library again later and asked her. Turns out she *is* related to Choko Hozumi. She told me Choko did in fact die at the age of eighteen in that institution. She hardly ate anything and got really weak, and then when winter came, she got a fever, and not more than five days later, she was dead. It was so sudden, everyone was surprised, the workers at the place, her family, everyone."

"So that's what happened."

"She told me there was nothing suspicious about it. Of course, this is all hearsay."

"But if she died in an institution, my grandma couldn't have had anything to do with it," I replied, taking out my notebook and drawing a line in pen through Choko Hozumi. Now there were four dead left.

"What about next weekend, Toko?" Yutaka's voice sounded kind of far away.

"I'm free."

"Okay, let's hang out on Saturday."

After hanging up, I flopped onto my bed and ran my eyes over my notebook. There were four names on the list: Namida, Yoji, Momoyo, and Kemari. I had drawn my lines in order of past to present, rapidly approaching the recently deceased looking for my potential victim. I got an email, so I took my eyes off the notebook and picked up my phone. It was from a friend I had recently made at the call center. The air in the room felt perturbed as though those four dead people left on the list were peeking over my shoulder with pale faces as I read the email. I had to find the victim. Unawares, a shudder of fear ran up my spine. I had to find the victim.

On Saturday night, I watched a movie with a friend and then waved goodbye in front of the bus stop before going off to stroll through town by myself. I went into that little bar on the arcade street, sat down at the counter, and asked for a cocktail. I felt a little weird going into a bar I didn't know by myself, and I really liked the atmosphere in this place. This time, the mustached owner didn't stare so much, so I didn't have to deal with the discomfort of the last time.

The place was empty. I let my eyes wander, and after a while, a man of the same generation as the owner pushed through the door. He was apparently a regular, since a beer appeared before him when he sat down at the counter even though he hadn't placed any such order. He was tall and thin, a middle-aged man with the air of having been handsome, who had then kind of aged out of that. As he drank his beer, he narrowed his eyes and looked over at me countless times, dazzled just like the owner had been when I first came in here.

"Sanjo," the owner said to the man quietly. "Alone again on a Saturday night?"

"Mm. You don't have to say the same thing every week, you know," the man called Sanjo replied snidely, furrowing his brow. The owner smelled like the capital, but Sanjo didn't. I got the impression somehow that he had always been in this region.

"You know, when I came back to this place, before I found you, Sanjo, I was a teensy bit depressed. All my old friends had families, and there I was, an old man. I mean, their kids were already in university." The owner spoke quietly. There were no other customers, so once he had placed the whiskey cut with water in front of Sanjo, he had nothing to do.

"Well, you know, out in the country like this, you don't generally see people who aren't married."

"But I went off to the capital. I had way too much fun, you know? Laughed my ass off. And I planned to keep it up too, so I staggered home all by myself, single. But everyone's so serious; it's so dull. It was such a relief when I ran into you, Sanjo. You're the same as you always were."

"We should be ashamed of ourselves, though. I mean, at this age?"

"You remember? In university. We used to have so much fun—every day was a party. We'd go to the beach, climb the mountain. The very notion that we would get old or die…the mountains…Oh!"

Simultaneously, the two middle-aged men whirled their heads to stare at me, looking like they had just put all the puzzle pieces together. They gazed at my face as I tipped back my glass. "Namida," they murmured from out of nowhere.

Smooth jazz played in the bar devoid of other customers. I finally understood why they had been staring so hard at me. These people knew my uncle Namida. And now that I was thinking of it, there was a student by the name of Sanjo in my mother's stories about the old days. I grew embarrassed, my face turned red, and I stared back at them. A smile came to the owner's face, but Sanjo got a strange look on his, as if angry or scared.

"Do we look alike?"

"Look alike? You two have the exact same profile. Aah, that was it. I knew you looked like someone, but I couldn't put my finger on it. So that's it…But you, you're what to Namida?"

"Uh, um, his niece," I replied to the owner's question in a small voice. "I'm his younger sister's daughter."

Sanjo narrowed his eyes abruptly. He observed my face for another thirty seconds or so before slowly lifting the corners of his mouth. He smiled. "Huh," Sanjo murmured.

The owner nodded. "This one started coming around last month-ish. I was sure I knew that face. It's been driving me nuts."

"Me too. It's been bugging me this whole time. I kept thinking I'd met her somewhere before. I get it. It's Namida's face."

"I'm surprised too... But it is a small town, after all," I replied. They both bobbed their heads in agreement.

The CD ended, and the owner put something else on. Jazz poured out of the speakers once again. New customers came in, so he showed them to a table and took their order. As he made their cocktails, he said, "All this time. I forgot about Namida. I was more of an acquaintance than anything else. But he was a quiet guy, the sort who was almost not there, you know?"

"I liked the way he was reserved like that. He was a good guy," Sanjo interjected. The owner nodded.

"Um, were you both there when my uncle Namida died?"

"Mm-hmm. That was when we were up in the mountains. We were both there. I was walking on up ahead, but Sanjo was right there with him. Namida was walking right behind him. Sanjo tried to jump off the cliff and go after him, but we all held his arms behind his back and stopped him.

"He was walking behind me, but I could feel him in my vision too." Sanjo slowly narrowed his eyes and peered into his glass. "But then he was suddenly gone."

"We all started running around like crazy people after that. But the thing is, no one heard him scream or anything. We didn't notice anything. It was such a huge shock. When you're that young, it doesn't even cross your mind that your friends can die. I mean, they're just as young as you are. Which is why we kind of thought he had maybe slipped off and gone home or something."

"He was just gone. That kind of departure, it's too awful. He could've at least said something," Sanjo murmured, and the owner got kind of a strange look on his face.

"Said something? Like what?"

"Aah…yeah, like what. Maybe goodbye or something."

More young customers came into the bar. Sanjo stood up and said in a small voice, "I'll see you later." I decided I would head out too.

The night road was frozen and silent. Walking on the arcade street at night, I saw how the steel structures were suddenly like creepy ruins, old and bent in different places, rising sluggishly up into the wintry night sky, almost like the abandoned bones of an ancient dragon. Chilly stars glittered above. Light leaked out of shops here and there, but really, this was a place meant for afternoon promenades, the wholesome daytime town of students. I walked slowly, looking down at my feet, and felt like I could hear echoes of the hustle and bustle of the people who prospered here in the long distant past. My own footfalls were surprisingly loud. I was thinking about how it was a little scary to be there at night when the shadow of a tall man appeared abruptly from the darkness and grabbed my arm. I froze to the spot, unable even to scream.

"Sorry. I didn't mean to scare you."

It was the middle-aged man from the bar before. Namida's friend. Sanjo. Looking at him in the gloom, illuminated faintly by the moon, I saw that he was still a handsome man. In his slender, almost womanly face, his almond eyes were dazzling, almost slits cut into his face. His half-open lips were thin and looked a little cruel.

"Oh, no, it's fine. It's just I didn't know who it was for a minute."

"Seeing you in the dark like this, you really do look like Namida."

"Huh. I do?"

"I have a car. I'll give you a lift," Sanjo said. "It's not safe around here at this hour. It's fine during the day, but there are a lot of abandoned shops around here and all." He started walking toward the parking garage.

I hurried after him. "Um, so, Mr. Sanjo, you went to high school and university with my uncle?"

"Mm-hmm. After high school, we went on to the same university together."

"Were you close?"

"It would have been physically impossible for us to have been any closer. We were that close," Sanjo said in a low voice, sounding angry for some reason.

He walked quickly through the dragon bones of the arcade street, and I was forced into a sort of trot to try and keep up with him and his long, slender legs. The moonlight shone dimly, turning him into a gangly, sad shadow figure. Looking at him from behind, I saw the hair hanging down to his shoulders was a little thinner at the top of his head. *Time just keeps pushing ahead*, I thought again. If I squinted a little, I felt like I could see a beautiful vision of the young Sanjo and the graceful Namida, the uncle I knew only from photos and old stories, side by side, walking together on quick legs. Once young and beautiful men. *Was anyone really that strong?* I wondered. Standing above everyone. Even the beautiful men.

Sanjo looked back at me, and his dry, creased face seemed a little looser and gentler than before. I sighed with relief and quickened my pace to catch up with him. The enormous form of the parking garage finally appeared before us, cutting the arcade street in half, slightly dirty and shining palely. I realized, belatedly, that going with a strange man was dangerous—much, much more dangerous than walking alone by myself at night on the arcade street, but I somehow got the sense that if the man were Namida's friend, it would even be okay if I got myself killed tonight. It was foolish, but in that instant, this was definitely the feeling that flashed to life in my heart.

The fact that I had only been born because Namida had died returned to my mind yet again. Because of the sudden death of the beloved oldest son, of whom so much had been expected, Kemari was married, and I was born, a truly dull girl. My own sorry self made my heart ache. Maybe the Akakuchiba family had been lost on the wrong path ever since Namida's death. Someone who had directly inherited Namida's blood should have been the heir to the main family. Tonight especially, I couldn't stop myself from having this thought.

Sanjo got in an old, fairly beat-up car and pointed me to the passenger door. He apparently used the car for work; the back seat was piled with a mess of papers and cardboard boxes and other things. The interior had that haze found only in the cars of smokers. Shuddering, the vehicle pulled out of the garage and raced into the night of Benimidori.

"We were very close," Sanjo said, suddenly, breaking the heavy silence. "Being in school was great. It was all great. Do you ever have that thought?"

"Yeah, I do. It's like...you're so free."

"I get that. You're free in what you think. You're free in love. Although the trade-off is you don't own anything."

"Um, my uncle died just a little before he graduated, right?"

"Mm-hmm. We were hiking up in the mountains, and Namida was behind me. I felt like he called to me. But really faintly. I thought it was just in my head, though, so I didn't turn around. Plus, we were trekking toward the top, so I was focused on that. And then he was just gone. I wish I knew whether he slipped or if he jumped. I've wanted to know that for so long. But you're his family and you probably don't even know that. This sort of thing, the people left behind, all we can do is carry on, not knowing. That's all we get."

"So my uncle definitely died then at that point?"

"What a weird question. It was definitely then. They got the general time of death from the autopsy, and the way they first found him was basically proof that he fell from the mountain into the river. That's how Namida left this world. Without even saying goodbye...It's been twenty-five years already. It should feel farther away than this."

The car slipped through the dark village, fat snowflakes starting to fall, flashing in the light, fireflies gently dancing down. We reached the hill road of the steps and started to ascend slowly. The engine roared.

"What's your name?" Sanjo said, abruptly, soberly.

"Toko. Written like child of the eye. Toko."

"Huh." Sanjo half opened his thin lips and sighed. He stopped the car in front of the gates of the Akakuchiba main house. Resting his elbows on the steering wheel, he looked over at me. "You should've been a boy. I hate it somehow that you have Namida's face even though you're a woman," he said suddenly, venomously, and his lips twisted into a sneer. "Get out."

I slowly slid out of the car. The battered machine shot down the hill road, shuddering, this time with the force of going too fast. I watched as it disappeared down the hill, nearly tumbling away. And then I stepped through the gates, went into the house, and walked down the hallway toward the altar.

I looked up at Namida's photo hanging on the wall. A somehow frail smile sat on his graceful face. I didn't think we looked alike. But maybe there were traces of me there somewhere. I guess that's what it means to be related by blood.

Then I went back to my room and took out my notebook. I drew a line through Namida Akakuchiba's name. The line shook a little. There were three people left: Yoji, Momoyo, and Kemari. All of whom had died when Manyo was about to march up and over the hill of fifty. Had she really killed someone at that age? And if she had, who could it have been? I didn't know. I threw down my notebook and fell into bed.

That night, I dreamed of her for the first time in a long time. A dream of a young Manyo frolicking with damp flowers in a valley of wild roses in the fullness of bloom. I grunted and groaned with the dream, and the Goldfish, aka Midori Kurobishi, appeared in the middle of it, glittering clothing fluttering and flapping. "Toko, Toko!" she said loudly. "Wake up, Toko."

I opened my eyes, and Midori Kurobishi was peering down at me.

"Toko, what're you makin' such a fuss about? I could hear you shouting all the way down in my room. Aah, you poor thing."

It was already dawn. The night was pale on the other side of the sliding doors. "I was dreaming about Grandma," I said as I sat up, holding my head.

"What?" A strange look came across Midori's face. "Manyo doesn't come to me in my dreams. I miss her so, I do. I wish I could see her again."

Still sleepy, I muttered, "Once your ride comes, you'll get to see her on the other side," and Midori gave me a sharp slap on the ass. I cried out and dove back into my futon.

But she stayed with me until I went back to sleep. "We were in the valley of the wild roses," I murmured.

"Well. I s'pose when I die, I'll head over there too," Midori replied, as if dreaming herself.

And then I fell asleep. Midori sang softly by my bed.

The snowflakes fluttered from the sky and began to pile up a little on the ground. The weekend. I saw Yutaka for the first time in a while. We went on a drive, then shopping, and then to our usual sky-blue room at The Chateau.

"I've been thinking about a lot of things," Yutaka said.

"Like what?" I asked, setting out on the table the juice and snacks we had bought at the convenience store.

"One thing, okay?" He paced around the circular bed. "One thing is all the stuff with your grandma. One thing is the possibility that she slipped some lies into those old stories. She was telling them to her grandkid, but she was hiding the fact that she killed a person, so she might have skipped over some bits on purpose or lied about just one part or something. I've been thinking about the fact that you can't believe everything she told you."

I was totally ready for him to start talking about work or life or something like that, so this was a letdown of sorts. "You've been thinking about that this whole time?"

"Yeah, uh-huh. I've been thinking." Yutaka nodded restlessly. "And one more thing. The difference between what Manyo 'saw' with her eyes and what she 'saw' with her gift. If you believe the bit about her being clairvoyant, that is. I mean, there's that story about being able to see the snapper on the sliding door of the Akakuchiba house from below on the hill road, but you can look up all you want and you're not ever going to be able to see the picture on the doors. There's the angle of the thing, and before anything else, it's just too far."

"Her eyesight was apparently really good."

"That's not the issue here. The problem is the angle and the distance. And I guess the same thing'd go for her being able to see the housekeeper giving birth in the branch house from the cypress tree in the yard. She probably 'saw' it with her clairvoyant eyes, rather than with her flesh-and-blood eyes. But I'm betting Manyo didn't make any distinction between the two and just remembered whatever she saw. Maybe some pieces of her stories aren't real things that actually happened in front of her, but like, distant events the clairvoyant madam saw or things that happened a little in the future." Yutaka stopped moving and sat down on the edge of the bed. "Basically, the idea is we can't trust all of the old stories. What do you think?"

I nodded. I took a sip of juice as I pulled out my notebook, in which the number of dead had decreased slightly since we last met, and handed it to Yutaka.

"So three people left," he said in a quiet voice.

I put on some music, and the constant din of cars passing by on the highway outside the window grew distant. I sat down on the opposite side of the bed and picked up a snack.

"Yoji," Yutaka murmured, still staring at the notebook. "Was he really decapitated?"

"Yeah. That's definitely true. It's a famous accident. The whole banquet train fell into the ravine, rescue teams showed up, there was a media helicopter up in the air; it was a whole thing. Some kind of steel something on the ceiling broke off and cut right through my grandpa's neck, and he died. Just like in my grandma's vision."

"Manyo didn't see the banquet train. Just his head going flying and him dying. She didn't foresee all the stuff with him getting on the train and the train being knocked into the ravine by the wind, did she?"

I gaped at Yutaka.

"Well, it's just, I mean, this is just what if, but maybe it's not wrong that the cause of death was his head getting cut off, but like, maybe the time is wrong or something. Like maybe, the dead body was placed in the banquet train with the head already cut off, and halfway along, the yamaoroshi blows and sends the train down, and in the end, it comes out as an accident. Or something."

"What?" I was dumbfounded. I had been thinking that Manyo couldn't have had anything to do with Yoji's death because she wasn't in the banquet train, but it wouldn't have been impossible if the time of death were different. But why would she have done something like that? And wouldn't that mean that everyone else on the train was an accomplice? I sat there, lost in thought.

Yutaka pointed at the notebook before continuing. "How about Kemari?"

"I'm pretty sure it wasn't her. I mean, I saw it."

"When she died?"

"Yeah. I mean, I saw right before she died and right after. She went into the next room, slid the door shut. And then I thought something was up, so I slid it open again, and she was already on the ground. There was nothing suspicious about the way she died."

"Really?"

"Really."

I stood up and went to put my half-finished juice in the fridge. When I opened the door, the inside of the appliance wasn't cold at all, which confused me, and I sat there thinking for a bit.

"The fridge's busted," Yutaka said casually, without taking his eyes off the notebook. "Since last week."

"Huh." I slowly closed the door and sat back down in one corner of the bed. I slouched there and didn't say anything for a while.

I hadn't seen Yutaka last week. I spent the weekend going to the arcade street by myself and catching a movie with a friend. What woman had Yutaka come here with? Tears threatened to spill out of my eyes, so I gritted my teeth hard and stood up. I put on my coat and grabbed my bag. "I'm going home," I said.

Yutaka looked up, surprised. "What's wrong?"

I shoved the notebook in my bag. "Who did you come here with? Last week," I asked.

"Ah," Yutaka muttered and fell silent.

I left the room, and he hurried out after me. He followed me into the elevator, still pulling his jacket on.

Neither of us said anything in the elevator.

"You won't be able to get a cab," he said, once we got outside. "I'll take you home."

That was true. I slid into the passenger seat of the Corolla, feeling miserable. The car pulled out onto the highway slowly, tires leaving black tracks as they packed down the snow covering the road. The sky was a dark gray.

The Corolla stopped at the gates to the mansion, and I hurried to escape through them. I could hear Yutaka calling after me, but I didn't look back. "Sorry, sorry, I'm sorry . . ." His voice felt like it was coming to me from a long ways away. My head was a mess. I walked through the backyard, where a thin layer of snow sat on the ground, and looked back at my own footsteps. And then I climbed the cypress tree.

The cypress tree that Manyo had climbed that long-ago day. I stood where the trunk forked into a Y and looked at the branch family house off in the distance. It really was far away, and the lattice-like painted wall of the storehouse faced this way, rather than a window of the main building; I couldn't see any part of the interior. Manyo hadn't seen the housekeeper Masago giving birth, she had "seen" it. *Huh, so that's what happened.* I was impressed with Yutaka, but I remembered everything in the next instant, and my shoulders dropped. What exactly had he been doing in the few weeks we hadn't seen each other?

I could call out "catch me," but I had no one who would do it, so I jumped lightly to the ground on my own. I floated for an instant, and it seemed like I would fly away, but then I faced the ground and landed. I felt like I had become a flying person somehow. *Grandma's most interesting vision was the one of Toyohisa flying,* I thought. Although I didn't know what that vision meant.

I crossed the veranda and went into the house, made some hot tea in the kitchen, poured some milk in, and took a sip. Something was bugging me about my mother, Kemari, and I started out down the hallway, mug in hand.

Soho caught sight of me. "Oh, you're home."

"Yeah."

"Although you look terrible. What happened?"

"Thanks. Hey, Tamo? Do you remember when my mom died?"

"Oh, I remember." He pulled a terrible face and started walking after me down the hallway. "It was a pretty big deal. Because Kemari Akakuchiba was such an important person. Although, come to think of it, she just holed up in this house and never went out, unlike other manga artists, so I don't think too many people had actually met the woman herself. Anyway, she had been serializing a hit manga every week for more than twelve years, from when she was nineteen until she was thirty-two. That'll take anyone out. But I do think it gave the industry a shake."

Soho spoke with a grim look that I never saw with his usual erudite chatter. We walked down the smooth hallway and came to the rectangular Japanese-style room Kemari had used as her studio. We stopped and stared into it for a while.

The smell of ink. The sound of the pens of the young assistants working silently, desks all in a row. This Japanese-style room had been some kind of secret manga factory in the recesses of the mansion. A large desk had been placed in the seat of honor, where Kemari had drawn manga every single day. With her whole heart. Without paying attention to her daughter. Without a look back for her husband. For more than twelve years.

The smell of ink, once so strong it made my head hurt, and the sweet body odor of the assistant girls no longer hung in the air; instead, a slightly dusty, damp air filled the room. There was nothing here anymore. No joy, no hatred, no desire, nothing. Soho and I stood there absently, after all these years, staring at a time past.

"The first time I met Kemmy, you know, she was still nineteen," Soho said abruptly. His voice was gentle somehow, and I looked up at his face in profile. "Younger than you are now, Toko. She was a total, complete kid."

Now that I was thinking about it, he was right. When my mother was my age, she had already long been a best-selling manga artist. A chill ran up my spine for some reason as I realized this all over again.

"She was a good kid. She seemed so grown-up, but then sometimes, she'd suddenly be so childish. You know? She had good points but didn't seem to have any confidence in herself, which is why— Well, that's why I figured I could make her into a pretty good manga artist."

"Uh-huh."

"Once she was that artist, though, Kemmy, she changed somehow." The gentle smile that had found its way onto Soho's face disappeared. "I wondered if maybe she wanted to run away."

"My mother?"

"Yeah. Because I was a runaway editor, right? I just got sick of everything: manga, money, artists, all of it. But Kemmy, she didn't run. I mean, drawing until you die, just think about it. You have to do something. But she knew she was too popular, she couldn't stop anymore. I know it's totally ridiculous, but back then, I felt guilty for making her into a star. I thought, she'll have to die if she wants to get away. And I told her that once too. That she should just pretend to be dead or something. That I'd help her. And she bust a gut laughing. But then she really did go and die."

"Uh-huh."

"The fact that she died after finishing the last chapter, though, that's very like her. That girl was a mess, but she finished what she started. And that's not a bad thing, you know? She put me through the wringer, but I could never bring myself to hate this part of her. Right up to the end." Soho stepped into the studio and stood where Kemari's desk had been.

"Kemari Akakuchiba," he muttered, looking down on a vision of the woman who was no longer there. "You did good."

I saw a vision of the large woman staggering like a ghost, shoulders shaking and walking this way. There were no assistants that day. There was only me, as a child. Kemari put down her pen, stood up, and walked this way. She opened the sliding fusuma doors leading to the nap room, lightly said "I'm going," and closed the doors. *Ah,* I noticed something, stood up, and when I opened the doors with a "Mom?" she was face down on the futon, already dead. I peered down at my fallen mother's face and held the palm of my hand under her nose. She wasn't breathing. I took her pulse the way I had seen others do. She had no pulse. My mother was leadenly heavy, like a dead animal. I hurried to call a grownup. I ran out of the room in the depths of the house, almost falling down the hallway, shouting, "Someone! Help! Mom's—"

I staggered forward like a sleepwalker and placed my hand on the fusuma door, just like I had then. Opening it slowly, I felt as though the vision of that day manifested once again in the fourteen-or-so-square-meter room, empty now. The shimmering of a dark red heat haze. It was a dreary sight, large futon set imposingly in the middle of the room, accompanied by only the trunk with changes of clothes in it. When she collapsed on the futon that day, my mother looked larger than usual. The hem of her skirt was flipped up, and her dark skin gleamed under the fluorescent light. Silky skin like chilled milk chocolate. Maybe I heard the sound of her collapsing on the other side of the doors. I don't remember. Was there a thud or some other noise? I don't know. I ran over to my mother, I called to her, but she didn't answer. She was dead. The moment after she finished her long serialization, she died.

Soho came to me slowly and put a hand on my shoulder. He seemed like he was still afraid of that distant day. "When I found out she collapsed right after the manga was finished, I thought, aah, she's finally managed to escape. I had the feeling she'd been running before that too. But she was a corpse. She was dead. I still can't believe it."

"Uh-huh." I nodded, trembling. At Soho's urging, I left the room. I felt dizzy stepping out into the hallway. The tea in my mug was ice cold.

"After that," Soho murmured, as if telling secrets, "I-I saw Kemmy's ghost, just once. Don't tell anyone."

"Mom's ghost?"

"On the day of the funeral, Kemmy came out, looking sharp, carrying a trunk. Everyone was so busy that no one else noticed. She was wearing a sort of loud dress and walking down the hallway like she was in a hurry. I stared at her dumbfounded, and she looked back and smiled. She waved at me. I started to go after her, but she stepped out of the entryway and that was that. She was such a bright ghost, I was astonished. I couldn't even call out to her."

"That—" I was about to say, *That was probably Aira.* Wool-gathering Soho had been convinced that man-stealing Momoyo was the ghost of a housekeeper right up until her funeral, and he hadn't known about Aira at all, that woman who looked exactly like Kemari. I had no doubt that the woman dressed in flashy clothes who left carrying a trunk on the day of Kemari's funeral was the body double. It wasn't that no one was looking; it was that everyone else knew her so no one was surprised. Soho, who had mistaken her for a ghost, was probably the only one who even remembered the scene.

Aira—

Right. Aira looked exactly like Kemari. Which was precisely why she had lived that bizarre life as a body double for the overworked manga artist. And after Kemari died, Aira disappeared from the mansion without anyone noticing. Because there was no longer any need for a body double. *So where was she now?* I wondered. Her visa would have expired long ago. Did she make it back to her own country? Or was she still somewhere in Japan?

Kemari's milk chocolate skin, so like Aira's. That sharply defined beauty—

I slapped my hand over my mouth and looked back down the hallway. The hallway I had just come down. And that time when I was nine, then too, I had raced down this hallway almost falling, shrieking for a grown-up. Shrieking, "Mom's not breathing!" There was only me and Kemari in the studio then. Kemari...

Trembling, I went back to the studio. Soho followed me.

That day, my mother went from the studio into the nap room farther in. She closed the fusuma doors. By the time I opened them, she had collapsed. I thought she had fallen with a *thud*. But I didn't know if the nap room had been empty before she opened the doors. There was no way I could know if there had been a dead body in there right from the start. Or if I had been helping paste tone that whole time in the room next to a dead body...

My mother went into the nap room and closed the doors. What if another woman—for instance, Aira—had already been in there, dead? A dead body wearing the same clothes. But even still, there would have ended up being two Kemaris. No. There had to have been someplace to hide.

I looked around the interior room. It was empty now, but I returned to the memory of what it used to hold. The trunk in the corner. Had it been, in the end, big enough for a large woman to hide in? I didn't know.

It had looked like a very big box to child me. At any rate, it might have been a hiding spot. My mother hid in the trunk. I came in and found Aira's body. I thought it was my mother's, I screamed, I ran from the room yelling for an adult. What did Kemari do? What would I have done if I was her? Obviously, I'd have come out from that corner of the room. And headed in the opposite direction I took down the hallway. Then the manga artist Kemari would be dead, and the real Kemari could live on as Aira. She wouldn't be the frantic manga artist anymore. Right, it was just like Soho had said, she "escaped."

Having gotten this far, I was suddenly troubled. Had Aira been murdered? This woman who had writhed in agony when I was born, as if on behalf of Kemari. Had she operated as the body double in secret right up until the very end? And what did my grandmother's "I killed someone" mean? Had she killed Aira? Had my mother then used the dead body as a stand-in for herself? Was it planned or did it happen spontaneously? My grandmother's last words "But it wasn't out of hate" could plausibly apply to Aira. It was unlikely that Manyo had any kind of grudge against the younger woman.

Shaking, I stood in this room where a murder may very well have taken place. *There's no way*, I thought abruptly. My mother hadn't been able to love or raise me very well, but still, I couldn't believe she would have set me up to discover her dead body. Kemari was a woman who finished what she started. I also couldn't help thinking that Manyo's murder was not just one of convenience like this. I went back to my room, took out my notebook, crossed out Kemari's name and, in its place, wrote "Aira" in small characters.

I wanted to trust the two women who were my roots. *This is wrong.* I shook my head. *Wrong. Wrong.*

Before supper, I popped in at one of the branch houses, the house Kaban had married into and currently ruled over. I went in through the back door. "Is Aunt Kaban here?" I asked, and the children Kaban—whose name meant "bag"—had given birth to came bustling out and yanked me along by the hand. "She is." These children had been given entirely normal names, but unbeknownst to my aunt, I called them Saifu, "wallet"; Denwa, "telephone"; Techo, "notebook"; and Kuchibeni, "lipstick." With the idea that these were all things that would come from inside a bag. My aunt would probably be mad if she found out. Although she didn't seem to hate her own bizarre name.

I stuck my head in the kitchen and found her in the middle of slicing burdock root with the housekeeper. She chatted at me about housework. "With four kids, just putting meals together is a lot of work." And then she asked, "Is something wrong?"

"Auntie, there used to be someone called Aira in the main house way back when, right?"

"Shh!" She hurriedly brought her index finger to her lips and came out of the kitchen. "Don't say that name," she told me in a low voice so that the housekeeper couldn't hear.

"Why not?"

"Because no one can know my sister had a body double. She was just so busy back then, so she would work in the mansion while Aira took care of all the TV appearances and magazine interviews and things. Aira's a secret."

"Huh. But she hasn't been in the mansion since Mom died, right? Tamo says he saw her leaving the day of the funeral with a trunk."

"Mm-hmm. She went back to the country where she was born. I remember it. There at the wake, we all talked about it. And Yoshio, he said how she had been such a help to his wife and offered her a pretty good retirement payout. Aira was basically indifferent to the whole thing as usual, and she took Kemari's passport and left."

"Her passport?"

"She pretended she was Kemari, got on a plane, and went back to the Philippines. Then she sort of disappeared into the night of Manila. There was a bit of a fuss that maybe a Japanese person had gone missing in the Philippines. But when they looked into it, the person in question was already dead in Japan, so they wrote the whole thing off as a stolen passport used for some kind of criminal activity or something, and that was the end of that. No one outside ever knew that Aira had been in the mansion, so it was easy to explain away as a simple theft."

"Did you see Aira when she was leaving too?" I said, as if it were no big deal.

"No...Now that you mention it, I didn't really see her. We were all running around like crazy. I didn't have too much time for looking around. I was pretty impressed at Yoshio's attention to detail, though. I mean, it would have been strange if Aira had stuck around after that, wouldn't it? This woman, the spitting image of my big sister who was supposed to be dead, lolling around the house. Yoshio called her into his study, and they talked for a long time. And you know, that day, we were all so busy that I'm pretty sure he was the only one who talked to her. Before I knew it, she had slipped out of the house and poof! She was gone."

"Oh, really," I said.

I was still only half convinced. Was the woman who left really Aira? If Kemari had taken her place, then she had pretended she was Aira, flown to the Philippines, and disappeared there. And then where did she go? Did she manage to completely escape like Soho said?

Kaban urged me to stay for supper, so I sat down between Techo and Kuchibeni and ate with the branch family. They still had something like family harmony and peace to them. I tried not to think about Yutaka, thought about Yutaka, and sighed from time to time. The burdock being cut earlier was scattered, brown, among the stewed dishes. The night grew late.

Work took my time and energy from Monday through Friday, so I stayed away from Manyo's notebook for a while after that. Talking with the strangers phoning in to the call center from anywhere and everywhere in the country was strangely exhausting. All day, every day, I had to respond as if I were an expert from whatever company on whatever product it was, so I couldn't let my focus slip for even an instant. I thought about working, about pride. All the things Yutaka was muttering about that night we slid down the embankment. Of course, I got nowhere with these thoughts. I hadn't seen Yutaka at all after that. He emailed or called sometimes, but I was somehow scared and I ran from him, leaving the emails unread, the calls unanswered. I was fainthearted in all things.

I met up with some friends from high school I hadn't seen for a long time, and we hung out over the weekend. The five of us went to an izakaya and drank, we went to karaoke, and finally, we set off some out-of-season fireworks under the pedestrian bridge in front of the station, running off before we were reported. At this age-inappropriate, irresponsible, childish behavior, I abruptly felt free. A gentle breeze blew through my head.

I had vague, drifting, selfish thoughts about how I wanted to live my life as a mere apathetic-ish consumer. I couldn't be a producer. I didn't want to be. I didn't want to have any social responsibilities. But even if I could manage to run from society entirely, I couldn't escape my relationships with other people. These connections we have with others are, in their own way, tiny societies themselves, and I had stumbled in this world as well, magnificently, shamefully.

The girl I had been closest with in high school slipped away from the group as dawn was breaking and whispered to me, "I guess Yutaka's really depressed."

"I wonder who he cheated on me with."

"I heard it was an older woman. Although I don't really know. The boys won't really tell me anything."

"Hmm," I murmured. I was proud of my youth, one of my few assets, so the fact that I had been cheated on with an older woman cut sharply into my shreds of self-confidence; I was deeply hurt. Like many women, I thought that everyone older than me was basically a grandmother. No matter how pretty, no matter how wonderful. They were just old things, after all.

But this was not a problem of love, but rather with my powerless, haughty spirit. It had nothing to do with Yutaka. As I struggled with all of this, I nodded in all the right places, pretending I wasn't interested, but this particular friend had known me too long and saw right through my sad show.

"I know it bothers you. I mean, the way you're acting."

"The thing is, okay? I mean, I've been going out with Yutaka for five years already and everything. But, like."

"He quit his job last week."

I kicked a rock on the road. Heavy and damp with winter, it tumbled along the asphalt making a dull sound. "He quit, huh?" I muttered.

My friend nodded. "He quit before too, right? Yutaka tries hard, but he snaps sometimes."

"He broke up with me that time too. And I heard about it then from you too."

"Hee hee! Information is a weapon in the war of love. And I've always been your spy, Toko." She made an exaggerated bow, and I cracked up. This tiny society around me. When I laughed, a few tears slipped out, which was embarrassing, but my friend kindly pretended not to notice.

The next day, it was still the weekend, and I was feeling the after-effects of hanging out the night before, so I was lying around the house when my phone rang. Yutaka. But of course, I was scared, and I simply stared at the phone as it rang and rang. In the afternoon, I went out, heading toward the port at Nishiki. To meet the retired paramedic.

The ocean rolled by Nishiki, pushing a chilly, salty wind onto the land. There was a nursing care center in a mixed-use building near the port, and the person I was looking for was sitting at the front desk, a man of sixty or so, hair half gray.

When he heard what I had to say, he smiled slightly. "The accident with the Akakuchiba president? Oh, now that caused quite the hullabaloo. Been twenty years or so already, hmm? You were born then, weren't you?"

"I was still too little, so I don't remember anything at all, though. Um." I tentatively asked about my grandfather's head being sliced off, and the man's face turned serious as he nodded.

"Nope, no mistake there. He died in the accident. This steel plate came off the ceiling and fell right on him. It was still stuck between the head and the torso when we got in there, and there were scratches and things on the plate. One look at the whole mess and you knew what happened. Of course, even if the plate hadn't taken his head off, you fall into a ravine like that one, you're not coming out of it alive, y'know? Everyone else in the train was dead too."

"Is that so..." I thanked him and left.

I went into a nearby café, drank some bukupuku tea, and opened up my notebook. I drew a line through Yoji Akakuchiba's name. Names added, names subtracted. There were two candidates left.

It was night by the time I got home. I snuggled into my futon and went to sleep. The next day, I grabbed ahold of my father resting his chin in his hand and drinking coffee.

"Is Mom really dead?"

My father spurted a lot of coffee at this question, coming at him out of the blue as it had. "What?" Deeply surprised. "Now? All of a sudden?"

"Oh, uh ... I was so little, I, uh, I wasn't sure."

"There's not being sure and then there's being ridiculous. You know, you really need to work on your confidence. Honestly."

"So then, she really is dead, right?"

"Yes, she is definitely dead. Honestly, what is going on with you, Toko? She's definitely dead," my father repeated, seemingly dumbfounded.

I got embarrassed and turned a little red. In a small voice, I asked him about the body double, Aira, who had lived here.

"Oh, Aira." He nodded. "Yes, she's really raking it in these days."

"Raking it in? What? Wait. Are you still in touch with her?"

"Of course I am. She did so much for us. That sort of connection, it can't be cut from our side. I talk to her every so often. It seems that business is good. Well, she did have some capital to start with, after all."

According to my father, after Aira went back to the Philippines, she used her severance pay to open a shrimp restaurant. About seven years ago, she brought in the Internet and turned it into a shrimp restaurant/Internet café. The place was apparently turning a tidy profit.

I followed my father into his study and peered into the computer monitor, waiting for the video call software to finally launch. A large, colorful woman appeared there. Huge, wonderfully black eyes. Her skin, the color of milk chocolate, was lustrous, and other than a wrinkle or two at the corners of her eyes, she looked very young still. Behind her was a restaurant type of wall with a large painting of a shrimp and a blackboard covered with characters I couldn't read, probably a menu.

"Hey, Yoh-sio," the woman said. Then she looked at me standing next to him gaping. "Who's this girl? Oh, she is maybe that kid?" Aira's Japanese, which had been fluent enough to work as a body double back when she was here in the mansion, had been washed away by the years and the world around her and was fairly broken now.

I stared at her hard enough to burn a hole right through her. She was as beautiful as ever, but she no longer looked very much like my mother. Her skin had gotten even darker, her eyes were damp like obsidian, and her frizzy, puffy black hair was exotic. She must have blended in when she was in Japan, a chameleon. Living in another country for a long time, she had simply developed a protective camouflage. With that removed, the body double of the shojo manga artist Kemari Akakuchiba could no longer be seen in the real Aira; she looked like nothing more and nothing less than the woman Aira herself.

So my mother really did die that day.

"How's business?" my father asked casually in Japanese. "Very good," Aira said in a teasing tone. "How about you?" "Mm-hmm," my father replied. "Not very good," and Aira laughed. It was an amicable exchange, warm with lingering memories of the past.

"I was just wondering if you were the one who died and my mother was still alive," I told her impulsively.

Aira clutched her stomach again and laughed loudly. "You wonder funny things. But okay, you just want your mother to be alive. I think I can understand that," she said. I could hear the many footsteps of customers trickling into the restaurant, and Aira stood up wearily. "Okay, talk to you again," she said and disconnected.

I went back to my room. And then I took out my notebook and drew a line through Aira's name. The names of the dead sitting next to each other. There was just one left.

Momoyo Akakuchiba. The woman of man-stealing lineage who died with legs bound and hands in hooks. So was it Momoyo? If it was, Manyo would have been fifty-five at the time. Could a mild-mannered woman pushing past middle age kill a woman on the cusp of thirty? Physical strength would have been on the side of the young. But Manyo had been a large woman. A mountain girl. I felt like serious power had to have slept in that solid physique.

Winter was moving toward its end. The new year started, and at the end of January, I quit my job at the general call center.

The more comfortable I got dealing with people on the phone, the more complaint work I was given. Calls came from all over the country, from people who had lost in the stock market, people whose computers had crashed, people who were angry for some unknown reason, all of them headed straight for our booths. If you made a call to a company's toll-free 0120 number and the support center on the other end of that number, your call was forwarded here, but the people who called to complain naturally believed they were connected to the head office in Tokyo or Osaka or some other major city. We weren't allowed to end complaint calls on our side; all we could do was offer the most detailed advice possible, repeatedly and earnestly apologize, and simply wait until the customer was satisfied and ended the call for us. A single call could sometimes take several hours. Although I got used to dealing with them and the work became routine, I gradually grew tired of these calls coming from all over the country to this single-story building plopped down in the suburbs of a provincial town.

On this particular day, the caller was an old man of fifty or so who had spilled sweet potato *shochu* liquor on his computer, and now it was all sticky. Why would you keep liquor that close to your computer anyway? He wanted a free repair, and the rule was that repairs due to neglect had to be paid for. But the old man was stubborn. I politely repeated the same thing over and over again. "I am extremely sorry, sir, but there is a fee for this kind of repair. Our company…"

"You Tokyo people are so cold!" he exploded, after about an hour and a half. "A thing like this and any neighborhood shop would be kind enough to just fix it for me. Come on."

I lost it. "This is Tottori," I immediately fired back. "I'm sorry, but you're not calling Tokyo here."

"What? Tottori? What on earth? Tottori…So I'm not calling the head office?"

"This is a call center. The people who work at the head office can't deal with each and every little call like this. They have jobs to do."

"Huh. How old are you?"

"Twenty-two."

"Ohh…Me, I'm in Yamaguchi. I'm calling way closer than I thought I was. You know, Yamaguchi's pretty close to Tottori. Quick trip by car. So, come on, go out with me. This is some kind of sign. Right?"

I slammed the phone down. The supervisor monitoring my booth lifted his face and searched me out. When an employee ended a call, that information flew over to the supervisor's computer. Having committed this sin, I would have my pay cut and be called into a separate room for a solemn lecture.

"I quit," I said before my supervisor could say anything.

"Toko, please wait a moment. Let's you and I talk about this," my supervisor said, in beautiful standard Japanese, raising one hand.

When I stood up and viewed the modern, sterile office like this, it was almost like a scene from some stylish TV drama set in the capital. Other employees in the middle of calls in the many booths were glancing up at me, likely wondering what was going on.

"Call centers like this are bullshit."

"Toko. Calm down. How about you and I go talk about this over there, just the two of us? Hmm?"

"This place isn't Tokyo's garbage dump. People in the city, they build a little office like this, and I mean, it's pretty at first glance, but then they throw all the work *they* don't want to do onto the young people out in the country. They take advantage of how bad the economy is and how there are no jobs, and they dump the shitty stuff on us in the country. This isn't a garbage dump. All these towns in the country, we have our own histories and our own pride. I won't do this kind of work anymore. I'm quitting for the sake of my pride."

My voice echoed across the entire floor.

My voice was more halting and saccharine than I thought.

The employees, who were generally my age, gaped at me, hung up their phones one after another, and stood up. They took off their headsets and, albeit slowly and rather lethargically, applauded. With so many calls being cut off halfway through, the short sound of buzzers came again and again from the supervisors' desks.

In the midst of the scattered applause, I was shy and hating myself, and I couldn't get anything else out of my mouth. Quitting for the sake of my pride, I mean, that was totally the worst, a complete and utter lie. I knew it only too well. I . . . I was running away. That was just an excuse. Just splitting hairs.

As we endure all kinds of things, as we take in the contradictions of society and resign ourselves to them, we drift into adulthood. We take it all in, good and bad, and we grow up. We present ourselves neatly to the world and enter into eternal battle against dull days. And this was something I couldn't do. Even though it was something everyone had been doing since the long distant past. Even though my grandmother's generation, my mother's generation, and even a certain percentage of my own generation already worked like this in society. I couldn't do it. The will to live and the readiness to fight had not been passed down to me from my parents. There was always going to be unpleasantness no matter where you went, but I wasn't prepared to be hurt by it. I had no confidence in myself, and so I ran away once more.

Several other young people left their booths with me, telling their respective supervisors, "I quit." There were many who looked over at me like they wanted to say something, but who did not stand up. Instead, they continued to move their mouths and deal with their phone calls. The people leaving. The people staying. I felt that both sides had their own conceits and thoughts that were too much for them. I left the office and breathed deeply of the outside air. *Aah, I failed again.* Round and

round, wandering lost, I was right back where I started. I cursed my
weak spirit. My feet were heavy on the way home, my heart was cold. It
felt like I would never reach the house.

When I told my family that I had quit my job, I was so despondent
that my father seemed to swallow the lecture he was on the verge of
giving me. As I looked up at that disappointed face, I remembered what
he had said, when was it, that morning, the day we talked about taking
down the blast furnace: "Everything's like that, after all. Starting something, continuing something, that's the really hard part."

Becoming an adult, becoming a productive member of society, this
thing anyone should have been able to manage was something I couldn't
do. Even though I didn't want to disappoint my father. Even though I
wanted him to be proud of me. I was ashamed of myself and looked
away first. My uncle Kodoku didn't say anything in particular.

I went to my room and, still depressed, emailed my friend, who
then spilled the most recent intelligence she had acquired through her
espionage. Apparently, Yutaka had gone back to his old job. I laughed a
little at that; why would he get rehired there, revolving door style? "Talk
to him already. Dating for five years, stuff happens," my friend said, and
I assented feebly.

The next day, I went to speak with the person who had pulled
Momoyo Akakuchiba's corpse from the sea; the old man at the nursing
care center had told me about him. He said that Momoyo had probably
bound her feet herself, so that she wouldn't be able to swim, left her suicide note, and jumped into the ocean. She was planning a lovers' suicide

and invited the man to join her, but when they dragged her up, she was alone. The man was nowhere to be found, but it was thought to be a lovers' suicide because of the note; the circumstances didn't lead anyone to think she might have been killed by anyone. I asked him if it could have been that someone else had bound her feet and thrown her in the ocean, and the man appeared startled.

"What?" he said in response. "Never even thought of that. I wonder."

I went looking for the would-be suicide partner, the young man from the rice shop. This had all happened over ten years earlier, so he was no longer a young man. He seemed uncomfortable when I told him that I was Kemari's daughter, but he responded to me very politely. As proof that Manyo's old stories were not lies, this rice shop man was, as expected, exceedingly ugly. I marveled again at my mother's deeply perverted tastes and stared at the rice shop man's face hard enough to burn a hole in it.

"Murder? Impossible. I mean, she fell into the ocean right in front of me."

"So my aunt was trying to commit suicide with you then?"

"She left the note there at Nishiki port, used some dried jellyfish as a weight, okay? She tied her feet, then tied mine real tight, and was all 'Okay, let's die now.' And then she threw herself at me. But I have a wife and kids—I can't just go dying with some other woman. I got scared and jumped to the side to dodge her. And then Momoyo's sweet face snapped. She turned into something like one of those Hannya Noh masks, right? Both of us had our feet tied together, so she jumped at me, howling. And then I jumped, sort of shrieking.

"Yeah, right around there. Nighttime at the port, big fat snowflakes falling, yeah, right here. The two of us jumping, dodging, jumping, dodging. Momoyo's face then, aah, it was like a demon's. Her eyes yanked up, tears flying away white on the winter wind, and her voice, the voice coming from those bright red lips. This deep, sort of masculine howl, it just never stopped. After a bit, she lost her balance and fell into the ocean right here. I panicked and I kept calling her name, but the winter sea was rough, and in the blink of an eye, she disappeared between the waves.

"I was scared out of my mind. I grabbed the note she left under the jellyfish and sort of rolled off down the street. Like this. I was pretty far from the port before I realized I could just undo the ropes myself. I was just so freaked out, you know? So I finally noticed, and then I undid the ropes. My knees just about gave out under me, but I held on and made it back home, and then I hid in the storehouse and shook. I felt like her pale spirit was still looking for me.

"And then in the morning, her body was pulled up, and everyone came looking for me; it was my wife who found me shivering in the storehouse. I gave Momoyo's note to someone from the main family. That adopted son. Right, I guess that'd be your dad. It had 'To Kemari' written on it. They must have been pretty close if she left a suicide note for her. Aah, it was really terrifying. Even now, I sometimes have nightmares about it. I hear Momoyo's voice calling me from the sea."

The rice shop man shuddered, and his shoulders shook. "Ocean's a dangerous beast," he muttered and turned his back on the port. Traces of an anguish that would never disappear came across his exceedingly ugly face.

The damp, salty wind marking the end of winter blew my hair up around me. When we parted, the man told me, "It was definitely a failed lovers' suicide. If you had to say that someone killed Momoyo, I guess that'd be me? I had feelings for her and everything, but I was also having fun with a brand-new affair. I was happy to have two sisters fighting over me. A man fooling around's the one who dropped Momoyo into the ocean. It wasn't murder, but someone is guilty for her death: me. That's what I think."

"And you're sure that my aunt's suicide note was addressed to my mother?"

"Yup. It said 'to Kemari' in really big, clumsy characters."

"You're sure?"

"Oh, I'm sure. How could I forget? It's burned into my eyeballs. Everything about that night is. How could I forget?"

I politely thanked the exceedingly ugly man, and on my way home, I racked my brains trying to remember every detail of my grandmother's story.

According to her, Momoyo's suicide note was brought back to the Akakuchiba main house and read aloud by Yoshio. It said, "We die together," and hearing those words, my grandmother fainted. That suicide note was even now carefully tucked away in a drawer in the altar.

Back home, I apprehensively went in to the altar. I opened the drawer and pulled out Momoyo's suicide note. It came out, wrapped in a scrap of paper.

Written on the envelope was "Madam Manyo."

Momoyo's suicide note from the story. Her suicide partner

remembers it being addressed to Kemari. So then why was the suicide note here now addressed to Manyo? Were there two suicide notes? There was no suicide note to her in any of her stories. Was this one of those bits Yutaka had raised the possibility of, one Manyo left out on purpose? If it was, then it had to be a part related to my grandmother being a murderer.

I sat by the altar and thought about this for a long time.

Momoyo had definitely fallen into the ocean on her own. Even if the purposefully hidden bit was connected to Manyo's murder, it wasn't Momoyo who had been murdered. I took out my notebook and drew a line in ballpoint pen through the name Momoyo Akakuchiba. I was finally out of candidates among the dead. The mystery of a suicide note addressed to the wrong person. A victim that didn't exist. The confession of murder that lingered in my ears. I clutched my head in my hands.

I went back to my room to let myself wallow in it. My cell phone rang. It was Yutaka. I answered it hesitantly. After a slow, awkward conversation, we decided to meet the following weekend.

My friend in espionage reported back to me, leaking the latest intelligence: the person Yutaka had cheated with was apparently that older librarian; he was sorry and wasn't seeing her anymore, and he said he couldn't live without me. "And, also, I'm getting married this year," she said abruptly. I was stunned. But she had been dating a man who worked at the village office since we were in junior college. And we were going to be twenty-three that year. It was about the time some people started to settle down. "I think the ceremony'll be in the fall. Come, okay? With Yutaka. Both of you," she stressed, and I replied in a small voice, "Okay."

Time kept marching forward. No one could stop it. The smiles of the old dead popped up and then gradually grew distant.

As if to announce the end of winter, the snow stopped that morning, and a dazzling white light shone down on patches starting to melt on the road.

I saw Yutaka for the first time in ages. He had gotten a lot thinner. He came to pick me up at the gates of the main family house, just like before, and stared at the mansion as if dazzled by it. I got in the car and silently fastened my seatbelt.

We didn't move; the car stayed where it was. Yutaka said nothing. In the end, I was the one to open my mouth.

"You quit your job, but then you went back?"

"Yeah... How'd you know that anyway?"

"That's weird."

I had plenty of scathing words to rebuke him with, but I was having trouble getting them out. I was stuck. I said nothing and hung my head. And then, Yutaka abruptly said something really strange.

"I cheated on you because I wanted to quit my job."

"Huh?"

Startled, I involuntarily looked at him. He had a serious look on his face. So apparently, he wasn't trying to be funny here.

"What are you—"

"I wanted to quit my job, but as long as we're dating, that's a bad thing for you."

"W-why is it bad for me?"

"People are going to say all kinds of things to you if I'm unemployed."

"*I'm* unemployed."

"That's fine for you. You're a member of the Akakuchiba main family. You basically don't even have to work ever. As long as I'm dating you, maybe they won't be trying to be mean or whatever, but people are going to say I'm a gold digger. I mean, some girls already think I'm lying to you. That I'm just after your status and money."

My jaw dropped and I kept staring at his face, resolutely turned forward. I had never once heard anything about this. Despite the fact that we'd been together for five years. I thought I was the one who had it rough, subject to some pretty harsh treatment back when Yutaka went to Koshien.

"It's fine as long as I have my shit together, but people are going to say all sorts of things to you if I'm not strong, not a man. That's why. I figured if I was away from you, Toko, I could quit. But that's actually pretty strange. I mean, you're the most important thing to me. I wanted to come back to you, so I went back to my job."

"That's weird, you know."

"Yeah."

"That time before, when you broke up with me that once, you quit your job."

"I did... I'm sorry. I keep doing the same thing."

Silence visited us once again.

The car slowly pulled out as if to get away from the awkwardness. I looked back at the red Akakuchiba mansion from the passenger seat.

It rose up haughtily; weighty, ponderous. This house would still be here long, long after this.

The former hero of Koshien, Yutaka, was silent; he simply drove. His thinking on all of this did have a certain kindness to it, but even so, I thought it was pretty antisocial. We ran along our seaside driving course, just me and Yutaka inside the Corolla II. Maybe because it was still chilly out, there weren't very many other cars on the road. The ones we did occasionally pass held young couples looking a lot like us. I wondered how many similar couples were out there in this country.

"I'm sorry," Yutaka said.

"Uh-huh."

"I'm really sorry. Please forgive me. I love you."

"Me too."

"I won't do it again."

"No, I'm sure you will."

"I won't. I will not. I totally will not. I understand now."

"I wonder."

Sitting there, I thought to myself how great it would be if I could just yell at him to shut the fuck up, jump out of the car, and just break up with him. The negligible pride I had, coming from my youth and nothing else, had been trampled by him and his cheating on me. No. This was a problem with the poverty of my own spirit. I was disheartened. It would all be so easy if I could hate him, but I loved Yutaka. That hadn't changed at all. My feelings for him were still the same as they were all those years ago in grade eleven, strangely unfaded despite the almost six years that had passed. I believed that I would continue to love him into the future—I was certain of it. It was the only true absolute in me, my love for this hopeless boy.

Having brought this tale all the way to the modern age at last, I, Toko Akakuchiba, had no new stories to tell. Not a single one. No turbulent histories of Benimidori, no fresh thoughts about work. All that was left to me were my extremely personal problems. And what a pathetic story they make.

However, if Yutaka and I did manage to stay together and get married in a few years, I'd be doing the one thing my grandmother and mother didn't; I'd be marrying for love, I realized suddenly. Although I had absolutely no idea what was going to happen from now on, what the future held.

As we drove, I talked to Yutaka about Manyo's notebook. When I told him that I had taken all the dead off the list of candidates and about the mystery of the two suicide notes that remained, he cocked his head to one side.

"So they say the same thing, but they're addressed to two different people?"

"Right. To Manyo and to Kemari. I don't really get it."

The car climbed the hill road of the steps, and when we arrived at the house, Yutaka followed me inside. He wanted to see the suicide note. I led him to the altar and pulled the note out of the drawer amidst the purple incense smoke that filled the room again today.

"Maybe the handwriting's different or something?" Yutaka said, taking the note from me.

"The handwriting?"

"Like, the 'Madam Manyo' on the envelope and the 'We die together' on the page inside were written by different people. Then you could explain it."

"I guess." I cocked my head to the side.

We unwrapped the scrap of paper around the suicide note, pulled the letter from the envelope, and unfolded it. We held our breath as we compared them. From just a quick glance, we could tell the handwriting on both was in the same, fairly skillful hand.

"Looks like the same person wrote them both," Yutaka sighed. "I'm even more confused now. What does this mean…"

"Well, it *is* a suicide note. That's how it usually goes, right? Why did you think the handwriting might be different?"

"I just thought maybe the envelope and the letter could have been put together from different letters. I mean, in those old stories of Manyo's you talk about, there's another letter, isn't there?"

"Is there?"

"You're so stuck on the suicide note, you can't remember. Not that, the farewell letter. You know, when the plant stopped steel production, that one worker went away? And he left a letter for Manyo?"

"Oh," I said, nodding. The story of my father, Yoshio Akakuchiba, stopping the fires of the blast furnace and of the night the worker Toyohisa Hozumi went away. He had left a farewell letter for my grandmother with "Madam Manyo" written on it. "I'm going far away," it said, and that was how my grandmother knew that Toyohisa, known as the hero of the blast furnace, had finally cast off the Akakuchiba Steelworks for greener pastures.

But in that case, what was the letter here all about? Toyohisa's letter had indeed been addressed to Manyo. But the details on the page inside were different from what he had written. This page had the text from Momoyo's suicide note. But the handwriting was the same. What on earth was this supposed to mean?

Yutaka and I looked at each other, turning the whole question over in our minds, but we found no answers.

Just as the snowy season ended, work to turn the plant site into a vacant lot gradually began. Kodoku was busy, leaving early each morning. Although they weren't related by blood, in his suit and from behind, I felt that he resembled my father somehow. It was decided that I would help out in the accounting department at Red Dead Leaf starting that spring. I hesitated at the idea, worrying that maybe I would put the grown-ups around me on edge, but my father insisted fiercely that it would be a good experience, so I decided to try it out for a while.

Things with Yutaka were as usual. He now went to work without grumbling about it, as if he had suddenly been able to get over some mental road block. Maybe he had had some kind of change of heart. I didn't really understand it. We would be turning twenty-three soon enough, and I had the feeling that even though we hadn't done anything big, our youth, this enormous asset, was gradually being eaten away. I mentioned this anxiety to Kodoku, and he grinned.

"It's no big deal, you know. Life keeps going even when you're not young anymore," he said—words that were not exactly encouraging— and patted my shoulder.

February was already half over, and then one night, I stepped onto the veranda and stared absently out at the backyard, still tangled with withered, skeletal branches, before going outside to look down on the plant site from the top of the hill road of the steps. The enormous blast furnace, that symbol of prosperity soon to be torn down, glittered gray in the night sky. I felt sort of up in the air somehow as I stared at it. Then I went back into the house. Kodoku had just gotten out of the bath, so I got in, got out, put on a coat, went back outside, and stared at the blast furnace again. The time to say goodbye was approaching. I wanted to look at it forever.

The night grew long. When I went to bed, I had a dream about Manyo for the first time in a while. Still a young country girl, she was in the middle of the hill road of the steps, looking up at the sky. Mouth hanging open. Yearningly. Eyes wet. I had never seen such an expression on her face before. I was a little surprised in the dream, and I asked her, *Grandma, what are you looking at?* Perhaps my voice reached her, as childish, unsophisticated Manyo looked back at me. And then she pointed at the sky with a thin index finger.

I looked up at what she was looking at.

Someone was floating there. In the clear afternoon, the dark pink petals of Mitsuba azaleas danced on the wind and colored the aqua sky like polka dots. Bobbing lightly in the middle of them was a middle-aged man. I knew that his clothing, the color of dry leaves, was the uniform of a worker, originally the color of vegetable greens that had grown old and discolored. His left eye seemed very kind, but the right had been cruelly crushed; it had essentially merged into the skin and become something like a single, long wrinkle. *Toyohisa*, I realized. I looked down at Manyo next to me. She was staring up, gaping, at the man in the sky with a soft expression like joy that she had never shown me.

The one-eyed man, Toyohisa, arms and legs spread out, in the shape of an X. He flew face down, letting the sky see his back and us his front. He looked like he was enjoying himself up there. Eventually, he slowly receded into the distance. Still smiling warmly. Manyo let out a sob with a hic. *What's wrong?* I asked my little-girl grandmother in the dream.

Toyo didn't know, Manyo said quietly. *Toyo didn't know I can't read. It was just, I was embarrassed. I was ashamed to let him know. Didn't say nothing.*

She began to cry and wiped her tears away with the back of her hand, in a very childlike manner. These were the same words my grandmother had murmured that final night, at her dressing table. Had my grandmother, on that night when she would soon die, come through the mirror and into my dream in the future? Had she come to see me? That night when I had been so anxious sitting in the hallway, shaking all over.

In the dream, as she cried, her hair fell further and further down her back, and her body stretched upward; she grew into the solidly built adult daughter of the mountains. Now the clairvoyant madam, Manyo called for Toyohisa in her adult voice. It was a terrifying call, the loud howl of an animal, enough to split the sky.

From off in the distance, Toyohisa, who had ostensibly flown away, zoomed back to us. Still in the X shape. His smiling face was now a little drawn and sad.

Grandma, I cried.

There was no expression on her face. The sky grew dark, and night, black like a sunless ravine, fell. Heaven and earth and Manyo rolled around. I let out a scream and crouched down. The night sky spun itself upside down, leaving Manyo and I above and the flying Toyohisa below. With the new angle, Toyohisa was lying face up, still in his X, and Manyo and I were looking down at him. In the blink of an eye, my hands were clutching something. Round, black, thick iron. Manyo and I had climbed up the scaffolding—that was what we were holding on to. I looked over my shoulder and shuddered.

We were at the summit of the blast furnace. On the very scaffolding I had climbed a tiny bit that day at the beginning of winter and then looked over my shoulder, gotten scared, and shimmied back down. Before I knew it, Manyo and I had scaled the towering furnace. With the concentrated black of the sky behind me, I looked back and saw the ground far, far below. Everything was dyed ultramarine, the dark color of the night. A thick darkness, a bottle of ink spilled.

Manyo was looking into the blast furnace.

I also peered inside the enormous chimneylike structure.

Toyohisa, who had flown gently and receded off into the distant sky high above before heaven and earth were inverted, was now lying face up, inverted himself, arms spread out, falling slowly into the blast furnace. His face sad. The remaining light from his lone eye turned to darkness and receded, glittering like a star burning, disappearing in an instant.

He wasn't a flying person.

Toyohisa hadn't been flying in the sky.

That childhood day, Manyo saw a vision with heaven and earth inverted.

She wasn't looking up at him. She was actually looking down at him.

Toyohisa wasn't flying. He was falling into the blast furnace.

He didn't go on a trip. He died. Toyohisa Hozumi himself was the dead person I'd been looking for. No one knew he died. Other than Manyo, who had killed him.

And most likely, Toyohisa Hozumi's dead body was sleeping inside the cold blast furnace even now. Inside that enormous chimney, that structure that stayed up throughout my grandmother's life, in the center of the abandoned plant.

I woke with a start.

I was drenched in sweat.

Midori Kurobishi's gold teeth glittered in the dark. I shrieked and jumped back. As my eyes grew accustomed to the dim light, I saw that Kodoku was also sitting there. Apparently, I had been crying out in my sleep, which woke them up, and they came flying into my room.

"It's nothing, it's okay," I told them.

"Well then," said Kodoku, and went to stand up, so I was quick to follow that with a question.

"Kodoku, when's the blast furnace coming down?"

"Huh? Er...It won't go as smoothly as all that. I think it'll take a while. Maybe by the time summer rolls around."

"Really."

"Why?"

"Oh, no reason. I'm still half asleep is all."

Midori also moved to leave, so I asked her in a small voice, "Hey, my grandma, she was pretty close with Toyohisa, huh?"

Midori Kurobishi looked back at me with a curious expression on her face.

"They weren't?"

"No, they were. Those two, oh, they had always loved each other, y'know."

"Really? In Grandma's stories, it didn't really—"

"Because she had a little thing called restraint. So did Toyo. But, well, they did, y'know."

I gazed at her, surprised. So then, was this what Yutaka was talking about, the bit Manyo purposefully left out?

"But, Toko. Why're you asking me about a thing like that?"

"Oh no, no reason."

When I was alone again, I pondered it all, shivering. And then I put on a coat and slipped down the hallway and out the door.

I stared at the cold blast furnace, looming in the moonlight. "What happened?" I murmured. The phantom of the person in flight was not a future vision of flying in the sky, but of plummeting into a pit. Manyo at the top of the blast furnace looking down on Toyohisa falling. Did she actually see him die with her own eyes? Or did she "see" it with her clairvoyant inner eye? At any rate, she probably hadn't actually witnessed him falling. But if she had, had she pushed him and killed him? No...

I staggered back into the house. No matter how far in I got, I had the feeling that the blast furnace, illuminated by the moonlight, continued to look down on me from somewhere. I went to the altar, still thick with the scent of incense, and took that mysterious suicide note out of the drawer.

This, I thought.

This is not Momoyo's suicide note.

But this is also not Toyohisa's farewell letter.

So then what is this?

I tried saying it out loud. In my sickly sweet, somehow childish voice.

"This is Toyohisa's suicide note."

Tears started to creep out. I wiped them away with the back of my hand.

"Toyohisa is dead.

"He is the dead person I've been looking for all this time.

"He was the murderer's victim.

"But Grandma didn't kill him.

"No one killed him.

"His suicide note is here. This is proof.

"Toyohisa took his own life.

"Together with the blast furnace.

"But Grandma could not read the suicide note."

I pressed my forehead against the tatami-matted floor. On behalf of my grandmother, I bowed my head to the one-eyed man who had written this suicide note, the flying man of the old stories, Toyohisa Hozumi.

Did my grandmother love you like Midori said? And then what? Was that why she hid the fact that she couldn't read from you?

"My grandmother thought she killed you. It ate her up.

"But please forgive her. Please comfort her and tell her she didn't if you meet her on the other side.

"Because it ate her up. So much. For so long."

My grandmother couldn't read. Toyohisa didn't know that. That day, a few days after the blast furnace was stopped, Toyohisa left Manyo his suicide note.

"We die together."

The words of the farewell letter before me came back to life in my ears in the voice of the man Toyohisa, a voice I couldn't have heard before.

"I'm dyin' with the blast furnace."

It wasn't a farewell letter. It was a suicide note.

A phantom Manyo appeared next to me. Her long silver hair hung down onto the tatami mats as she sat there heavy-hearted. I continued to bow my head to Toyohisa's suicide note on the tatami before me.

That night, Manyo must have gotten the letter, but being unable to read it, had probably jumped to conclusions. The murderer's lie in the old stories that Yutaka talked about, Manyo's lie to hide her murder, was this single point. That she had gotten a farewell letter from Toyohisa that said "Madam Manyo" on the envelope and "I'm going far away" on the page inside. She wouldn't have been able to read the farewell letter. She was illiterate. But Manyo, not thinking that Toyohisa would die, jumped to the conclusion that it was to say goodbye before he left on a trip far away.

For a long time after that, Manyo probably had no idea that

Toyohisa had died that night. She was most likely convinced that the man was living somewhere in some distant town. She was clairvoyant, and yet she didn't know. She had jumped to the wrong conclusion.

It would have been after six years had passed that she learned the truth about what was written in that letter from Toyohisa. In the winter of 1998. The winter of the suicide pact of Momoyo Akakuchiba. Momoyo was the only one to die and returned to the house cold. Yoshio read out loud the suicide note written in the hand of her lover/would-be suicide partner. Momoyo had written the same thing as Toyohisa. When Yoshio read out, "We die together," Manyo's face drained of color, and she fainted. She learned then what was in the letter from Toyohisa. She could tell by looking that the two letters held the same characters.

Manyo must have thought that if she had been able to read it when she got it, she could have pulled Toyohisa back from the edge. And although this was certainly tragic, it wasn't murder. She hadn't been able to save Toyohisa, but she didn't murder anyone.

But she was the type to agonize over things like this. The phantom floating hazily next to me at that moment cocked her head sadly and stared at Toyohisa's suicide note.

"Grandma," I murmured. The phantom stirred slightly. "You didn't kill him, Grandma. Manyo Akakuchiba was a descendant of the mountain people, the clairvoyant madam of the main family, my grandma... Not a murderer. You didn't kill anyone."

Had I untangled all this properly?

Was I right?

I wouldn't know the truth of the matter until the blast furnace was torn down. But I felt sure this was it. When dawn finally broke, phantom Manyo shimmered like a dark red heat haze, and then, my grandmother's bright red spirit glittered and disappeared as if absorbed into the morning light. Even after it was full morning, I stayed like that for a while, sitting quietly by the altar. Coming to light the morning incense, Midori found me sitting there vacantly, suddenly very feverish, and tucked me into my futon, where I was laid up for about three days.

The work to take down the blast furnace continued.

5. BEAUTIFUL

As I lay sick in bed, out of the corner of my eye, chilly, frozen Benimidori gently thawed at the arrival of spring. The sound of the water left behind after the snow melted, churning violently as it filled the riverbed of the Hino River, meant it was officially spring. Buds sprouted on the trees; the season for planting rice in the paddies drew near. And at some point along the way, a dazzling light managed to pierce the clouds of even the smoky sky of the San'in region to cast pale illumination over the mountains.

I was finally able to get up again, so I took a shower, put myself together, and went out. As I descended the hill road of the steps, I abruptly looked back toward the mountain.

Deep in the mountains my grandmother had once climbed with Midori. They went up, perfectly at peace with the idea of never returning, and they arrived there: the valley of the wild roses. Was that a shared dream? Or was there really a valley filled with the boxes of the dead hidden away in the mists?

Were they there even now, those people, in the yawning Hoki woods, unchanged since ancient times? The mountain people, the ones the folklorists call "Sanka," "Nobuse," "Sangai." No one knows whether they're there or not. They're not laborers holding the country up. They don't pay taxes. They don't build society. They just are. Human beings who simply flow along, almost invisible from the perspective of the nation.

But they exist. Just like I exist here now.

I narrowed my eyes and looked up at the mountain for a while before turning on my heel again and starting down the hill road of the steps slowly.

I walked through Benimidori, its arms open to the arriving spring, to the cemetery behind the temple on the outskirts of town, where the plum blossoms bloom. The plums were flowering all over the graveyard, the ancient tombstones were covered in moss, the wet scent of the earth hung in the air. I headed straight for the Akakuchiba main family's magnificent tombstone. Standing before it was a thin middle-aged man I had seen before.

Sanjo. In a worn-out suit, carrying a briefcase. The merciless afternoon light highlighted cruel cracks in his beauty. I could see his pale scalp through his thinning hair. He narrowed his eyes, dazzled, and looked at me.

"So we meet again."

"Mm-hmm...for my uncle?"

He had offered a bouquet of red roses and a bottle of wine. Sanjo nodded. "Wine and roses," he said.

"Huh..."

"I'm only too well aware of how pretentious it is, which is why I snuck them in. But then, of course, here you are to find me out. I can't do anything bad."

"It's not bad—"

"Toko, was it?"

"Uh-huh."

Silence fell. The spring sun shone down harshly on us. On the aging of Sanjo, who had continued to live, and on my half-asleep young woman's face.

A bird chirped off in the distance.

I suddenly couldn't stand it anymore. "It's Toko," I said quickly. "But the truth is, my name was supposed to be 'Jiyu'; it was supposed to be 'Freedom.' Jiyu Akakuchiba. That's pretty great, huh?"

"Hmm. Namida and Jiyu. Tears and freedom."

"Uh-huh." I nodded. And then I placed the flowers I had brought and lit some incense. Since I was already there and everything, I also cleaned up around the tomb with Sanjo's help. As we polished the tombstone and pulled up the weeds, I wondered why.

Why did my great-grandmother Tatsu try to name me Jiyu? Tatsu believed that names didn't change destinies, but rather that destiny chose the name. In which case, was there a fight over freedom in my future? Would I find freedom? But in the coming era, what even was freedom for us...

Sanjo was apparently the meticulous type; he neatly yanked up the weeds I had missed, and the cleaning was done. We started walking alongside each other. It was a nice day.

"Um, Sanjo," I said quietly.

"Hmm?"

"It was because my uncle died—that's why I was born. My uncle was amazing, and everyone had high hopes for him, but then he was gone so suddenly like that. So then his younger sister, my mother, she ended up having to get married. It really should have been my uncle's children who inherited the main family house."

"Namida wouldn't have had kids. He only loved men. If he had lived, either way, the children of one of his brothers or sisters would have inherited," Sanjo replied offhandedly. He spoke as if shooting down my whole thesis. Hearing such a thing so bluntly shut me up for a moment.

"Do you really think so?"

"I don't say anything I don't think."

"Right." I smiled a little.

I kicked a rock at my feet. Sanjo chased after it, and we shot this one rock between the two of us as we walked through the cemetery.

"But well, at any rate. I was born because Namida died."

"Well, either way." Sanjo kicked the rock and looked at me. Wrinkles came up at the corners of his eyes. As if he were smiling. He seemed a little gentler than he had earlier. "Welcome. To the *beautiful* world of Benimidori."

Caught off guard, I gaped up at Sanjo, and he gradually lowered his head. His face in profile steadily turned red.

"So that ended up sounding snotty, huh? It was supposed to be a joke."

The bird chirped off in the distance.

The plum blossoms swayed in the wind.

In the next instant, I couldn't walk anymore, and enormous tears began to spill out of my eyes. So many tears, I couldn't even see. But I didn't know why I was crying. Sanjo reached a hand out and, gently, stroked my back.

"Don't cry. Come on…"

I was sobbing so hard I couldn't speak. For a while, Sanjo stroked my back with a troubled look on his face, like he just wanted to be done with me but couldn't walk away. Finally, he hugged me as if pushed by a sense of duty. "Stop crying, how about you stop now, what the hell, are you still crying, *tch*, what am I supposed to do," he muttered.

"Welcome," I whispered as I cried.

Welcome. Welcome. To the beautiful world. Welcome to a world with plenty to worry about. We'll all live together forever from now on. Right. The world, it has to be at least a tiny bit beautiful.

Around the end of spring that year, the bleached bones of an unidentified man were discovered at the bottom of the blast furnace during the large-scale work to take it down. He wore the uniform of a worker, but it was so old that the name on the badge couldn't be made out. The police started investigating. My father and Kodoku were troubled, so I quietly mentioned that I felt like it might be Toyohisa Hozumi. Finally, they learned from dental records and identifying marks on the body that it was, in fact, Toyohisa, and the remains were handed over to his family. Although I felt weird about it, I asked the librarian descendant of the Hozumi family for a favor and secretly had a bit of the bones given to me. I gently placed this in the altar drawer with Toyohisa's suicide note.

"You didn't kill him, Grandma," I said, closing the drawer. There were no more on my list of the dead now, and her spirit didn't seem to be wandering around the mansion. I couldn't feel any strange auras in the peaceful house, but I continued speaking as if trying to convince myself. "No one killed him. Toyohisa climbed the blast furnace himself. So that he wouldn't change, I'm sure."

Can we only live as people from our generation? The men and women of the village who had been a part of the tatara world flowed with the era in which they lived. Human beings are such awkward creatures. Just looking back at myself, I have to wonder, *Honestly, why I'm such a total mess, I don't even know.* And yet I can't quite manage to break free of this total mess of a self. Change is hard. Growing is tough. *But I've got to keep fighting,* I told myself.

A little after spring arrived, the empty branches of the trees in the backyard of the Akakuchiba main house belatedly started to sprout tiny new buds. More and more green leaves popped up, shivering as though it were still too chilly; each time the wind blew, they shook and rustled. The snowmelt flowed in the brook, and from time to time, a flock of birds took off all at once into the air.

Because I had gotten the identity of the body right, rumors spread in the village that the daughter of the Akakuchiba main family was apparently a little clairvoyant. When the seniors asked me about it, I made a curious face and nodded, "Perhaps I am." A little clairvoyant. That's not a bad way to be known. Things would be really interesting if it were true.

Here ends the investigation into the flying man my grandmother saw some sixty years ago and the tale of the murderer, told through my uncertain groping for a future. I may not be as reliable as my grandmother or my mother, but this is still the story of a spirit of Benimidori, guided by iron, bright red in its own way.

My future, the future of Toko Akakuchiba, starts now. As does yours. And so, I hope that in this future, this land into which we were all born together is the same strange, mysterious, beautiful world it's always been.

Kazuki Sakuraba was born in 1971. She began publishing while still in college. Her early *Gosick* light novels were best sellers and translated into English, and her adult fiction is also popular and critically acclaimed. *Red Girls* won the Mystery Writers of Japan Award in 2007, and *Watashi no otoko*, a suspense novel about an incestuous relationship, won the Naoki Prize for popular fiction in 2008.